I0772320

Throne of Blood & Lies

K. C. Preston

Book Cover by Etheric Designs

Illustrations by Etheric Designs

Edited by Starweather Press

ISBN Hardback 979-8-9893621-2-7

ISBN Paperback 979-8-9893621-3-4

ALSO BY K.C. PRESTON

Daughter of Fire & Storm Series:

Daughter of Fire & Storm
Throne of Blood & Lies

ONE
DAMIYUN

THROWING A LOG ONTO the fire, I checked the perimeter of my small camp, making sure the torches remained lit. Settling onto the ground, I leaned against a tree, the scent of sap and pine drifted down on the light breeze. Digging into a saddlebag, I pulled out a sack filled with dried meat, hard cheese, dried fruit, and crusted bread. Pulling a cork out of a bottle of Serpent's Venom, I took a long drink and looked out into the dark, my sight of the Fallen One, or so some called it, allowing me to see clear as day. Though the woods were silent, I knew it would not last as the darkness blanketed the land.

Xander crept closer, settling down beside me, and I scratched his ears. He no doubt knew the dangers that lurked in the forest and the darkness. Even without that, he knew my need for comfort. Companionship.

Running a hand over my face, I took another long drink. My keen ears picked up movement in the woods as darkness descended.

A scraping of feet.

A grunt.

A growl.

Xander snorted as I got up to check the perimeter again. "Just keeping us safe, boy," I said.

A scream pierced the silence, the sound like that of a child being disemboweled. Wraiths.

The howls of wolves echoed in the distance, growing ever closer. Fuck, but it was going to be a long night. Not that I was immune to sleeplessness. The only thing that kept Themesis from torturing me was drink, but there was nothing to keep the memories of my Lil, her scent, her feel, at bay.

No. Those memories haunted and tormented me more than anything Themesis could do. Her eyes haunted my sleep. Her scent filled the air in the manor, and her presence was with me always.

"Damiyun."

The word drifted on the breeze, and I froze.

"Damiyun, where are you?"

No. It couldn't be. It wasn't her. I took another long pull of the bottle. It was a trick of Themesis. His demons were fucking with me, but then, she stepped out of the shadows. Her hair like fire. Eyes the color of the purest emeralds, and skin white as marble and smooth as silk.

"Damiyun?" Her voice rose, pleading as if looking for me.

"Lil?" I called out. Rising, I took a few stumbling steps toward the perimeter. Toward my Lil. Xander huffed, and I heard him rise, stamping his hooves in displeasure, maybe even in warning.

Stop. A voice rang in my mind. I ignored it and took another step forward.

"Where are you, Damiyun?" Her voice called out again, and I ran toward it.

Stop, you fool, the voice said. It was one I knew, and again I ignored it.

"Please?" Lil begged, and then there she was. The woman I loved beyond all reason, the woman who was the object of my desire, and my demise, stepped out of the woods. I gazed upon her. The moonlight cast her in an ethereal glow; the shape of her body silhouetted beneath the sheer white slave dress she wore, the hundreds of emeralds on the collar around her neck glinted in the silver light.

Though I knew she was a specter, a vision of Themesis made to torment, it did not stop me from walking out of the protection of the fire. Xander let out a loud whinny, a warning I ignored.

"Lil." I choked on the word. Choked on the lump forming in my throat. My eyes burned, and I wiped away the tears on my sleeve like a child.

Stop, Damiyun. This isn't real. That nagging voice echoed in my head again.

"Lillyanna," I said again, taking a few stumbling steps toward her. "I'm here. I haven't left."

Her eyes met mine, and a smile curled her lips. "I miss you."

I stumbled closer still. "I miss you too. The gods damn me, but I only wish to hold you again."

She opened her arms to me. "Then come to me, Damiyun."

I didn't have to will my legs to move forward. I broke into a run toward where she stood, but every step taking me closer, took her farther. The wind picked up and the scream of Wraiths, the howling of wolves seemed much closer than they were before. My heart pounded, my palms turning clammy as the sounds grew closer. I cursed myself for chasing a specter. I didn't want to be outside my perimeter any longer. Turning, I saw in the distance the specks of firelight from my torches that were slowly dying. Fuck. How far had I run?

"You betrayed me," Lillyanna's voice came at me and I stumbled back. Her words hit my heart like a dagger. I turned back, my eyes meeting Lil's, who seemed so far away. The wind whipped her hair around, looking like a mass of flames around her head. A snarl curled her lips, and she held her palms out.

"Lil, no. I'm sorry. I never meant to hurt you." I took a step closer.

No. Stop, Damiyun. It's not her. You know this to be true.

Again, that voice rang in my head.

Go back.

To my left, something growled. To my right, a hiss. Red eyes peered out of the darkness. Clouds rolled in, fast and furious, blocking the rays of the full moon. The wind howled, and I raised my arm, shielding my eyes from flying dirt and debris. Thunder rumbled in the distance. Lightning lit the sky, lit Lil, her veins glowing. Her eyes pinned me; blackness and silver swirled within the depths.

"You did this to me, Damiyun Rayne." Her voice echoed through the forest.

The beasts to my left and right growled. Leaves crunched beneath hooves. Forks of lightning surrounded Lillyanna. Sparks danced across the forest floor toward her, crawling up on her.

Into her.

"You killed me." Her voice came from everywhere.

The beasts moved ever so close.

"I had to. You know this." I reached a hand out. Her black, soulless eyes pierced me. Her skin glowed silver from the lightning that flashed around her. Within her.

"You denied me what was mine. I was a queen."

I grit my teeth at her words. My magic, the warmth of the fire, filled me. "You were his slave."

"He loved me."

I clenched my fists. "He used you. Controlled you."

"You will kneel before us both, Damiyun Rayne, and we will show you no mercy."

My head snapped to the left at the sound of feet moving closer. A giant beast with sharp talons curled into the ground, a massive skull for a head and flames for eyes. Steam spilled out of its empty nostrils and a long, forked tongue licked decayed lips.

A screech came from above. I looked up briefly and saw a being the size of two draft horses, silver scales glinted in the moon's light briefly peeked through the ominous clouds. Giant leather wings flapped, and red eyes peered about. Its mouth opened and let out another ear-piercing scream. The beasts that advanced hesitated, as did Lil. A voice rang in my head.

Run.

This time, I obeyed.

TWO
ABRAHAM

"**G**o," I told my demons. They pulled away, slinking out into the shadows. I watched Damiyun sprint back to his camp. A screech came from above.

Bel. My companion and my familiar. I watched him circle, eyes on the beasts in the shadows of the forest. He would take care of them.

Stepping out of the shadows, my eyes went to the specter of Lillyanna. My heart constricted as I looked at her. At the beautiful woman who was a slave to Themesis in death. A slave to Damiyun in his love. Thunder crashed, and the sky lit up. She lit up.

"Lillyanna," I called out.

The red mane of her hair flew about her head and her soulless eyes met mine. "Zedekiah."

The name slammed into me like a brick, but I showed no emotion. The sound of demons howling filled the air. My demons taking control of the night.

"You betrayed me. Betrayed your father," Lillyanna's voice echoed in the air.

Though I knew her to be a specter, a ghost to torment Damiyun, her words pierced my soulless body. The sound of demons screaming, the cracking of bones and tearing of flesh, could be heard.

"Damiyun, help me. Zedekiah, he... no." Lillyanna's eyes were on me as she projected her words out. I felt Damiyun race to the safety of his camp.

Don't. Please, Damiyun. You know the truth. She is gone.

The wailing of demons faded, save for one. The sound of wings flapping filled the silence. I looked up to see Bel circling the woods. I felt his eyes on Lillyanna. A question ran through my mind. My eyes went to the woman before me and though, like Damiyun I wanted to believe, I knew it wasn't her.

She raised her palms to the sky again. The lightning that had retreated came fast and fierce. Thunder screamed in the sky.

"Bel," I called out, my voice rising above the wind.

He swooped down toward Lillyanna, claws out, body aflame. Crashing into her, she fell to the ground, the storm quickly retreating. Bel shrank down and hopped to my shoulder. I looked down at the bones wearing the slave dress, the emeralds of the collar glinting in the silver moonlight. Bel whined, and I scratched his head.

"I don't know what he is about, but I will gain his trust and find out."

Bel purred and rubbed his head against my chin.

"Let's go keep an eye on him," I said. Pulling the shadows close, I drifted to his camp.

Zedekiah, you son of a fucking whore, bring your sorry ass here.

The words vibrated in my head.

My fucking father.

Bel growled at hearing the voice. Grasping him, I looked into his red eyes.

"Watch him."

Bel huffed his displeasure but obeyed. Scampering off, he settled next to Damiyun. Xander snorted, his eyes going to Bel, then to me. A silent agreement crossed between us as he settled down.

Taking a deep breath, I called the shadows. My demons surrounded, a comfort as their boney arms embraced me, hot breath caressing as they brought me to the Abyss.

To my father.

F UCK, BUT I HATED it here. The heat. The oppression of my father's tomb. It was like a ton of obsidian weighing on my shoulders.

I never wanted this. I never asked to be who I am. He made me a soul collector.

If my mother were alive, I know she would have fought against it.

Against him.

But she was dead, and Themesis claimed me long ago. When my magic manifested, he knew. He owned me, and there was nothing I could do.

"Zedekiah," a voice hissed.

A demon rose from the molten river of lava. His giant head brushed the rocks above. Arms stretched out and leathery wings spread.

"King." He bowed at the waist, head touching the river of flames. Smaller demons scuttled about, bowing as they passed. The words "King" resonated through the corridor.

But I was no king. I did not rule the Abyss, and yet these demons who resided here, who were slaves of my father, saw me as such.

"I am no king."

Laughter echoed through the hall. "You are."

I looked at the beasts, the twisted souls who were once a man, a woman, a child who sold their souls for love. For riches. For selfish reasons. But now they knew. Now they had regrets, and they looked to me to free them. What happened here with Lillyanna weakened the binds, but it also weakened my father, and somehow my magic grew stronger, and so did those who resided in the Abyss. Souls I had brought to the Abyss to serve Themesis.

I shook my head. "I am not your master."

Laughter rumbled through the largest demon's chest. He was one of the first souls brought here. A leader to those who came after. "So, you think."

Zedekiah, I know you are here. Throne room. Now. Don't make me tell you again.

Shit.

Sighing, I began walking toward Themesis' throne room. Demons trailed behind. Some slinking into the shadows, others surrounding me with tendrils of smoke. A loud chirp pulled my attention, and I looked down, seeing Bel scampering behind. Pausing, I held out my hand, and he leaped into my palm. I pulled him to eye level.

"You are supposed to be watching Damiyun."

Bel chirped and growled, his little wings fluttering. I had forgotten time moved slower in the Abyss, being almost mid-day above with Damiyun well on his way to Va'l'Victorus. Running up my arm, he buried himself beneath my beard. I drew up to the doors to the Throne Room. The demons who surrounded me hissed and fell into the darkness. Bel growled and jumped down from his perch, landing on the floor. Red eyes looked up at me.

"Stay," I said. He growled, fluffing himself up two sizes. I laughed. Always he was my protector. "Only come and bring the others," my eyes met the demons who melted into the dark, "if necessary." Bel shook himself with a purr, but did not shrink down.

Taking a deep breath, I pushed open the obsidian doors. Striding through, I looked around. Demons were working on repairing the walls and ceiling. Piles of obsidian littered the floor. My eyes went to the center. Dried blood filled the channels.

Lillyanna's blood. Her body was no longer there.

"Zedekiah." My father's voice brought my attention. He stood amid the pieces of his broken throne, Night Shade. The gold of my own throne glinted beneath the rock.

"You did this," he snarled, stalking toward me.

I felt Bel's anger deep inside me. *No.* I sent out.

"I did nothing," I said, folding my hands behind my back.

Themesis' eyes narrowed on me. "Jaylynn," he called.

I froze at hearing her name. "She has nothing to do with this." Falling to my knees, I bowed my head. "Please, father." The words felt like venom on my tongue.

"You will pay for what you did."

I risked a glance and saw a knout whip appear in his hand.

Fuck.

I removed my shirt, bearing my back to him.

"Jaylynn," he called out again, and my blood ran cold. I heard her soft feet as she padded over to my father.

"Master?"

The sound of her voice, the word master, almost undid me.

"Whip him," Themesis ordered. "Fifty lashes and make sure he calls them out. If he skips one, start over."

I watched him hand the whip to my daughter. He knew how to hurt, but I wouldn't let it. My eyes met hers—deep chocolate orbs once so full of sunshine, now devoid of life—vacant. Devoid of any recognition. Shadows moved to my left. Bel had grown to the size of three draft horses and he had brought demons.

No, I sent to him. He cocked his head in confusion, but he obeyed and shrank back into the shadows, as did the others. His eyes peered at me with sadness from the darkness as my daughter raised her arm and struck me with the whip. Barbs tore into my flesh, but I would not give my father the satisfaction of flinching. Of screaming.

I appreciated the presence of my demons, of Bel. Now was not the time for rebellion. I had to figure out what was going on here. Why had Themesis lived? We needed better information.

"One." I called out. I made sure to call out every number of every strike as they bit into my back. Blood dripped from my wounds. I looked up, my heart breaking at seeing my daughter look at Themesis with eyes filled with adoration.

"Good girl," he crooned, as he took the whip from her. "You are done," he said, and she obediently left the room.

Themesis stood in front of me. Gripping my jaw, he jerked my head back so my eyes met his. "Remember who owns you, Zedekiah. You think your stunt four Moon Cycles ago worked? It did not." He released my jaw with a laugh. "No. It only made me stronger. Her blood runs through my veins and I will break free."

I wanted to laugh. Break free, yes. Stronger? I looked to the shadows, to Bel, and the demons who were now mine. And I felt the magic, dark and powerful, in my veins.

"You are right, Father." Rising, I bit back a wince. The warmth of blood dripped from my wounds, stinging as I moved, but I would not give him the satisfaction of seeing my pain. "I will be by your side when these walls crumble and you walk amongst the humans. They will bow to us both."

My eyes caught the glint of the golden throne that lay amongst the rubble. While Night Shade was completely destroyed, somehow, my own throne survived. I shuddered at what it meant, but at the same time, I knew this was my place. My domain. And when I struck my father down and this, the Abyss, became mine? I would unite the gods, so we were one again.

My eyes went to Bel, whose wings fluttered. His sharp teeth glinted in the light in a grin, and the demons? They bowed, and I knew I had them, had the Abyss, but I had to play a part, like I had before. I'd play it better this time and this time, I would not betray my friends.

Themesis smiled, and my wounds were healed. Snapping his fingers, two glasses of spirits appeared in his hands.

"I'm glad you see it the way it is," he said, handing me a drink. "To my reign." He raised his glass in a toast, and I raised my own.

"To your reign," I said, taking a sip of the proffered drink, the demons in the shadows hissing their displeasure at my words. Bel scampered across the rubble, small as a mouse, running up my leg to my shoulder. Small chirps hit my ear; a soft tongue licked my cheek as he dove beneath my beard. He let out a soft growl, and the demons in the shadows each bowed again in turn and melted into the rock.

I turned my attention back to my father. "What do you wish of me?"

He smiled; a look that made my blood run cold.

"Kill the Wielders and bring Damiyun's soul to me."

THREE

B EL'S LITTLE WINGS FLUTTERED as I pulled the shadows and darkness around, drifting back to Howling Cove. As I made my way through the vacant streets, a scream echoed off the buildings. Bel let out a roar as he leaped off my shoulder, shooting toward the sound. Racing after him, I saw the shadow of three figures in the dark alley. Two large frames I knew were men, knelt beside a woman. Another scream echoed down an alley that stank of piss and something dead.

"Shut the fuck up or I will cut your fucking tongue out," the man who knelt by her head growled, drawing back his arm and striking her hard across the cheek. A whimper escaped her lips.

"That's better," he said, pinning her arms above her head. The second man spread her legs wide, and I heard a belt being undone. The woman kicked and struggled, but she was no match for their strength.

Carefully drawing my sword, I slipped through the dark on silent feet, running the man on top of the woman through. The one who held her arms looked up, eyes widened in surprise, a permanent look on the face of the head that rolled away.

The woman's lips trembled. Wide, tear-filled eyes looked up at me. "No. Please." Her voice shook. I kicked the dead man off her with my boot. Her delicate hands tried to hide the naked flesh exposed beneath her torn and tattered dress.

I held up my hands. "It's alright. I'm not here to hurt. I am here to help."

Sobs wracked her body and tears streamed down her cheeks. Sitting up, she rose to her feet, then collapsed back to her knees.

"Easy." Removing my cloak, I wrapped her up inside and scooped her up in my arms. Her body shook, her hot tears soaked my neck. Holding her close, I strode through the vacant streets of Howling Cove to my home.

Entering, I made my way upstairs to my bedroom and placed the woman gently on the bed. Brown eyes filled with fear looked up at me, but she did not try to leave.

"It's alright," I said again. "My name is Abraham. What is yours?"

"Palma." Her voice was so soft I strained to hear her.

"Rest. I am going to draw you a bath," I said, pulling a blanket up and tucking it around her. She said nothing, eyes watching me as I lit the lamps and started a fire in the hearth. Slipping out of the room, I went downstairs to the kitchen. Lighting the stove, I went to the laborious task of heating water, bringing the numerous buckets up the stairs to fill the tub.

When the tub was filled, I gently shook the sleeping woman. Her eyes snapped open, and she bolted up in bed. A scream echoed through the room and she clamored to get away.

"Easy," I said in a soothing tone. "You're safe. I drew you a bath." I gestured to the copper tub filled with steaming water. Her eyes followed, and her body relaxed, if only slightly.

Rising, I made my way to the door. "Have a soak. When you are done, come downstairs for something to eat."

I returned to the kitchen, my eyes going to Bel, who sat in the middle of the table. He cocked his head to the side as he watched me pull items from cabinets and the icebox. Grabbing a knife, I began chopping carrots. Bel perched on my shoulder as I worked; catching the scraps I tossed to him.

With the soup cooking, I poured myself a glass of Faerie's Blood and sank down on my worn and comfortable couch. Bel jumped up beside me, curling up on the cushion. I scratched his head, and a loud purr vibrated through him.

The soft sound of footsteps drew my attention. Looking up, I saw Palma entering the room wearing a blue shirt of mine. Her long, brown hair hung down her back in damp waves.

"Thank you," she said. "I-I'm staying at the inn. I will be out of your way." She turned and began walking out of the room.

"I made soup. At least have some before you leave," I said, rising from the couch. She hesitated a moment, then nodded.

Heading to the kitchen, she took a seat at the table. I filled bowls with steaming soup and cut a hunk of crusty bread. Placing the food on the table, I took a seat at the opposite end. Bel scampered up my arm, nestling beneath my beard. His red eyes looked curiously at Palma, who shoveled the food into her mouth. When she finished, she placed her bowl in the sink.

"Thank you," she said again. "You've been too kind, Abraham." Her voice hitched, and her shoulders shook.

Rising, I slowly crossed the short distance to where she stood. Tear-filled eyes looked up at me.

"I will leave you now." She made to leave, and I gently grabbed her arm, stopping her.

"It's late and I have a bed here. Go rest. You can leave in the morning."

Her lower lip quivered, and tears spilled down her cheeks. "Thank you." Her voice was barely above a whisper. Turning, she made her way to the stairs. I heard her feet as she ascended, and the soft click of the door as it closed.

Rubbing my eyes, I ascended the stairs shortly after, going to the spare room. Stripping out of my clothes, I slipped beneath the covers. Weariness set in my bones. Closing my eyes, I slipped into sleep.

"**G**OOD MORNING." I GLANCED over my shoulder at Palma, who entered the kitchen. Her hair was a tangled mess, and she still wore the shirt she took from my wardrobe.

A shy smile curled her lips.

"Sit," I said, motioning to a chair. Pulling it out, she slowly sat down. I slid a plate filled with pastries, cheese, cured meats, fruit, and boiled eggs in front of her with a hot cup of tea.

Placing my own plate and mug on the table, I sat down across from her. "Did you sleep well?"

She nodded as she nibbled on a pastry. She wasn't much for words, though the silence between us wasn't uncomfortable. Bel jumped down from his perch beneath my beard, landing on the table in front of me. Palma's eyes widened, and she dropped the egg she was eating.

"Wh-what's that?"

I often forgot the fright Bel gave to some, being used to having him around.

"His name is Bel."

He chirped at hearing his name.

"What is he?"

"He's a demon."

Her eyes grew wide, and her hands shook. "Demon? Who are you? What are you? Are you going to kill me?" Her voice rose with hysteria.

"What? No. Bel isn't going to hurt you, and neither am I."

"How can I be sure?"

"I didn't hurt you last night, did I?"

She licked her lips. "I'm sorry it's just... it's just demons attacked the village I was living in. So many innocents dead. So much blood." She swallowed hard. "I was able to flee with what I had on my back. I stopped for the night here with the last bit of coin I had when..." her voice trailed off. Tears glistened in her eyes, and my heart broke for the woman across from me. The woman who lost everything because my fucking father wanted to break free.

"I'm sorry."

Wiping her nose, she pushed her chair back and rose. "I should go. I'm going to see about finding work since I used the last of my coin on the room at the inn."

"And where will you be staying without coin to pay? What will you do if you cannot find work?"

Her shoulders slumped, and she sank back into the chair.

"I have room here. You are welcome to stay." I don't know what possessed me to offer her my home, only that there was a part of me that did not want her to leave. I had been living in this house alone for longer than I could remember. After what happened in the Abyss, after what happened between Damiyun and me, the loneliness had grown deeper. I didn't realize how much I enjoyed Damiyun's companionship until he was gone. And though I had Bel check on him from time to time, I respected his wishes and kept my distance, only involving myself when necessary.

"I couldn't impose like that. I will figure it out," Palma said.

I chuckled. "I wouldn't have offered if it were an imposition. Truth be told, the silence in this house begins to become maddening."

Palma chewed her lip in thought. "Alright," she said after a bit. "But only until I find work and have enough coin to pay for a place to stay."

Relaxing at her words, I smiled. "Welcome to your new home, Palma."

FOUR

T HE SOUND OF OFF-TUNE humming coming from the kitchen hit my ears as I descended the stairs, and I smiled. Palma must be baking. She either hummed or sang when she did, her off-tune voice always filling my heart with warmth.

It had been four Moon Cycles since I found her. Since I asked her to stay and though she found work with the apothecary in the village making elixirs and helping the sick, and though she had made enough coin to rent a room, or even a modest dwelling, she didn't leave.

And I didn't ask her to.

If I were to be honest, I did not want Palma to leave. I had become used to her presence. Her routine. Bel was also enamored with Palma, spending more time with her than me. I couldn't blame him. There was something about her that drew you in. Made you comfortable and not wanting to leave.

"Stop eating my fruit," I heard her chastise Bel, who growled. "If you eat it all, there will be no pie, and I know how much you want some."

Bel chirped.

"No, he doesn't know I sneak you sweets. He would have my head if he did."

Holding back a chuckle, I crept to the doorway of the kitchen. Bel sat on his haunches in the middle of the table, catching the cast-off bits of fruit Palma threw. Her eyes met mine, and a smile split her face.

"Abraham."

Bel chirped, then ran to a corner, curling up on a cushion Palma made for him. Traitor.

Palma brushed a lock of hair from her face, leaving a smudge of flour on her forehead. I had to resist the urge to wipe it away. As much as I did not want to admit it, I cared for Palma. I had not felt this way since my Lenore, and it frightened me, as much as it thrilled.

I felt a tug in the back of my mind. That invisible string connecting me to my father.

Fuck.

Zedekiah, I am calling a contract.

I froze. The words from the night prior when I was in the Abyss rang in my head. *Bring me Damiyun's soul* he had said after ordering me to kill Wielders. Innocents who just happened to hold the magic that kept the binds on his tomb sealed.

Though between the Suppressors, the demons, and Lillyanna's death that was for nothing, those binds crumbled still. I didn't know exactly how close they were to completely failing. The demons that roamed still told me it wasn't too far off.

A contract appeared in my hand. Palma blinked at seeing it.

Shit.

"What's that?" She motioned to the rolled-up parchment.

I rubbed a hand over my face. "I have something to do."

"What?" Palma shook her head, cheeks turning pink. "I'm sorry. I have no right to ask, but that," she gestured to the parchment, "appeared out of thin air." Her brown eyes met mine, a question within.

The tug became stronger. *Zedekiah, do not disappoint me.*

Closing my eyes, I sighed. I wanted to keep who I was from Palma out of fear she would leave, but mostly because I am Abraham. I rejected the name Zedekiah. I rejected who I am, who my father is. Though I could not shake the picture of my golden throne glinting beneath the rubble in the Throne Room while Themesis' throne was destroyed. The implication sent a chill down my spine.

Opening my eyes, I looked at Palma as I stowed the paper in my shirt. "You have every right to ask. I promise, when I come back, I will tell you everything."

"That sounds ominous," she said, a wavering smile crossed her lips.

And perhaps it was. What I told her when I was done would determine if perhaps my caring feelings, no, the love, I felt was foolishly placed with her. And if it was? Well, I would live out my lonely days in this house that held nothing but sadness.

"Perhaps. We will see."

Bel jumped to his feet. I looked at him and shook my head. "No. Stay with Palma."

His back arched, wings stood erect, and he let out a high-pitched screech of displeasure. His small body grew one time its size, and Palma's eyes widened.

"No, Bel. Stay here. She's making sweets. Don't you want them fresh out of the oven?"

He growled, shrank back to his small size, and scampered across the floor, leaping onto Palma's shoulder.

"You will know everything when I get back. You have my word, Palma."

Striding down the hall, I called the shadows, the bony arms of demons wrapped around me, bringing me to the one whose contract had been called. I only hoped it wasn't Damiyun.

I WALKED THROUGH THE streets, sighing with relief that it wasn't L'Ochal. Grateful Damiyun's soul was safe.

For now.

The scent of rot, piss, and semen drifted on the air and I held back a gag. It was a poor town; the buildings that lined the street dilapidated and abandoned. I gripped my dagger as I walked through the streets.

A shoe scuffed behind me, and I paused.

"I would think twice about what you think you are going to do," I said. Glancing to the shadows, red eyes peered at me. A demon rose, wicked talons out, ready to tear flesh.

The person behind me laughed. "If you cooperate, the only thing that will leave you is your purse. If not? Then your purse and your life."

For the love of the fucking gods that hate me.

I rubbed my eyes with a sigh. "I will only tell you one more time. Think again about what you are going to do."

"Or what?"

A hand grabbed my hair and jerked my head back. The low moonlight glinted on the blade that pressed against my throat.

"So, I guess it's your purse and your life. Hand it over, old man."

I laughed. The fool who held the knife could slit my throat, and I would let him, if only to give him the satisfaction of thinking he won, but I could not die. At least, not by a slit throat.

"I may be an old man, but I assure you, you are making a big mistake."

My eyes went to the demon who sat in the shadows. Forked tongue licked decayed lips and sharp talons dug into the cobblestones. The man jerked my head back further still, pressing the blade deeper against my throat, nicking my skin.

"Have it your way, then."

My eyes went to the movement in the shadows. My demon slunk across the street. Sharp teeth glinted in the moonlight, talons scraped across the cobblestone. Its massive dog-like head turned in my direction.

"Mine?"

It wasn't so much a question, rather an affirmation.

The knife clattered to the ground. Releasing me, he took a step back. "I was just—"

"Too late." I nodded to the demon. The beast crossed the divide in two great strides. The man didn't have time to scream as talons cut through flesh, sharp teeth sank into bones.

Leaving the demon to his meal, I continued on, making my way to the tavern. Grasping the handles, I pulled the door open, a wall of heat hitting me, along with the scent of sweat and body odor.

I looked around the tavern packed with ruffians, similar to the one I just encountered. Those with wealth, though few and far between, held their coins close. Whores weaved their way through the crowd, picking the visibly intoxicated patrons and relieving them of coin.

I did not need to look at the contract to find the one I was to take. The cheers that rose from around a table in the back told me he was there. With much reluctance, I crossed the floor to where the man sat. Shaking a cup, he tossed the dice and scattered them onto the table. I watched them roll, each one settling on snake eyes, a winning throw. His opponents cursed, tossing coin on the table, while an old and haggard whore ground her tits into his side.

The idiot had sold his soul for the Luck of the Fallen One, something I had, though it was something I was born with. Why Themesis called this contract, I couldn't say, but here I was and there was nothing I could do about it.

Sighing, I pulled out the contract and unrolled it. "Santael," I called out.

He tossed the dice on the table. Four sixes. A losing hand.

"Santael," I called again.

His eyes went from mine to the paper I held. The color drained from his face as recognition set in.

Pulling out the golden quill, I cleared my throat. "Santael, you sold your soul for the Luck of the Fallen One. I am here to unfortunately tell you your luck has run out."

"No," he said, raising his hands.

"You knew the terms, and the house always wins."

Grabbing his hand, I stabbed my golden quill into his flesh, drawing his blood in. Placing the parchment on the table, I wrote the words *Contract Fulfilled* in the blank space at the bottom. The words lit up, and the man convulsed. The people around him jumped from their seats, screaming in terror. I held out the obsidian box, watching the man's soul spill into it. Closing the lid, I left the tavern and, pulling the shadows and demons close, I drifted to the Abyss to deliver the soul to Themesis.

FIVE

T HE HOUSE WAS SILENT when I entered. What had seemed like a few moments in the Abyss, hours had passed here. Was it a day? I didn't know.
When I brought that soul to my father, he was pleased with me, as he should be. Once again, I was playing a part. One that was the most difficult for me to play. It was easy to deceive Damiyun and Lillyanna, though when I told her my truth, I feared she would expose me. Damiyun was justified in his rage. I did not want to keep him in the dark, but if I were to play my part, my cards right, he could not have known who I was.

And now I sat in a similar position with my father. I was still being deceitful, though that deceit was for him, playing the part as the dutiful son.

The heir to the Abyss.

Shaking the oppressive thoughts and closing the door, I crept up the stairs. Opening the door to Palma's room, I sighed in relief at seeing her figure beneath the pile of blankets, Bel curled up beside her head on the pillow.

Closing the door, I made my way on silent feet to my own room. Stripping off my clothes, I slipped beneath the covers, my mind going over what I was going to tell Palma in the morning; my heart hoping she understood and accepted me as I am.

I SAT AT THE table eating a slice of the pie Palma made the day prior, the sweet fruit and flaky crust melting on my tongue. The sound of footsteps drew my attention, my eyes going to Palma, who entered. Bel jumped down from his perch on her shoulder, landing on the table. Red eyes focused on the sweet in front of me. Pushing my plate toward him, he dove into what remained of my slice.

Taking a seat, Palma picked up the fork in the pan and dug into the last piece. The tension in the room was thick, or perhaps it was just me who was tense.

"Did everything go alright last night?"

I sighed. "I told you, no promised, I would tell you everything."

Bel launched himself onto my shoulder, wrapping his tail around my neck. A soft purr rumbled through him, and he rubbed his head against my cheek.

I took comfort in him, knowing he understood how hard this was. It had been a long time since I felt the stirrings of desire like this. Not since my Lenore. The glances and soft touches Palma gave made me believe, no hope, she felt the spark between us. My confession would lay it on the table, show my trust and vulnerability and let me know the truth of how she felt.

The silence stretched. Taking a deep breath, I began. "My name is not Abraham. It is Zedekiah." Bel's tongue flicked against my ear. Palma's eyes never left mine. "Themesis…Themesis is my father."

Palma sat back. "I'm sorry?" It was a question, not pity.

I barked out a laugh. "As am I."

"So why do you go by Abraham?"

Though it was early, I felt a stiff drink was necessary. Rising, I grabbed the almost empty bottle of Faeries Blood.

Bel Growled.

"Yes, I know it's early. No, I don't care," I said.

Huffing, he jumped down from my shoulder, running to where Palma sat. Holding out her hand, he jumped into her palm, then ran to sit on her shoulder.

Fucking traitor.

"Because Zedekiah is a name I do not accept, nor one I want."

Reaching across the table, she grabbed the bottle, draining the remnants. Rising, I went to the cupboard and pulled out a fresh one and poured two glasses, sliding one across the table to Palma.

"So?"

Settling back, I began my tale. "My mother was a whore," I said, my voice loud in the silence. Grasping my glass, I tossed back my drink and poured another for courage.

"Her father sold her when he couldn't pay a debt. She had healing magic, much like yours, and it was very attractive to Themesis."

Why wouldn't he want a woman who was nothing but goodness and light to break and corrupt?

"He took her away from that life. Showered her with jewels and what she thought was love, but when he asked, no demanded, she be his queen, she rejected him. He left her with nothing else except to go back to being a whore. Then I was born, and he claimed me as his, giving me the name Zedekiah."

Fuck, but I hated that name and everything it meant. Palma tossed back her drink and refilled her glass. Bel wrapped his tail around her neck, and she scratched his head.

"So why do you go by Abraham if your name is Zedekiah?"

"Because when my mother was murdered, I was taken as a slave. I was given a number that became my name." My hand unconsciously rubbed the brand on my chest. Four two four. "When I escaped, I took the name of a friend who was killed by our Master. Perhaps it was a way for me to free him, I don't know."

Rising from her chair, Palma came around the table and knelt beside me. Bel trotted off to his cushion. Taking my hands, she looked up at me.

"I don't care who you are, who your father is, or what your real name is. You are my Abraham. The man who appeared in my time of need. The man who offered me a place to stay and never told me to leave." She kissed my hands. "I love you."

And damn, if her words didn't undo me. Gathering her in my arms, I pulled her close.

"Fuck, Palma. I love you too. I didn't want this, truly I didn't, but I won't fight it."

Sinking into my arms, she laughed softly against my chest. "I know."

Pulling her close, my lips met hers, hard and desperate. Lifting her up, I placed her on the table. Her hands worked the laces on my trousers, pulling out my hard cock.

"Now," she panted against my mouth as she stroked me. Pushing her skirts up, I yanked her forward. She gasped as I filled her, legs locking around my waist as I slammed into her.

While I frequented whores who satisfied my needs, there was something very different about claiming a person you cared about. One you loved. I slammed into Palma, the table scraping across the floor with each thrust. Gripping her hips, I gave one last thrust, grunting as I spent myself inside her. Holding her close, our ragged breathing filled the silence, the scent of sex filled the air.

"Abraham," Palma said, pushing me away with a gentle shove.

Frowning, I looked down at her. "What is it?"

"You didn't give me mine." Her lower lip jutted out in a pout and if I had not just claimed her, that look alone would have driven me to it.

"I will make sure to give you yours. More than you can handle. The day has just begun," I promised, biting her lip.

She sighed, her mouth opening in a hungry kiss.

"I love you, Palma."

The words filled the air and a weight settled in the pit of my stomach. I spoke the truth and yet, I felt a twinge of guilt. An image of Lenore surfaced, her brilliant smile. The memory drifted and I sighed.

Palma softly touched my cheek. "And I love you, Abraham. My heart."

Turning, I kissed her palm. "And you are mine."

Bel screeched, drawing our attention. His little wings fluttered, and he let out a series of chirps.

"Fine," Palma said, rolling her eyes. "I will make a pie just for you."

White teeth glinted in the sunlight spilling through the windows, then Bel settled back on his cushion while Palma rummaged through the cupboards for ingredients, her off-tune singing filling the void.

I sat back in my chair, sipping my drink as I watched her make the dough for her pie. Happiness spread through my chest. It was not something I had felt in a long time and I hoped, probably foolishly so, it would not be taken from me. That for once I could have what I have craved. What I once had and lost.

A family.

SIX
SERAFIN

TWENTY-ONE GRAND PASSAGES LATER

Sunlight spilled through the windows. Stretching my arms over my head, I slipped out of bed and looked outside. The sun sat high in the clear blue sky; the rays glinting off the snow on the ground. Elves loaded crates of ornaments and other decorations into carriages bound for the town's central square.

It was the first morning of my twenty-first Name Day celebration. My stomach flipped and a thrill ran down my spine. Traditionally, the Shadow Elves hosted grand parties for a twenty-first Name Day. Seven days of celebration with scheduled activities lasting from sunup to well past sundown. Games, dinners, grand balls, the hunt, and finally for an heir —the coronation. Most Shadow Elves looked forward to their twenty-first Name Day celebration. They knew what to expect. Me...I fidgeted with the edges of my nightgown as I watched the last carriage leave the courtyard. Would anyone attend my celebration?

Memories from my twelfth Name Day flooded my mind. Hands yanked me from the depths of sleep. The room was black as pitch; my assailants, dressed in black with masks and hoods, were but shadows. I fought against them, kicking and screaming. Something cold circled my wrist. Familiar words were whispered, and my magic disappeared.

They had attached the Sigaa'Lean.

I screamed.

"Shut up, you fucking half-breed," a deep, gravelly voice growled. It was vaguely familiar, though I wasn't quite sure who it was. A dirty rag was stuffed in my mouth, my arms yanked painfully behind my back and bound with rope, and I was tossed over a shoulder. I squirmed, kicked. It was no use.

Phabian. I reached out with my mind to my father's advisor and most trusted companion. Daggers shot through my body, red hot and painful. I had forgotten about the Sigaa'Lean. Tears burned my eyes and ran down my cheeks. What was happening?

Tossed on a horse, I bumped painfully along for what felt like hours, until the beast finally stopped. Hands pulled me off, and I was dragged along, my bare feet numb from the cold ground, the wind whipping through my light sleeping dress.

"Four days, Serafin. Survive and live." A voice growled. "Count to thirty, then remove your hood. Best of luck to you." The rope binding my wrists was cut, and I listened to the retreating steps of the man and horse.

Counting to thirty, I removed the hood. My heart pounded in my chest and my stomach dropped. I was in the middle of the woods. Wrapping my arms around myself, I tried to quell the shivers that overtook me as the wind whipped about my ill-dressed body. I looked around, my eyes spying a bow, one arrow, rusted blade, a pair of warm boots, and a tin cup.

Survive and live, the person who brought me here had said.

This was a test, though the reason for it was lost on me.

Shivering against the cold, I pulled on the boots. But what next? Phabian's voice rang in my head from the many times he had taken me into the woods for a hunt.

"The first thing you want is warmth," he had said.

Digging a hole, I gathered thick branches, twigs, brush, and arranged them inside, then went to task of making a bow drill. Finding a relatively dry dead branch, I made a hole with the rusted blade, then, finding another branch, filed an end to a point. My hands were frozen, causing me to drop the knife and wood several times. My teeth chattered and my body shook from the cold and wind that whipped through my light clothing.

I had to get this done or else I would freeze to death. Not having any idea exactly where I was with regards to the palace didn't help much either. While I could wander about, follow the hoofprints in the snow for the Elves who brought me here, it would mean failure, and I was not about to fail.

Stuffing the hole with tinder, I wrapped the bowstring around the other stick, placing the pointed side in the hole, and spun the stick in an attempt to cause enough friction to light the tinder. After what seemed like an eternity, I saw a spark, then smoke. Grasping the wood with the burning tinder, I blew on it until a small flame sparked, then carefully transferred it to the pile I had made.

"Come on. Come on." I blew on the tinder, urging the embers to light the brush, almost crying with relief when flames grew. I fanned the flames, tossing small pieces of wood and brush onto the fire until it grew to a size where I was able to put larger pieces of wood on. I scooted closer to the fire, warming my hands and body.

With fire established, my next task was to secure shelter. As the sun crested the horizon, I had finished fashioning my shelter out of logs and conifer branches. With shelter and warmth done, I sat down on a rock and thought about my next steps. I needed food, I knew, but with only one arrow, it would be next to impossible to catch game. Sighing, I spent most of the morning making more arrows. Though I knew the bark fletching wasn't as good as feather, it was all I had to work with. I hoped my skill with the bow would compensate for it.

The rest of the day was spent trying to catch game, but to no avail. I sat down beneath the shelter I made, tossing a few logs on the fire, and ate a dinner of a handful of berries and nuts that I had gathered after missing a sure catch. Phabian would be so disappointed in me for my miss. The thought of him, the thought of my warm and comfortable bed inside the palace, made me want to weep. Why had this happened to me? Did whoever did this expect me to not survive? I didn't know; though when I returned, I would make the one who brought me here pay.

I watched the sun dip below the horizon, and as the darkness fell, so came the beasts. Wolves howled in the distance, growing ever closer. Grunts and growls came from all around my camp. Red eyes peered out at me from the woods. Sweat broke out on my skin. I unconsciously pulled at my hair. My heart raced and I could barely catch my breath.

I was going to faint.

The howls and growls grew ever closer. I wanted to curl up in a ball and cry, but if I did? Then whoever sent me here won. I couldn't let that happen.

Taking a deep, calming breath, I grabbed two logs. Wrapping them in dried tinder, I set them aflame. While I would have liked to set a flaming perimeter, the ground was too hard, so I was forced to keep the wolves, the demon beasts, at bay on my own. I spent the entire night keeping my torches lit, waving them when something came close. I even hurled rocks at whatever crept near.

"We will have you. You are his. You are hers," a ghostly voice hissed as the night drew to a close. And as dawn crested the horizon, I threw my torches onto the almost dying embers of the fire I had made and, crawling beneath my shelter, I curled up and fell asleep.

D URING THE DAY, I hunted, finally bagging game. Though it was small, it kept my belly full and gave me much needed energy for at night, that's when the wolves came. When the red-eyed beasts advanced. Gravelly voices taunted. Goaded, chilling my blood. They came disguised as people I knew. My father, the king of the Shadow Elves and the only reason I still lived. Phabian, my keeper. Krall and Lazaro, the king's men who rarely hid how much they despised me.

Shadow Elves were not known to accept outsiders and my mother, she had been a human.

Another voice called to me. My blood froze. A woman's call who I knew like a distant memory. I was an infant then.

"Serafin? Daughter. Why are you out in the cold?"

My heart pounded in my chest and my mouth went dry.

"Come to me. I have a cloak. I will take you home."

It's a trick, I knew, and yet I couldn't stop my feet from moving. I couldn't stop myself from walking forward to the flaming perimeter I set up. I peered out into the darkness, my eyes catching a woman with long, red hair standing in the darkness, holding out a red cloak, a smile on her lips.

"Come, daughter," she said again. "You cry for me at night. You ask questions about me and receive no answers. I am here now. I will take care of you. I will take you away from here."

Closing my eyes, I took a deep breath. "It's not real. It's a trick." I said over and over again as I stepped back into the safety of the torches.

"Serafin, how can you leave me, your own mother? Or have you accepted the Bitch Queen as your mother?" Her voice turned angry.

"You're not real," I called out. As much as I wanted to believe she was really here, I knew it was a trick.

"Come see for yourself, Daughter."

I shook my head. "No. Go away. Why are you doing this to me?"

"Let me take you home. Raise you like I should have."

Damn it, but I wish I had my magic.

"Serafin." Her voice was closer, her silhouette several feet away from me. "Come, give me a hug."

I grabbed the nearest torch and held it out. "Go away. I know you're not her."

A growl vibrated within her chest, and I watched the woman claiming to be my mother change. Her eyes turned red and her fiery hair turned into flames. Leathery wings sprouted out of her hunched back. Fingers turned into claws, feet to hooves. I backed further into the confines of my perimeter, tossing logs onto the fire, fanning it until it roared. For the rest of the night, I kept the torches burning, while I tried to block my ears from the howls of wolves, the wailing of whatever lurked beyond. During the day, I slept as much as I could. I hunted and kept the fire going, and every night I kept the torches burning to keep whatever was out there at bay.

On the fourth day, the sound of hooves roused me from my sleep. It was about mid-day, far too early and bright for wolves and monsters. I cautiously slipped out of my shelter. One hand gripped the rusted dagger, the other shielded the sun from my eyes. I watched a horse approach, a tall figure seated in the saddle.

"Stop. Who are you?" I called out.

"My Little Princess survived." Phabian's voice drifted on the breeze.

Anger filled me at seeing him sitting so casually astride Maximillian, a smug smile on his face.

"What the fuck was this about?" I yelled as I charged at him. Swinging down from Max's back, he caught me in his arms before I could hit him, though my small fists were no match at my age, I tried to strike his face.

"You, Sera. If you could survive the wild alone, then you can survive the wild that's going to come when you are named queen. Every chosen heir has to go through a test halfway to their twenty-first Name Day. It is to see if they have what it takes to be strong. To rule."

Throwing a cloak around my shoulders, he gestured to Max. I climbed up onto his back. Phabian swung up behind, slipping an arm around my waist, and clicking his tongue, urging Max around.

"What would have happened if I had not survived?" The thought of dying, of being picked off by the beasts in the forest, brought a chill to my bones. I pulled the cloak closer, trying to keep whatever warmth I could find.

"I'd never let that happen, Serafin. I was close. I would have saved you. Protected you like always." His breath was warm in my ear.

"Serafin, Serafin, did you fall back asleep? My guess is no, too excited for the week." A sing song voice filled the room, pulling me from my thoughts. The woman stepped closer, and I raced across the room, throwing my arms around Cwella, my personal maid and dearest friend. "Are you ready to start your week?"

Pulling away, I slipped my hand in hers and tugged her to the window. I was no longer a twelve year old girl but a grown woman. "I'm nervous, Cwella."

She squeezed my hand. "Why?"

Shaking my head, I sat down in a chair Cwella plopped herself on my lap. "I'm a half-breed. The ones who are participating in the celebration are only doing so because it's a party and my father has made an exception in the law. If the queen had borne a true heir, I would not even be here. Their participation will have nothing to do with me." I looked down at my hands.

Cwella grasped my chin and jerked my head up. "Yes, you are a half-breed, but do you not see the women who support you? Lazaro's wife, Kayah. Krall's wife, Felina, and so many other women. I hear them talking. You are the queen, half-breed or not." Cwella leaned forward and kissed my cheek. "Phabian supports you, as does your father, the king. She slid off my lap. "Now get up, highness, and dress for the first day of your celebration."

"But—"

"I will not take any negativity or doubt. Get off your ass, wash up, and let's go."

"Fine." I rose and held my arms out. "Prepare me for my celebration."

SEVEN

C WELLA AND I MADE our way across the atrium.

"Stop fidgeting," she scolded.

But I couldn't help it. I knew the elves were only at the celebration to drink and party. It had nothing to do with me.

"Sera," a voice called out. I looked up and saw Phabian standing at the door. His white hair was loose, brushing his broad shoulders. The light blue shirt he wore brought out his eyes; the purple trousers fit his muscular legs like a glove. A smile curled his lips as I ran across the room, throwing myself into his arms.

"My Little Princess," he said as he lifted me up, spun around, then set me back on the floor.

"Phabian." I pulled away and looked up at him. "I'm not a little princess. I am to be queen." I tossed my head.

A smile tugged his lips again. "Apologies, highness." He dropped to a knee, and I laughed, dragging him back up. Grasping Cwella's arm, we made our way to where our mounts waited. Phabian swung up on Maximillian's back and I swung up onto Yasmine, hefting Cwella up behind. She wrapped her arms around my waist, and, looking at Phabian, I heeled her forward.

What's wrong? Phabian's voice echoed in my head.

Sitting taller, I gripped the reins. Yasmine tossed her head with an irritated snort.

Sera?

Nothing.

Phabian chuckled. *My Little Princess can't hide anything from me.*

I sighed, knowing how true his words were. If he didn't see it in my eyes, he felt it in my soul. *Why am I doing this? Why am I making a show?*

It's the week of your twenty-first Name Day.

It was my turn to laugh. *Right. Because all these elves are turning out to celebrate a half-breed's acknowledgement as the heir.*

Phabian sighed, an annoying sound within my mind.

Yasmine tossed her head again and snorted, showing her own annoyance.

"What do you know?" I snarled. "Everyone loves you. Me? Not so much."

Yasmine bucked, almost tossing Cwella and me. "Bitch," I snarled as I got her back under control. She let out a low whinny, an amused sound coming from her.

Phabian snorted. *Sera, stop thinking that way.*

You know I am right. Why am I doing this?

Phabian's sigh echoed in my head. Pictures flashed through my mind.

Phabian holding me as a wee babe.

Me, cuddled on my father's lap as he read me my favorite book, *The Story of Jayne.*

Other pictures flashed. Elves, male and female, bowing their heads in silent respect. Silent support, as I passed.

Stop it, I snarled, glaring at Phabian who looked for all the world like he didn't do a thing.

Just enjoy it, Sera. He paused for a moment. *I took your mother to a solstice celebration when you were a babe in her womb. She had such a good time, and she ignored the slurs thrown her way, as will you.*

Entering the square, we dismounted, handing our mounts off to the stable hand. Phabian turned and grasped my chin.

"You are going to be the queen. Fuck those who throw shade on you. Hold your head high and show no fear." He smoothed a hand over my hair. "I may call you my Little Princess, because to me, that is what you are. To them? You are their future queen. Act like it, Sera."

I looked up at Phabian, the one constant in my life besides my father. He shielded me from the harsh words spoken. He held me when I cried. He believed in me. Loved me.

Taking a deep breath, I smoothed my hands down my silk skirt. Grasping Cwella's hand and holding my elbow out to Phabian, I tossed my hair.

"Let's go."

W E STRODE THROUGH THE throng of people, my hand entwined in Cwella's, Phabian's arm around my waist. I leaned into him and he smiled down at me. He didn't know or understand what he meant to me.

He had known my mother. He was the only one who spoke of her. Even my own father, the man who loved her most, brushed me off when I brought up her name, Lillyanna.

But Phabian? He told me the stories about her. He was open about his feelings.

"My Little Princess." His voice drew me out of my thoughts. A sad look crossed his face. "Not so little anymore."

Tears stung my eyes at his words. Would my being queen change the way Phabian felt about me, the way he saw me? Was that something I even wanted?

I shook my head. Definitely not. Phabian was like a brother—no, a second father—to me. I looked up to Phabian, the man who all but raised me. Who held me while I cried when I wasn't invited to parties because I am a half-breed. Phabian was there for me. I loved him for that, and he would never see me as anything other than his Little Princess.

Pulling to a stop, I wrapped my arms around him and buried my face in his chest.

"Promise me, no matter what happens, I will always be your Little Princess?"

He pressed a kiss to my temple. "Always," he said, voice choked with emotion. Pulling away, he wiped the tears from my cheeks. "No crying. This is a celebration, isn't it, Cwella?" His eyes went to my friend. She smiled and grasped my hand.

"What would you like to do, highness?" Cwella said with a giggle.

I laughed, lightness filling my heart. "I think—"

"Phabian," a deep voice boomed.

I froze at the sound of the voice, my eyes going to Lazaro, Phabian's lover, and one of the elves who despised me the most. He was tall, with broad shoulders. The pink shirt he wore beneath his read cloak strained against his muscles. My eyes traveled down his muscular chest to the yellow trousers that were, if I were to judge, two sizes too small. My gaze went to his face, the chiseled jaw had a bit of stubble, white hair touched just below his shoulders, the sides pulled back in braids, his deep blue eyes gazing at Phabian. If I didn't hate him as much as I did, I'd consider him handsome.

Phabian embraced him, lips meeting in a brief kiss before they pulled away.

Lazaro's eyes went to me. "Princess. Or should I say queen?"

I gripped Cwella's hand, maybe a little too hard, as she winced.

"Lazaro," I ground out.

He laughed.

Why was he being nice to me? I glanced at Phabian. He must have told him to, though that has never stopped him from throwing slurs at me in the past. He must have something up his sleeve. Something planned to hurt and humiliate me.

I tensed at the thought. A chill ran down my spine, and the brief happiness I felt evaporated. The music seemed too loud. Too joyous. The scent of food turned my stomach, and the crowd of people closed in. Suffocating.

I wanted to go back to the palace. Back to my room, where I was safe. Where no one could hurt me. I glanced at Cwella, who looked up at Lazaro in adoration.

She had a crush on him, though why was beyond me. Sensing my gaze, she looked at me, concern pinching her brow.

"Are you alright?"

I forced a smile. "Of course, I am. Let's go have fun."

Cwella grinned, and we pushed our way through the crowd, Phabian and Lazaro trailing behind. Elves browsed booths lining both sides of the street, purchasing food and trinkets. Performers weaved their way through the crowd.

One elf on stilts juggled four colorful balls made from magic. Another, naked from the waist up, swallowed flaming swords. Off to the side, a third performer walked a tight rope six feet in the air with a stack of plates balanced on his head. Music filled the air. Lutes, wind instruments, drums, and voices singing songs about times past.

As Cwella and I walked, the unease I had felt moments ago subsided slightly as the festive mood weaved its way inside me. I looked around, my eyes going to a group of children seated in front of a stage ten feet wide and five feet high. Puppets on strings bounced around and laughter filled the air. I smiled at the sight. The puppet show was always my favorite attraction during the Solstice Celebrations, my father sitting patiently beside me, watching for hours.

"Look." I pointed to it. Cwella's eyes followed. "Let's go watch." I tugged her toward the show.

"No." Phabian's voice stopped us. I turned toward him. "That is for children. You are a grown woman, Serafin. Far too old for childishness."

The tips of my ears burned at his words. I bit my lip and looked down at my shoes. "Of course."

"Let her go," Lazaro said. I looked up at him and frowned. Phabian's eyes went to him as well. "Did you not just say she is a grown woman? Does that not mean she can make her own decisions? Yet here you are, treating her like a child by telling her what to do."

Phabian's eyes narrowed. "What will it look like to have the future queen sitting on the ground watching a children's show?" His tone was sharp, and Lazaro flinched.

"I—I just meant she should be able to do what she wants," Lazaro muttered.

Phabian's nostrils flared. "Fine." He glanced at me. "If you want to crawl around the ground and watch a children's show, then go."

Turning, I hurried away before he changed his mind, dragging Cwella along. I glanced over my shoulder. Phabian had Lazaro's chin in a tight grip, his face inches away. Anger rolled off him as he spoke, his words low and unintelligible.

I snorted at the sight, a bit of happiness spreading through me at the thought of Lazaro being chastised.

"I don't know what the problem was. I love the puppet show," Cwella said. "And the way Lazaro stood up for you..." she closed her eyes and sighed.

"I don't trust him. He hates me, so why is he being nice?" I said as we made our way to the front, sitting on the ground in front of the stage.

Cwella shrugged. "Maybe because you're going to be queen some day and he knows you could sentence him to death."

The thought made me smile.

A hush ran through the crowd as a puppet appeared on the stage. "I am Terrin Trounde, King of the Shadow Elves," a voice boomed as the puppet bearing the likeness to my dead grandfather bounced around the stage. Another puppet popped up, this one was female bearing a resemblance to Rahina, my dead aunt.

I sat back and watched the play unfold. It was a time in our history when Rahina, who was the chosen heir, poisoned Terrin to take the throne. When her treachery was discovered, my father had her thrown into the dungeons to be executed. Taking the throne himself, he discovered there were elves procreating outside our race, hiding their illicit families in villages. He waged a war against those who went against our laws, rounding up families and publicly executing them, while banishing the elves they belonged to.

Though I knew all about the event, seeing it unfold through the puppets made my stomach turn. I understood the law was the law, but the massacre of innocents was too much. And yet, here I was. Someone who went against the law. Someone who, had I been born during that time, would have been executed.

How could my father hold up the law for them, yet bend it for me? It did not make any sense, nor did it sit well with me. And though the thoughts disturbed me, it also lit a fire inside and I vowed to abolish that law when I took the throne, despite the consequences it would bring.

The play ended, and Cwella and I made our way back to the street. Phabian and Lazaro stood against a wall, eating a battered sausage on a stick.

Phabian held one out to me as we approached. "Enjoy the show?" He pushed off the wall and began walking down the street toward the town square.

I shrugged as I ate my food, though I had no appetite.

Phabian said nothing as we walked down the road. The sound of music and laughter grew louder as we drew closer, the black marble pillars marking the square came into view. People spun around, feet pounded, and hands clapped as elves danced in the square.

Bright colored streamers and jars with orbs of magic light, illuminated the square as dusk settled, decorated the entablatures.

The white marble statue of my father standing ram-rod straight, hand resting on the pommel of his sword, right hand gripping a scepter, loomed in the background. His face was stern, eyes staring out at the horizon. A crown bearing the

Shadow Elf crest sat upon his head; emerald serpents with ruby eyes glinting in the dim light, wrapped around thorny roses carved from obsidian, formed jagged peaks. The statue was decorated with garlands of flowers and strings of lighted jars. The shadows cast from the light made him look frightening. An ominous pall weighted my shoulders. Nausea threatened to make me toss the food I ate.

"Shall we dance?" Lazaro's voice pulled me back. He held out a hand to Cwella who hesitated, stumbling when I shoved her toward him, catching herself before falling into his chest. She cast me a glare over her shoulder, cheeks red as she took his hand.

Phabian held his hand out to me and I took it, letting him guide me to the floor. The song was a jaunty tune, and we clapped, stomped, and twirled to the beat. Pulling me close, Phabian then spun me out, releasing my hand. I twirled down the line, arms catching me and pulling me in. I looked up to see who had me, a pit of ice forming in my stomach as I looked up at Lazaro.

A tight smile stretched his lips. "Serafin." He spun me out, then pulled me back against his hard, muscular chest.

"Why are you being nice to me?"

"Phabian gave me orders."

I laughed. "Since when have you listened when he's told you to be nice to me?"

Lazaro's lips curled into a snarl.

"There he is. It must be killing you to not be able to call me the daughter of a whore or half-breed cunt."

I was pushing my luck, I knew, just as sure as I knew he would not take my bait. Whatever Phabian had threatened him with was keeping him in line. For now.

His nostrils flared, but he said nothing.

I bit back a smile. Phabian must have threatened him good. No doubt Lazaro knew he would delve into his mind to make sure he kept his word. It only made me want to push him all the more.

I opened my mouth to goad him more, when screams rose above the music and stomping, the sound bringing everything to an abrupt halt. An ear-piercing screech punctuated the silence. A mighty figure flew above. Massive wings flapped stirring up the air below. A serpentine neck swung a giant horse head around, red eyes searching the crowd below. Its mouth opened, jagged teeth glinted in the moonlight and sharp talons curled at the end of long toes.

Lazaro scooped me up, tossing me over his shoulder and ran through the crowd as Elves scattered, searching for safety from the demon above.

What was going on?

"Ours," the demon snarled and my mind went back to when I was twelve and the demons circled my camp. How they said I was theirs.

I bumped around on Lazaro's shoulder as he ran to the stable.

"Go to the palace. Warn the guards of what is happening."

Nodding, I swung up on Yasmine's back. Digging my heels into her sides, she surged forward, racing toward the palace. Wings flapped above and I risked a look up. My throat went dry as I saw the demon circling above.

"You are his. You will be his," it hissed before shooting up into the air and disappearing.

The words vibrated deep inside me and somehow, I knew who he was.

Somehow, deep inside, I wanted to go to him.

Shaking the thoughts, I raced through the open gates, eyes on the stunned guards. "Demons," I called out as I raced past. Heading to the stables, I jumped off Yasmine, then hurried to the safety of the palace.

"Filthy, ugly, half-breed." A voice hissed as I headed for the stairs. My ears burned at the slur, but I ignored it, continuing down the hall. "Do you think people will bow to you? Accept you as their queen? A half-breed will never rule."

Slowing down, I turned around as the voice came closer. An elf wearing a black dress, white apron tied about her waist stood with her hands clasped behind her back, a snarl on her pretty face. Denalla. Mouranda's maid servant.

"No one will accept the daughter of a whore." She took a step closer, and I had to stop myself from stepping back. Tossing my hair, I gave her my nastiest glare, though inside I was shaking.

"It doesn't matter if they do not accept me. I am the heir. I will be their queen and they will kneel." I smiled at her. "At least I am not barren. I will be able to produce an heir. Maybe I'll have two."

Denalla's fists clenched her skirts. "How dare you," she snarled.

"How dare I what? Speak the truth? Everyone knows Mouranda is defective. She couldn't even do the one thing the women of our race are forced to do." Yes, I said ours. I was an Elf too.

Her eyes narrowed, and a cruel smile curled her lips. "The only reason anyone is going to this sham of a celebration is because the king ordered it. No one wants you, Serafin. No one will kneel before you. I'd watch my back if I were you, lest a knife ends up in it," she said, roughly shouldering me out of the way as she passed.

My eyes stung and my ears burned at her words. Taking a deep breath, I hiked my skirts and ran through the halls to my room, not letting the torrent of tears flow until I shut the door behind.

I could put on a brave face, pretend the words didn't hurt me, but deep down they cut like a knife. I took a deep, shaking breath. When I became queen, I would exact my revenge on those who spoke ill of me. Those who called me the daughter of a whore, a half-breed cunt. They would regret ever speaking those words.

EIGHT
DAMIYUN

The ride to Oaken Leaf Castle was long and tiring. Violent snow squalls delayed me, and on more than one occasion, the thought of going back home to Pine Crest Manor in L'Ochal crossed my mind, but I had traveled far and the damn binding promise—the promise forced out of my mouth by magic—Barlack put on me would not allow that.

Finally, after what felt like an eternity in the saddle, Va'l'Victorus came into view. Oaken Leaf Castle loomed above on a hill. The rays of the rising sun glinted off the white marble. Tall spires marked the four corners of the palace, large metal bowls where warning fires were set graced the tops. Sentries walked along the walls high above, alert eyes watching the horizon. Arrow slits were cut into the walls where I knew archers waited, though what sort of danger would befall this castle, aside from the demons lurking in the dark, I did not know.

The city of Va'l'Victorus was just waking up. Elves and humans went about opening their shops and setting up booths. Wagons filled with fruit, meat, reams of cloth and other items to sell ambled by. The scent of fresh baking bread filled the air. My mouth watered. I longed for something other than the hard cheese, cured meats, and dried fruit that made up my meals when I wasn't eating bland stews, moldy bread, or mutton that had turned days before in seedy taverns.

Guiding Xander through the streets, I looked around. The opulence of the city proper never ceased to disgust me, knowing on the outskirts there were those who lived in squalor. Many were servants of the castle, making just enough to get by, if only barely. It boiled my blood knowing the stocks of food that was beginning to turn or any leftovers from a grand event were incinerated. Though L'Ochal was mainly an affluent city, there were poor sections, and I always made sure to feed and clothe them. Zenith had found it disgusting. Though it was a scandal for her to wear a dress from a prior season, it was much worse to see a poor person in it. I rode on, passing the city square. A large, red marble fountain took up the middle, empty for the winter. A statue of Barlack standing on a pedestal rose up from the center. He stood erect, head held high, with hands resting on the pommel of a sword. His long hair blew in a breeze and a crown of vines and antlers curling up from the sides sat atop his head. Benches carved into the base and large urns made of gold, currently filled with small conifers and berry bushes, marked the four corners. Scattered about the square were tables and chairs, a few having some sort of game set up.

The sun rose higher in the sky, the yellow rays lending warmth. The city woke as the sun rose, humans and elves scurried from their homes and bustled down the road, dodging horses and carts. Eyes cast in my direction, many smiling and waving as I passed. A group of four young and very pretty women, elves and human, appraised me. I winked, and they erupted in giggles, faces turning red as they hurried on. I chuckled, mentally memorizing what they looked like. Perhaps one, or all four, would be enticed to grace my bed.

Pulling up to the pathway that led to the castle, I swung down from Xander.

"Let's get this over with," I said, patting his neck. He snorted, tossed his head, and stomped a hoof.

Taking the reins, I began the ascent. "Trust me, boy, I know. If I had my way, we would be back at Pine Crest Manor. At least you will get a good rub down, grain, and a warm blanket. Maybe that brown mare you had eyes on will be here."

Xander's head pushed me in the back, and I stumbled forward. I glanced at him. "Hit a nerve?" He whinnied, and I laughed.

The stone path crunched beneath my feet as we made our way up to the castle. Rose bushes lined each side, the branches arching over the walkway forming a canopy. When the days turned warm, the path would be fragrant from the white flowers, the buzzing of bees gathering sweet nectar, and birds making nests to lay eggs. But now, the branches were bare. A few birds twittered and flew around, but for the most part, the only sound was that of our feet.

Finally, the colossal iron and thick oak gates came into view. Though they were open, a guard stood at each side. I looked up at the palace, the glint of metal catching my eye through a slit. Elves with arrows knocked, strings at the ready.

"Damiyun," a guard greeted, bowing his head. "Welcome back."

"As if I had a choice."

"We will take care of Xander. The king is in his study."

Scratching Xander's nose, I handed the reins over, then made my way through the courtyard. It was a grand expanse of space, a fountain similar to the one in the square graced the center. Wooden benches dotted the green grass. When the weather turned warm, the empty flower beds would fill with colorful and fragrant blooms. The bare trees would overflow with various fruits. Apples and pears. Cherries, peaches, and plums.

A few people occupied the benches, people played a board game, two elves rolled dice in the corner. A few reclining in lounge chairs acknowledged me with a nod. Most ignored me, which suited me. I never wanted to come here.

Striding up the white marble steps to the palace, I pushed open the cherry wood doors and stepped into the atrium—a grand, circular room. High, vaulted ceilings were painted with pictures of nature, scenes were carved into the red marble walls depicting battle scenes and celebrations. Stained glass windows at the peak, let in colorful morning rays to illuminate a massive stag with golden antlers and red eyes in the middle of the floor.

The Wilde Elf crest.

Everything about the palace was ostentatious. Gaudy. From the blood red floor with pure gold inlay, to the oak and cherry furniture, intricately carved with vines and flowers and embossed in pure silver and gold. Thick tapestries lined the hallways, golden thread glinting in the light of five-tiered crystal chandeliers hanging above. All the coin it took to make this palace could have fed thousands. The thought sickened me. Though I was considered very well off by most standards, I did what I could to give back, sending leftover food, buying warm cloaks, gloves, and boots along with bundles of wood in the cold months to the poorer people in L'Ochal. I knew Barlack did not show the same sympathy.

The halls were relatively quiet, only the servants and a handful of warriors passing through. The men dressed in polished armor wearing helmets with tall ears, bowed their heads as I passed. The servants scattered like frightened mice, refusing to look me in the eyes.

Fucking Barlack. I knew he had put the notion in the heads of the elves I was to be their future king.

Drawing up to the door of the study, I grasped the handles and pushed them open. Barlack sat behind a grand, oak desk across the room, head bent over a piece of parchment, quill flying across the paper. A fire burned in the hearth behind him, lending warmth. Shelves crammed with books and rolled up parchment lined both sides of the room, the ones on the left side separated by windows, the sunlight illuminating the Wilde Elf crest carved into the desk.

My boots scraped across the marble floor as I walked to where he sat. Glancing up from his paper, he sprinkled sand on the parchment before folding it and stamping it with wax.

"Damiyun," he said, putting the stopper in the bottle of ink and wiping the nib on a rag. "Welcome back."

Stifling a laugh, I took a seat in front of the desk. "As if I have a choice. How long is this to go on? I would very much like to spend more than a few days at my home."

Barlack folded his hands and leaned forward. "As long as it takes for you to know and understand our history. As long as it takes for you to learn how to become a leader. It is imperative you become king."

I grit my teeth. "I am not going to rule."

Barlack laughed. "So, you say, but I chose you and per Elven law, that makes you heir."

I rubbed my eyes. I was tired from the trip. Tired from sleeping on the cold, hard ground and hard beds at the inns. I was tired of having to come here.

"Surely that is not the only reason you have forced me to come here when you beckon?"

"No. You need to know who you are and where you come from. You need to understand the laws of the Wilde Elves. You need to know our history, and you need to learn how to wield your new power."

I sighed. "I know where I come from. My mother was a Shadow Elf, and I am half."

Rising from his chair, Barlack crossed the room. "Come," he said as he walked past me.

Rising, I followed him out of his study and through the halls. Sturdy furniture of cherry and oak crowded the walls, tall windows lined one wall facing a training yard where soldiers fought each other, pummeled training dummies, and ran an obstacle course. Further on, stained glass windows and tapestries lined more walls depicting more battle scenes, hunts, and celebrations.

Finally, Barlack drew up to a large oak door that had the Wilde Elf crest carved into it. I had been before this door enough times to know it was the library. Pushing it open, I followed him inside. The scent of must and books filled my nostrils. It was a cozy room. Dark rugs dotted the marble floor. Shelves made of deep cherry crammed with books lined three walls. Comfortable chairs sat around low tables. Low windows broke up the shelving on one side. Barlack disappeared amongst the shelves, and I went to task of building a fire in the cold hearth. Pouring a glass of Serpent's venom, something I knew Barlack would frown upon, I took a seat in a soft, leather chair. Barlack returned and slapped a book down on my lap. It wasn't anything special, a plain book with a black velvet cover. No words written to say what it was.

"What's this?"

"Your mother kept journals. I found them after she left and bound them in a book. I guess you could call it a Tome of the Queen of sorts."

Opening the book, I looked at the neat and even flowery script gracing the paper. I ran my hand over the pages my mother had once touched so long ago. I pictured her sitting at the desk in her room, my room now, long white hair curtaining her face as she poured over the pages.

Sipping my drink, I settled back in my chair, the sound of Barlack's feet retreating and the click of the door plunging me into silence. Flipping back to the beginning, I began to read.

*A*FTER WHAT FELT LIKE *an eternity, I finally made it to Va'l'Victorus, arriving with my faithful maid, Dulce. I didn't know what happened to my six guards and could only surmise they perished.*

While the battle between my race raged, Dulce along with six of my guards, freed me from my prison, using a secret tunnel beneath the castle to escape. Though once we broke through to the surface, we were far from safe.

The battle raged within, and without, the palace walls. My brother, Allendaire, had waged a war against those who procreated outside our race. Battle cries pierced the night, as well as screams from the wounded.

The dying.

We bolted toward the tree line, my heart in my throat as we ran. My eyes went to a female elf named Flanka, a woman I had been close to. An arrow protruded from her chest, and I watched the Life Force leave her as she collapsed to the ground.

There was no time for tears. No time for mourning. Clutching Dulce's hand, I pulled her along as we raced to the forest, my guards flanking me. The sound of screams and metal on metal rang through the night. Picking up my skirts, digging in deep, Dulce and I raced through the night. We stuck to the darkness of the woods, resting only long enough to catch our breaths. Only when we were far enough away, did we stop to make camp, though I did not sleep.

What Allendaire did to me was out of anger and jealousy, I knew. Being a man, he had assumed our father would choose him as the heir. As such, he showed no interest in running a palace. No interest in the politics, keeping peace, and keeping the treaty between our people and the Suppressors in place, which included providing the Sigaa'Lean.

No. He assumed too much. I, on the other hand, was very interested and such, Father saw potential in me and named me heir, which enraged Allendaire. So much so, that he poisoned our father, blamed me, and locked me in a cell. With any luck, with the chaos of his war, I would be thought dead.

And now, after many Moon Cycles of running, hiding, and dodging patrols, I was safe in Va'l'Victorus at Oaken Leaf Castle. Barlack had welcomed me with open arms, promising to keep me safe, promising he would ensure others thought me dead.

And to one day ensure my resurrection as queen.

I FLIPPED THROUGH THE book, skimming entries about parties my mother attended, men who courted her, councils she sat in on, until I got to the last one.

I T IS WITH MIXED *emotions that I make this last entry. I enjoyed the many Grand Passages spent at Oaken Leaf castle. I enjoyed Barlack's company, and his attention and though I had many admirers, and lovers, something was missing inside me.*

That was, until I saw him.

I ran into Kallen Rayne one sunny afternoon while I was taking a walk. He was in the woods practicing with a sword. His long, black hair was tied back and sweat slicked his naked torso. As I watched him move, fluid like water, I felt a tug inside me. A pull toward him, and though no words were spoken, I knew one thing for certain. He was my mate.

And so, in a bold move to meet him, I challenged him to a duel. He declined with a laugh, though when I pulled my blade and attacked, he had no choice but to defend. Though I would like to say he beat me fairly, in truth I let him win. But I would never tell him that.

And now, after one and a half Grand Passages of courtship, it is time for me to move on from here. Time for me to take my place as Kallen's wife. Oh, I do not intend to leave this place for good. No. Someday, when Barlack deems it, I will rise as queen. Perhaps returning with the future heir in tow, securing my legacy.

But for now? For now, I embark on a new adventure.

NINE

I LOOKED DOWN AT the pages dotted with tears I did not know I had shed.

"Mother," I whispered. "How I wish you could be here with me now. Perhaps had you lived, my life would have been much different. Perhaps Arden would have been a brother to me. Perhaps the darkness that invades my soul would not have been."

Fuck, but being here brought up feelings I did not know I had. I yearned for my mother the way a small child would. I wanted to feel her arms around me, holding me close. I wanted her to tell me everything would be fine.

That she loved me despite the badness inside.

I shook the thoughts and wiped my eyes. The sooner I left, the better off I would be. I glanced at the book again, one thing I read nagging in my mind. Rising, I crossed the room, slipping into the corridor to find Barlack.

As I stepped out, I almost collided with a serving girl carrying a stack of towels. "Excuse me, highness," she said, skirting away.

The palace was far busier than when I arrived, the sun sitting high in the sky. Servants bustled about, some carrying linens, others carrying clean chamber pots. I walked on through the halls, dodging the bustling staff. The scent of food wafted toward me, and my stomach growled. I followed the smell to the grand dining room. Barlack sat at the head, various elves sat around the table. One of Barlack's brothers, Mative and his advisor and his wife, Della. Grimm and Joidal, two council members as well as a few high Elves, lords and ladies who I did not know.

On the table was a roasted suckling pig partially picked apart, root vegetables, fresh bread, lard and a decanter of wine, thank the gods. I needed something to numb the feelings coursing through me. Barlack looked up as I entered. The chatter stopped, and all eyes turned to me, and I shrugged off the uncomfortable feeling as I crossed the room, taking the empty seat to Barlack's left, no doubt left empty for me.

The conversations thankfully resumed, and I piled food on my plate. Taking a bite of the suckling pig, I sighed as the flavor exploded in my mouth, the tender meat melting on my tongue. Gods, it seemed like forever since I had a decent meal. Filling my glass, I sipped the dry wine, ignoring the disapproving look from Barlack.

The chatter was nothing more than a buzz in my ears as I ate my food and drank my wine. My mind kept going to the journal entries I had read, and I wondered what would have happened if Mother hadn't died. I could not help but feel guilt for it. After all, she had a child, a girl named Aznai born three Grand Passages before me, whom Arden killed. Mother survived that birth. Perhaps Arden had been right. Perhaps it was my magic that killed her.

The low chatter filled the room along with the sound of silverware scraping dishes. No one paid me any mind, and I was grateful for the peace.

Pushing his empty plate back, Barlack rose, his eyes on me. "Let's go, Damiyun. There is much to do today," he said, bowing politely to the others at the table.

Sighing, I pushed back my chair and stood. "Lead on, then," I said. The gods only knew what Barlack had in store for me this day. I followed Barlack down the halls, the sound of shoes following made me look. Mative trailed behind, eating a flaky jelly filled pastry. I found it curious he was following.

"Where are we going?"

Barlack glanced at me. "You will sit in on hearing the grievances of my people. It is an important task for a king to listen to his people and dole out fair and balanced solutions."

This would be interesting, seeing as Barlack seemed to be anything but fair and balanced. At least where the poor were concerned. We pulled up outside a set of grand double doors, where two guards stood, and led us into a grand ballroom. It was empty, save for a long table with three chairs at the opposite end. A sideboard with crystal decanters filled with red and amber liquid and several glasses sat against a wall to the right. A set of doors on the left led out to a marble patio. Urns filled with small conifers and winter flowers sat at the corners.

Large windows spanned the entire room, the midday sunlight reflecting off the white and red marble floor. A twenty-tiered crystal chandelier hung from the ceiling; crystal sconces sat between the rows of windows. I looked around the huge room, noting guards clad in silver armor, the Wilde Elf crest pounded into the breast plate. Helmets with long, pointed ears covered heads. Hands rested on hilts and eyes peered about the room. There were ten guards total, two at the outside of the doors, two inside, one in each corner, and two standing behind the lone table.

Barlack strode across the room, the click of his boots echoing off the bare walls, followed by Mative. I made my way to the sideboard and grabbed a decanter of amber liquid and three glasses before I took the vacant seat to Barlack's left. His lips pursed as I poured the liquid into the glasses, passing one to him and Mative, who hesitated a second before taking a sip, much to Barlack's dismay. I sipped my own drink, expecting a comment, but he said nothing.

"So, what happens now?" I looked at Barlack who shuffled a stack of papers in front of him. Mative opened a ledger, pulled the stopper from a jar of ink and placed a quill in the bottle. A guard stepped into the room.

"Rogot Ac'Ran and Citgen Prise," the man announced in a rich baritone that filled the room.

Two men entered, backs straight and eyes forward. Neither looked at the other as they crossed the room. The tension between them was palpable. Barlack folded his hands and looked at the men as they drew up in front of the table.

"State your issue," he said in a clipped tone.

"Citgen cut down my sogna fruit tee." One of the men said. He was tall, with sharp features. A long, pointed nose, pointed chin, and eyes set a bit too close together, his brown hair thinning at the top.

Citgen glared at Rogut. He was two hands shorter and where Rogut was thin, Citgen was stocky. His face round, eyes small within the flesh, long blonde hair pulled back.

"It was dead. The damn thing was near to falling down with the next wind. It would have landed on my house. I did Rogut a favor."

"It was not dead. It still produced fruit. You were just sour because I never shared with you."

Citgen snorted. "Yes, it produced fruit you let rot on the branches, stinking the air and bringing all sorts of unsavory insects about. I can't even sit on my porch when the days are warm."

"You had no right to cut down my tree."

On and on the men bickered. Barlack should have said they were petty grievances. I sipped my drink, boredom filling me as the men argued.

"Enough," Barlack's voice snapped, pulling me back. The men stopped. Standing up straight, they looked at Barlack whose eyes went from on to the other, settling on Citgen.

"Citgen, you had no right to cut down Rogut's tree, dead or not."

Rogut smiled.

Barlack's eyes went to him. "Rogut, it is selfish of you to not share your bounty and let the fruit rot on the branches." Barlack sat back, eyes on the men. "Citgen, you will plant a new sogna fruit tree for Rogut and Rogut, you will not let the fruit rot and you will share your bounty with Citgen. You are dismissed."

The men glared at each other but said nothing as they left the room. The sound of Mative's nib scratching across paper as he wrote down Barlack's decree filled the void. Though Barlack's decision had been set in paper, I wondered how he would enforce it. I opened my mouth to ask when a guard stood in the doorway.

"Rayanne Silas and Joreen Lindt," he announced.

Two women walked through the door, heads held high. They were finely dressed, the silk of their dresses swishing softly as they walked, their footsteps light on the floor. They stood in front of the table, eyes on Barlack.

"State your issue."

"Two days ago, I was at L'Rounge's dress shop looking at a lovely silk dress. It was a soft green with a fitted bodice, the skirt flowing like water to the floor. The color brought out my eyes and the fit accentuated my figure," one woman said, running her hands over her voluptuous hips. "I went to look at other dresses when Joreen," Rayanne glared at the other woman, "came in and bought the dress right from under my nose."

Joreen sniffed. "She had no claim on it. If she wanted it that bad, she would have taken it."

I snorted into my glass, which earned me a sharp look from Barlack.

You have to be fucking kidding me.

I couldn't believe I was being forced to sit here and listen to petty squabbles. More so, I couldn't believe this was a thing Barlack did. No doubt it was just a show to make the folks feel better. If I ever decide to take the throne, this bullshit would be the first thing I'd end.

"I walked away for a moment. That dress was mine."

Joreen folded her arms. "And now it's mine, bought fair."

The two women bickered back and forth, and I had to try hard not to laugh. Though the scene before me was likely something Zenith would have complained about, if she were granted council with someone to hear.

Finally, Barlack held up a hand. "Enough," he said. The women stopped and brought their attention to him. "Rayanne, if you wanted the dress, you should have claimed it. Joreen did nothing wrong. There is nothing I can do. You are dismissed."

The women turned on their heels and stalked out of the room, their low, angry voices echoing softly off the walls.

On and on it went with humans and elves bringing their ridiculous problems for Barlack to solve. Though I suppose having a king tell you what you must do puts an end to it, it was ridiculous and boring, none the less. I tuned out the people who came and went, my mind going to my mother and the journals I had read. Seeing her flowing script and reading her words made me feel closer to her, as did staying in her rooms.

At first, I balked at the accommodations. The room was almost a shrine in her memory, and I felt uncomfortable staying there. No doubt Barlack was trying to pull my heart strings, possibly hoping this would make me stay. But as I went through her things, touched the items her hands held so many Grand Passages ago, I began to feel closer to her and my want to know more grew.

I looked out the window, noting the sun hung lower in the sky. How the fuck long had I been sitting here? The ache in my back and ass told me it had been more than a few hours. How much longer would this go on?

"Lord Penton D'orn and Illia Roust." The announcement pulled me from my thoughts. My eyes went to the two people entering the room.

Lord Penton was tall and thin, his white hair cut short and blue eyes piercing. He wore a yellow tailcoat, pink shirt, light blue trousers, and red boots. Though the colors were clashing and comical, they denoted his station as a High Elf. The young woman, Illia, was small in height and frame. Her long, white hair hung limply past her waist. Blue eyes were large in sunken sockets, and she wore a dress two sizes too big, hanging off her thin frame. The dress was soiled and the many patches sewn into the fabric showed it had seen better days, possibly passed down for a few generations.

"State your issue."

Lord Penton stood up straight and adjusted the cuffs on his coat. "Illia Roust has been caught stealing my winter stores of fruit and vegetables."

Illia looked down at her feet.

"How many times?"

"Three, by my count."

"Six, actually," Illia said, lifting her head and looking at Barlack. "The people are starving. We barely have enough rations to make it through the rest of winter. Lord Penton and others have more food than they could ever eat."

Barlack pushed a lock of hair from his forehead. "There is nothing stopping you from growing your own food."

"Nothing stopping..." Illia's jaw clenched, and her nostrils flared. "Nothing stopping us but poor soil riddled with boulders and roots. He," she gestured to Lord Penton, "he has plows and oxen to ready his fields. We have hands and shovels. We would never be able to move the large boulders and if, by some miracle, we did, the soil is too poor to grow everything. Even weeds will not grow."

"You haven't tried, so how can you know?" Barlack said. "Stealing is a crime. For that—"

"I only took what was needed to give to the people."

"Be that as it may, Lord Penton's crops and stores are for his family."

"A family of six. Lord Penton," she spat, "has enough store to feed my people three times over."

"Even so—"

"If I may?" I cut in. I had heard enough, and I had seen enough in the city to understand this young woman's plight. While Lord Penton, and the likes of him, lived in luxurious homes in what I imagined to be hefty plots of land, Illia, and those like her, lived in falling down shanties with holes in the roof. Many did not even have glass for windows, rather rags hanging down in the summer, and planks nailed up in the winter.

Barlack sat back and folded his arms. I looked at the couple who stood in front of the table.

"While stealing is wrong, hoarding stores of food that will inevitably go bad and end up being tossed is worse."

Lord Penton bristled. Barlack leaned forward, folding his arms on the table. I felt his eyes on me. *He thinks I should be king, so I will show him what a right and fair king I would be.*

"Lord Penton," I said, looking at him. He looked down his nose at me and I wanted to laugh. "I see no reason to not share your bounty with Illia's people."

His nostrils flared. "I worked hard on my fields and crops."

I raised an eyebrow. "Did you? I hardly think your hands have seen a minute of hard labor."

"That crop belongs to me, regardless of who tended the field. This woman is stealing my food. She should be punished." He cast a glare at Illia.

"Out of desperation and hunger." I folded my hands. "Lord Penton, put yourself in this young woman's position, and tell me, what would you do?"

Lord Penton laughed. "I would never be in her position."

I shook my head. "Circumstances happen. One cannot rest on their laurels thinking their lives won't take a turn. I am certain Illia did not ask for the hand the gods dealt her."

"And it is not my fault either. Her lot can grow their own food just as I have."

"She already stated that is impossible." I leaned forward, my eyes going from Lord Penton to Illia. "This is what I propose, Barlack." I turned my attention to him. Barlack looked at me, his expression unreadable. "Barlack will give Illia and her people a substantial plot of land in which to grow crops and fruit. He will also provide them with livestock. Cows and sheep, goats and chickens. Horses and oxen to pull the farming equipment will also be provided by the king."

Barlack's eyes narrowed. "Damiyun—"

"This will allow you, Illia," I said, turning my attention to the young woman, "and your people to grow food and provide for your village. It will also allow you to sell wool and eggs. Milk and excess bounty at the market for coin."

"This is preposterous," Lord Penton sputtered.

"It is fair," I said. I looked at Barlack. "What say you? Will you lock this desperate woman in prison for trying to survive, knowing others will follow in her footsteps? Or will you allow them to provide for themselves?"

The choice was clear, at least to me it was. If Barlack chooses to lock Illia up, he would be viewed as a tyrant. If he chooses to give them land and livestock, he will be viewed as a fair and just king.

"Who are you, to dole out judgement?" Lord Penton snarled.

My eyes locked on his. "I am your prince." His eyes widened, but he said nothing.

Barlack mulled over my words, then turned his attention to the couple. "Damiyun's judgement stands. I will draft up the deed to a plot of land and provide you with livestock and farming equipment per his decree."

Lord Penton spun on his heel and stormed out. Illia looked at me with tear filled eyes.

"Thank you, highness. You are most gracious," she said, executing a low curtsey before turning and running out.

Mative's nib scratched across the paper as he logged the judgement in the ledger.

"What were you thinking?" Barlack growled.

I sat back in my chair and looked at him. "I was thinking of the poor people in your overly affluent city. The people who are overlooked and neglected. The people who work in your castle cleaning chamber pots and scrubbing dishes for a few coppers that won't even get them a crust of bread. I was thinking of the people who are starving while you burn your excess food and food that's turned. I was thinking of Illia who has to resort to stealing to provide for her people because you are not."

Barlack pursed his lips. "You were to sit here and observe, not interfere."

"If my interference means some people will be able to pull themselves out of squalor and live a decent life, I would do it again, ten times over. Are we through here?"

Without waiting for an answer, I pushed my chair back. Rising, I strode out of the room. I wasn't sorry for what I had done, or for putting Barlack in a no-win situation. At least for him. For Illia, it was a bountiful win.

I walked through the palace, ignoring the people who called "my highness," the ones who bowed and curtsied. Climbing the grand, marble staircase, I made my way down the empty hall to my room. Slipping inside, I closed the door and let out a sigh. The sun was sinking below the horizon. An entire day wasted listening to people squabble. Rubbing my eyes, weariness settled in and I crossed the room to the dresser that held decanters of spirits. Pouring a glass, I knocked it back, then filled another. Tossing a log on the dying embers in the hearth, I used my magic to reignite the fire, and to light the many lamps in the room. Sinking into a leather wing-backed chair, I propped my feet on the table and sipped my drink. The warmth the spirits spread through my body relaxed me.

There were so many things wrong with Barlack's rule. He was willing to throw Illia in prison for trying to survive and feed her people. I sipped my wine. He had been angry with my decision. Be a tyrant or come off as a fair and just king. I didn't rightly give him a choice.

Sipping my drink, I again thought about my mother and wondered what sort of a queen she would have been. Would she have followed in Barlack's footsteps, or would she have taken a different stance? A kind and fair stance? I couldn't imagine her being any sort of a tyrant, locking innocents up for trying to put food on their table. No. I'd like to think the kindness inside me, however small, came from her.

Weariness settled further in my bones, and I yawned. Though my stomach growled, begging me for food, I did not wish to sit at the table with Barlack and withstand his scrutiny and displeasure with what I had done.

Draining my glass, I pulled myself out of the chair. Pulling on night clothes, I slipped beneath the warmth of the heavy covers. Though I had only been here a day, I had seen enough. On the morrow I would prepare to leave.

TEN

I FOLLOWED BARLACK THROUGH the halls to the amphitheater. Barlack had brushed off my request to leave, and the fucking binding promise forced me to stay. Only Barlack had the power to allow me to go, and as I should have known, he refused.

I had been at Oaken Leaf Castle for almost ten days, far longer than I wanted to stay. Though I was allowed the freedom to go where I pleased, I still felt like a prisoner within these walls.

Along with sitting in on the petty grievances, Barlack dragged me along when he went to collect the taxes. It was yet another black mark against the poor. Though he granted them leniency in what I knew to be a false magnanimous gesture, I knew there wasn't any way the people would ever catch up on their payments.

"What happens if they cannot pay?" I had asked Barlack as we rode back through the city on tax day.

"They have one Grand Passage to gather the coin for their tardy payment, and another six Moon Cycles for what they owe currently. If they cannot pay either?" He shrugged. "They will go to debtors' prison."

I clenched my jaw but said nothing further. Barlack liked to think himself a good and generous king. It was something I couldn't wrap my head around. Perhaps it was because of where he came from, born into being a High Elf. He only knew opulence, though one would think a leader would be for all the people and not biased against one group.

There were a lot of things about Barlack's ruling I did not agree with, but I held my tongue. After all, it was not my kingdom. I rejected who I was and therefore it was not my place to voice my opinion.

I shook the thoughts and followed Barlack down the halls. This was an area of the castle I had not explored. The light poured through the stained-glass windows projecting a rainbow of color across the white marble floors. As with all the other windows in the palace, they depicted grand hunts with elves standing next to giant stags and elk they felled, grand celebrations of the Solstice, and wars from many Grand Passages ago. One portrait memorialized in glass caught my attention, and I stopped. It was of a woman dressed in a royal blue gown, standing before a grand throne. The arm rests were emerald serpents with ruby eyes, wrapped around black roses. Emerald serpents wrapped around black roses rose up from the back forming points. Men dressed in armor, emerald serpents with ruby eyes wrapped around a black rose was emblazoned on the breastplate. Helmets with long, pointed ears covered heads.

The men flanked the woman in blue, holding her arms. Her chin jutted defiantly, her long white hair spiraled down her back in soft waves. A man sat on the throne dressed in bright colors. Orange shirt, blue trousers, and purple boots. A fur cape of purple sat upon his holders and a crown, emerald serpents wrapped around black roses, the heads of the flowers and snake forming points sat atop his head. He pointed a finger at the woman, his face contorted in anger.

"What's this?"

Barlack stopped and drew up beside me. "That is your uncle, the tyrant Shadow Elf king, Allendaire Trounde. It's depicting a time when he denounced your mother to death."

"I read about that in her journal. He poisoned my grandfather and blamed Mother. All because she was chosen as heir. Then he waged a war on those who procreated outside the race."

We began to walk on. "Where were you during all of this?"

It had occurred to me Barlack was a Trounde, once a Shadow Elf, though he changed his surname and called himself and his people Wilde Elves.

"I was ensuring my own family was safe. Your uncle," he spat the word, "rounded up the human and elven families that many elves had and publicly executed them. I wanted my own to be safe and was able to get them to another place far away."

I frowned. "You knew what he was going to do."

"I was his personal guard. He was free with his words around me."

My mouth went dry, and my heart pounded in my ears. "You knew he poisoned my grandfather and placed the blame on my mother, and you did nothing?"

"There was nothing I could do. Had I gone against Allendaire, my head would have been on the block. I regret I could not help your mother, but she escaped."

"And you fled like a frightened child," I said. A bitter taste filled my mouth.

"There was nothing I could do. Your mother did not fault me. She fled here to live. She even promised to come back when the time came for her to take her place as queen."

I said nothing. Though Barlack's words made some sense, I would not admit it. Perhaps he could have stopped what happened. Alerted my grandfather of what Allendaire was going to do, or perhaps it was done and Allendaire was merely bragging. I wasn't sure I wanted to know the truth, just as I knew Barlack would most likely not tell it.

The silence between us stretched as we walked down the halls, the scuff of our shoes on the floor echoing off the walls. Finally, we drew up to an enormous half-circle door. Barlack pushed it open, and we made our way down a long, dark corridor. Turning a corner, the light of the sun spilled through a rectangular opening ahead. We stepped through the doorway into the amphitheater. It was enormous. Hundreds of rows of seats rose up the curved walls. The high ceiling was made of clear glass, and windows let in a breeze, giving the illusion of the amphitheater being outdoors.

Tapestries with the Wilde Elf crest—a giant stag with red eyes and golden antlers—and pictures of various royals and what looked to be competitions in this very arena, hung on the walls and from the bottom of the upper tiers of seats. Iron gates closed three of the four doors round the arena where Barlack and I stood.

I looked around, noting a variety of training dummies scattered around the arena. Barlack crossed the dirt floor to one, and I followed, standing in front of it.

"We are going to work on using your Elven magic. We will work on your wielding it, as well as using the magic with your sword." He gestured to the weapon strapped to my back.

Shadow Blade was its name, and it had belonged to my grandfather. Barlack had given it to me as it was passed down to the true heirs and he felt it was time one should wield it again.

"Now, push your natural magic down, and focus on the Elven magic burning inside."

Though it was difficult to do, I pushed the flame that burned inside, the fire that was a part of me, deep down and focused on a foreign feeling. It was a pulse, a tingle, a buzz bubbling within. It was a far different feeling than the flame. Where that felt natural, the fire coming without my having to think about it, this magic that pulsed inside was odd. Closing my eyes, I concentrated on the feeling, bringing it closer. Closer. My body buzzed. My veins burned, but it was not like the flame. No. This was an uncomfortable feeling, an energy racing through my body that stung. I heard a crackling, and lights flashed behind my closed lids. Opening my eyes I looked down, gasping at the colorful light circled around my wrists.

"Good," Barlack praised. "Now, make a ball in your palm."

Holding out my left hand, I concentrated, picturing a colorful ball. The light that circled my wrist slowly drifted toward my palm, the circle closing, forming a small ball of light that hovered above my palm.

I smiled at the sight.

"Not terrible for a first try," Barlack said.

I tossed the ball at him. It hit the ground in front of his feet, exploding on impact. Dirt flew in the air and Barlack was tossed backwards.

"Are you trying to kill me?"

I stared at the hole the ball made. "I had no idea it was that powerful."

"Well, now you know. This magic is not something to play around with. You need to learn how to use and control it. Loss of control could have catastrophic implications." Barlack brushed the dirt off his clothes. "Now, I want you to make another, bigger ball, and throw it at the dummy over there," he said, pointing to a figure a few yards away.

I concentrated, bringing the magic forth and making another, slightly bigger, ball. Pulling my arm back, I aimed and launched it at the dummy. It missed by a long shot, hitting the ground behind, exploding in a plume of dirt and color.

"Again," Barlack commanded.

Over and over again he had me make balls of light and power and launch them at the dummies. Dirt and light flew in the air.

"Damn it, Damiyun. Focus," Barlack snarled as he used ice magic to put out the flames burning a nearby tapestry. The stag's legs singed.

"I am focused," I snarled. Sweat coated my naked torso. The breeze blowing through the open windows caused me to shiver. I had to keep my fire magic at bay in order to draw the new, and foreign, Shadow Elf magic. I had to bury the flame deep to draw the Shadow Elf forward. I panted from the effort.

"If you were, then you would not have set another tapestry on fire."

"Why the fuck would you hang tapestries in an amphitheater set for magical competitions?" I spun in a circle, arms sweeping around, taking in the many seats.

"That is our history. Those who come here can see the competitions and battles of the past. They know where they come from. You," he poked me in the chest.

I grabbed his hand and twisted his wrist. I was hot and tired. I did not need Barlack to berate me for lacking control of a new magic, the fucking hardass. It would not kill him to turn his critical eye upon himself for a change. I smiled at the thought.

"Do not assume I am one of your trainees, someone you feel you can mold to be what you want." I called the flame, pulsing heat through my body into my hand. Barlack cried out, pulling from my grasp, and I had to stop myself from laughing.

"You are a rogue Wielder," he said, shaking his head. "Your mother would be disappointed in you."

Flexing my hand, I let both the flame and Elven magic fill me. "How can a dead woman be disappointed in a son she never knew?" A ball of energy and fire formed on my palm, and I hurled it at Barlack. The light and flame exploded on the shield he erected.

"Good," he said, a smile curling his lips.

Fucker.

I let my anger grow and threw ball after ball at his shield until it weakened and cracked. A ball flew through, hitting Barlack, who flew back, slamming against the wall.

"What were you saying again?" Colors swirled around my wrists. Flame danced on palm.

Barlack pulled himself to his feet. Blue eyes pierced me. "That wasn't very nice, Damiyun."

I tossed the flame from palm to palm. The energy around my wrists flared. I shrugged. "You said I was weak."

"I never said that."

"You said my dead mother, I'm sorry, the dead queen, would find me a disappointment. As far as I'm concerned, the only disappointment to her would be Arden."

I bounced the flame on my palm. Gods, but I loved that magic. The fire. The warmth. The air left my body and burning pain radiated through my mid-section as a ball of energy hit, tossing me in the air and onto my ass.

"That wasn't very nice, Barlack," I growled.

A shadow fell over me. I looked up to see Barlack glaring down at me, arms crossed and stance wide. "You are a rogue Wielder. You can't even make a shield to block attacks."

Pulling myself to my feet, I looked down at him. "You're right. I am."

"I think we are done here," Barlack said. "It is time for your history lesson."

I rolled my eyes. Gods, it was like being a child back in school. At least my obligation to Ayelay was approaching. If I didn't have that out, I don't know if Barlack would ever let me leave. He'd probably put me on the throne if he could.

I followed him through the halls, the late afternoon sun spilling through the windows. We drew up to the door of the library where my blasted lesson would take place. He wasn't teaching just the Wilde Elf history, which spanned a scant few centuries. He was teaching all the history. Dark Elf, Shadow Elf, and Wilde Elf. He felt I needed to be well versed for when I became king. Barlack pushed the door open to the room, the scent of must and books filled my nostrils. Barlack made his way to the back to get what I knew was the Wilde Elf Tome of the Kings.

While he gathered the book, I made a fire in the hearth and took my seat. Grasping the decanter of wine, I poured a drink for myself and Barlack. Though he thought me a pathetic drunk, he at least did not take drink away completely, though he never let me have too much. No. That was saved for the night when I was alone in my room.

I counted the seconds. So much time between now and the night hours. Might as well be eternity. Barlack returned carrying the heavy Tome and took the seat beside me, resting the book on his lap.

"Tell me what you learned from our last session," he said, taking a sip of wine.

Damn if his voice didn't transport me back to another lesson, another place. Wren's Keep. The suppressor Compound. A place I wished never to return. A flicker of a memory flooded my mind. The musty scent of books. The metallic scent of ink. The instructors cold eyes turned to me "Recite the five principles and one hundred articles." Their voice cracked like a whip. Gods forbid if I had ever stuttered or forgotten one. My arms ached from the thought, standing in the corner, arms outstretched to hold piles of books for the whole ten-hour class.

Taking a sip of wine, I pushed the memories away. I had escaped the Compound and yet, still I remained captive. I idly rubbed the left side of my chest where the brand, a big, ugly "S" was. I might have defected, but I could never truly leave. "Aside from being an inbred, genocidal lot? Not much." At least I kept my voice steady.

Barlack pursed his lips. "I will not tolerate insolence."

I chuckled as I refilled my glass, much to Barlack's dismay. "I am not a child who needs their knuckles cracked or who has to hold heavy books for hours for being insolent," I said, stressing the word. Leaning closer to Barlack I locked eyes on him. "Do you really want me to recite what you have told me?"

Barlack said nothing.

"Very well then." I rose, assuming the position I was taught as a Suppressor, stance wide, hands behind my back, eyes forward.

"The Dark Elves were the first elves known. Some were born different. They thought themselves superior and bred within their race. Karrinian gathered your lot and traveled to Il'Ekhester, where he encouraged the inbreeding to continue. Then he unleashed a magic plague on the Dark Elves to eradicate them. Later his son Bodwin killed him in a hunting accident, and he in turn was killed by his brother Halston. And then, more history, brothers raping sisters, women forced to breed, Terrin is poisoned, my mother is blamed for it and imprisoned, Allendaire waged a war," I paused, my eyes going to Barlack. "My mother escaped, had a daughter who Arden killed, then I was born, and now it's present time." Breaking form, I grasped the decanter and took a hefty pull, my eyes never leaving Barlack.

"You're pathetic," he spat.

"Did I miss anything?"

"Your mother—"

"Would be disappointed in me? Most likely," I said as I took another drink. Barlack glared at me.

"Would you rather your brother be the prince? The king? Someone who hates women, who rapes—"

"Much like your lot?" I finished the wine, then crossed the room and grabbed the bottle of Serpent's Venom. Pulling the cork with my teeth, I took drink. "He'd make a splendid king."

"You are nothing more than a pathetic drunk."

I took another long pull. "Pathetic? Maybe. Drunk? Not yet."

Barlack grabbed the bottle and smashed it on the floor. I watched it shatter, the amber liquid spilling onto the floor, and I laughed.

"Feel better?"

Barlack's lips pursed into a thin, white line and I knew I had pissed him off, but I didn't care. He thought to use my dead mother as motivation. A woman I never knew.

"You are the pathetic one, Barlack. You are trying to guilt me into a position I do not want."

"I named you king."

I clenched my jaw and pulled my magic close. The flame danced on my hands and energy circled my wrists. "I did not want that." I sent a ball of energy in his direction. It hit its mark and Barlack flew across the room, hitting a shelf, heavy books raining down on him. I made my way to where he lay, a pathetic king buried beneath books.

"You think me something I am not. A prince to a mother who is dead. I am no prince and I sure as fuck don't want to be king. I don't care what you claimed. I am not that," I said turning away. "I am nothing more than a pathetic drunk."

Crossing the room, I stepped into the hall and made my way to my quarters. Kicking off my boots and stripping out of my clothes, I slipped beneath the warm and heavy blankets and, closing my eyes, drifted off to sleep.

ARMS CIRCLED ME. HAIR tickled my nose. Looking down I saw a mane of red nestled against my chest.

Lil. My Lil.

Brushing a hand over the silky smoothness of her hair, she stirred. Pulling back, eyes black as night looked at me.

"You killed me. You betrayed me." Her voice boomed inside my head.

"No. Lil—" I reached for her, but she changed. Her eyes sank into the sockets. Her skin melted off from her leaving decay and bones.

"I will have you Damiyun Rayne. You will pay for what you did.

I BOLTED UP IN bed, my body slick with sweat, heart pounding in my chest.

Another fucking nightmare. Reaching toward the night table, my hand closed round the bottle that always sat there. The only thing that chased my demons.

A movement caught my eye and, pulling on my magic, calling the flame, I lit the candles and lanterns, seeing the figure of a woman wearing a pink dress standing in front of the windows. Long white hair spilled down her back. A circlet sat upon her head, the white diamonds glinting in the moonlight. Though I did not recognize her, something deep inside told me who she was. Was it a specter? I couldn't rightly tell.

"Mother?" I barely heard the words I spoke. She turned, a smile curling her lips and blue eyes gazed upon me.

She was radiant. The moonlight made her look ethereal, and my chest constricted.

"I'm sorry." Tears choked my throat.

Her head cocked to the side in confusion, and she floated across the room, sitting on the bed beside me.

"For what, Damiyun?"

My eyes burned. "For killing you."

Smoothing a hand over my hair, she laughed softly. "You did no such thing. Yes, it was a hard birth, but I gave myself over. It was what I had to do to save you."

Wrapping my arms around her midsection, I buried my face in her neck and wept a lifetime of tears.

For her, who died.

For me, who took the brunt of her death.

For my father, who lost the woman he loved.

And for my brother, Arden, for losing the only mother he knew.

And when my tears were done, I laid down on my bed. Mother clutched my hand, and my walls were filled with fantastical pictures of unicorns and centaurs. Giant birds and stars. Her soft voice filled the silence, singing a haunting melody.

Hush my child
Close your small eyes

Fall to sleep
Let darkness rise
Hid in shade
Wants you to come
Fall to him
You will succumb
Do not fight
You cannot win
Razor claws
Tears off your skin
Sharp teeth glint
From his large maw
Crushing bones
In mighty jaws
Hush my child
It's just a dream
Hush my child
Hush your loud screams
Wake my child
Today anew
See my child
The beast is you.

And as my eyes closed again, as I drifted back into sleep, her voice rang within my head.

You are the heir, Damiyun Rayne. I named you when you were born.

And despite everything I rejected, I could not ignore this.

Fuck.

"I REGRET MY TIME here is at a close," I said to Barlack at the morning meal.

Barlack put his fork down and folded his hands. "Your training is far from done. We have only just begun."

I bit into a pastry; the sweet jam filled my mouth. "I know. However, I have another obligation. You know this."

"Yes but—"

"I cannot ignore it, Barlack. I am bound to the Fae." *Much like I am fucking bound to you.*

Barlack pursed his lips. "There is much more for you to do."

I sighed. My obligations weighted heavy on me. All I wanted to do was go home, spend the rest of my days in solitude with the occasional woman on my knee. But the fucking gods never let me rest.

Pushing my chair back I rose. "I am sorry, but I must leave. I will return. Does your binding promise not ensure that?"

Barlack sighed. "Fine then. You are free to go."

"Goodbye, Barlack," I said. Not waiting for him to change his mind, I left the room and traveled down to the palace courtyard.

Making my way to the stable, I smiled at seeing Xander.

"Hello, boy."

He stepped forward, pressing his muzzle into my chest with a snort. "Don't worry boy. We're leaving," I said, nodding to the stable hand who went to task of saddling him.

"Let's go," I said, swinging up on his back. He snorted again, and began walking toward the entrance to the barn.

"Safe travels, Prince Damiyun," the stable boy said. I grit my teeth.

"I am not a fucking prince," I snarled over my shoulder.

Barlack, who stood outside the stables, laughed. "So, says you. See you in a Grand Passage," he called out as I guided Xander past him and out the gates of Oaken Leaf Castle.

"Do you think me a prince, Xander"

He tossed his head with a snort, and I laughed. "Exactly."

It didn't matter who my mother may or may not have been. It didn't matter that fucking Barlack named me the prince. I wasn't. I didn't want any of that shit. What did I know about running an entire kingdom? Fuck, I couldn't even run my own manor.

Xander trudged on out of the Wilde Elf lands, and I dropped the reins, guiding him with my legs as I pulled a bottle of Faeries Blood out of a saddlebag. The drink, I felt, was apropos for where I was heading.

Fuck, but how did I get myself bound to Ayelay? Not that I was disappointed in having to see her. She was sweet and she was the one who saved my neck when Zedekiah left me to take the fall for his actions.

Zedekiah. The traitor. Themesis' son.

How I didn't see his betrayal was beyond me. I should have. All the signs were there. He was a Shadow Walker tied to the Abyss and he owned my soul. But I foolishly trusted him, as did Lillyanna. Lil. My Lil. The only woman who loved me despite my flaws. Despite the darkness inside. Despite my betrayal that made her lose herself. She still loved me. He had not reached out to me, nor had he tried to find me. And if he were to show up on my doorstep, I would gleefully take his head and drop it at his father's feet.

Finishing the bottle, I tossed it into the woods and pulled out another. Xander snorted and tossed his head in disapproval.

"Oh, go on with you. Judging me now then? I guess we spent too much time with Barlack."

Xander huffed and I laughed. Taking a drink, I settled in for the long journey back to Willowshire.

Back to Ayelay.

ELEVEN
SERAFIN

I WALKED THROUGH THE palace halls to the atrium where I knew Phabian was waiting to take me on the traditional Name Day hunt. It saddened me no one else would be accompanying us. Usually, two dozen elves accompanied the leader, or the chosen heir such as I was, on a hunt that lasted three days. But for my time, it would only be Phabian and instead of the three days, it would be one—today.

The presence of beasts and demons made it too dangerous to be outside after dark. Though we had taken precautions for the celebration, digging trenches filled with lit pitch around my Name Day festivities, and lit torches further out marked the perimeter, it did not stop a flying beast from attacking, something we had not considered.

Sadly, six elves had perished in the attack and the celebration was brought inside the walls, though on a smaller scale. Fear and grief kept many celebrants away. I did not partake, the pall of the attack weighted heavily on me, as did the thought the event was an omen. I couldn't shake the feeling deep inside something terrible was going to happen. But what, I did not know.

I walked with my head down, eyes watching the creamy white marble floor pass beneath my feet. Something slammed into my shoulder, and I let out a startled gasp. I looked up, seeing two familiar High Elves. Lord Fa'vak Trounde stared down his nose at me. His bright orange cloak shifted as he nudged me out of the way.

"Saunac coaaughhom a'r oa llha'mo," he snapped.

My ears burned at the words. Stupid daughter of a whore. Oh, I heard it all. Filthy half-breed, human, Wilde Elf. But the worst slurs, those were saved for Phabian's brother, Krall and Lazaro. They favored calling me a half-breed cunt and sullied blooded bitch. Of course, those words were said rarely when Phabian was around.

They didn't have to sling insults for me to know I was different. That was obvious from a young age. I was much smaller than the others who towered over me. My hair color, while white, it had red streaks running through it and my unique eye color that could be blue, or green, or a combination of the two, the colors reflecting my mood, marked me as different.

It also proved the queen, Mouranda was not my mother, something my father confirmed when I was a child of nine.

"Serafin. You are growing up to be a beautiful girl," he said. It was a sunny summer day and we were walking through the palace gardens, my hand in the crook of his arm. Pulling up to a marble bench, Father sat, patting the spot next to him. I lowered myself onto the seat beside him. The sound of birds chittering filled the air, the scent of flowers, lilacs, lilies, and roses drifted on the breeze. I looked at Father. His gaze was far away as though he were reliving a past memory, and a sad smile curled his lips.

"Father? Are you alright?"

He looked at me and smoothed a hand over my hair. "You are so beautiful. You look so much like her. Your birth mother, Lillyanna."

Though I should have been surprised at his words, I wasn't. somewhere deep inside I had always known my mother was someone else.

"Who was she?"

He smiled, and his look became far away again. "She was a human who wandered into our lands. Though she should have been executed, she was alone, and I saw no harm in letting her live," he said. "She enchanted me. Bewitched me and I fell in love with her and through that," he grasped my hand and looked at me, "you, my beautiful, perfect daughter, you were born."

"What happened to her?"

Father pursed his lips. "When it came out, Mouranda forced her to agree to give you up and leave our lands."

Heat flushed through my body at his words, as did my new hatred for Mouranda. Surely, she knew he loved my mother. Why else would he have taken her to his bed? True, it might have been awkward to let her stay, but Father and Mouranda didn't share a bed and they were rarely together as it was.

"Where is she now?" My voice broke the silence. Perhaps I would be able to find her one day. The idea took root and grew in my mind.

"I don't know. I suspect she was reunited with her lover. Or perhaps she went back to Howling Cove."

The memory sparked the desire to find my mother again. Then, I was too small to go out alone and certainly not off our lands. But now? Now I was a woman, the future queen and desire reared its head again, igniting my soul. I needed to find her.

Tucking the thoughts deep inside me, I crossed the atrium. It was a large, square room painted white with high, vaulted ceilings. Busts of all the kings since Karrinian, including one of my father, lined the marble walls. Colorful tapestries with scenes of nature and celebrations hung from the ceiling. My eyes went to Phabian whose arms were wrapped around Lazaro in an intimate embrace. He was dressed in his hunting clothes, similar to mine, the greens and browns a drab comparison to the bright clothing Lazaro wore. His hair was tied back in a low pony tail, making his sharp features more prominent. Phabian's eyes met mine and he smiled.

"I will see you when I return." Phabian softly kissed Lazaro, then turned to me.

"Majesty," he said, bowing.

I laughed. "I am still a princess."

"Fucking cunt is more like it," Lazaro snarled.

Faster than I could blink, Phabian grabbed him and slammed him against the wall. "Apologize to Serafin."

Lazaro's nostrils flared. "No."

Phabian ground his teeth, and he leaned forward, his nose inches from Lazaro's. "We will discuss this when I return." He jerked back, shoving Lazaro away, who stumbled, catching himself before he fell. Casting me a glare, he stalked out of the atrium.

"I'm sorry, Sera," Phabian said as we stepped outside and walked toward the stables.

"It's alright. It certainly isn't the worst I've heard."

Phabian's jaw clenched. "He should know better. Trust that he will be reminded when I return."

I said nothing as we entered the barn, the scent of hay and dung filling my nose. Our horses were saddled and waiting, and I walked to where Yasmine stood. Scratching her nose, she leaned into me, nuzzling my neck.

"Are you ready to get a big buck, girl?"

Yasmine snorted and tossed her head. Laughing, I swung up into the saddle and followed Phabian out. Anticipation and excitement filled me, and I forgot no others would be joining us.

This was my first big hunt, and I was determined to kill big game to prove I was a worthy queen.

WE RODE DOWN THE road, the chattering of winter birds filled the air as the sun began to crest the horizon, spraying the sky in pinks and orange.

"Are you ready to be named queen?" Phabian's voice startled me.

I chewed my lip. Was I? It certainly was my birthright, and it would force all those who spat at me and said nasty things to kneel before me. They'd have bowed heads before clearly speaking, "your majesty."

"Serafin?"

"I think so. I mean, it will force everyone to acknowledge me as heir and their queen."

"But?"

I took a deep breath. "I don't know. Something feels wrong. Ever since that demon attacked, I've had a bad feeling in the pit of my stomach."

Phabian chuckled. "It's just nerves. It's a big day for you. Of course, you are going to think the worst of it. I assure you. Nothing bad is going to happen."

His words lightened my mood, if only a little. "You're right. As always," I said, flashing him a smile.

Phabian guided Maxamillian to the woods, and we picked our way through to a clearing beside a river. He pulled his mount to a halt, and I reined Yasmine in beside him.

"Ready?"

We swung down from our mounts, tethering them to a tree. I pulled my bow and the quiver of arrows from where they were stowed on Yasmine's back and strung the bow.

"Let's go. I'm ready to get a big buck."

Phabian grinned. "Lead on, then."

I crept through the woods, the soles of my fox fur boots crunching on leaves and sticks with each step, and I cursed the sound. Scanning the forest, bow held loosely in hand, I steadied my breathing, calming myself. My senses took over. Pine needles swayed in the breeze, millions of them. Tree sap flowing like blood through veins. A rabbit hopped softly from a copse twenty paces away. I felt the scuttle of squirrels running on branches. The smell of them invaded my nose. Fowl scratched in the snow. I heard the twitch of whiskers and the footpads of a wild cat trotting across the snow as loud as my own footfall. The natural world consumed me momentarily, as it always does, before I shut it out. Only one animal remained.

Him.

The buck stood to my right, grazing on a patch of grass poking through the snow. Lifting my bow, I took a deep, calming breath and nocked my arrow. The deer's head lifted, and his eyes locked on me.

Brown, beautiful eyes.

Innocent eyes.

Eyes that pleaded with me.

Don't, they said.

And I hesitated, just long enough for a blue-fletched arrow to imbed in his chest.

"You hesitated, Serafin."

I lowered my bow and glared at Phabian, who sauntered up to me, a smile playing on his lips.

"No, I didn't." The buck's life force fluttered. I felt it.

He laughed as he made his way to the buck. "You hesitated." He removed his arrow, inspected it, put it aside to be fixed later, then pulled his dagger and began removing the internal organs.

I watched him as he worked, knowing his words were true. I hesitated, but I couldn't exactly explain why.

"You can't let them do that to you, Serafin."

"Do what?" My voice cracked. I knew hunting was a necessity, but my connection with nature made it difficult to kill. His heart fluttered in my chest, a soft feeling like a bird fluffing its wings, and then it was gone. He was gone. I blinked back the tears that burned my eyes. Pushed down the guilt over taking a life.

"You know what. If you were to listen to every animal who pleaded with you for their life, you would be a shit hunter. And I know you're not."

"I was going to shoot him."

"You hesitated," he said for a third time as he sat beside me, folding his long legs beneath him. "If I hadn't shot, he would have gotten away."

I sighed. "Fine. I hesitated. But his eyes —"

"They all have eyes, or a cute face. You need to control what you feel, Serafin."

I watched Phabian as he dressed the deer. He was beautiful with his sharp Elven features, prominent nose, and strong jawline. Long, graceful fingers curled around the hilt of the dagger. His arm muscles bulged against the brown shirt he wore as he worked. He slid the blade between the folds of fabric from his trousers to remove the blood and then Phabian strung the buck on a tree branch. Quickly he washed up in the nearby stream.

"Come on. Let's have some lunch." Shaking the water from his hands, he made his way to where the horses grazed, grabbed a blanket, and spread it out on the ground.

I turned away from the buck's body and focused on Phabian, who was pulling items out of a sack.

I chewed on a piece of dried beef and shrugged out of my cloak. Though it was winter, it was far warmer than it should have been, the day feeling more like spring. We ate our meal in silence, my mind on the kill I didn't score, knowing the feeling—the connection I had with the animal—came from my mother's magic.

I knew little about her, only that she had magic, what people call a Wielder, and it was powerful. I had inherited her magic along with my father's—the King of the

Shadow Elves—and I could feel the constant battle of power coursing through my blood. The goodness of my mother's power and my father's dark Elven one.

"Joyous Name Day, Serafin," Phabian's voice pulled me from my dark and confusing thoughts, and I turned my attention to him. He held out a black velvet box tied with a white ribbon.

Every Name Day since I was small, Phabian bought me a piece of jewelry. Intricately designed bracelets, necklaces, earrings, and circlets. I treasured his gifts, knowing he handpicked them. Knowing they were made with care, and I looked forward to opening them.

Smiling, I opened the box. My eyes darted from one sparkle to the next. Gold, obsidian, rubies, and emeralds formed an intricate serpent and rose. The Shadow Elf crest. It was a stunning neckpiece. The head of the emerald serpent with a sparkling ruby eye lay next to the black rose flower, the tail and the stem went up, winding twice around my neck.

This was far more than anything he had bought me in the past.

"I can't." I set it back in the box. "It's too much."

Phabian laughed as he took the box from my hands and opened it back up. Removing the piece, he moved behind me.

"Phabian." I smiled and shook my head as I lifted my hair and let him secure the necklace around my neck.

"Nothing is too much for my Little Princess." His words were soft in my ears. Looking into his vibrant blue eyes as he moved in front of me, I shivered at the soft caress of his breath on my face.

"I am not a Little Princess. Today I am twenty-one. I am a woman, and I will be queen." I sniffed, looking down my nose at him. "It will force everyone to show me respect, including Mouranda." I longed for respect and acceptance. I wanted the queen to finally acknowledge me. To admit the throne and title were rightfully mine. She hated me. There was no denying that. I was the product of her husband's infidelity.

He smiled. Damn him for that engaging grin. "You will always be my Little Princess," he said, his blue eyes dancing with amusement. A breeze blew a lock of white of his hair free from the leather thong that held it back and I brushed it aside.

Phabian had been by my side for as long as I could remember. He was the only friend and ally I had, being a half-breed amongst the Shadow Elves. He had befriended my mother, and he promised to take care of me. Promised to protect me from the cruelty she knew I would endure.

"Are you alright?" Phabian's voice pulled me from my thoughts, his eyes concerned.

I stretched out on my side, resting my head on my hand, and looked up at him. "I was just thinking about my mother. My Name Day always makes me think about her."

Phabian pushed a lock of hair behind my ear. "I know. It's only natural you would," he said, stretching out and facing me.

I looked away from his penetrating gaze.

He reached out and cupped my chin, turning my head to face him again. "What is it, Sera?"

"Do you think me a Wilde Elf?"

He released me and frowned. "Why would you think that?"

"My mother was human, and they mate with humans. That's why they were banished." I bit my lip and looked down. "And I have heard some call me that."

"You are a Shadow Elf, Serafin. Regardless of what Lillyanna was. Your father loved her."

"I know but—"

"Stop. I will hear no more of this today," he commanded, his voice gentle.

I flopped onto my back and looked up at the fluffy white clouds that lazily drifted across the brilliant sky of blue.

"So, you're twenty-one today," Phabian said, drawing my attention again. "Have you thought about who you will lay claim to?"

I groaned. "You sound like my father, and no. I have given no thought to who I will lay claim to."

Phabian looked down at me. "Hmm. Not even Cal?" He raised an eyebrow, and my face heated. "Don't think I haven't seen the two of you sneak off. Or that your hair is mussed, and clothes wrinkled when you return."

The fire in my face grew. I will admit Cal was a handsome Elf who I allowed certain liberties, though never letting it go too far.

"You're too nosey for your own good," I pushed Phabian away. He fell onto his back with a laugh. "I wouldn't lay claim to Cal, anyway. His designs are not for me, rather for the throne." I sat back up. I knew this to be true when he didn't bother to come see me, let alone wish me joyous Name Day when I passed him in the hall.

"Well then, who else?"

I shrugged. "What if I don't want to be Blood Bound?" I chewed my lip. "What if... what if the man I choose takes over? What if I am forced to... to breed?"

Phabian cupped my face with his hand. "Your father has the authority to grant or deny your union. He also swore an oath to your mother, and you know he is a man of his word. A man who upholds the law. He would not let that happen to you."

I opened my mouth to speak, my words cut off by the snap of a twig. We both grabbed our weapons and jumped to our feet. "To my left," I hissed to Phabian, seeing a rustle in the woods. We both slowly turned, aiming arrows at a human man who approached on horseback.

"Halt." I called out. The tall, black-haired man continued to advance. "I said halt." I loosed an arrow. It skimmed his shoulder.

He touched the wound, licking the blood from his fingertips. Ice-blue eyes narrowed on me. "Bitch." A snarl curled his lips.

While Phabian was all kindness and rugged strength, this man had jagged edges. His horse black as night. The sword sheathed on his hip dangled broad and long. One hand curled around the hilt. Heat gathered in the hollow of my neck and flooded my chest. The man smirked, and I glared at him. This man had an ego larger than Il'Ekhester.

I nocked another arrow. "I said halt. Twice. Which you did not."

Phabian snorted. The man reined his horse several yards away, and I noted the black trousers and black shirt. The two swords crossed over a scarlet "S" on the left side of the chest.

Suppressor.

"What are you doing on our lands?" I leveled the arrow at his heart.

He turned his attention to Phabian. "I have come to renegotiate the treaty we have with your kind."

"The treaty doesn't expire for two more Grand Passages," I said.

The man's eyes flicked to me for a moment, then he addressed Phabian. "There are things that need discussing. Things which will benefit both of us. If you don't mind taking me to your king?"

"I told you the last time you were here. We are not going to tell you how to make the Sigaa'Lean."

I frowned. What was Phabian talking about? I narrowed my eyes on the dark-haired man. "The king is away. I am regent in his stead. I will be more than happy to look over what you are proposing."

He smirked. "I will not conduct negotiations with a child."

I moved the aim of my arrow and let it go, grazing his other shoulder. His eyes narrowed dangerously on me—a depthless, icy stare to make me shiver—and he walked his horse forward a few paces.

"It would serve you best to watch yourself, little girl." His hands clenched the reins. "I can easily write your servitude to me in the treaty for your lack of hospitality."

I laughed. "Try it. I am sure my father—the king—wouldn't let his only daughter go so easily."

A slow, evil smile spread across his face. "Oh, love. You have no idea what I will threaten until I get what is mine," he said, voice low and menacing. "And I always get what is mine."

I swallowed hard at his words, a sliver of fear creeping up my spine. I didn't doubt them to be true.

Phabian leveled his arrow at the man's head. "That's quite enough. The king is not here. Leave the document and he will look it over and respond in kind."

"That will not be necessary. I will be back. That I can promise." His eyes swept over me as he clicked his tongue and heeled his mount around, back in the direction he came.

Phabian lowered his arrow, and I shivered, the surrounding air suddenly cold. Bending down, I picked up my cloak and pulled it around me, hugging it close.

"Not bad, Princess. You will be quite the leader."

"He's been here before," I said.

Phabian nodded as we began to pack up the picnic, securing the items on our mounts. "Yes. He was here twenty-one Grand Passages ago. He wanted to know how to make the Sigaa'Lean, which would negate our treaty. I suspect that's what his intentions were today." He glanced at me as he swung up onto Maxamillian. "Your father would never allow such a thing."

"I know," I said as I swung up on Yasmine's back. Excitement filled me as we headed back towards the palace. In a few hours I would be acknowledged as the heir and queen. I smiled at the thought as we rode in silence. Entering the palace grounds, we handed off the horses to the stable hand. Phabian hoisted the buck onto his shoulders.

"You're going to escort me to my party, right?" I placed a hand on his arm. He looked down at me, a smile lit his blood-stained face. Licking my thumb, I wiped off some of the mess. Laughing, he grabbed my hand and kissed my palm.

"Has there ever been a Name Day when I didn't? I'll be there, Serafin. I promise."

TWELVE
PHABIAN

"**P**HABIAN," MY BROTHER KRALL'S voice called out as I left the smoke-house.

"Krall," I greeted with a smile.

He wrinkled his nose. "You're covered in blood and smell awful."

I laughed. Krall was never one for hunting. No doubt he didn't know from where the meat for the table came. "It was the Name Day hunt. Of course, I'm going to be covered in blood. Serafin felled a big buck." I pointed at the carcass that hung from hooks in the beams. Though it was I who killed the deer, I knew had she not hesitated, her arrow would have pierced him.

Her mother's magic, while beautiful and amazing, allowing Serafin to do such things as make flowers grow in the winter, produce rain showers, and know what ails an animal, it was a detriment when it came to hunting. Her connection with nature made her feel everything. I was certain she had felt the life leave the buck. Her face said as much.

It pained me that no one wanted to go on the hunt with us, and the way most of the elves treated her boiled my blood. I heard the names hurled and saw the hurt, the tears in Serafin's eyes. She put on a brave face, pretended the words didn't sting, but I knew. She might be able to hide her feelings from others, but never from me. Always her eyes told me the story. Always her eyes showed her pain.

Though I was able to keep my brother and Lazaro somewhat in line with my threats, there was nothing I could do with the others. And when either man stepped out of line, I made sure they felt my wrath, something Lazaro would be feeling for his blatant insolence. And I couldn't help but wonder if the king heard the words spoken, and if he did, why didn't he do anything about it? After all, he punished those who called Lilyanna the King's Whore. He even executed those who tried to kill her. Those who tried to cut Serafin from her womb.

I shook the negative thoughts from my head, making a mental note to ask the king. This was a happy day. The day my Little Princess would claim her birthright. Where had the time gone. It seemed only yesterday I was holding her as a wee babe in my arms, reading her stories and singing her lullaby's. And now she is a beautiful young woman. A petulant, rebellious young woman who I loved with all my heart. A woman who would one day lead the Shadow Elves, and I would serve her just as I have my king.

"Phabian. Where did you go?" Krall's voice brought me back.

"Sorry. I have to go wash up for Serafin's celebration," I said, striding past him.

Krall grabbed my arm as I passed. "No, you don't." Turning, I looked at him. "Trespassers have been seen on the eastern border. We need to go take a look."

I pulled my arm from his grasp. "Then get Laz to go."

Krall shook his head. Reaching into his pocket he pulled out a folded piece of parchment, the violet wax seal—the Shadow Elf crest with the letters *AT* in flowing script—denoted it was from the king. Frowning, I opened the paper and read the short note:

Phabian, trespassers were seen on our eastern border. You are to accompany Krall in the search for them.

I folded the decree with a sigh. Why the king wanted me to go was beyond me. While Krall commanded the king's guard, Lazaro had second. It was his place to go, but I could not ignore a royal order.

"Fine. Let's go then and make it quick. I have to escort Serafin to her party."

I made my way to where Maxamillian waited, still saddled from the hunt, and swung up onto his back. Krall swung up onto Mist, and we heeled our mounts down the road and out the gates. I rolled my shoulders, trying to shake the creeping feeling of something not being right.

Forming a picture of her in my mind, I reached out. *Sera? I might be a little late in retrieving you. Please wait for me,* I sent out. There was no response, which made my trepidation grow.

"Why did the king ask me to go with you? Why not Lazaro? He is the second in command. Patrolling is one of his duties."

"Lazaro has other tasks to attend to." Krall's eyes remained forward, though I noticed he gripped the reins a bit harder.

Closing my eyes, I took a deep breath. Opening them, I looked at Krall. Something told me he wasn't being forthright with me and, focusing on him, I reached out with my magic, curling it around his mind to gently probe for the truth.

And I came up on a block. Krall's nostrils flared. I knew he felt me. I gripped Max's reins, trying to quell the shaking in my hands. The only reason he would have a block is if there were something to hide. Sweat trickled down my back and my heart pounded in my ears. I took several deep breaths to calm myself. To stop me from leaping off Max and plunging my dagger deep into Krall's heart, though that would do me no favors. I still would not know what he is hiding from me.

A light snow began to fall, the soft sound of the flakes hitting the ground filled the relative silence between Krall and me.

"Krall—"

"You know I protect myself around you. Many of us do," he said, his tone terse.

I sat up straight in the saddle. "If you have nothing to hide from me, let me in."

Krall's lips pursed, and he gave a curt nod. Once again, I reached out with my magic, wrapping tendrils around his mind, gently probing. Pictures flashed in rapid succession. Krall in a tavern in Duenney with a whore on his lap. Another of him and one of his eldest sons sparring in the training yard. Krall in an intimate moment with a male elf.

On and on the memories flashed, and then I saw him in the king's den. Allendaire was speaking as he handed Krall the sealed parchment. The memory flashed so fast, I could not hear the words spoken between them.

My fear began to turn to panic.

"Satisfied?"

Don't let him know you are still suspicious. "Yes," I said, flashing a smile.

Krall slowed Mist down as the eastern border came into view. Pulling our mounts to a halt, we both swung down and securing them to a tree, we made our way to the edge. Stepping into the woods, I crouched down, examining the brush and leaves that covered the ground for any signs that someone had been through here. I moved through the woods, stopping now and again to examine the terrain, Krall trailing behind.

"No one has been here."

"One of the sentries said he saw a group of humans walking through the woods."

Rising, I wiped my hands off on my trousers. "No one has been through here. There are no foot prints or broken branches that would indicate a person has passed. There are only game trails."

"Check again." I folded my arms and leveled my gaze on Krall. "Are you doubting my ability to track? By all means, Krall, go on in and tell me what you see." My irritation with my brother was high, as was the feeling this was a falsity.

"Check again, Phabian."

I had enough of his games. Of his evasion and what was becoming clear to be an effort to stall me. I took a few steps toward him.

"What is this about, Krall? Why have I been brought on this sham of a search?"

His gaze dropped to the ground. His gesture confirmed my suspicions. This had to do with Serafin and her twenty-first Name Day. I rushed to Maxamillian.

"Phabian, wait." Krall's voice called from behind.

I ignored him as I swung up in the saddle. Krall grabbed Max's reins. Max tossed his head, shoving into him and knocking him on his ass. If I wasn't so angry, I would have laughed. Grabbing the reins, I pulled my mount around. Digging my heels in, I urged him into a gallop and raced back to the palace.

I hoped, no, prayed to those deities I did not believe in, my fear was unfounded. I prayed when I got back to the palace, I would find my Little Princess in her rooms preparing for the celebration.

Please, I begged. *Please let her be alright.*

THIRTEEN
MOURANDA

S INKING BACK AGAINST THE tub, the warm water enveloped me. My body relaxed, any kinks, any stress I had felt dissolved as the warmth embraced. Closing my eyes, I rested my head against the back of the tub.

Today was Serafin's twenty-first name day. The half-breed daughter of a whore who never should have been born would be recognized as the heir.

The future queen of the Shadow Elves.

I tried to love the girl, truly I had, but as a babe, she did nothing but scream when I was around. As she grew older, I tried harder. Though her reception was cold, I still had hope inside she would accept me. Like her mother, she favored the library, reading the same book Lillyanna read, *"The Story of Jayne."*

I remember once when it was just shy of her twelfth Name Day, walking by into the warm confines of the library.

The scent of leather and paper hung in the air. Serafin sat curled up on a chair in front of the windows, that blasted book open on her lap. She looked up when I crossed the room, taking the chair opposite her. Closing the book, she folded her arms. Blue-green eyes glared at me.

"Have you come to make fun of my ignorant human self for reading the same book again and again?"

I blinked, taken aback by the hostility in her words. I had done nothing but sit down. I glanced at the book in her lap, the cover worn, binding broken, and pages stuck out in a haphazard way.

"Of course not," I said. "I know that book was a favorite of Lillyanna's. It only seems natural that you would favor it too. Tell me, Serafin. What is it about? What makes you like it so?"

She picked up the book, stuffing the pages back inside. "Besides the fact that my mother held it in her hands?" Green eyes met mine. Eyes the color of Lillyanna's. My cold heart shattered for a moment as I remembered the girl's mother almost begging me to let her hold Serafin after she was born. But I didn't out of fear of Lillyanna bonding with the babe.

For all the good it did me. She hated me regardless.

"It's a story about a fierce warrior woman whose heart of ice was melted by a mortal," Serafin said bringing me back. Her hand caressed the worn cover. "It's a beautiful story about love and two people from different backgrounds overcoming their differences and letting love win."

Her eyes met mine again and though I wanted to tell her I did love her, I knew she would think those words false.

Rising, she strode across the room, putting the worn and well-loved book back on the shelf, her fingers caressing the spine in reverence. I watched her walk out of the room, head held high, back straight. Always the regal princess. She didn't cast a look back. Didn't offer a good-bye and my heart constricted. I knew she hated me, but what else was I supposed to do? Keep my husband's whore under the same roof? Let her bond with her child? Though that didn't matter as the girl never bonded with me. Never me. It was Phabian and Allendaire, but never me.

Rising from my chair, I crossed the room and pulled the book off the shelf. The pages Serafin shoved in fell to the floor. As I watched the pages flutter and fall, an idea formed in my head. Scooping them up, I put them back where they belonged, tucked the book beneath my arm and made my way back to my room.

Over the course of the next few days, I spent all my spare time reading The Story of Jayne. I had to admit it was an entertaining story. Sweet, and at the same time, tragic. When I finished the book, I took it to a book restorer in town.

"This book has seen better days." The man behind the counter adjusted his glasses and peered down at the worn book.

"It's well loved," I said.

"It would probably be best to buy a new one."

"This book has sentimental value to my daughter. I would like it repaired as I wish to give to her as a surprise for her Name Day."

"Very well," he sighed, taking the book.

Leaving the shop, I then made my way through the streets to the tapestry weaver. I wanted to memorialize a scene in the book for Serafin to hang on her wall. It was a beautiful scene of the Blood Binding between Jayne and her mortal lover, Bennington. The description of the scene was stunning, and reading it brought me to tears. I thought the beauty of it perfect for Serafin.

While she was on the traditional Name Day hunt with her father and Phabian on her twelfth birthday, I slipped into her room, hung the tapestry on the wall and left the book wrapped in green paper on her bed, and I waited patiently for her to see her surprise.

But she never said a word to me about it. No thank you. No daughterly hug. Instead, she tore down the tapestry, leaving the bundle in front of my room and the book? Well, the girl was upset that I fixed it. That I had taken her mother's essence from the pages, making it something sterile and foreign. But she did not give it up.

The memories faded and I rose from the now tepid water. Drying off, I pulled on a warm, plush robe and padded across the room, the marble tiles cold on my feet, and sat down at my desk. The wind blew shaking the windows, white snow swirled, hissing against the glass. Slipping a chain over my head, I unlocked a drawer and stared down at the Tome inside. Pulling the book out, I traced the winged beast with scales made of emeralds on the cover. Ruby and citrine plumes of fire poured from its mouth, obsidian eyes looked at me, and the diamond talons glinted in the light. It was a book from the Dark Elves, a race long eradicated by the Shadow Elves. Why a book that contained dark and forbidden magic was tucked in the furthest stacks in the library was beyond me.

When I found it, the layers of dust and cobwebs told me the volume was long forgotten.

A knock at the door made me freeze.

"My queen? Are you there?"

I relaxed at the sound of Denalla's voice. "Come," I called.

The doors opened and Denalla stood on the threshold, her eyes going to the book I cradled on my lap. A frown drew her lips down.

"What's wrong?"

I placed the book back in the drawer. Shutting and locking it, I held the key in my hand. Pulsing magic through, I felt the metal heat. The fire burned my hand, but I did not let go. I pulsed more magic through until it was nothing but liquid. Until the key that hid my secret was no more.

"Everything is as it should be," I said, rising from the chair.

Denalla smiled, holding her hand out to me.

"Shall I get you ready for the celebration?"

My fingers danced across my abdomen as I took her hand. "Yes. You shall."

Denalla placed the crown in the form of the Shadow Elf crest upon my head and stood back, hands folded in front of her, and a smile on her lips. I turned to the mirror, taking in my black dress. The severe bun, and the ruby eyes of the serpent that glinted in the lamplight. My eyes met Denalla's.

"Ready, my queen?" She said with a curtsey.

Turning from the mirror, I held out my hand to her. "I am more than ready."

FOURTEEN
SERAFIN

"Ow." I jerked my head out of Cwella's hands, rubbing the spot where the pin had poked.

"Stop fidgeting, and you won't get hurt," she said, pulling me back.

"I'm just nervous." I wiped my sweaty hands on my dress.

Cwella squatted in front of me and took my hands. "Take a deep breath, Serafin, and stop wiping your dirty hands on your dress. You're going to ruin it."

I took a deep breath, and slowly exhaled, though it did not calm me. It was more than just nerves. I couldn't shake the foreboding feeling. It was more than the beast that had attacked ruining the celebration. It was more than me failing to kill the deer during my Name Day hunt. It was a feeling deep within my bones something horrible was going to happen. It was a voice inside my head telling me to run and never look back. I wanted to tell Cwella of my fear, of the reason I was so nervous, but I knew she would brush it off. Just like Phabian had.

Cwella placed a circlet on my head, a delicate and much smaller version of the royal crown, made in the shape of the Shadow Elf crest.

"You look absolutely beautiful, princess." A smile curled Cwella's lips as she stepped back. "You look just like the queen you are. If you have not picked a suiter yet, I guarantee by the time the night is over they will be lined up fighting for your hand."

Laughing, I rose and turned to the full-length mirror. The long sleeved off the shoulder white dress shimmered, the tiny diamonds and pearls sewn into the fabric caught the sunlight, making the dress look as if it were glowing. The necklace from Phabian nestled between my collarbones, and the circlet rested atop my head. The emeralds that made up the serpent sparkled, its red eyes glinted in an almost menacing way, bringing my trepidation that briefly left, back.

A knock at the door made both Cwella and I jump. Rushing across the room, I pulled it open. My heart raced at not seeing Phabian standing on the other side ready to escort me to the ballroom, rather Samel and Lazaro stood outside. My mouth went dry, and my stomach turned.

"W-where is Phabian?"

"What's going on?" Cwella's voice came from behind.

I turned and looked at her. "I don't know." My voice shook. I looked back at the men who stood in the hall. "Where is Phabian?"

"We were told to fetch you for the celebration," Lazaro said, ignoring my question.

The hair on the back of my neck stood up, and a chill washed over me. Reaching behind, I grabbed Cwella's hand and gripped it. It was too late to slam and lock the door, though I wanted to do just that.

Standing up straight, and willing my hands to stop shaking, I stepped out into the hall, Cwella beside me, giving my hand a gentle, reassuring squeeze. Samel and Lazaro flanked us as we walked through the halls. I glanced at Cwella who chewed her lip, eyes darting around, and I knew she was nervous too.

Pulling up a mental picture of Phabian, I reached out to him. There had to be a reason he wasn't here.

Phabian, where are you? Something is very wrong. I need you.

Silence followed my words.

I gripped Cwella's hand, clutched my skirt, and took deep breaths, trying to calm my racing heart. We stopped at the closed doors of the ballroom. No noise came from within. No music. No voices, or laughter. I took a step back. Lazaro's hand clamped down on one arm, Samel's on the other

"What is the meaning of this? Let me go." I jerked in their grasp.

"Let her go." Cwella grabbed Lazaro's arm. He glared down at her and shoved her away. She stumbled back, falling hard on her backside. Samel pushed the doors open, and I was dragged into the room.

I looked around, my legs shaking at seeing the room not set up for a banquet. Rows of chairs lined the floor, every seat occupied by an elf. Those who did not get a chair stood. At the head of the room was a table, behind which sat Mouranda, with my father to her left. Sweat broke out on my body as realization hit me.

This was a trial. My trial.

Lazaro and Samel dragged me to stand before the table. Stumbling, I caught myself before I crashed to the floor.

"What is going on?" My voice broke the stony silence. "Father?"

Whispers rustled through the room.

"Father?" I stepped closer to the table.

He sat with his hands folded, eyes forward, and jaw clenched. He did not look at me.

Did not acknowledge me.

Mouranda's lips pulled back into a smile. Pure hatred flashed in her blue eyes. She sat ramrod straight, hands folded on the table. Her hair was pulled back in a tight bun. The light of the late afternoon sun glinted off the diamonds in the crown that sat on her head. The black high-necked dress she wore brought out the whiteness in her skin, making her look ghostly. Frightening.

"It's so nice of you to join us all for your...celebration." She gestured to the people who chuckled at her words.

"What's going on?" My voice sounded weak to my ears. The room became uncomfortably warm. I could smell the odor of sweat emanating from the elves in attendance. I looked out at the sea of people who hissed at me. At the High Elves of the court dressed in their finery, the bright color glaring to my eyes.

Phabian, please. Where are you? I need you desperately.

Again, I was hit with silence.

"You are no longer welcome in the palace or our lands."

My head whipped in Mouranda's direction. What did she mean?

"You never should have been born. Your whore mother should have been executed when she stepped foot on our lands, but she wasn't. My husband's infidelity produced you, and though everything about the relationship and your birth went against our laws, your father," she spat the word, "bent them so he could have an heir to preserve his legacy." She sat back in her chair, her hands resting on her abdomen. "It seems the healers were wrong. After countless Grand Passages of miscarriages, of not having my husband's seed take, I now carry the true heir. A full blood Shadow Elf who will be king."

A cheer rose up through the room at her words. She looked at me with a satisfied smirk.

Coldness washed over me like a bucket of water. I shook my head. Wrapping my arms around myself, I tried to block out the murmurs that grew increasing louder. Increasingly angry.

"Kill her. Kill the filthy half-breed daughter of a whore."

Rushing forward, I threw myself onto my knees in front of the table. "Please, Father," I begged.

Rising, he looked out at the rowdy crowd. "Silence," his voice boomed, bringing the chatter to an abrupt halt.

Hope bloomed inside as I slowly rose to my feet. Hope he was going to oppose the queen. Hope he was going to assert my birthright.

But that light of hope was dim and fading. He did not look at me. Did not smile as he addressed those in attendance.

"The law is clear," his rich, powerful voice rolled through the silence. "Though I made an exception, bent the law for my daughter to secure an heir, the tides have changed. The queen is with child. She carries the full blood prince. Any title, any land and anything previously designated for Serafin Trounde, now goes to the unborn child. And henceforth," his cold, blue eyes penetrated me. "Henceforth,

I denounce Serafin Trounde as my heir and I will uphold the law as it is written. Upon the morrow, Serafin Trounde will be publicly executed in the square."

The room erupted into pandemonium at his words, though I hardly heard anything over the pounding in my ears. My vision tunneled, my legs grew weak, and I collapsed to the floor. Sickness rolled through me, and I emptied the contents of my stomach onto the high polished white marble.

This couldn't be happening. It's just a nightmare.

But I knew it wasn't. The feelings that had not left me from the first day of the celebration had been valid. Something horrible indeed happened.

And where was Phabian? Why wasn't he here?

"Get that filthy half-breed out of here," Mouranda's voice snapped.

Lazaro grabbed my arm and jerked me painfully to my feet. I fought against him, trying to yank my arm from his grasp as he secured a bracelet on my wrist.

"Rorla'rro ho rloagha rma'rl ho Waorcom," Lazaro spoke the words "remove the magic from the Wielder." I inhaled sharply as my magic rushed from my body, encapsulated within the obsidian bracelet.

Samel grabbed my other arm and jerked me forward.

"I think I can handle this," Lazaro said. "She has no magic, and I doubt this puny cunt could hurt me."

Samel shrugged and released my arm.

"Let's go," Lazaro snarled, dragging me across the room. As we exited, I heard my father's jovial voice.

"Let us all celebrate the life that grows inside the queen. Let us all celebrate the rightful heir. To our future king."

Cheers rose up, and music started, the sound fading as I was dragged through the halls. Tears stung my eyes, but I refused to let them fall. What would be the point to wallow in self-pity when I wouldn't be around once the sun rose on the morrow? And reaching out to Phabian did no good. I don't know why he did not respond and could only surmise he had turned his back on me.

Lazaro led me down a flight of steep, stone steps. Inserting a key in the door at the bottom, he pushed it open, the hinges screaming in protest from lack of use. Grabbing a torch off the wall, he lit it and pulled me down a dark and dank hallway. It smelled of earth, mildew, rot, and death. The echo of water dripping from somewhere began to grate on my nerves. The torch cast ghostly shadows on the moss-covered walls. Faceless beasts with sharp teeth and claws undulated in terrifying ways.

Lazaro came to an abrupt stop. I hadn't paid much attention to where we were going. Why should I? It didn't matter, as I would be locked in a cell. I looked around, noticing we were in a small alcove. Lazaro leaned forward toward a wall and whispered words. The alcove shook, dust and debris fell from the ceiling. The sound of stone scraping on stone echoed off the walls. A breeze rustled my hair bringing with it a stale, musty scent. Lazaro turned to face me, stepping to the left revealing darkness beyond an open door.

"What is this?" I looked from Lazaro to the opening, not comprehending fully what I was seeing.

"This corridor stretches beneath the palace. There is a door at the end that opens to the outside on the northern border."

I blinked. What was he saying? "What?" I had no other words.

"Yasmine is tethered in the woods. Keep as much of a straight line as you can, and you will find her. I made sure to hide her well. I have loaded her with your dagger, bow and quiver of arrows. There's a cloak, warm boots, change of clothes as well as a sack of food and coin."

Grasping my wrist, he leaned forward, speaking the words to remove the Sigaa'Lean. My magic filled me with a rush. I stared at Lazaro. At the person who hated me the most. The one who despised my mother just as much. What was this about? My mouth went dry as a thought occurred to me. This could be a trap. Perhaps he was leading me not to freedom, rather to my death. What would it matter if I was executed in the morning, or hunted down and killed for sport this eve? Dead is dead.

I took a step back. "Take me to my cell."

"Serafin—"

"I want no part of whatever death game you plan on playing. Take me to my cell."

Lazaro ran a hand through his hair. "I don't blame you for your thoughts, nor do I blame you for not trusting me, but I am asking you to do just that. Just this once. I promise I am not up to anything nefarious."

"How can, I be sure?"

He shrugged. "You can't, but I promise you I am not. Take the tunnel, Serafin. Run fast and run far. Don't go to Duenney or Theonaus. Run until you are far away from these lands. Run until you feel you are safe and only then should you stop."

I swallowed past the lump in my throat. Something in his words made me believe, if only slightly, he was being true.

"Why are you doing this? Why are you helping the half-breed daughter of a whore?"

He winced at my words. "Maybe I am doing it for Phabian. Maybe I think something is wrong about the queen being with child." His blue eyes bored into me. "Or maybe I am saving the true heir to the Shadow Elf throne."

Tears stung my eyes and this time I let them fall. "Thank you, Lazaro. I won't soon forget this."

He gave a curt nod, and a half-smile curled his lips. "Before you leave, I need you to do something, and I think you will like it."

I frowned. "What is it?"

Lazaro's grin widened. "I need you to beat me up a bit."

I blinked. "What?"

"Beat me up. It has to look like you put up a fight and then escaped. You're not going to get another opportunity like this."

I stared at Lazaro, his words sinking in. He was right. I was going to enjoy it. I thought about all the nasty slurs he threw at me, the looks he gave me, let my anger, my hatred fill me. Making a fist, I pulled back my right arm and punched him in the jaw. It was like hitting stone. My hand smarted, but damn, it felt good.

Lazaro's head snapped to the side, and he rubbed his chin. "Impressive."

I launched myself at him, kicking, punching, and scratching, the sound of my fists hitting bones and flesh and his grunts filled the small area. I assaulted him with twenty-one Grand Passages of pent-up fury from the way not only he treated me, but everyone else. I punched, kicked, and scratched until my arms were sore, my hands hurt, and my breathing became ragged.

"You were right. I did enjoy that."

Lazaro laughed, a sound that turned into a wheeze, and he winced with pain.

"Go, Serafin," he said, grabbing another torch from the wall. Lighting it, he handed it to me. "Don't turn around and don't stop running until you are far away and safe."

Taking the torch, I nodded. "Thank you, Lazaro."

He smiled. "Stay alive, highness. I have a feeling we will need you."

I stepped into the corridor, and the door slid into place. My ears rang in the deafening silence. Holding the torch out in front of me, I began to walk, hoping that Lazaro was being truthful and I would be heading to freedom.

FIFTEEN

THE CORRIDOR WAS DAMP, the air thick with a musty, rotten smell. The torch light danced off the mossy wall, casting my shadow in an eerie, menacing way. The scratching sound of critters scurrying around echoed through the hall. I did not want to think about what they were.

Quickening my pace, I hurried on. I wondered what Lazaro would tell the king. Would he send elves out to search for me to bring me back to the dungeon to await execution, or would he dismiss it in the hopes I would perish at the hands of the demons and monsters when night fell?

Tears pricked my eyes, and I swiped at them like a child. How could a day with so much promise go so wrong? I did not understand how the king could throw me away, sentence me to death. His words denouncing me rang in my ears. I could not get the sight of his cold, blue eyes out of my mind. And where was Phabian during all of this? Did he abandon me on purpose? Was he afraid of being sentenced to death if he stood beside me? The thought shattered my heart. I shook my head. There was no use crying over what happened. It was done. Wiping the tears from my cheeks, I pushed down my self-pity and let my anger, my hatred, grow into a cold, hard stone next to my heart.

And through all of this came the least likely ally I could have ever imagined. If it came down for me to choose who would have helped me, Lazaro was most certainly not on that list. And yet, he did. His words played over in my head, one thing he said in particular. He felt something was wrong with Mouranda being with child. Though I hadn't had time to think about it, his words gave me pause. The reason I was born, the reason the king bent the law and allowed me to live was because Mouranda was barren but now she was with child? It didn't make sense, though it was no longer my problem.

I trudged on through the hall. The air was hot and stale. Sweat poured off my body. My dress clung to me, and my hair stuck to the back of my neck and face. Gathering it up, I piled it on top of my head in a make-shift bun, bending the flimsy circlet around to make it stay.

How much further did I have to go? I feared my torch light would extinguish, the hiss and sputters that came made me think it was close. Though I could use my magic to light the way, I did not know how much further the end was. I did not want to deplete my energy as I would need all the strength I had when I had to flee.

Finally, after more moments, I saw the outline of a door just ahead. Relief flowed through me, and I rushed to it. Stopping in front of it, I brought the torch light closer. I hadn't thought about how I would get it open but now faced with the only barrier between me and freedom, the thought loomed over me like a thunder cloud. The torch sputtered, then went out, plunging me into darkness.

"Damn it."

Tossing it aside, I held out my right hand. Calling my magic forth, a bright, white orb filled my palm, the corridor exploding in a wash of white light. The door came into perfect view, allowing me to inspect it. It was tall and wooden with a rusted lock and handle. Looking closer, I noticed small holes in the wood where insects of some sort had bored in. Reaching out, I touched the wood. It felt soft. Spongy.

My heart raced. The wood was rotten. Extinguishing the light, I took several steps back. Lowering my body, I ran at the structure, putting all my weight behind my right shoulder. I hit the door hard, but it did not budge. Stepping back further, I ran at it again.

Nothing.

The thought of using my magic to blast it to pieces crossed my mind, but I did not know if there was a search party beyond and I did not want to draw attention to myself. Again and again, I threw myself at the door. I was not going to give up. I couldn't. This was the only way out of the tunnel. It was either break it down or die a slow and painful death.

Finally, after the fifth try, I heard a crack. Bolstered by the noise, I ran at full speed, putting everything behind my body and launched myself at the door again. The wood exploded and I sailed through the other side.

Right into a thicket of briars.

Thorns scraped my face and hands drawing blood. They caught on my dress, tearing it up. I scrambled to my feet, pulling the brambles off me, ignoring the stinging in my hands and face. Ignoring the blood that ran. There was no time to take care of my wounds. I carefully picked my way through the patch, my eyes on the woods that seemed so very far away. Woods that I needed to get safely to.

"She couldn't have gone far," a voice close by—too close—said. "It hasn't been that long. The bitch is probably cowering in the woods."

I quietly backed up behind the briar patch. Squatting down, I peered out between the branches. Up ahead and a bit to the left was a party of six soldiers, all dressed in armor.

Fuck.

Hunkering down even further, I willed the group to pass by. Eyes scanned the area, horses danced impatiently on their hooves. I held my breath as I watched the group.

A pair of blue eyes met mine. I did not know who it was, the helmet they wore preventing that, but I knew he saw me. The blood rushed to my head. My chest constricted. I couldn't move.

I called my magic, feeling the rush of power course through me, and held it close, ready to unleash it. I would kill whoever tried to capture me. I would not go back. I would not be executed. Anger flowed through my body, calming me.

I would fight to the death.

The man turned his attention back to the group, walking his mount forward. "She's not here. Let's join the others at the eastern border."

It was Lazaro. He was taking his group far from here to allow me to escape, I knew. Gratitude flowed through me, and I silently thanked him for not betraying me. For not misplacing my trust.

I waited until the cold seeped into my bones. Until I was sure the party was far away, then I pulled my cramped body up, and bolted for the woods, keeping a straight line. Branches caught my dress, the fabric tearing when I pulled it free. Roots caught my feet and more than once I fell, scraping my hands on rocks and debris. Pulling myself up, I kept going. My legs ached and my lungs burned, but I was not going to stop.

Fuck. Where is she?

Finally, my eyes caught a flash of white hidden beneath the bows of a massive pine tree. I stumbled, catching myself before I fell again, and hurried to where Yasmine was. A warm black cloak and boots sat on the saddle. Bulging saddle bags were secured across her back, along with my bow and quiver. Kicking off the thin leather shoes I wore, I stuffed them in the bag and pulled on the boots and threw the cloak around my shoulders. Untethering Yasmine, I swung up into the saddle.

"Let's go, Yaz, and make haste. I want to be as far from here as I can get and safely tucked into a warm bed at an inn. I do not wish to be caught out in the woods at night.

Yasmine reared up, then took off like a bolt through the woods, leaping over logs and dodging trees. I ducked and weaved beneath low branches as she raced on. Yasmine stuck to the woods, as if she knew the importance of my staying hidden.

Though I was sure the search parties were far away, if not given up for the day, I did not relax and kept a constant eye on my surroundings. We raced on, stopping on occasion to briefly let Yasmine rest and drink. I knew I was running her hard, something that could be to her detriment, but I needed to put as much space behind me as I could.

"You're doing good, girl," I said as I rubbed her down on one of our stops. She tossed her head and let out a low whinny. "I know I'm running you hard and I'm sorry. Please. I ask that you find the strength to just go a little further."

And she did.

We raced for a few more hours, then rested once again.

"That's it. No more racing," I said, scratching her nose. Pulling away, I picked through the dense woods. Peering through the branches I saw what looked to be a road several yards away. Returning to my mount, I swung up on her back, turning her in the direction I had come.

"There's a road just past that thicket. With any luck it will lead to a village where we can stay for the night." I looked up at the sky, noting the sun's rapid decent toward the horizon. I did not wish to be caught out when darkness fell.

Clicking my tongue, I kicked my heels into Yasmine's sides, guiding her forward to the road and toward what I hoped would be a village and a safe place to rest for the night.

THE JOURNEY WAS QUIET, Yasmine and I the only ones on the road for a long time. After a while, I passed covered carriages with people bundled up inside, some people walking, while others were on horseback. All signs a village was near.

"This is it, girl," I said, patting Yasmine's neck and pulling her to a halt at a sign that read Miller's Pass. "This looks to be as good a place as any to bed down for the night."

Yasmine snorted her agreement and ambled forward. I did not know what sort of town it was, if it were a town filled with Nons, or if there were Wielders within. Using my illusion magic, I made my ears look like those of a human. We walked down the road where people bustled about, closing up booths and hurrying to their homes. I knew they were trying to get behind closed doors before the darkness fell. I urged Yasmine on, my eyes scanning the many shops that were closed. Up ahead I saw a few people coming out of one building. Heeling Yasmine into a trot, I drew closer to the establishment, sighing in relief at the sign that hung from a rusty chain: Miller's Pass Tavern & Inn.

Swinging down from Yasmine, I guided her behind the establishment, finding the stable and stable hand. I handed the young girl the reins and relieved Yaz of her burden. Rummaging in one of the saddle bags, my hand closed around the coin pouch, a very full one at that. Pulling out a silver, I handed it to the girl, said good night to Yaz, and made my way to the tavern.

The tavern was fairly empty. A bard stood in the corner strumming his lute and singing to the few patrons at the table. I made my way to the counter where a thin man with gray hair stood. Watery brown eyes appraised me as I approached.

"Rough night, eh?"

I looked down at my tattered dress and pulled my cloak closed. "I'd like a room, if one is available."

"Aye. There's room," he said. Reaching below the counter, he pulled out a ledger. Dipping a quill in a pot of ink, he scribbled on the paper. "How many?"

"Just me."

"Aye. You might'n want to barricade your door. A pretty lass like you will stir up trouble," he gestured to the room. Turning, I noted a few of the men seated at tables eyeing me.

"Thank you. How much?"

"Two coppers and a silver."

Handing him the coin, he gave me a key and directions to a room down a hall in the back. I made my way to my room and opened the door. It was a small room, not that I was expecting luxurious accommodations. It held one small bed covered by a thin blanket, and a dresser with a mirror above, a wash basin and pitcher on top. Locking the door, I pushed the dresser against it to ensure none entered during the night.

Dropping the saddle bags onto the bed, I sat down. My mind raced. In a handful of hours my whole life had changed. Tears burned behind my eye, but I would not let them fall. How could things have gone so horribly wrong for me? How could the king revoke my claim on the throne and sentence me to death?

How had Mouranda become with child? If the most skilled Elven healers were unable to assist her for all these Grand Passages, how had she done it?

And where was Phabian during all this? The man who all but raised me. The one I was the closest to and who I loved like a father. The one who defended me against the others. Who taught me how to use a sword, and fight with my hands. How to survive in the wild with nothing more but one arrow, a pair of boots, a tin cup and a rusted dagger.

Why had he abandoned me in my time of need?

Pushing the thoughts aside and pushing down the tears that threatened to spill, I unpacked the saddle bags. Lazaro had packed me a shirt, and a pair of trousers. A sack of dried meats, hard cheese, and crusty bread. I found my dagger nestled within the bag, and slipped it beneath the thin pillow. I pulled out the bag of coin, the heft telling me there was a significant amount, and finally, my hands closed around a book. Pulling it out, I looked at the title, tears making it hard to read, though I knew what it was.

The Story of Jayne.

It was a book my mother had loved, and one I read over and over. Though I could recite it by heart, I still read the words my mother's eyes saw and touched the pages her hands caressed. Lazaro, who often made fun of me for reading the book as much as I did, had thought enough to include it in the pack.

I did not know what had changed his mind; why he was being kind to me. Perhaps, as he said, he was doing it for Phabian, but the inclusion of the book felt like much more than that. Putting the contents back in the pack and placing it on the other side of the bed, I wiped away the tears I shed and slipped beneath the thin blanket.

Tomorrow I would assess my situation with fresh eyes.

Tomorrow I would come up with a plan of action.

SIXTEEN
MOURANDA

I WATCHED LAZARO DRAG Serafin out of the room, taking her to the dungeon to await her execution on the morrow.

She didn't scream, nor did she cry when Allendaire passed his judgement. She didn't crawl on her knees, clutch at his trouser legs, and beg him not to do it. She barely fought Lazaro when he grabbed her and put the Sigaa'Lean on. I might have admired her stoicism, her stubbornness had it been anyone else. But Serafin never allowed me to be a mother to her. She always snubbed my attempts at affection. Always she went to Allendaire or Phabian with her scrapes and bruises, or when she had a bad dream. Never did she come to me. Never did she want me.

As soon as Lazaro had her out of the room, Allendaire announced the celebration to be for the life growing within me. For the prince, the full blood Shadow Elf who would one day rule. Those in attendance cheered. A string quartet set for Serafin, played for me, for my unborn child. Servants entered, carrying trays piled with food and drinks for all who packed the room. True joy shined in their eyes.

Allendaire sat back down beside me and took my hand. I had to resist the urge to snatch it back, but I had to keep up appearances for the sake of the child I bore and for the sake of the half-breed sentenced to death. I looked at Allendaire who sipped a glass of wine and tore at a boar's leg with his teeth. He was as pathetic as he was useless. If I were to be truthful, Allendaire banning me from his bed was one of the best things to happen. No longer would he touch me. No longer would he force himself on me. My defect had freed me from him. But my defect also meant there would be no heir and the Trounde name, our legacy that has survived thousands of Grand Passages would end.

It was something I could not allow to happen so when Lillyanna was found on our lands, I launched a plan. Denalla was furious with me when I told her, and I should have listened to her. I saw the way Allendaire looked at Lillyanna. How he had made up excuses to see her, and though it shouldn't have bothered me when he began to share her bed, it did. Lillyanna showed me all the ways I was wrong. Broken. She showed me I never really meant anything to Allendaire.

And when she became with child, she showed me the black mark against me. She showed me I could not even do the one thing that made me a woman. And

Denalla, for all her love and loyalty she had for me, knew my sorrow. She knew my folly with what I did, and she tried to make sure not only would the child not be born, but Lillyanna would die as well.

Her plan had failed. Damn Lazaro for hearing Lillyanna's screams and saving her. Denalla came to me after, frightened and crying.

"My queen, I am so sorry. I thought I could get rid of them both and now…" tears poured down her cheeks. Burying her face in my skirts, she sobbed.

"Stop," I said, gently picking her head up.

"They will be executed. I will be executed."

Leaning forward, I kissed away the tears that wetted her cheeks. "You won't. I promise, Denalla. I will protect you."

Pulling her to her feet, I guided her to the bed where we slipped beneath the covers. "No one will ever know," I said softly, kissing her neck.

And when Lillyanna gave birth, all my insecurities, all that I wasn't, all I lacked as a woman was exemplified in the tiny being I held.

"What are you thinking, Mouranda?" Allendaire's voice brought me back.

Smiling, I kissed the knuckles on the hand that held mine for anyone who saw us. "I am thinking of our future. Of the king that will be born and rule." Pushing my chair back, I rose.

"Where are you going?"

"I am tired. It has been a long day, and the child steals my energy." It wasn't a lie. I found myself more exhausted than normal since becoming with child. "I am going to retire to my quarters."

"Do you want me to join you?" Allendaire made to get up, and I placed a hand on his shoulder stopping him.

"No. Enjoy the celebration for our heir."

Pushing my way through the crowd, I exited the ballroom and walked through the halls to my quarters. Sinking down in a plush chair in front of the roaring fire, I thought of the events that happened. I had no regrets about any of it. No regrets about my deception.

Allendaire was a fool. When I told him of my condition, he was elated. He did not question my words. There was no reason to. After all, we had copulated several times over the past four Moon Cycles.

Or at least that's what he thought.

Oh, I thought of everything where this was concerned. I made sure to cover my tracks. To make what I had done believable to a certain elf who has the habit of delving uninvited into others minds. I was very careful in my moves. The only one who knew was my sweet, loyal, Denalla.

"How can you be sure he will believe what happened?" Denalla sat up in bed and looked at me.

"How can he not, when he wakes up naked in his bed? All I have to do is fill in the blanks for him. How can he not believe me when I tell him he kept saying Lillyanna's name as he forced himself on me?"

"But—"

I kissed Denalla. "Trust me, darling. Everything will be fine," I said, slipping a hand between her legs. Denalla sighed, any protest she had was lost in her pleasure.

The next evening, I put my plan in motion. I knew he would be in his den, like every night, in front of the fire with a drink. Most likely he was thinking about Lillyanna.

"Are you sure about this?" Denalla asked for the hundredth time. She sat on the edge of my bed watching me dress. I had chosen a long-sleeved scoop necked dress of blue silk. My hair was loose, flowing down to my waist. Slipping my feet into a pair of shoes made of soft calf leather, I knelt in front of Denalla. Taking her hands, I kissed her knuckles.

"I am very sure."

She opened her mouth to speak, and I silenced her protest with a kiss. "By now he will be three drinks in and getting a little drunk." Rising, I crossed the room to my vanity table and picked up a black marble pipe. "A few more drinks and a little bit of Sal'va," I held up the pipe, "and I will have him."

Denalla pursed her lips but said nothing.

I loved her for the way she watched out for me, but I always made sure to cover my tracks. I would never plan something if there was the smallest chance of it not working. The smallest chance of getting caught.

Leaving Denalla, I walked through the halls to Allendaire's den, opening the door and slipping inside. As I thought, he sat in his favorite worn chair in front of the fire. An almost empty carafe of wine sat on the table beside him, next to a full one. Finishing the glass he held, he poured the rest of the wine in and took a healthy sip. Crossing the room, I grabbed a glass from the sideboard. It hit another one beside it, the sound causing Allendaire to turn. Glassy eyes looked at me, a frown creased his brow.

"Mouranda? What are you doing here?" His speech was slurred. It appeared he was further into the drink than I thought. That was a plus.

Crossing to where he sat, I took the chair beside him and poured a glass of wine. I had thought up a valid story for my presence and based on his condition, I was certain he wouldn't question it.

"Can't I visit my husband without being questioned?"

Reaching over, he refilled his glass. "We do not spend time together. What is this about?"

I looked at him over the rim of my glass. "I have been visiting healers again," I said, eyes watching him.

He rubbed his eyes. "Mouranda—"

"I have been drinking a tea to aid in fertility. The healer told me of its success, and I have spoken to women for whom it has worked. It is my fertile time now." I took another sip of my wine.

"Serafin is the heir. I have named her as such."

My nostrils flared. "And the girl is a half-breed. It goes against everything we are."

"I bent the law for her. You know that Mouranda. You were the one who suggested it."

Yes, I was, and I have regretted it every day since that daughter of a whore was born.

Pushing down my anger, I took a deep breath. "It does not hurt to try now, does it?"

"I have had far too much to drink. I doubt I could even find my cock right now."

"I assumed as much, and I came prepared." Pulling the pipe out of the bag I carried, I lit a piece of timber in the fire and lit the pipe. I took a long draw, though I made sure not to inhale. I could not afford to not have my wits about me. Blowing the smoke out, I held the pipe out to Allendaire.

"I have heard you have not taken anyone to your bed since that—since Lillyanna has left. Surely you are craving the presence of a woman. I am here, offering you myself."

Allendaire grasped the pipe and took a long pull from it, holding the smoke in before letting it out.

I smiled to myself.

I had him.

T HE WINE AND SAL'VA relaxed and aroused him. He stumbled over to where I sat, hands groping me, mouth crushing mine, his tongue assaulting. I stifled a gag, and the urge to knee him in the groin, reminding myself why I was doing this. Reminding myself nothing sexual would occur.

Pulling away from another painful kiss, I held his face in my hands. "Let us go to your quarters and continue what has been started."

Allendaire stood clumsily up almost pitching backwards into the fire. I rose, slipping an arm around him, supporting his weight to keep him upright. Swiping the new full carafe of wine from the table I guided Allendaire out of the den and up to his room. Entering his quarters, he grabbed me, pressing his body against mine. His hands took liberties with my body, his mouth devoured my neck.

Extracting myself, I took a few steps back. "Let's have another drink first," I said, bringing the wine to my lips and taking a sip. I held out to Allendaire who took a healthy pull.

"Come. Sit on the bed."

I took his elbow and guided him to the bed. He grabbed me, pulling me down, his body covering mine.

No, no, no. This is not how it was supposed to go. I struggled beneath his bulk trying to close my legs against the hand that grabbed me. I heard the sound of his belt buckle as he undid it with the other hand.

And then, he was still. A soft snore came from the body crushing me, and I sighed with relief. Wiggling from beneath him, careful not to wake him, I rolled him over and stripped off his clothes, scattering them across the room in what I hoped would look like he stripped them off in a fit of passion. Pulling a blanket over him, I left the room, knowing I would not have much convincing to do.

A flutter in my abdomen brought me back. I placed my hand on my dead womb, feeling another soft flutter beneath. My child may have been got through nefarious ways, through dark and abandoned magic, but I was with child. I carried the heir.

That was all that mattered.

SEVENTEEN
PHABIAN

I MADE IT BACK to the palace just as the sun kissed the horizon. Screams and wails echoed through the forest as dusk settled. Krall did not follow me, and I only hoped he was tucked away safe in the tavern in Duenney with a whore on his lap.

Jumping off Maxamillian and tossing the reins to the elf in the stables, I raced to the palace taking the steps two at a time. Pushing open the sturdy doors, I rushed inside. The sound of music drifted through the halls and I followed it, drawing up to the ballroom where a grand celebration was taking place. Elves danced and ate and drank. Chatter and laughter filled the room. Pushing my way inside, I scanned the room, searching for a head with white and red hair but I did not see it.

Perhaps she went back to her room. Perhaps she had enough.

I rushed through the halls, flying up the stairs to Serafin's room. Throwing open the door, I looked around her dimly lit quarters. She was not there. My eyes went to Cwella who sat in the middle of the floor. Tears stained her face and my breath caught.

"Cwella?"

Looking up at the sound of my voice, she jumped to her feet and ran to where I stood. Throwing her arms around my waist, she buried her face in my shirt, her body wracked with sobs. Untangling her, I held her at arm's length, my eyes searching her face.

"Cwella? Where is Serafin?"

She shook her head, sobbing uncontrollably. Realizing she was too distraught to answer, I placed my hands on both sides of her head. Closing my eyes, I trickled magic into her mind.

What I saw filled me with a cold sickness. Pictures of Serafin being dragged into the ballroom by Samel and Lazaro. She stood before a table behind which Allendaire and Mouranda sat. Mouranda's words hit me, and I stumbled.

She was with child, but how?

I saw Serafin looking around, looking for me, I knew, and my heart shattered.

Allendaire stood up, calling the room to silence and the words he spoke…I could not believe he said them. And with those words, with his denouncement of Serafin, any respect, any love I had for my king shattered. I watched Lazaro put a Sigaa'Lean on Serafin, then he dragged her out of the room.

Removing my hands from Cwella, I sank to the floor. My chest tightened and my ears rang. Allendaire had sentenced my Little Princess to death. I could not wrap my head around that, or Mouranda being with child. She was barren. It was the whole reason Lillyanna was not executed when she stumbled here. It was the reason Serafin was allowed to be born.

It did not sit well with me. The only person who could tell me the truth was Allendaire. Rising, I brushed past Cwella and stalked through the halls to find him. How could he do this to her? How could he sentence his own daughter to death? He loved her, I knew. When she was small, he spent almost all his time with her reading, playing games, and rocking her to sleep. And when she was older, he had her listen to the petty grievances of the people, even asking her for her thoughts. She accompanied him a few times to collect the taxes of the people and sat in on council meetings.

And in the blink of an eye, he turned his back on her. It did not make sense.

"Phabian."

I stopped at the sound of Lazaro's voice. My blood boiled and my magic surged. White light wrapped around my arms, snapping and crackling.

"Come with me," he said, voice low as he walked past.

Grabbing his arm, I sent a tendril of my magic through. He cried out in pain, jerking his arm back.

"How could you, Lazaro?" I snarled. I held my hands apart, drawing more magic and making a ball.

Lazaro held up his hands. "Stop, Phabian. Please. I need to speak with you. It is extremely important. Please."

"What could you possibly have to say to me that is more important than Serafin being executed in the morning?"

He took a step toward me. I clutched the ball in a hand, ready to launch it at him.

"Please, Phabian. I need to explain what happened."

"So, explain."

He looked over his shoulder in a furtive way. "Not here. Please?" He said again.

Something about the desperation in his tone, the way he looked around, fearful almost, made me let go of my magic.

"Fine. I will go with you."

A look of relief washed over him, and he strode down the hall. Stopping at the door to his quarters, he opened it and slipped inside.

Following behind, I closed the door. "Speak, Lazaro."

He crossed the room to a table in front of the hearth, and poured two glasses of amber liquid. Handing me one, he took a long sip.

"I said, speak."

Lazaro took a deep breath. "Serafin was sentenced to death. The queen is with child."

"I know this. I delved into Cwella's mind. You have exactly ten seconds to tell me what is so important before I blow you apart with my magic."

Lazaro's throat bobbed as he swallowed. "She's not here. There will be no execution tomorrow."

I lowered my glass. "What?"

Lazaro crossed the room to the chairs situated in front of the fire. Tossing a log on, he took a seat. I lowered myself into a chair beside him and filled my glass back up.

"I took her to the dungeons. I purposely told Samel I could handle it. There is a secret passage beneath the palace exiting at the northern border."

Secret passage? "What are you talking about? I've been to the dungeons hundreds of times. My brothers and I used to play in them as children. I never saw a passage."

"Because it is hidden."

I sipped my drink, the warmth of the Faeries Blood spread through me. "How do you know about it?"

I was beginning to doubt his story. The thought occurred to me he fabricated it to keep me from going to see Serafin to set her free.

"That doesn't matter."

I clenched my fists. "Laz—"

"What matters is Serafin escaped through the tunnel. I am the one who opened it. Before the... before what happened, I packed up Yasmine with supplies and tethered her in the woods. I told Serafin where she could be found when she got to the other side."

I stared at Laz. He had to be lying. He despised Serafin. Why would he help her?

"Delve into my mind if you do not believe," he said, as if reading my thoughts.

And so, I did, and when I was done, I sat back on my haunches. Grasping the bottle of spirits, I took a healthy swig. "Why?"

He shrugged. "For you. For Serafin. I don't know. Phabian, something isn't right about all of this."

Putting the bottle down, I rose. "I know. I was on my way to confront Allendaire about it," I said, making my way to the door.

"He is at the party. He won't be available until tomorrow." I heard the rustle of clothes as Lazaro rose and stopped, my hand on the doorknob.

"I don't think there is any good reason for you to leave now." His breath was a hot caress on my neck. He slipped his arms around my waist, lips grazing my ear.

Turning around, I looked at him. Lust pooled in his blue eyes, my own desire rising in turn.

"You're right. I don't." Lazaro leaned in to kiss me, and I stepped back. Eyes on him, I undid my belt, pulling it free from the loops. Holding it out, I snapped it, the leather hitting like a whip crack. Laz jumped and I smiled.

I took a step toward him, and he took one back. Step for step he matched me until his back was against the wall.

"Did you forget about the discussion I said we would have for your insolence?" Lazaro swallowed hard.

"Get on the bed," I ordered, stepping away. Laz crossed the room, lying down on his stomach.

Though he may have helped my Little Princess escape death, I would show him just how bad his words hurt her.

And when she came back, perhaps he would think twice about saying them again.

EIGHTEEN

Extracting myself from Lazaro's limbs, I slipped out of bed and rooted around the floor for my discarded clothing.

"Where you going?" Lazaro's voice was thick with sleep.

"I am going to wash up, then go speak with Allendaire," I said, pulling on my trousers. Grabbing my shirt, I slipped it over my head and shoved my feet into my boots.

Lazaro yawned, rolled over and buried himself beneath the blankets. I chuckled, kissing his head, then slipped out of the room. Though the night spent with Laz helped calm me, stopped me from going off half-cocked and possibly doing or saying something I might regret, the new light brought it all back, as well as my rage. I was ready to confront Allendaire and force him to tell me why he did what he did.

And then I would go look for my Little Princess and when I found her, I would keep her safe.

Even if that meant turning my back on my own people.

Standing outside the doors to the den, I took a deep breath. Pushing them open, I strode into the room. Allendaire sat behind his obsidian desk. A fire blazed in the hearth behind him. The scratch of the nib across parchment reached my ears. Sturdy oak furniture graced the room, bright tapestries hung on the walls depicting elven hunts and pictures of past kings. Though the hangings were cheerful, they lent little warmth to the otherwise stark and sterile room.

My boot scraped on the marble floor. Allendaire looked up from the paper, a look of shock and guilt flickered across his face. I ground my teeth at the look.

"Phabian," he said, placing the quill in the pot of ink. He folded his hands, eyes on me. "What can I help you with?"

Striding across the room, I stood in front of his desk. Oh, how I wanted to put my hands around his neck and choke the life out of him.

"How could you? How could you sentence Serafin, your daughter, to death?" I ground out between clenched teeth.

"Mouranda is with child. She carries the full blood Shadow Elf heir. Serafin never should have been born. I did what should have been done. I was wrong to bend the law." He took a sip of the wine in front of him. Drinking away his guilt. As far as I was concerned, the world could never produce enough wine to hide his crimes. What he had done was criminal regardless of the law—it was immoral. There was no denying, Serafin existed for his whims and he so casually sentenced her to death. What a betrayal. Even for we rigid Shadow Elves, our customs, our laws, he'd bent them for a legitimate purpose. He could have exiled her, spared her.

My nails bit into my palms as I tried to control the shaking. "She is your daughter. You loved her."

Allendaire's eyes narrowed. "She is a half-breed. Mouranda carries a full Shadow Elf."

Placing my hands on the table, I leaned forward. "You sentenced your daughter, your blood, to death. She is the heir. You named her as such."

"A half-breed will never rule." He sat wooden, like stone.

My heart pounded in my ears. I could not believe what he was saying. Could not believe he would toss his own daughter away like garbage.

"Damn it, Allendaire." I grabbed the carafe of wine and hurled it at the wall. "Will you fucking listen to yourself?

I wanted to pummel him. Grab him by the neck and choke the Life Force out of him.

Allendaire's blue eyes flashed with anger. "Do not speak to me like that. Remember your place, Phabian Trounde. I am your king. You will show me respect."

"Respect," I spat the word. "You lost that when you doomed Serafin. You care more about your fucking bloodline than you do your own daughter. You are not my king, Allendaire. Not anymore."

Turning, I stalked out of the room. Allendaire's angry voice called after me, but I did not stop. Hurrying to my room I rummaged through my wardrobe, grabbed clothing and shoved them and several other items into a bag. Filling a sack with a substantial amount of coin, I quickly made my way to the door, my heart plummeting at seeing Krall on the other side, sword drawn. It certainly didn't take Allendaire long to summon him, nor for him to get here.

"Move, Krall," I said, hoisting the bag on my shoulder.

"I am on order by the king to escort you to the dungeon."

"Don't do this."

"I am following our king's orders. Now, come with me, Phabian. I would hate to hurt you."

I pulled my magic close. "Your king, Krall. He stopped being mine when he sentenced Serafin to death."

Krall smirked. "Didn't you hear? The bitch escaped."

"I heard, and I know Allendaire will send soldiers to find her and bring her back so he can take her head."

Krall pursed his lips. His hand gripped the hilt of his sword harder. "She will be getting everything she deserves."

"Are you mad? Serafin did not break the law or even alter them. Allendaire did." My brother was a stubborn mule. I clenched my fists. "Get out of my way, Krall. I do not wish to hurt you. But I will."

Krall did not move.

I drew in more of my power, feeling it race through me and down my arms. Light crackled around my wrists and hands. Lunging at my brother, I grabbed him, pulsing my magic through. It came out in a tremendous burst of light and energy. Krall flew backward, slamming into the wall across the hall. His head hit with an audible crack, and his listless body crumpled to the floor.

"I'm sorry, Krall but you gave me no choice." Hefting my bag, I hurried through the halls. Exiting the palace, I raced to the stable where I quickly saddled Maxamillian and swung onto his back. Digging my heels into his sides, I urged him into a gallop. I raced through the streets, elves jumped out of the way as I barreled through the city. I urged Max on, urged him to go faster, not slowing and not looking back until I had put considerable distance between me and Il'Ekhester.

I would search the entire land for Serafin if I had to, and I would not stop until I found my Little Princess.

IN THE MORNING, I scoured the village I stopped at for the night, searching taverns and shops. I watched the people, looking for a head of white hair streaked with red. For a pair of eyes that were a combination of blue and green. I even stopped people and asked if they had seen her, but none had.

I made my way back to my room, heart shattered and shoulders heavy. Packing up my things, I mounted Max and headed on to the next village. None of what had transpired sat well with me. Allendaire could easily change the law with the stroke of a pen. He pushed aside tradition with Lillyanna, but not his own daughter. There had to be something more. Something to do with Mouranda.

I traveled through the village, heading in no direction in particular, a heavy feeling fell over me. I stroked Max's hair. We travelled new roads, new woods. Leaves budded on the trees as spring approached.

I had failed her. I wasn't there to escort her to her party—her trial—and I wasn't there beside her to plead her case. The one person she trusted—she loved—wasn't there for her when she needed them most. I sighed as I guided Max off the road to a clearing near a stream. Swinging down, I rolled my shoulders as the nagging suspicion reared its head again.

The queen was barren, and now she was with child.

My chest tightened, and a coldness fell over me. *Something wasn't right. Something wasn't natural.*

My thoughts were swiftly pulled back to the present as Maximilian suddenly reared up, hooves pawing at the air.

"Easy, Max," I soothed, gripping the reins, and bringing him under control. I grabbed the bow that was slung over my shoulder, loosely nocking an arrow while I attempted to soothe my agitated horse, wishing that I had Serafin's knack with animals. Max tossed his head and pawed at the ground as I scanned the woods. Seeing movement to my left, I turned in that direction. Movement to my right had me whipping around to assess an additional threat.

"Well, wouldya lookit wha' we 'ave 'ere," a voice on the left said and I turned back, training my bow, heart sinking as six men stepped out of the woods.

"We gots one o' dem pointy eared fellers. Are ye' lost?" A voice to the right said, and I glanced over, heart sinking further at seeing six more men casually coming out of the brush.

"I mean no harm. I am only passing through." I eyed both groups as I slowly lowered the bow, knowing I could still take out at least three at a moment's notice, but that would do Serafin no good.

"Ya hear dat? He's only passin' through," A burly man on the left stepped casually forward. "The question be, whada fuck is yer lot doin' so far 'way from home?"

"That is not your business. I have done no wrong. Let me pass." I casually shouldered my bow, placed the arrow in the quiver and pulled my magic close.

"No, our bidness, eh?" He glanced around at the other men, who chuckled. "Da problem we 'ave 'ere is ye's one o' dem magical lots. We don' take kindly ta yer sort 'ere."

"You are either very brave or very stupid to think you can defeat a Wielder." I glanced around at the ragtag group. I pulled my sword out and twirled it. Taking a fighting stance, I held it in front of me. The men drew their own weapons, and

I sighed. "Stupid fools. Very well. Let's get this over with." I marked the men who would die with my eyes. I took a step forward, pausing a moment as the wind suddenly picked up. Clouds raced across the sky, covering the mid-day sun, and plunging the clearing into darkness. The blue fire of my blade glowed eerily in my hands. A movement to my right caught my attention, and I turned, eyes peering into the darkness of the woods. A figure advanced and as it—as she—drew closer, coldness fell over me. She lifted her arms, blinding light flashed, and a loud boom sounded followed by a concussion that threw me to the ground. Then silence. Blinking against the black spots that floated in my vision, I looked around the clearing at the men who were lying on the ground, knocked out or dead, and I dragged myself to my feet.

"Phabian Trounde," a voice said from behind, and I turned. My heart raced and my legs were like water as I looked at the woman who stood before me.

She was as beautiful as the stories I had heard, and the pictures I had seen. Long, white hair cascaded down her back. Eyes so blue they were almost white burned through me; blood-red lips curled up in a smile. And her skin. Her skin shimmered in the sunlight that dappled through the leaves above, looking as though she was made of diamonds and starlight.

"Do you know who I am?" Her voice, smooth as silk, soft as down and with an edge as sharp as a blade, washed over me.

"Yes," I said, my voice barely above a whisper as I dropped to my knees at her feet, pressing my forehead to the dirt in subjugation.

NINETEEN

M Y EYES FOCUSED ON the canopy of blood red as I slowly woke. Curtains encased the unfamiliar bed. Frowning, I sat up and pushed aside the curtains, and looked around the large room, quickly realizing this room was much too nice to be an inn. Fire danced in the hearth near some cozy chairs. A tray with glasses and a decanter of red liquid sat on a table. To my right, I noticed an enormous wardrobe and a table with a porcelain bowl and pitcher. Open doors led out to a grand balcony, and I slipped out of bed, having no recollection at first of how I got here. I remembered guiding Maximilian through the woods. Remembered the twelve men who threatened to harm me and the flash of light and loud thundering boom that knocked me to the ground.

And the woman.

The beautiful, elegant Elven woman who stepped out of the trees, voice smooth and soft and dangerous.

I remembered falling to my knees before her. Her voice echoed in my head saying just one word: sleep.

And now I had woken up in this strange room.

I noted my bow, quiver of arrows and sword propped against the wall. Felt the pulsing thrum of my magic course within me. It was apparent they did not deem me a threat. Slipping my bow over my arm and strapping the quiver to my back and sword at my side, I pulled open the door.

"Ahh," a voice said. I looked around, seeing a man—human, not Elf—casually lounging against the wall, picking his nails with a dagger. "I was wondering when you were going to wake. It's half past mid-day," he said, eyes flicking to me.

"How long have I been here? And where is here?"

"That I will let her answer. As for how long you've been here? A little over a day now, most of which you've slept through."

Over a day? "Well, if it's all the same to you, I'd like to leave."

"So, it would seem," he said, nodding to my weapons. He pushed off the wall and turned towards me. "Though I regret to inform you you can't leave yet."

I bristled under his words. "Oh? Says who?"

"You know." He smirked and walked away.

I didn't move. I was not completely sure if what I saw in the forest was the truth "No. I don't know."

He stopped and turned. "You will know soon enough, though I suggest you follow me. She does not like to be kept waiting for long."

I followed him through the halls, firing questions left unanswered. Finally, he stopped at a set of doors.

"Should I leave my weapons?"

He smiled. "There's no need. You won't raise a sword—or magic—to her." He pushed open the doors and with no other choice, I stepped into the cozy study. A fire warmed the place. The wall to the left had a row of windows from floor to ceiling. Tapestries hung on the walls showing Elven tales and depictions of animals, and earth tone rugs were scattered about the floor. Finally, my eyes were drawn to the desk across the room.

To the woman who sat behind it.

Her hands were clasped in front of her, a smile on her full ruby lips. Her crystal blue eyes bore through me, but I was more distracted by the circlet that sat atop her snow-white hair. It was the emerald serpent with ruby eyes wrapped around the stem of a black rose.

My mouth went dry at the realization of who she was. This was not a dream. "Arybelle," I whispered, eyes widening as I took in the first Shadow Elf queen. The woman who was married to Karrinian Trounde. A woman who was long thought dead.

Her smile grew. "So, you are not so naïve, Phabian," she said.

I blinked, not truly comprehending. "But you—"

"Took my life?" She raised an eyebrow and motioned to the servant I didn't see who scurried across the room, bringing two glasses of amber liquid to us.

Arybelle—Queen Arybelle—crossed the small room to the hearth, taking a seat in a chair, watching as I slowly sank into another.

"One would think that," she said, answering her own question, lips curling into a smile as she took a sip of her drink.

I shook my head as I sank into the plush cushions of the chair. "I don't understand."

She folded her legs beneath her, fanning her ruby red silk skirt out, eyes growing dark. "Karrinian was a bastard." She clenched her jaw. "He was my brother, and he came into my room on my eighteenth Name Day and forced himself on me. I should have known by the way he looked at me, though there would have been nothing I could do, regardless. He forced the mating bond, and I had no choice. I was now his," she said. "He owned me and he used me as he saw fit. It included letting others... have me." She took a drink; her eyes were dark and face tense.

"I don't understand," I said again, feeling foolish for it. She refilled our glasses and settled back with a smile. "But you took your life and Vanla's. They burned your bodies."

"Bodies were burned, yes," she said, nodding to a servant who scurried out of the room.

I rubbed my temples. "I don't—" I stopped myself before I uttered the words understand once again, even though I didn't.

"So why have you remained hidden for nearly a thousand Grand Passages? Why did you not come out when Karrinian died? Why not try to put Vanla on the throne?"

She cocked her head to the side. "Do you think I would have been well received? Welcomed back with open arms? As for Vanla—" the sound of the doors opening cut her words off. Her features softened, and a smile graced her lips.

"Vanla," she said, and I turned and watched a breathtakingly beautiful woman enter the room. Tall and thin, her long white hair spilled down her back to her waist, the sides secured with diamond combs. She wore a dark blue velvet dress, the long sleeves cut at an angle, the low-cut bodice embroidered with flowers of white lace and pearls. The garment fitted at the torso and flowed out at the hips to the floor. Panels of periwinkle flashed as she walked—no, floated—across the room to Arybelle.

"Mother," her soft voice sang as she grasped Arybelle's hands and kissed each cheek.

"Say hello to my guest, Phabian Trounde."

Vanla turned, blue eyes so dark they looked violet, appraised me. "Welcome, Phabian," she said, taking a chair to the right of her mother.

"As you can see, Vanla is also alive and well."

"But—"

"The bodies?" She quirked an eyebrow. "There were those who hated Karrinian as much as I did. It took little to find a Shadow Elf woman willing to escape the cruelty endured by sacrificing herself and her daughter," she said, refilling our glasses again.

I tossed my drink back, gripping the empty glass in my hand. A dull ache began forming in the back of my head. I didn't understand anything that was happening right now, and half thought perhaps something had been slipped into my drink when I was at the tavern, and all of this was a dream.

"But... they would have looked nothing like you. Your deception would have been revealed. You would have been hunted and killed, deemed a traitor at best, Wilde Elf at worst."

"I survived, Phabian." She smoothed a wrinkle on her skirt with her hand. "I am a woman. I am no more important than the chair you sit upon. My role was beside Karrinian. I was to obey him and produce his children. Do you think he cared? Do you think he would have been distraught? Mourn my death? Shed tears over my body? He was fucking his young cousin when he received the news. He paused long enough to say, 'Wrap the bodies and burn them.'" She said, blue eyes hard.

I looked away from her pinning gaze, saying nothing, though my face heated with shame at the truth of her words.

I was no better than Karrinian in thoughts and actions. The things I did to my sister as a child came rushing back, and I despised myself for it. My actions as an adult—claiming her against her will, forcing her to give me children—drove my Anya to take her own life and my only daughter's, like so many others and now, I understood why. I understood the suppression of the women and it shamed me. At the time I had known no other way. I liked to tell myself.

My eyes met hers. "It is what we are taught. It is what we know. I am not saying it makes it right. I... I'm sorry."

Arybelle smiled, though it didn't reach her eyes. "You haven't treated Serafin that way."

"No, I haven't. I promised her mother I would take care of her. Raise her like my own. I love her. I would never... I would never treat her the way I treated my Anya. I will never treat another woman like that again."

"Perhaps there is hope for your race, Phabian. You and the princess can change this."

And I knew we—she—would do just that, and my need to find her became even more urgent.

"I still don't... how is it you came to me?"

"I kept track of the Shadow Elves throughout time, and when I found you, Phabian, you were the one I kept an eye on the most. You were closest to Allendaire."

So that's how she knew about Serafin. I looked at Arybelle and Vanla. The stories of how she took hers and Vanla's life went through my mind. And yet, they were sitting here... where was here?

"Why am I here?"

Arybelle glanced at her daughter, then waved to the servant who placed a fresh bottle of spirits on the table.

Reaching forward, I refilled our glasses. Arybelle took a sip, then settled in her chair, folding her legs beneath her.

"We are descendants of the Dark Elves," she started. I sipped my drink. Her declaration was not new to me. Every Shadow Elf knew this, but I did not say anything.

"The Dark Elves have dark hair and white eyes. They are sensitive to the light and must keep themselves covered at all times." She paused, taking another sip of her drink. "Their life span is not as long as ours. They are more susceptible to sickness. Something as innocent as a scrape could breed infection, which could lead to death."

Interesting. Our own magic healed things like wounds and broken bones. Sometimes the healer is called to lend help in the case of more serious injuries, such as when Allendaire was injured in the attack on his Name Day hunt but never had any of the Shadow Elves died from a simple scrape or sickness. Pouring more spirits, I took a healthy sip. Arybelle shifted her position, rearranging her skirts around her legs. Vanla sat silently sipping her drink.

"As time went on, some elves were born different. Their hair was white. Eyes blue They weren't sensitive to the light, and they outlived the Dark Elves. Because of that, some decided to procreate with each other out of fear of birthing a Dark Elf. The children produced looked like their parents, and so it continued."

That was information I had not known. It was conveniently left out of our history.

"Why were some born different?"

Arybelle shrugged. "We do not know. All we know is the breeding within did not produce a Dark Elf." Leaning forward, she held her glass out, and I filled it. She took a long drink, then began speaking again.

"Our numbers grew as the Dark Elves diminished. It was Karrinian's idea to leave Naar'Glon. He had sent people over to Ay'Arinia to find a place to settle. When Il'Ekhester was claimed and named, he sent workers over to build the palace. When it was finished, he gathered those who followed him and set sail to the place he now called home. He called his people Shadow Elves, because though we came from the Dark Elves, we were not them completely, rather we were a shadow of who they were. And, well, I am sure I do not need to tell you the rest."

I rubbed my eyes, a headache forming behind them. While I knew we were descendants of the Dark Elves, I did not know the whole of it. There was no reason for me not to believe Arybelle. After all, she came from Naar'Glon with Karrinian.

"There have only been three true kings throughout history. Karrinian, Nehem, and Terrin," Arrybelle said. "I am sure you have heard the story of how Rahina poisoned her father, Terrin, but it wasn't her. It was Allendaire."

I shook my head. What she spoke was borderline treason, though why should it matter? She was thought to be dead anyway. Placing my glass on the table, I rose. "Thank you for the history lesson. I regret I would like to retire. I am quite tired."

Arybelle smiled. "Of course. It has been an exhausting day, and I have armed you with much information. Go rest."

Nodding, I exited the room, making my way through the halls to my quarters. Pulling open the doors to the balcony, I stepped outside. A soft breeze rustled through the oak tree's branches lining the courtyard below my room. Warm air caressed my skin. It moved thick and carried the scent of rain. The distant rumble of thunder and periodic flashes of lightning confirmed the advance of a storm.

I stared out into the night, but not really seeing anything. I had spent several hours with Arybelle and Vanla, listening—and not quite comprehending—the tale told to me. A dull persistent ache pulsed in the back of my head and the more I tried to understand what I had been told, the more the ache throbbed.

Arybelle's tale was outlandish, bordering on treason and as much as I wanted to reject what she had said, the long dead and forgotten queen and her daughter were alive.

If only I could close my eyes and go to sleep. If only I could wake from this bizarre dream and find myself back in my room at the palace or lying next to Serafin on the grass, listening to the thunderous roar of the water tumbling over the rocks above before crashing into the crystal blue waters of the lake below. I blinked hard. Life was not a dream.

The silence stretched, the rolling thunder grew closer, and I heard the soft patter of raindrops hitting the roof above. I went into the room and grabbed a decanter and a glass. Sitting back down, I filled it and took a long drink. I didn't know how I ended up here, nor did I understand how the very first Queen of the Shadow Elves and her only daughter could be alive.

My head throbbed, the pain as if battered by a hammer. The odd winter storm drifted eastward, the rain a soft patter upon the roof. The air was thick and heavy with humidity, the feeling more like summer than winter. Arybelle had left me with more questions than answers. What they claimed had to be true, though I didn't want to admit it. What a disaster.

I rolled my shoulders, the tension between them heavy with everything I had learned in a short amount of time. Information that destroyed the history I had known and had been raised on. The history written within the pages of the Tome of the Kings. It was a diary written by each king since Karrinian. It was a detail of their thoughts throughout their reign. It was all a lie.

Rubbing my eyes, I made my way back into the room to sleep. In the morning, I would break my fast with the queen, then leave this place and continue my search for Serafin.

And when I found her, I would hold her tight if only to reassure myself that she was alive and then I would take her away from here. I would close myself off from my brothers and live a modest life with my Little Princess.

When I found her.

"DID YOU SLEEP WELL, Phabian?" Arybelle watched me as I crossed the large room. Windows spanned the wall to my left from floor to ceiling, stained-glass depicted scenes of nature and elves, both Shadow and Wilde. The morning sun filtered through, painting the scattered rugs in brilliant color. A large table split the room in half. It was more suited for an elaborate banquet, piled with pastries, trays of fruit, boiled eggs, and an array of meat. Arybelle and Vanla looked small like the dolls from Serafin's old nursery.

"I slept like the dead," I said, taking a seat to Arybelle's left. I grabbed a plate and piled it with food.

"So," Arybelle said, folding her hands upon the table. "Have I answered your questions?"

I looked at her as I nibbled on a pastry. "No," I said, swallowing my food. I pushed my plate away and sat back in the hard and uncomfortable chair. Arybelle raised an eyebrow. While I slept well, my thoughts raced before darkness claimed me and even after, my dreams were those of treachery, murder, and treason.

And the questions that churned in my mind? There was not enough time for me to sort them and even if I did, I knew Arybelle's answers would only give rise to more.

"Speak, Phabian." she said.

I rubbed my neck. "There are not enough hours in the day for me to ask my questions, let alone have them satisfactorily answered. Where does that leave Serafin? If the king isn't the True King, then is Sera the heir?" I was reluctant to admit what I had been told confused me. With the throne being generationally usurped, I feared what it meant for Serafin, who I knew would bring our race to greatness.

When the Shadow Elf women were taking their lives and that of their daughters so as to stop being forced to have children, the population began to dwindle. Elves began procreating outside their race and when Allendaire became king—though it was through nefarious ways—he waged a war on his own people and banished those who did not abide by their law. Those that lived fled and called themselves the Wilde Elves. Perhaps Serafin would bridge the gap between the Shadow and Wilde Elves and unite them.

"I thank you for your hospitality, but I regret I must leave. I must continue my search for Serafin."

"No," Arybelle said as she rose to her feet.

"But—" my words were cut off by her sharp look, eyes narrowed and danger-ous.

"You will return to the castle and figure out what is wrong."

"Do I just forget about Serafin then?"

"Of course not, but your duty is not to find her. Not yet," she said. "Return to Trounde Castle. Stay close to Allendaire and Mouranda. Keep an eye on the child when it is born."

"But Sera—"

"Will be safe," Arybelle said, her tone less harsh. "What would you do if you found her, Phabian? You know she cannot go back home. Not yet."

I admit I hadn't thought about the fact Serafin couldn't go back home. I took a deep breath. "Alright then. I will do as you command." How could I not? She was, after all, the queen, even though she was thought to be dead. Rising, I began walking to the door, then stopped. "How do I keep you updated with what, if anything, I find?"

Arybelle smiled. "You will know when I request information."

Resisting the urge to roll my eyes at her cryptic answer, I nodded then exited the room, making my way to the stable to get Maximillian ready for the trek home.

TWENTY
SERAFIN

MY EYES FLUTTERED OPEN, an unfamiliar ceiling coming into focus. The events of the day prior crashed down on me. My chest tightened and I pushed back a sob. It wasn't a horrible nightmare I was going to wake up from.

Sitting up, I winced at the pain that shot through me. My body was stiff, my back sore from the hard bed I slept on. A far cry from the luxurious feather mattress I was used to sleeping on at the palace.

Stop it, Serafin, I chastised. *That life is in the past.*

Slipping out of bed, I went to the window. Wiping off the grime, I looked outside. The sun was rising and folks bustled about the streets. Carriages with goods raced by and people opened booths, setting out their wares for sale. Using the cold water in the pitcher to wash, I pulled on the trousers and shirt Lazaro had packed. I looked at the dress I had worn. The once beautiful snow white was spattered with dirt; the fabric torn with diamonds and pearls missing.

It was a reminder of what was supposed to be a joyous day but turned into one of death. Balling it up, I threw it in the corner of a rom. It was a memory I did not wish to keep. Throwing my cloak around my shoulders and stuffing the bag of coin in an inside pocket, I moved the dresser and exited the room.

The scent of food—eggs, bacon, and baking bread—drifted from the tavern kitchen. My stomach growled. I hadn't had anything to eat since the small lunch with Phabian. Though I was hungry, the thought of a hot meal alluring, I exited the tavern and stepped out into the bustling street to explore the town.

It wasn't an affluent place, but neither was it poor. It was a working town, and a friendly one from what I gathered by the smiles and nods people gave me as I walked by. I strolled down the lane, stopping at various booths for a look. There were booths with trinkets, some selling jewelry, others sold reams of cloth, food, and pastries. Stopping at one such booth that sold sweets, I bought a round, sugared pastry filled with lemon custard. My stomach moaned its thanks as I ate the treat. Wiping my hands on my trousers, I walked on.

This was a quaint village, my thoughts going to the possibility of staying here. It started to take root and grow into a solid plan. Turning around, I made my way back to the inn. As I drew closer, I heard a ruckus up the road. The crowd in the streets parted. Horses and carriages drew to a halt. I stopped walking, frowning as I watched people scramble out of the way of... My eyes widened. My heart raced, and my mouth went dry. Sunlight glinted off helms with pointed ears and high polished armor that bore the Shadow Elf crest.

Twelve mounted warriors made their way down the street, heads swiveling left and right.

I knew they were searching for me.

Pulling my hood up and drawing my magic close, I dove into the sea of people crowding the sides of the streets. Weaving around bodies, I headed back to the inn, silently thanking the crowd for their cover. Entering the establishment, I headed toward my room.

"Aye. Wait a minute, Lassie," a voice called.

Stopping, I turned to see the man I spoke to the evening prior coming out from the kitchen, wiping his hands on a towel tucked into his apron.

"There be some funny lookin' fellers come in here askin' 'bout a young woman wit white n' red 'air."

I froze. My stomach lurched, bringing up the pastry I had. Covering my mouth, I pushed it back down. The man's brown eyes never left me. I looked at the door. I could run, but then where would I go? Into the hands of the king's warriors? That wasn't an option. Swallowing hard, I looked back at the man.

"I—"

"I tole 'em I hadn't an idea of who dat be. Surely, I would 'member a lass wit unusual 'air color."

I blinked.

"It were clear ye 'ada rough night when ye come," he said. "I don know what it be, but I reckoned dem funny fellers 'ad somethin' ta do wid it?" He raised an eyebrow.

"Yes," I said, my voice barely a whisper. I didn't know what else to say. Why would this man, this complete stranger help me? He had no reason to, and I was certain the king had put a price on my head.

"Thank you, but why?"

The man shrugged. "We be a peaceful town. I din no wan trouble. Fer me, no fer ya." He rubbed the back of his neck.

Tears stung my eyes, and I blinked them back. Nodding, I hurried down the hall to my room. Shutting and locking the door, I pushed the dresser back against it. Pulling out *The Story of Jayne*, I settled back on the uncomfortable bed to read and to try and to keep my mind off the warriors in the town searching for me.

When it was clear, I would saddle Yasmine and run far from this place. Clearly, it was far too close to Il'Ekhester.

Clearly, I was not safe.

I would run and keep running until I found a place far away that I could call home.

I WAITED UNTIL THE next day before I moved. I wanted to ensure the king's warriors were truly gone. After eating a hearty morning meal, I went out to the stable and saddled Yasmine. I felt a little sad leaving the village. It was a quaint and friendly place, and I had hoped to stay here longer, but it was too close to the palace. Too close to danger.

When I left the village, I turned Yasmine toward the woods. I did not know what direction the warriors went, and I did not wish to encounter them on the road. The deafening silence of the woods proved useless against the thoughts tumbling in my mind.

Though I tried to push the events of the day prior—was it only a day? It felt like it happened many Moon Cycles ago—out of my mind, they slowly weaved their way in until it consumed me and it was all that I could think about.

I did not understand how Mouranda was with child. The healers told her she would never conceive, and now, after twenty-one Grand Passages, and many more prior, she is with child. It did not make sense. Less so, did the king's decree of my execution.

Pictures flowed in my mind unbidden. Pictures of me as a small child sitting on the king's lap, snuggled in his arms as he read me a story. Me, hiding behind a thick curtain, trying not to giggle as he looked for me. On and on the memories flowed until the final one.

The one where he denounced me and sentenced me to death. And though sadness settled over my shoulders for the man who loved me once, anger and hatred spread through my body for the man I no longer knew. The man I no longer respected or loved. I kept that anger and hatred close, wrapping it around the cold stone beside my heart.

One day I would return to Il'Ekhester, not as the broken princess sentenced to death. No. I would come back as a queen with an army of wrath that would rain down upon Trounde Castle. I would one day claim my birthright through blood and death.

Yasmine snorted, pulling me from my sullen thoughts.

"What? You don't think I can command an army?"

She tossed her head.

"You will see, Yaz. You and everyone else will see what happens when you toss me away. When you throw slurs and spit on me. Every single one of them will pay."

Yasmine let out a low whinny of agreement, and I laughed.

We rode on through the woods, stopping every now and then to rest and eat. The food rations Lazaro had given me were getting perilously low. I looked at the sky, noting it was late afternoon. In a handful of hours, the sun would begin its rapid descent toward the horizon. I did not wish to be caught outside at night.

Guiding Yasmine through the woods, we made our way back to the main road. Though I did not know how far ahead the warriors were, or which direction they headed, the need to find a place to stay, if only for the night, superseded my fear of being caught.

We ambled down the road, the occasional cart and people on horseback passing by. Thankfully, none were warriors in polished armor. As the sun slipped closer to the horizon, I saw the glint of a signpost. Guiding Yasmine forward, I stopped and read the weathered sign, the name of the town all but illegible; Voodomecism.

It sounded like as good a place as any to lay my head.

Using illusion again to hide my ears, I coaxed Yaz forward. The town was bustling, people rushed about, and carriages flew by. Booths lined the street, the voice of people hawking their wares filled the air. Slipping off Yasmine, I took the reins and walked through the throng.

"Fine fabric made from the best silk on Arnagalon. Fabric made from the tiny hands of the A'arnas Fae. The silk got from the Gaalon spiders."

Curiosity got the better of me and I wandered to the booth. I knew the clothing made by the A'arnas Fae to be infused with their magic. A cloak made from their thread would keep the wearer warm on the coldest of days. Clothing would resist holes and tears. Looking down at the merchandise, I choked back a laugh. The items the man sold were not what he claimed, rather a cheap imitation made from the silk of the Wonthen spiders, woven by human hands.

I had no doubt there would be some unhappy customers when their clothing frayed, and the wind whipped through their cloaks. Shaking my head, I moved on. The constant clang of a metal hammer hitting steel rang through the noise. The scent of burning coal mixed with cooked meat drifted on the air. My stomach growled at the smell of food. After eating cured meat, cheese, dried fruit and hard bread, the thought of real food made my mouth water.

I let the scent of food guide my nose, stopping at a booth where small, unknown animals with heads still on, dead eyes looking at the sky, and toes curled, spun on a spit turning over a fire.

"Oy, lil' gurl. Wha' kin I gitcha?" A large man with arms the size of tree trunks turned around, wiping hands on a towel slung over his shoulder.

I eyed the unknown meat, feeling wary as I looked. "How much for that?" I pointed to the animal.

The man looked me up and down and crossed his arms. "Five coppers," he said.

I reached into my pocket and pulled out my pouch of coin. The man's eyes locked on it.

"Five coppers for that shit? It's not worth even half."

I jumped at the voice, turning to see who spoke.

"Maybe if you were to catch some decent meat and offer a good gravy, it'd be worth that much, but this is garbage? I wouldn't feed it to my dog." He motioned to the pot of brown liquid.

"Oy. Git on witcha." The big man waved his hands. "Yer chasin' me coin 'way wit your talk 'bout robbin' pe'ple."

The man to my left jerked his head, and I slowly followed, falling in step beside him, leading Yasmine along.

"I'm Brock Rheinstad," he said with a smile, a small dimple dancing in his cheek. He was tall and muscular with short blonde hair. Green eyes glanced down at me.

"Serafin."

"I noticed you when you walked by my forge. A fine, well-to-do young woman like you could get herself into serious trouble, especially when you're hefting a bag full of coins out in the open. At the least, you'd be relieved of it."

I looked at him out of the corner of my eye. "And how do I know you're not leading me into trouble?"

He stopped and looked at me. "You don't, but if you want to keep on showing you've got coin, have at it, and then see where you stand in the morning."

I sighed. "Where are you taking me? Hopefully, some place with food."

"There's a tavern and inn just up a way. You can stable your horse and have a meal while you wait for the rest of your party to catch up." He sounded different from the man with the strange meat. No strong accent. I eyed Brock, keeping my peripheral searching for a sign of a dagger.

"It's just me," I said, immediately cursing myself for telling this stranger I was alone. Well, he had stopped me from buying questionable meat. I wrinkled my nose at the thought. He had also warned me of thieves. But then he might be a thief himself.

"Ran away, did you?" His eyes swept over me. "It must have been something major for someone like you to leave what I presume to have been a comfortable life. Or are you only trying to prove a point?" He circled me like he was examining a prized horse. "Run away, I think. Trying to prove a point." He smiled.

"You're quite nosey," I said with a sniff.

He laughed. "I prefer to call it... friendly."

"You didn't happen to see any warriors wearing armor come through?" I asked. I felt as though I could trust this person. He did save me from consuming what he considered sub-par food.

He glanced over at me. "Ah Definitely a runaway then," he said, the dimple in his cheek peeking out as he smiled. "And no, I have not seen anyone like that."

Exhaling in relief, I followed him through the village. People called out friendly greetings or nodded at him, which eased my apprehension somewhat. Finally, we stopped at a building. The sign blowing gently in the breeze read The Impious Seductress.

"You will find a warm bed and food here. Ask for the venison stew and tell them Brock sent you. If not, they'll lie and say they're out." He reached for Yasmine's reins. I clutched them tighter.

"Why are you doing this? What are you looking for in return?"

He grinned and winked. "Maybe just a golden road to the gods." He gently tugged Yasmine's reins. I reluctantly released them and relieved her of my belongings.

"The barn is behind this building. You have nothing to worry about, Serafin," he said, and I could have cried at his kindness. At this stranger who—for whatever his reason—helped me. I reached into my cloak, removed my pouch of coin, and took out two golds, and pressed them into his hand. Brock's eyes widened at the sight, and he made as if to give them back.

"No," I said, offering a smile as I backed towards the tavern's entrance. "You have helped me tremendously." I stifled the urge to cry. No need to open the floodgates here.

Pocketing the coin, he bowed slightly, then guided Yasmine toward the stable as I pulled open the tavern door. I looked around the almost empty room. A blazing fire warmed the place, and I shrugged off my cloak as I took a seat in the corner. The scent of fresh baked bread and meat drifted from the back and my painfully empty stomach whined in displeasure. Taking Brock's advice, I ordered the stew, and it was delicious. I made a mental note to thank him.

Hunger satiated, I secured a room where I unpacked my meager belongings, then exited the room, eager to explore the village. Stepping back outside, I looked around. Where to go? What to explore? Turning right, I struck out in the opposite direction from which I came, heading toward what I guessed would be the center.

The town was larger than I first thought. Tall buildings made of stone, brick, and wood lined the streets, shops advertising their wares in the windows. Pastries and bread from a bakery, fine fabric, suits and dresses from the haberdasher. Vegetables sat outside another shop, a boar and rabbit hanging from hooks in the window. I took my time exploring the different stores and booths, buying a few useful items. A dagger from the weaponsmith's shop, beautiful fabric in different colors to make dresses, shirts, and trousers. I stopped at the bakery shop and bought a chocolate hand pie to satisfy my sweet tooth. The folks in the town were a friendly sort, smiling and saying hello as I passed, and I quickly became comfortable here, the thought I perhaps found my new home taking root in my mind.

"Serafin," a voice called out. Turning, I smiled at seeing Brock walking toward me. A petite woman with mahogany skin, a head of unruly light brown curls, and golden eyes walked beside him.

"Brock," I said in greeting as he drew closer. "That venison stew was delicious. Thank you for the suggestion."

Brock smiled, then turned to the woman beside him. "This is Uma Barnstable," he said, throwing an arm around her shoulders. She held her hand out to me with a smile.

"I'm Serafin," I said, grasping her warm hand in mine.

A frown creased her brow, her eyes widened, and a sad look crossed her features. Releasing my hand, she dropped it to her side.

"It's nice to meet you, Serafin." Her voice was soft.

She and Brock began walking down the street again, and I fell in step beside them.

"I was heading to my store to work. I could use a bit of help. I have to check in and record some books a trader brought in. You could help make it go faster," Uma said, brushing a curl from her forehead.

I didn't need to think about it. I wasn't doing much besides exploring the town, and when I was through, I'd only go back to my room. "Sounds fun."

Uma smiled, as we pulled up to a building, the sign hanging read Nonpareil Opus. I smiled at the name that meant one of a kind place.

"Well, this is where I leave you ladies," Brock said. Leaning forward he kissed Uma's cheek, then continued down the street. Uma pulled a key from her cloak pocket and unlocked the door.

Stepping inside, I looked around. It was a large store, the musty scent of old books filled my nose, and a comforting feeling fell over me. Rows upon rows of shelves lined the walls, the other shelves dividing the shop in half and on the floor were stacks of books and overflowing boxes. Uma disappeared in the back, and I took the opportunity to look around. Wandering through the aisles, I ran my hand along the spines, tilting my head to read the titles. While many of the books were in the common human language, many were foreign to me. My eyes found one book whose title was written in flowing Elvish script. Pulling it off the shelf, I looked at the cover. A castle on a cliff loomed in the background, the foreground a dense and eerie forest with tree branches reaching out like claws, red eyes peering out from the shadows. A pretty young girl with long, blonde hair dressed in a long, black dress knelt in front of a pond looking into the water. The face reflecting back was that of an old hag with white, stringy hair, long, pointed nose and watery eyes. The title read *The Witch Princess*, a spooky elven faerie tale.

The sound of Uma's shoes scraping on the wood floor pulled my attention. Putting the book back, I made my way to a table in a corner where she placed a long ledger, quill, and ink.

"Alright. That pile," she pointed to a stack on the floor, "contains books I need to record, then put in the empty spaces on the shelves. The rest will go in the back."

I looked at the pile spread out on the floor. Uma was right. This task would take an eternity for one person. She gestured to the table, and I sat behind it. Opening the ledger, I looked at the page that was broken up into columns, the headers reading title, date, seller, and condition. Uma went through the books, reading off the information on the slip of paper tucked inside, which I wrote down, filling the parchment. She seemed to know many of the languages, something which impressed me.

Pulling out another book, she looked at it, a frown creasing her brow. "I'm not sure what this one says. There are a number written in this strange language. Though I can't read it, I have had patrons buy them."

I glanced at the book. "That's Elvish. The title is *The Demon Beneath The Bed*," I said without thinking.

Uma looked at me.

"I—I don't—"

"Don't worry Serafin. I'm not going to tell anyone."

I stared at her. "What do you mean?"

"I got your story when I shook your hand. I see auras around people and when I touch someone, I get visions of them. Sometimes it's their past. Sometimes it's their future, or even both. I'm sorry about what happened to you. It really wasn't fair," she said, handing me the book and the slip of paper that was with it, and I recorded it in the ledger.

"You were smart to do whatever you did to hide your ears."

I frowned. "Why?"

Rising, Uma went behind the counter and pulled out a bottle of wine and two glasses. Pouring the liquid, she handed me one, then settled back on the floor.

"Voodomecism is predominantly a Non town, and they work closely with the Suppressors. There are Wielders who reside here. We keep to ourselves, hiding who we are so as not to be turned in."

"Why do you stay if it's a Non town?"

Uma shrugged. "The folks maybe misguided, but they're friendly. They can't help the poison they've been fed. And it keeps us safe. There's no need for the Suppressors to bring Feelers with them."

I sipped my wine, realizing how sheltered I was at the palace. My people were the only ones who inhabited Il'Ekhester. Perhaps that kept us safe from the Nons. Though there was nothing the Suppressors could do to us without breaking the treaty and causing a war, the Nons possessed the ability to harm us.

Uma waved her hand. "That doesn't matter. As long as we stay low, we will stay undetected. Now," she said, pouring more wine in her glass. Holding the bottle out, I took it and refilled myself. "I could really use some help around here. I have a beast of a time finding people who want to work here. Most days it's slow and the books that need to be recorded is a never-ending job. Plus, you speak Elvish. The books written in that language rarely go out the door and they're taking up space. Perhaps if you could provide a translation, they might become more appealing."

I thought about it for a moment. I did want to stay despite finding out it was a Non town, and I would eventually need to find a way to earn coin. "Why not?"

Uma smiled. "Good. That's settled. Now, the second issue is a matter of where you're going to stay. You can't live at the inn."

I chewed my lip. "I hadn't really thought about that."

"Right," Uma said with a nod. "I have a spare room you can move into. You can pay me out of your wages for the room and we'll split food and chores."

"I—"

"Good. That's settled then. We will gather your things when we're done for the day," she said, picking up another book.

My eyes stung at her words, at the friendship and kindness this stranger offered me. Uma's eyes met mine and she smiled.

"Welcome to your new home, Serafin."

TWENTY-ONE
ABRAHAM

"**M**UST YOU LEAVE?" PALMA'S arms slipped around my waist and teeth grazed my earlobe. Turning my head, I caught her mouth with mine and kissed her slowly. Her fingers danced down, down, down, grasping between my legs and stroking me back to attention.

"Yes," I said, reluctantly pulling away and removing her hand. "The sooner I get this over with, the sooner I come back to you." I pushed a lock of ash blonde hair behind her ear.

She sniffed. "You'll be gone the better part of the day. Can't someone else do it, Abe? Bones or Sam?"

I sighed, wishing it were that easy, but it was my contract. My soul to deliver.

"I'll make it up to you."

Palma's lips curled up into a smile. "With a pretty?"

"Whatever you desire. You know my wish is only to make you happy," I said, looking down into her brown eyes.

"You do, Abraham. I've never been happier in my life."

Kissing her again, I reluctantly rose from the bed. I quickly washed, pulled on my clothes, and gathered my weapons. I cast one last look at Palma, who was settling back down beneath the covers, and slipped out of the room and headed out to go collect a soul. My father had needs and I didn't want to disappoint. I dared not.

The village of Howling Cove bustled. People rushed to their destination. Horse-drawn wagons flew by, Suppressors milled about patrolling streets, eyes scanning, hands resting on sword hilts. I wandered through, stopped at the bakery for a chocolate sweet cake, my one guilty pleasure in life—aside from Palma—and bit into the cake. Turning down a side road, I drew closer to my destination. Licking the chocolate off my fingers, I drew up to my quarry's home. It was rundown. The paint chipping in places, and the porch sagged. The windows were grimy, and one was boarded up, and the yard overgrown with weeds. I stood in the shadows and watched the happy family go on with their life, unaware I was here.

Unaware that, within minutes, I would be taking a life.

I watched the small boy tottering after his father. A tow-headed girl running to her mother. The mother. I was here for her.

The woman's eyes found me.

She didn't look shocked. The color didn't drain from her face. She looked... ready. She put the child down, eyes never leaving me.

"Go to Papa."

"But—"

"Go," she repeated, voice firm, gently swatting the child's backside, sending her in the man's direction who stood stock still.

"I have been waiting," she said as she slowly made her way toward me. "How does this happen?"

I glanced at the man who scooped the two children up and began making his way toward the house. He paused, eyes on me.

"It's all right. I have been expecting this for some time," she said to him, brown eyes sad. Running a hand through her short, chestnut hair, she looked at me once again. "How does this happen?"

I looked at the man bringing the two children into the house. At the girl who looked over his shoulder, brown eyes focused on her mother's back, those same eyes focusing on me for just a moment.

"How does this happen?" The woman's voice persisted, tinged with annoyance.

I wanted to turn and run. To write the words *Null and Void* across the parchment, breaking it and giving her soul back, but I knew I couldn't. My father made his displeasure clear the first time I voided a contract for a woman named Yarnnalay. He made sure I paid for the deed in pain and blood, something I did not wish to go through this day.

I knew this contract was a test. He knew the children would pull at my fatherly heartstrings, like Yarnnalay's son had, but I turned a blind eye to it, though it was a difficult task. I needed to gain my father's trust. I needed him to believe I was on his side, that I would take the golden throne and rule beside him when he broke free.

Reaching into my cloak I pulled out the contract and my golden quill.

"I need your blood," I said. She held out her hand and I stabbed her finger, drawing her blood in. Unrolling the parchment, I placed it on the nearby table.

Fuck, but it would be so easy to write *Null and Void* across it. So easy to give this woman, who sold her soul to bear her children, her soul back. Though some might think it selfish, think she deserved what she got, I did not. And now I had to take her from her family. From the children she so desperately wanted.

But I had a part to play. I had to be the dutiful and obedient son. I had to do what I was told, and in a convincing way if I were to execute my plan when the time came. Grasping the quill, I wrote the words *Contract Fulfilled* across the page.

The woman's eyes widened; her hands clawed at her throat. Her mouth opened and her soul poured out in a smoky mist. I held out an obsidian box, her soul drifting into it. Closing the lid, I made my way to the darkness of the woods. As I pulled the shadows close, as the demons clawed at me and wrapped around my body, I heard the woman's husband scream. Heard the cries of her children as I drifted to the Abyss.

I fucking hated my job.

"**Z**EDEKIAH," THEMESIS CALLED OUT as I entered the throne room. It was almost back to its full glory, the demon slaves working steadily to put it back together. Nightshade had been rebuilt, though it did not look as majestic as before. Themesis sat upon it, his fingers drumming on the armrest. The golden throne, my throne, sat to the right. The gold gleamed brighter, the seat looking a bit larger and grander than Nightshade.

Or perhaps it was my imagination.

Demons lurked in the shadows, eyes on me, heads bowing as I crossed the room to stand in front of my father. As always, he was smartly dressed. His black hair was pulled back, he wore a velvet tailcoat the color of smoke, black shirt, white trousers and boots polished to a shine. His blue eyes pierced me, and I resisted the urge to look away from him.

The one saving grace I noticed upon entering was the absence of my daughter, Jaylynn. I did not look where she often knelt to the right of his throne. That would make him summon her, something I did not want.

"What do you have for me?" Themesis said, as if he didn't know.

I pulled out the obsidian box and he smiled.

"I admit I thought you would disobey me and void her contract. You surprise me, Zedekiah."

I clenched my teeth. "I am your servant. My job is to obey."

Bel hissed at my words, and I did not blame him. Just saying them made the bile in my stomach rise.

Opening the box, a mist poured out, coalescing into the form of the woman. She looked around. Her eyes weren't filled with fear. She didn't cower, nor did she cry. She looked resigned, as if she knew tears and fear would do her no favors.

"Themesis," she said, looking up at him.

Themesis' eyes narrowed on her. He gripped the armrests, his jaw clenching and realization hit me. This woman was not afraid of being here, nor was she afraid of Themesis, and that angered him.

He fed on fear. On terror. He loved to see the ones brought before him cry. Grove. Beg him for forgiveness and this woman did not do any of that.

"Take her to a cell. I will decide her punishment later," he snapped.

Two demons crept out of the shadows, one taking an arm. She didn't resist. She held her head high, walking with them to her cell. Themesis drummed his fingers again. His nostrils flared. I wanted to laugh at how much the woman's lack of fear bothered him. What would happen when he breaks free and no one kneeled? No one cowered? It was an amusing thought.

"The Suppressers are not doing an adequate job of annihilating Wielders. Forcing them to join does me no favors. That silly bracelet can easily be removed. I need a river of blood—their blood—flowing through the lands. Their death will be my rebirth."

I suppressed the urge to roll my eyes.

"I would have been free a long time ago if Damiyun did not kill my queen." His knuckles turned white as he gripped the armrest hard.

"Are we done here?" I was growing impatient and did not wish to listen to the ramblings of an insane man.

He nodded, and I pulled the shadows and demons close, drifting back to the world of the living before he could change his mind. It was midafternoon when I arrived back at Howling Cove. I thought about what Themesis said about Lillyanna, and a pang of sadness settled over me. She was a sweet young girl who foolishly gave herself and her love to Damiyun, who did not turn her away.

I feared his feelings for her would drive him to not complete his task, but in the end, he drove the dagger into her, ending her life.

And it was all for naught, something that did not settle well with me. Her death did not seal the binds on Themesis' tomb like the gods, like Felicity, the Goddess of Nature said it would. That bothered me greatly, more so, the thought the girl was sent to her sacrifice for nothing. For a test of Damiyun's will and loyalty.

I needed the truth as to why Lillyanna was born. Why her sacrifice did not work and get the gods to tell me what, if anything, they planned to do when Themesis escaped. My prior conversation heeded no answers. The girl's death had done nothing. Monsters roamed attacking innocents all across the land. Demons multiplied, some still in service to my father. The gods had to admit their failure.

Though Felicity forbade me from going back to S'aehe, I felt it was time to pay another visit to the gods.

TWENTY-TWO

"W HAT ARE YOU DOING here?" Oohlrich, the Keeper of the Cave hoisted his battle ax in a defensive manner.

I clasped my hands behind my back to show him I had come in peace, though if he attacked, I would not hesitate to defend myself.

"I seek council with Felicity."

Oohlrich's jaw clenched, and he gripped the ax tighter. "She told you to not dare entering S'aehe again."

"True, yet, she is the only one with answers about her daughter."

Oohlrich's nostrils flared. "The Goddess of Nature banished you from here. I will not allow you to pass. Go back from whence you came, Zedekiah, Son of Themesis."

I stepped out of the darkness of the cave. Oohlrich held his ax higher, eyes on me. Fear flickered in his eyes. He licked his lips and gripped his ax. I was no mere mortal to command.

I pushed past Oohlrich wo did not try to stop me, for all the threats he gave. "I trust Felicity is in her garden?"

"Yes," he said. I suppressed a satisfied smile as I heard the clink of the ax head hitting the ground as he dropped it.

I made my way down the walkway toward where I knew Felicity would be. Though S'aehe was the home to the gods, including the lesser ones, Felicity, the narcissistic cunt, had inserted herself as the leader, much like what my father tried to do. The other gods and goddesses did not question her. I suspect having Sarlay, the God of War in her bed and under her control helped. Who would go against the man who commanded armies and who could cut you down with the swipe of a blade that never dulled? Felicity might have the others in fear, but she did not have me.

The scent of lilies, roses, and honeysuckle drifted on a light breeze. Bushes trimmed into the shape of beasts, unicorns rearing up, a minotaur holding a shield and sword, and a centaur with a bow and arrow lined the path. Light reflected off the white marble statues of the gods.

Sarlay, the God of War in his heavy, majestic armor stood tall, broad ax strapped to his back, right hand resting on the hilt of his sword. Euphina, the Goddess of Healing held a basket of herbs. Dhala, Goddess of Fertility, nursed a babe in her arms. The God of the Sea, Leoatle, stood proud, trident in one hand, a huge wave looming behind. Vatra, the God of Fire held flames and Samanka, the Goddess of Dreams, sprinkled dream dust on a sleeping figure.

And in the center of them all stood Felicity, the Goddess of Nature. Her long hair spilled down her back in waves. She wore a low-cut, tight-fitting dress, and a seductive smile curled her lips.

Seeing the statue of Felicity filled me with disgust. While she had not waged a war upon the gods, she was no different than my father.

As I walked toward the pavilion where I knew she would be holding court, lesser gods scattered in fear, whispering Zedekiah behind hands. Though the reactions, the whispers should have angered me, it only bolstered me. By now the news of my being here should have reached Felicity's ears and I was sure she was fuming inside.

A grand structure of marble and oak with a high peaked roof marred the beauty of the garden. As I suspected, Felicity was inside, though she did not lounge against the many push pillows decorating her sanctuary.

No. She stood in the middle, blue eyes angry. Her blonde hair flowed down her back, the sides secured with golden combs. The turquoise dress she wore hugged her curves, the neckline dipping low, an invitation to any man who could not resist such a display.

"Zedekiah." A snarl curled her full lips. "I told you, you are not welcome here."

Stepping into her sanctuary, I grasped the carafe of wine sitting on the low table, pouring the liquid into an empty glass. Taking a sip, I settled down against the plush pillows. Her eyes flashed with fury.

"Who do you think you are walking into S'aehe as though you own it?"

I took another sip of my wine, my eyes on her. "I am Zedekiah, son of Themesis, a god who once sat amongst you. Or have you forgotten who he once was?"

She clenched her fists, and I dare say she almost lost her decorum. But being who she was, she visibly calmed herself.

"He was tossed into the Abyss, never allowed here. Much as you."

I laughed into my glass. "You know only my name and who my father is, but you do not know me. But I know you, Felicity." I rose from my spot. Her eyes traveled up to my face, fear flashing in them for a moment. I did not want her to be afraid, not really, but I played on what she showed me.

"You made a daughter with a human for the sole purpose of defeating my father. But it didn't work, did it?" I took a step toward her. The other gods flinched but she remained cool. Impressive.

"You knew her sacrifice was not going to work, yet you sent her to her death anyway."

Felicity shook her head. "No. It was going to work but those damned Suppressors going after Wielders, it weakened the binds. You know this."

I clenched my fists. Of course, she would push her failure off on another. Of course, she would sacrifice someone who could possibly usurp her.

Lillyanna was strong in her magic. Far stronger than her mother, so why not sacrifice her?

"The Suppressors had nothing to do with Lillyanna's death. Don't you even care? Don't you think about the person you birthed?"

"Of course, I do." Her voice rose. Lesser gods passed by, glancing to assure themselves their goddess was alright. "You think I did not love the child I birthed? That I did not watch her? Care about her?"

Crossing my arms, I pinned her with my gaze. "You left her after she was born. That tells me just how much you cared about her."

Her eyes narrowed. "I had to."

I laughed. "You didn't. I do not know how no one can see what a narcissistic cunt you are."

Her nostrils flared. "Is this why you came here, Zedekiah? To tell me what a horrible mother I am? To sling insults at me?"

I shook my head. "Your plan did not work. Your daughter," I emphasized the words, "died for naught. My father's binds weaken. Surely you are aware demons roam the mortal world, multiplying, spreading.

Felicity sniffed. "Yes, we are aware. We hear the desperate prayers of the humans, begging us to help."

What you all have wanted. You have wanted the humans to recognize you again. To pray to you again.

The thought sickened me. Mankind had long since turned their backs on the gods. Very few believed in them. Those that did, those that still prayed and asked for help weren't enough to matter to them. The few prayers answered wouldn't be enough to change the minds of the non-believers. It would just be chalked up to luck. A good summer for a good harvest. A well place bet for a windfall. A grand ball to keep the haberdasher busy for a Moon Cycle.

"What do you plan to do when Themesis breaks free?"

Felicity laughed. "Do you think we would allow that? Allow him to launch another war against us so he can rule S'aehe and the Abyss?"

"Your plan with sacrificing Lillyanna did not work and his bind are weaker still." I should know.

Felicity tossed her hair. "I am done with this discussion. Leave, Zedekiah."

Of course, you are.

Brushing past her, I exited her pavilion and made my way back toward the cave.

"Zedekiah," a voice called out. Stopping, I turned to see Samanka hurrying toward me. She held her long skirts in her hand, her short black hair bounced around her heart shaped face. She stopped a few feet in front of me, sweeping a few tendrils of hair from her forehead.

"Samanka," I greeted.

"Zedekiah, I—we—are truly sorry for what happened to the girl, Lillyanna. We...we truly do not know what to do. We know Themesis is close to breaking free, but Felicity," she cast a fearful, furtive look over her shoulder. "Felicity," she said again, voice lowered, "will not let us do anything. We see the chaos below. The demons and monsters feeding on the people. If Themesis breaks out, there will be a war to rival the one before. I don't know if we can win. If he rules the Abyss and S'aehe..."

She didn't have to tell me what would happen. I was all too aware. Stepping forward, she grasped my forearm, golden eyes meeting mine, silently pleading with me. "We need your help, Zedekiah."

I said nothing as I pulled away from her, making my way back to the cave. I did not wish to reveal my plan to her. To any of the gods. Felicity forbidding the others from doing anything told me she had something nefarious up her sleeve. Lillyanna was made to make my father stronger, to assist him. Felicity had helped him to regain worshippers.

Stepping past Oohlrich, I entered the cave. Pulling the shadows and monsters around, I slipped back to Howling Cove. My talk with Felicity made my charade of being the dutiful and loyal son much more important.

If I could gain my father's trust again, I would have it all, and he would be so blinded by power, he wouldn't even see what I planned.

TWENTY-THREE
ARDEN

S WEAT ROLLED DOWN MY back as I walked through the hall. The black obsidian walls rose high, the light from the molten rivers of rock reflected off the smooth surface. A shadow passed over me from above. Looking up, I saw a giant, winged beast, wicked talons protruded from curled feet. A giant hawk head sat on a long neck. Fiery eyes peered about as it flew. A scrape to my left drew my attention. A half-human, half demon being stood in the shadows. Its flesh hung off skeletal remains. Wings protruded from a hunched back. Fingers curled into sharp claws and its feet were turning into hooves. Its face was twisted, its nose and mouth forming a long beak and darkness filled the holes where there were once eyes.

I should have been terrified of the grotesque beasts creeping out from the darkness, but I was not. Something about them gave me a strange and quiet comfort. Perhaps it was the thought one day I might end up here in the Abyss, a twisted monstrous soul joining my brothers and sisters who looked at me with curiosity, I did not know.

I just knew—felt—they were not here to harm.

I drew up to an obsidian door, at least ten feet high and fifteen feet wide. A large iron ring hung in the middle. Grasping it, I pushed, and the door swung open on silent hinges. The room was enormous. Torch light danced on the smooth, black walls, a sideboard holding crystal glasses and several decanters filled with liquid was the only furniture. Tapestries lined the walls, depictions of the war between the gods, and multicolored rugs covered the floor.

Carved into the middle of the floor was a large triangle within a circle, surrounded by odd words and pictures. Four channels ran from there across the room to the walls. The channels were caked with a reddish-brown substance.

And at the other end of the room, seated on a large throne of obsidian, looming above, larger than life on the raised dais, he sat.

Themesis.

The throne was black, the armrests and legs carved into the shape of Griffins. A string of delicate purple flowers curled around the base lending a hint of color. Flowers after which the throne was named.

Nightshade.

My eyes went to Themesis, my skin prickling at seeing him. His black hair was pulled back in a low ponytail. He wore a blood red satin tailcoat, and a black shirt beneath, the red buttons looked like drops of blood. Black trousers sheathed his legs and boots polished to a shine; silver buckles glinted in the torch light completed his ensemble.

A lump formed in my throat as I gazed up at him. He was beautifully majestic. His ice-blue eyes bore through me, neatly manicured nails tapped the armrest.

"Arden Rayne," his voice boomed, vibrating through my body.

Dropping to my knees in front of the dais, I pressed my forehead to the floor.

"Master," I said, rising to my feet again.

I looked up at him. At the most powerful god to ever rule. A chill ran through me as realization hit that Themesis, the ruler of the Abyss summoned me to stand before him.

I felt blessed.

"Your order is a disgrace my name," he spat. "You are to kill the Wielders, not block their power. That does nothing for me. Their magic still flows even if they cannot summon it."

Clasping my hands behind my back, I met Themesis' eyes. "I am well aware, Master. It is Vel who gives them the choice to live or die. If I had my way, all Wielders would be destroyed."

Themesis propped a leg on his knee. A smile curled his lips. "You are one of my faithful disciples. I have watched you, Arden Rayne. Your dedication to destruction is unwavering. It is why I called you here."

My heart bloomed at his words.

"You will be my vessel. Destroy every man, woman, and child with magic. Kill them."

I smiled at his words. At being chosen—blessed—by Themesis to carry out his orders. I would do exactly what he commanded. A dead Wielder is better than a captured one. I would make sure their blood painted the world in a river of red.

O PENING MY EYES, I stared up at the royal blue canopy above my bed. Themesis' words rang in my head. He had chosen me to carry out his orders. He had called to me because of my dedication. I was truly blessed.

Tossing off the covers, I slipped out of bed. Washing up, I pulled on a clean uniform, buckled my sword around my waist, and exited my quarters. The halls were quiet, the sun hadn't woken yet. Most of the Suppressors were tucked away in their warm beds, but not me.

No. The dream I had, no, the reality I entered in my sleep, filled me with purpose. My body buzzed with power. Shadows from the lamplight danced on the black marble floor as I strode through the halls, passing busts and paintings of Elders and Eminences past. Pausing at a bust of Zachariah Farnsworth, I kissed my fingertips and placed them briefly on his lips before continuing on.

Coming upon a winding staircase, I ascended to my torture room. It was a tall tower on the eastern side of the Compound, Wren's Keep. The crack of a whip and screams of pain echoed down the stairwell. I smiled at the sound, pushing the heavy metal door open, the hinges groaning beneath the weight. I looked around the room. My sanctuary.

Tall, open windows overlooked the forests and mountains beyond, a cool breeze blowing in chilled the room. A woman hung from the ceiling, wrists shackled to a chain. Her naked torso dripped sweat, blood trickled from the wounds on her back and deep knife cuts to her torso. Puddles of crimson gathered on the floor beneath her.

The metallic scent of blood filled my nostrils. Closing my eyes, I inhaled the delicious perfume, my head spinning with giddiness. Opening my eyes, I crossed the room and stood before the hanging woman. Leaning forward I licked a trail of blood, savoring the sweet honey on my tongue.

I lifted a hand, chuckling as she shrank back. "Comfortable, Love?" I said, pushing a lock of sweat and blood-soaked hair from her face. Her eyes narrowed at me, lips pulled back in a snarl. Her spit hit my face, and I casually wiped it off on my sleeve.

"You are a monster," she spat.

I flashed a smile. "Thank you, Love. I appreciate the compliment."

"How can you live with yourself, doing what you do? How can you sleep at night with the blood of innocents on your hands?"

"Oh, I sleep just fine," I said. "You are far from innocent. Magic is a blight upon the pristine world. A disease that chokes the goodness from everything."

I should know. My brother Damiyun's birth choked the goodness, the life out of my mother.

"Are you not a Wielder too? Do you hate yourself as well? We have done nothing wrong. We keep to ourselves. How can you treat us this way? We have never hurt a Non." She rambled.

Crossing the room, I stood in front of the long table spanning the wall. On it laid devices used to extend the torture. Pliers with sharp points on the inside, blades to cut through bones. Hammers to smash hands and limbs. Sharp knives to cut and slice. Hanging above the table was an array of whips, my favorite being the knout whose many barbs tore and ripped flesh. In the fire rested a length of metal, the steel glowing red.

Picking up one of the knives, I turned back to the woman who quickly stopped speaking. Crossing the short distance, I stood in front of her. Looking deep into her eyes, I slashed the knife across her throat. Blood sprayed, and poured from the wound, her mouth opened and closed, a sickening gurgle coming out. Her eyes stared at nothing as her Life Force left.

Tossing the knife on the table, I exited the room, heading toward the training yard to work off my pent-up energy.

"Regulator Rayne," a voice called after me.

Turning, I saw Suppressor Farnsworth striding down the hall, right hand on the hilt of his sword.

I smiled at the young man.

At twenty, he had shown great potential and promise as a Suppressor and not just because his blood could be traced back to Zachariah Farnsworth, the founder of the Order. Ghent was bright and eager. He was good with a sword, though not yet an expert by any means. He was certainly better than others his age. He eagerly took on any task, even those not asked of him. I knew he wanted to rise in the ranks. Though he was often loyal and obedient, he did frequently forget himself, being occupied by the fairer sex, causing me to whip him into submission.

Ghent Farnsworth embodied what it was to be Suppressors and everything we were.

"Suppressor Farnsworth," I nodded.

"Elder Castille wishes to see you," he said, stopping in front of me.

I nodded and followed Ghent down the hall in the direction he had come. The rising sun glinted on the stained-glass windows, throwing a kaleidoscope of color upon the white polished marble floors. "In a few weeks' time, I will head to Voodomecism for recruitment. Being a Non-dominant town, they are always eager to join," I said to Ghent as we walked. "I will request for you join me. It will be your first time out with me. I want to see what you can do."

"Of course, Regulator Rayne. Just let me know when."

I smiled at his response.

At his obedience.

"You're a good Suppressor, Ghent. I suspect you will rise quickly in the ranks."

He shrugged. "I'm a Farnsworth. It is what they expect of me."

I chuckled. "Surname aside, you have ambition and dedication." Ghent said nothing. "If recruitment goes well, I will speak with Elder Castille about broadening your duties," I said as we stopped outside the closed door to Vel's office.

"Thank you, Regulator Rayne." Ghent bowed slightly and backed away. Turning the handle, I pushed open the door and strode inside. I glanced around the sparsely furnished room. An enormous stone fireplace sat to the left, the heat from it warming the room. To my right was a large ornate sideboard made of cherry. A pattern of vines and flowers in gold leaf adorned the doors and legs, the same pattern replicated on Vel's desk and chairs. Upon the sideboard sat crystal glasses and a decanter filled with red wine, the candlelight from the diamond chandelier above glinting off the glass. As I looked around the room, I made mental notes of what I would add to the empty room once I became Elder, a pen for my playthings being one. My eyes went to Vel who sat behind a large mahogany desk, head bent over papers. The light of the setting sun pouring through the wall of windows behind him glinted off his gray hair. I crossed to the sideboard, the sound of my feet muffled on the worn mismatched rugs—those would be the first to go—and poured two glasses of wine.

"You wished to see me?" I said, handing him a glass when he looked up, and then settled into the high-backed chair in front of his desk, the wood hard and uncomfortable beneath my backside.

"How are things going?"

I took a sip of wine and looked at Vel over the rim of the glass. "Another Wielder is gone."

Vel's nostrils flared. "You are supposed to be turning them, not killing them."

I laughed. "A dead Wielder is better than a captured one. Their death is what will break Themesis free. As long as they live, as long as the Sigaa'Lean can be removed, he will stay bound in the Abyss by their magic," I said. "Of course, had your plan with your daughter worked, we wouldn't be having this conversation."

Of course, I did not know what happened to Lillyanna. I did not see her when I was in the Abyss in my dream, though the reddish-brown substance caking the channels of the triangle gave me pause. Was it possible it was her blood? Was it possible she was killed and that is why Themesis was still bound in the Abyss?

I pushed the thought aside for the time being.

Vel's eyes narrowed on me. "Watch your tongue, Arden. You are walking a precarious line right now. You will continue to capture Wielders and force them to join.

Placing my glass on his desk, I rose. "Are we done?"

Vel gave a curt nod, and I exited the room, stalking through the halls to my quarters. He didn't know who he was dealing with. He didn't know my orders came from someone much higher than him, nor would he.

Slamming the door to my room, I poured a glass of wine. The sound of rattling filled the room, stoking my ire. Putting my glass down, I crossed to where I kept my Play Thing. Black eyes glared at me as I squatted down and looked at her naked body crouched within the small confinement, wrists shackled to the wall. She jerked against the shackles again, rattling the cage, panting with the effort.

"I'd stop that if I were you. You're going to hurt yourself, which will not please me. I am the only one who causes pain around here."

Her eyes were like daggers piercing through me as she struggled and tried to speak, her closed mouth making the noise a grunt.

I laughed. "Sorry, love, but I had to bind your mouth. You scream when I want you to scream. Now, if you behave like the good girl, I know you can be, you will be afforded some liberties. I can remove the cage and allow you to speak for a few hours a day, though the chains must remain. I am not a savage. Not completely. The more you submit, the easier your life will be." I stood up. "The choice is entirely up to you."

She grunted and rattled the chains once more before defeat flashed in her eyes and her body sagged.

"Good girl. I may even feed you for this," I said, crossing back to the couch. Tossing a log on the fire, and sat in a chair, kicking my feet up on the table and sipped my drink. My thoughts went to my conversation with Vel. I did not know why he would rather force Wielders to join the Order instead of ending their lives. The Sigaa'Lean might block their magic, but they were still a plague on this world. They could easily be released, and their magic would fully secure Themesis in the Abyss for eternity.

Their death would remove the taint choking the land, and it would set Themesis free to unleash his terror, his punishment on man.

I sipped my drink, letting the dark thoughts invade my mind.

The day I stopped believing in the good of magic was the day my brother was born.

Which was the day my mother died.

She was sweet and beautiful. She had a smile that lit up a room, soft ruby lips and skin as white as snow and as smooth as marble. I loved to feel her skin against my cheek. Her supple breasts a soft pillow for my head.

She was pure and loving and when her light was extinguished? It was as though all light had left with her. And when my beautiful shining angel—my love, my life—was taken from me, I only saw darkness.

I only saw the taint and evil of Wielders.

And I only wanted to cause them pain and torment.

But above all, I only wanted one to suffer the most. I only wanted one to rue the day he entered the world. I only wanted one to never forget all he had taken from me.

And so, I turned my hatred on my brother torturing him day after day. The euphoria of making him suffer made me lightheaded. The need to inflict my pain upon him gave me pleasure and his screams—his screams were a potent aphrodisiac.

My father believed Damiyun was evil, something I had planted in his mind. I had him convinced Damiyun was born from the Abyss, from Themesis.

He seemed to have disappeared after his visit to Kraagswell Mountain, but I would find him again, and when I did? He would suffer worse than he ever had. I was done playing with him. This time, the pleasure I took would be watching him suffer and die by my hand.

Clenching my jaw, I slammed my drink down upon the table; the glass shattering on impact. Shards sliced through my flesh, stinging pain blooming through my palm. I reveled in the feeling of the dull, pulsing ache, and licked the blood. Droplets spilled upon the floor. I did not bend to lick those. The salty metallic taste filled my mouth and with it came lust, desire, and the need to inflict pain.

I got up and crossed over to my plaything. Her eyes were closed, and I saw the steady rise and fall of her back as she slept. Unlocking the door, I reached inside, grabbed a fistful of her hair, and yanked her head back. Her eyes snapped open, wide with fear, and she tried to open her mouth to scream. Unlocking her wrists, I dragged her out by her hair and threw her face down on the bed, securing her to the shackles on the post. She thrashed about. She craned her neck to look at me, wide eyes showing mostly the whites, and her body shook as I stood above her. Her jaw moved again as she tried to speak.

"Don't worry, Love," I whispered softly in her ear. "You'll get your chance to scream. I promise."

I pulled away and pressed my lips to her temple. Placing a hand on her back, I let loose my magic. Her body convulsed beneath my touch, her screams piercing the quiet of the night. I closed my eyes and lost myself in the symphony of pain.

TWENTY-FOUR
SERAFIN

S ETTLING INTO MY NEW home and a new routine didn't take long. The friendship I found with Uma and Brock made it feel as though I had lived here my whole life. In many ways, Uma reminded me of Cwella. In her unruly curls and how she could distract me when my thoughts went south, making me laugh and, for the moment, forget. And Brock? He had taken me under his arm my first day and looked after me as if he were my brother.

Much like Phabian.

Sadness shot through me at the thought of him. Of the person who had been there for me from the start. When I was just a babe in the womb, he was there, and after I was born, he took care of me. Watched over me. Protected me.

"Stop, Sera," Uma said, her hand gripping my arm. "That is in the past." Her face screwed up. "I don't think he abandoned you. He wouldn't. Something stopped him." Shaking her head, she removed her hand. "You were like a daughter to him. He loved you. He wouldn't abandon you, let alone allow you to be sentenced to death."

As much as I loved Uma, sometimes her ability was a bit invading.

"I'm in the mood for a hand pie," I said. Rising, I grabbed my cloak and made for the door. Pulling it open, I stepped out onto the porch. The sun shined bright in the sky taking off the winter chill.

"Elf Girl," Brock said, slinging an arm around my shoulder. "She can't help what she sees. Don't take it personally."

The porch creaked as Uma stepped out. "I don't," I said. "As she said, it's in the past." Shoving Brock away, I strode down the porch. "I swear to all that is good if the hand pies are sold, someone is going to pay."

Uma's house sat on the outskirts of the principal town on a parcel of land surrounded by woods. It had a broad porch and flowers lining the stone walkway, giving it a quaint feel. Threadbare carpets dotted the floor, and the furniture was well worn, but I adored it. The simplicity of it was a stark contrast to the grand opulence of the palace and her home's warmth made me see how cold and uninviting my former home was. If I were to be truthful, I didn't really miss it, either. Being on my own had shown how sheltered my life had been. I never had to think about the cost of items, nor did I have to think about doing anything for myself, and now I was.

Though, had it not been for Uma and Brock's guidance, I would have been fleeced within the first few days. We walked on toward the town's center, Brock's arm wrapped round Uma's waist, mine linked through her elbow.

"Sera," Brock said. I leaned slightly forward to look at him. "You have been here for three Moon Cycles. Tell me how it compares to where you came from."

"I was pampered. I was a princess living in opulence. I had a maid, Cwella who was like a sister to me, and though I was pampered," I looked at Brock and Uma. "This is real."

Uma smiled and squeezed my hand as we pushed through the crowd, ignoring the harsh words and glares. We bought our hand pies, the proprietor swiftly closing up his shop as soon as my coin hit his hand. I noticed other shops were closing up as well, which I found odd as it was early in the afternoon.

"What's going on?" I bit into my hand pie, the sweet peach jam filling my mouth along with the powdered pastry. I watched people move to the side as a parade of men dressed in black sitting astride horses trotted down the street.

"Shit. I forgot that was today," Uma said.

I glanced at her as I watched the procession, my eyes going to the man leading. He sat straight in the saddle, one hand loosely holding the reins, the other rested on the hilt of his sword. Blue eyes scanned the crowd, narrowing on me for a moment as they walked on.

"Let's go," Brock said.

My eyes followed the man leading who I recognized as the Suppressor who had come to Il'Ekhester asking about the Sigaa'Lean.

"No. I want to see what they're doing here."

"They're here to spew their anti-Wielder bullshit. Let's go," Uma said, tugging my arm. Pulling away, I pushed through the crowd, ignoring Uma and Brock who called after me. "Sorry," a deep voice said as he bumped into me. The hand pie I carried flew out of my hand and landed in a muddy puddle.

"Oh." His voice dripped with dismay.

I looked up from where my ruined treat lay. A pair of hazel eyes locked on mine.

"I am so sorry. I wasn't watching where I was going."

"Nor was I,"

"I'll buy you another one."

"Suppressor Farnsworth." The icy blue-eyed man's voice cracked like a whip.

The other straightened up, clasping his hands behind his back and standing wide. "Regulator Rayne," he said, voice loud and official.

"It's time to start."

Suppressor Farnsworth nodded, following the man to the raised platform in the center. Climbing up, he stood at attention beside Regulator Rayne, who looked out at the crowd. The other Suppressors staggered out behind him.

"Welcome," Regulator Rayne said, his rich voice carried and quieted the crowd, their attention fixed on his ruggedly handsome features.

"I am Regulator Rayne and I head the Suppressors." A small smile played on his full lips. "Once again, we are here to gather those who despise Wielders. Those who would like to see every one of them eradicated."

I cringed at the cheers and voices rising in anger following his words.

"Kill the evil Wielding bastards!"

"Send them to the Abyss where they belong."

"Feed them to the wolves."

The crowd's anger, so different than their day-to-day, startled me. It was much like the palace back home. The Shadow Elves hatred mirrored the town's anger here. I remained rigid, watching.

Rayne smiled, a cold and cruel look as his eyes scanned the angry crowd. I glanced up at Suppressor Farnsworth, who stood stock still, eyes ahead and jaw clenched.

Regulator Rayne held up a hand, and the crowd settled down. "I am sure many of you know what our organization is about, but for the younger ones in the crowd who don't, we are a righteous Organization. We are the law. We are the ones who stop the evil taint of Wielders from further infecting our world," he said, voice carrying across the crowd who cheered.

I laughed. His head turned at the sound. An icy, depthless stare chilled me to the bone. Stepping down off the platform, he stood in front of me.

"Did you find something I said amusing?"

I looked up at him and met his icy stare.

"I did, actually."

"Sera." Brock hissed to my right while Uma elbowed me in the ribs on my left.

Regulator Rayne crossed his arms. "Oh? What part, exactly, did you find amusing?"

I gestured with my hand. "All of it. What exactly makes a Wielder evil? What is this—taint—that is infecting the world? You're quite vague, you know."

Brock groaned, and Uma cursed under her breath. I ignored them.

"They are tainted. Their magic is dirty. They spread like a virus, choking society. Spreading their evil." He hissed.

"Do you know any Wielders?"

"I am a Wielder," he said.

The crowd gasped.

"And you believe the bullshit you speak?"

"The world would be a better place without them." His jaw clenched.

"And yet here you stand. An evil, tainted Wielder," I said, crossing my arms to quell the shaking. "If what you speak is the truth—that your organization is trying to rid the world of them—why wouldn't you just kill them? Why bother giving them the option to join? Your entire Order is a contradiction."

A smile curled his lips, and I shivered at the look. "They will no longer be offered the option to join. All Wielders will die by the Order's hand. A dead Wielder is better than a captured one."

A raucous rippled through the crowd. People cheered and clapped, and again, many called for blood and death.

Regulator Rayne leaned forward, lips close to my ear. "I would watch my tongue if I were you, Love, lest I cut it out. Your father's lands do not protect you, princess. Perhaps I will call you out right here. Let the crowd do as they wish with you." He pulled back, his lips twisting into a smile, his eyes raked over my body, and I had to stop myself from trying to cover up. "Or perhaps I will spare your life and take you instead. You would be a stunning addition to my menagerie of playthings."

Stepping back, he focused on the crowd again. "Those who wish to join, may speak with myself or the others at The Impious Seductress where you can sign up and be sworn in immediately." His voice rolled over the crowd which began to disperse, many of the villagers heading for the tavern. I knew it was not to quench thirst with drink.

His eyes met mine for a brief moment before he stalked off, snapping orders to the Suppressors who jumped and scattered like ants.

"Damn, Serafin. You must have a death wish. That guy does not like you," Brock said. "How does he know you're a princess?"

I chewed my lip. "I—we've met before. He came to my lands to negotiate a treaty we have with the Suppressors."

Uma frowned. "Treaty?"

I took a deep breath. "The Elves provide the Sigaa'Lean. It's our magic that is infused into them, and because we make it and provide it to them, we are granted immunity. The Suppressors cannot touch us, though Rayne came onto our lands twenty-one Grand Passages ago and wanted to know how to make it and he returned not too long ago."

Uma blinked. "Why would you do that?"

"I don't know. I have never read the treaty. It was put into place thousands of Grand Passages ago. But...if they're not going to force the Wielders to join, they won't need it anymore. I don't know what that will do to the Elves. And, well, because I am not in Il'Ekhester, I am not protected by the treaty. He...he can do whatever he wishes with me." The thought twisted my stomach. "I'm sorry. I don't agree with any of it." And when I reclaimed my birthright, I would figure out way to get out of the treaty, while still keeping the Elves safe on our own lands.

"Excuse me. I don't mean to interrupt, but I felt bad for making you drop your treat." Turning, my eyes met with a pair of hazel ones belonging to Suppressor Farnsworth. He held out a bag, a sheepish smile on his face. "I didn't know what flavor you had so I bought one of each."

"Thank you, Suppressor Farnsworth."

"Ghent," he said, long fingers pushing a dark curl off his forehead.

"Serafin. This is Brock and Uma," I gestured to my friends who stood to the side, arms crossed and eyes on him. Taking the bag he offered, I held it out to him. He hesitated a moment before pulling out a sweet. I held it out to Brock and Uma. Brock took one, though Uma shook her head.

"We're going to the tavern," she said. "I could use a stiff drink. Coming?" Her golden eyes went from me to Ghent and back.

"I'll meet you there."

Casting one last glance at us, they followed the stragglers who made their way down the road. Ghent took a bite of his hand pie, a smile splitting his face. "Blueberry. My favorite."

I took a bite of mine, the sweet chocolate filling coating my tongue, and looked up at Ghent through lowered lashes. He was definitely handsome in a rugged sort of way. Strong features and a face browned from the sun, a bit of stubble gracing his jaw, and curly black hair shading his hazel eyes. He was tall, broad, and muscular causing his uniform to strain.

"Are you thinking of joining?" He wiped his hands off on his black trousers and began slowly walking toward the tavern.

I licked the chocolate off my palm. "What? No."

Ghent chuckled, the corners of his eyes crinkling up. "I didn't think so, based on your questions."

"I guess I don't understand the Orders hatred toward those with Magic. You wear the uniform so you must agree with the rhetoric spewed."

Though Ghent was a Suppressor, and though I should be afraid of him, I wasn't. Perhaps it was the absence of Rayne, but I felt comfortable with him at the moment. Though if he somehow found out I was a Wielder, an elf off her lands, I was sure he would sound the alarm and I would lose my head. And perhaps the underground network of Wielders would be compromised because of me. I had to be careful.

He shrugged. "I have no thoughts on it."

"So why did you join?"

Stopping, he turned and looked at me. "Because I am a Farnsworth. My bloodline can be traced back to Zachariah. I have no choice."

"Everyone has a choice."

He laughed. It was a hollow sound. "Maybe you do, but I do not. Every Farnsworth must join, making our way up the ranks until we become Eminence."

We began walking again, the tavern coming into view. Striding up the steps, Ghent pulled the door open, standing aside to allow me to enter. The room was hot and packed shoulder to shoulder with people. The scent of sweat and body odor choked me and I gagged. Scanning the room, standing on my toes to see over heads, I spotted Brock and Uma sitting in a corner. Pushing my way through the crowd, ignoring the angry growls, I made my way to where they sat.

A bottle filled with amber liquid, the label showed it to be Serpents Venom, something I hadn't heard of, sat in the center. A glass sat in front of Brock and Uma, whose eyes were glassy. I tentatively sat in the vacant seat across from them.

"Am I still welcome here?"

Brock frowned. "Why wouldn't you be?"

Pulling the bottle close, I poured myself a glass and tossed it back. The heat rushed down my throat, hitting my stomach like molten lava. I sputtered and coughed, much to Brock's amusement. Pouring more, he raised another glass and I took a smaller sip, the liquid going down smoother than the first.

"I—because of the treaty."

Brock shook his head, and grabbed my hand. "You had nothing to do with that, Sera. And it doesn't matter anyway. Despite who you are, or were, you're with us now and we don't toss those we care about aside."

He lifted his glass, and I lifted mine. Uma grasped hers and raised it as well, the liquid slopping over the side as she waved her arm back and forth.

"Congradu-fucking-lations," she called out. Eyes turned in our direction. "You fucking shits happy with yourselves? Does your fucking hatred help you sleep at night?"

A shadow fell over the table. "Do you have a problem, bitch?" A man with a long, gray beard and shoulders two ax handles wide loomed over our table.

Uma tried to stand but only crashed back into her chair.

"No," Brock said, slipping an arm around her. "My girl is drunk. She meant nothing."

"The fuck I didn't," she muttered, though the man had thankfully backed away.

Tossing coin on the table, I followed Brock and a very drunk Uma through the crowd.

"Serafin? Is everything alright?"

A voice stopped me. Turning, I came up against Ghent's broad chest. "Yes. Uma is just drunk. We are taking her back home."

Disappointment flashed in his eyes. "Oh. Alright then. Do you want help?"

Yes. "No, I think we can handle this. It was nice meeting you, Ghent."

He smiled and I noticed a dimple playing hide and seek in his cheek. "Same, Serafin. Take care." Turning, he pushed his way through the crowd to where Regulator Rayne stood, fists clenched, and eyes narrowed. Grabbing Ghent by his collar, Rayne slammed him against the wall, jaw clenched.

Turning away, I weaved my way back through the patrons and outside to where Brock crouched next to Uma holding her hair as she vomited in the street. Shaking my head, I joined him in helping her up, supporting her beneath my arm as we walked through the town.

Though the events were somber, happiness spread like fire through my chest as I made my way back home with my found family.

TWENTY-FIVE

A N ICY DRIZZLE FELL from the sky, the drops hitting the windows with a soft ping. Though a fire roared in the fireplace, the room held onto the chill. Pulling my thick cloak close, and wiggling my cold toes in my fox fur boots, I dipped my quill back into the pot of black ink, continuing my translation of another elven faerie tale.

Since accepting Uma's offer to work at the store, the elven books, previously unsold, were flying out the door, with many buyers coming back looking for more. It was tedious work, though many of the titles were familiar to me. It brought back comfort and warm memories of a time when I was cherished and loved.

Shaking the thoughts, I rose from my chair, stretching the kinks out of my body, and tossed another log onto the fire. The bell above the door tinkled, drawing my attention. The weather had kept people tucked in their homes or the tavern, the slowness allowing me quiet to do my work.

The person pushed back the hood of their cloak, and my heart skipped at seeing who it was.

"Ghent."

Smiling, he shook off the ice, crossing the room to the fire, and held his hands out for warmth.

"Serafin. How is your friend, Uma?"

"Sleeping off an aching head." I bit my lip. "I hope you didn't get into too much trouble with Regulator Rayne. He looked pretty angry when I left."

Ghent's nostrils flared. "Arden is an arrogant prick with too much power. He needs to be knocked off his pedestal," he said, wandering around the store. Stopping at the table I was working at, he pushed the papers around. "What's this?" He pointed to the open book I was working on.

Rushing over, I shoved the papers into it, shut it and placed a blank stack of parchment on top.

"Just cataloging some books in the back," I said, moving around the table. Ghent glanced at the covered book but said nothing. "What can I help you with?"

"I'm looking for a book."

I looked around the shop. "That's too bad. We don't have those here."

He laughed, a rich sound that filled the shop. "Cute and a sense of humor. I like that."

My face heated at his words.

"Red looks good on you." A smile twitched, the dimple in his cheek peeked out, and the heat deepened.

"What exactly are you looking for?" I brushed past him, walking to the center of the shop.

"A book for a special lady friend."

I squelched the feeling of disappointment, but what was I expecting? We only just met. Clasping my hands in front of me, I looked everywhere but at him. "What does she like to read? What is she like?"

He slipped his hands in the pockets of his cloak and rocked back on his heels. "I think she'd fancy a whimsical tale," he said. "As to what she's like? She's educated, possibly high born based on her speech and manners. She's beautiful and seems to be a sweet, kind woman. I'd like something to honor her uniqueness and beauty."

"Tall order," I muttered, pushing past him and looking over the shelves and piles of books. Ghent hovered casually by my side, his broad shoulders brushing me on occasion, something that made me flush.

My eyes fell on a book on top of a stack. It was one I had my eye on but hadn't yet bought. It was thick and heavy with a cover made of black velvet. The picture on the front was in a circle, a golden tree with purple flowers in bloom. A snow-white unicorn stood beneath it, waif-like female Elf reaching out in the beast's direction and an ugly witch hid behind the majestic tree. I picked the book up and ran my hand over the front, noting that on closer inspection the circle that contained the picture wasn't a circle at all, rather a gaping maw of a demon, long sharp fangs making up some of the tree limbs, red, fiery eyes gleaming in the background. The flowing golden script of the title read *Monsters, Witches and Magic*. I flipped the book open, trying hard to ignore Ghent, who peered over my shoulder looking at the gold leaf pages. The book was, unfortunately, both beautiful and unique.

Ghent took the book from me and flipped through, running his fingers down the pages, eyes taking in the brightly colored pictures.

"It's perfect."

"It's expensive. Four gold pieces," I said, hoping the price was too high.

"That's fine." He handed the book back to me.

Sighing, I made my way to the counter. Ghent handed me the coin and I wrote up the slip, then wrapped it in thick, blue paper, tying a bow with golden twine.

"I hope she's worth it." The words flew out of my mouth without thinking and I wished I could take them back.

Ghent grinned as he tucked the book beneath his arm. "I guess I'll find out."

I watched him leave, kicking over a stack of books. A sour taste formed in my mouth just thinking about the beautiful and unique woman who would be getting the book, my book, as a special gift.

Pushing it out of my mind, I threw myself back into my task, not stopping until the candles burned low and a chill seeped into the room. Packing up, and working the kinks out of my body again, I closed and headed home. The streets were quiet, only a handful of people rushing about, trying to get home. I eyed the sky, quickening my steps as I noticed the sun sinking lower. Shadows loomed ominously across the cobblestone.

A rustle sounded to my left. A growl to my right, and a howl echoed far too close. The hair on the back of my neck rose at the feel of eyes on me. My mind conjured nasty beasts with sharp teeth and lethal claws. Breaking into a run, I raced toward home. I heard footsteps pounding behind. A snarl. A snort. A growl. I didn't dare turn around. Didn't dare stop.

Digging in deep, I ran harder. My heart pounded, lungs burned, and my legs ached. I cried in relief at seeing Uma's home come into view, a trail of gray smoke spiraling up from the chimney. Racing up the steps, I crashed through the door, slamming and locking it before collapsing on all fours, gasping for breath, my head light.

"Sera," Uma cried, rushing to my side. Helping me to my feet, I shrugged out of my cloak and followed her on still shaking legs to the cozy living room, where she poured wine, pressing the glass into my hand. I took a long drink, sinking down into the well-worn and very comfortable couch.

"Are you alright? I was worried about you. I hoped you wouldn't walk home. Prayed you would stay at the inn, or even the store."

"I'm fine. It wasn't that dark when I left," I said, pouring more wine. Leaning back on the couch, I kicked my feet up on the table.

"Oh, I almost forgot. Someone left a package for you." Rising, Uma disappeared into the front hall, returning moments later, handing me a rectangular parcel.

A parcel wrapped in heavy blue paper, tied with gold string. A card was tucked beneath the twine, the letter "S" scrawled on the front.

"Well? Are you going to stare at it or are you going to open it?" She plopped down beside me. Pulling the card free, I opened it.

S-

I'm not sorry I bumped into you at the recruitment event, or making you drop your treat. It allowed me to linger a bit longer and talk. I hope you accept this gift, a gift as unique and beautiful as you are and I earnestly hope I will see you again.

-G

(And yes, I do think you are worth it.)

Flames danced beneath my skin. I shuddered, delight filling me.

"So? Who is it from?" Uma snatched the card from my hand.

Smiling, I pulled the paper off, my eye taking in the book. "Ghent," I said, running my hand over the cover.

Uma elbowed me in my side. "That boy wants to fuck you."

I shoved her back with a laugh. Regardless of what he wanted from me, on the morrow, I would go to the tavern and thank him.

THE NEXT DAY, I made my way to The Impious Seductress. I took a deep breath and opened the door. The heat from the blazing fire came at me like a wall. Stepping inside, I looked around the packed room. The Suppressors were still taking names of those eager to join and it was clear—based on the amount of people still waiting—why they came here every other Grand Passage.

Scanning the crowd, my ears picked up at the sound of a familiar laugh as it rose above the din and I pushed my way through to find him. My eyes went to where Ghent was, and my heartbeat quickened at the sight of him. He sat at a table, chair tilted back on two legs, arms crossed over his chest. An amused smile lit his lips and black curls fell in his eyes.

His gaze found me. Dropping the chair to the ground, he nodded at the Suppressor he was speaking with, and the man slipped away.

"Serafin," Ghent said, a smile breaking his face as I slowly approached.

"Ghent." I suddenly felt shy. "Thank you for the book." His grin widened, and the dimple deepened. He motioned to the chair across from him and I sat down.

"You are very welcome."

"I admit I was sad when you bought it. I had been meaning to purchase it for myself but hadn't gotten around to it," I said. "How did you know where I live?"

Ghent's eyes danced with amusement. "Easy. I just asked where the most beautiful woman in the village lived."

I raised an eyebrow. "Do all Suppressors expect others to believe the bullshit they spew?"

"Well. It looks like intelligent needs to be added to the list."

"Oh? You have a list?"

"It's getting longer every time we speak."

"Hm. So how do you know where I live?"

"I don't. I saw your other friend Brock and gave him the book."

I shook my head. "Why didn't you just give it to me at the store?"

He smiled again. Damn, but I liked it when he did. "Because you would have thanked me and sent me on my way. Delivering it to your home made you come here to find me and now we are sitting down having a delightful conversation."

I smiled. "Well, thank you again. I wish I could do something in return."

He tipped back in the chair again and laced his fingers behind his head. "Just promise you'll think of me every time you read it."

I opened my mouth to respond, eyes going to Regulator Rayne, who stalked in our direction. "I—I should go," I said hastily, pushing the chair out and getting ready to stand.

"What? Why? We—" his words were cut off as Regulator Rayne swiftly kicked the legs of the chair, sending Ghent crashing to the floor.

"Get off your ass and get to work." He glared down at Ghent.

Ghent glared up at him as he rose to his feet and righted the chair. "You know I am not working today."

Rayne crossed his arms. "Well, now you are."

Ghent clenched his jaw, and his nostrils flared at the words.

"Every second that passes, another lashing is added to your punishment for your continued disobedience while here." The corner of Rayne's lips turned up in a smile.

Ghent turned towards me, face tense and eyes blazing. "I apologize, Serafin, but it looks like I'm on duty."

"I understand. I can come back later when your shift is over."

His face softened, and he smiled. "I'd like that. Come back in a few hours," he said, then turned to Rayne. "Unless I am to work all night as well?"

Regulator Rayne's jaw clenched, and his eyes flashed as Ghent walked past, shouldering him out of the way. Rayne placed his hands on the table and leaned down, pinning me with his icy stare.

"I don't like my subordinates being preoccupied by anyone but me," he said, voice menacing.

I shook off the fear and held his gaze. "Well, then perhaps you need a better hold on them. Or maybe you're just not suited for the job," I said. "You lack respect for them, and it is obvious they don't respect you."

An ugly snarl twisted his handsome face. "I do not need respect. I need obedience."

"And you think berating them—humiliating them—will get you that?"

"No," he said, drawing the word out and smiling. "My whip and magic will."

I shivered at the words. "Based on what I have seen, it appears those tactics aren't working for you. Perhaps you should step down and let someone competent take over," I said, unable to stop what I had started.

A cruel and cold look crossed his face and faster than lightning, he reached out, fisted my hair and yanked me forward. I winced, hands going to his, clawing at them in an attempt to get free.

"Oh, Love. You have no fucking idea who you are dealing with," he said, voice cold. A small cry escaped me as he tightened his grip and pulled me closer. Our faces were inches apart and I could see red flecks—burning embers—swirling in the depths of his blue eyes, and his breath was hot on my face. "And if you don't shut that pretty little mouth of yours, I will cut your tongue out. But not before you grovel on your knees and beg me to forgive your insolence. I do enjoy that last moment of regret—that moment of fear—everyone has before I cause them great pain and agony and I can assure you that yours will be horrific," he said, releasing me with a shove as he rose to his feet and sauntered away.

I exhaled, wiping my sweaty hands on my trousers and tried to calm my pounding heart.

Good job, Serafin. I didn't know what possessed me to speak, but like two days prior at the recruiting event, once I started, I couldn't stop. Taking a deep breath, I pushed away from the table and stood, briefly scanning the room for Ghent, who sat at the table, head bowed down as the quill scratched across the parchment. I pushed my way through the crowd, ignoring the prick between my shoulder blades which I knew was Rayne's angry gaze watching me as I exited. Stepping out into the street, I took several deep breaths, the soft drizzle cleansed me. I picked my way down the road in the store's direction, carefully avoiding stepping in puddles and being splashed by the carts that ambled by. The day was still overcast, though, the brightening sky offered hope that it would clear.

With my thoughts on Ghent and the possibility of seeing him again this evening, I made my way across town to the bookstore to spend what I knew would be an excruciatingly long day of work.

T HE SUN SAT HIGH in the sky, as I settled onto the bench where Ghent waited. The bench was in the park, facing a small stream. Patches of ice floated down the water like barges.

"I'm sorry for getting you in trouble," I said.

Ghent pushed a curl from his forehead and smiled. "You didn't do anything, Serafin."

"What is Rayne's problem, anyway?"

Ghent sighed. "Arden thrives on control and power. He's also the Master Torturer and, believe me when I say he thoroughly enjoys the job. The more power he has over someone, the bigger an ass he becomes. And being in line to be the next Elder?" He shook his head. "It wouldn't at all surprise me if something were to befall Elder Castille."

Master Torturer. I could see how a man like that would relish the position. I thought about his cold, soulless eyes. The threats he made to me and the flash of pleasure—however brief—when I winced in pain as he fisted my hair.

"He scares me."

Ghent raised an eyebrow. "Really? Because your words and actions definitely belie the claim." he shook his head with a chuckle. "No one goes up against Arden the way you did. I'm surprised you still have your tongue."

"Well, he threatened to cut it out," I said.

"You are brave, I'll give you that."

It was my turn to raise an eyebrow. "Brave? Brock and Uma all but called me stupid."

Ghent's face softened, and he reached out and pushed a lock of hair behind my ear. His fingers brushed my cheek and my skin burned where he touched.

"You are anything but stupid, Serafin." His breath was a warm caress, and I felt my face heat at his words. He dropped his hand with a sigh and ran it through his hair.

"I better get going. I'm sorry I didn't get to spend more time with you and unfortunately Arden wishes to leave at daybreak."

My heart sank at his words as I chewed my lip. "Of course. I don't want you to be in any more trouble."

He took my hand and grinned. "Trust me. Whatever punishment awaits me when I get back will have been worth it," he said. "Regardless, I am going to get expanded duties, which means I will have my own team and patrol. I know there's a town a few miles from here and I plan on convincing Elder Castille to let me claim it."

My heart leapt into my throat. "But Rayne—"

His grin widened. "Can't say a damn thing when the order comes down from the Elder."

"And if he doesn't agree?"

"I'm a Farnsworth. Elder Castille will do as I ask, or he will answer to my father."

I shook my head and laughed. Ghent rose to his feet, pulling me up with him. He stepped forward, and we stood just a breath away from each other.

"I have had a delightful time here, Serafin."

I looked up at him. "As did I."

His eyes searched mine briefly, then he lowered his head and pressed his lips against mine in a soft kiss.

"Until I see you again," he whispered as he pulled away. "Think of me when you read your book. I will be thinking of you too." He turned and strode away in the inn's direction. I watched his retreating back until it disappeared, my heart hammering in my chest, the feel of his warm lips upon mine lingering.

Smiling, I made my way towards home, a shot of excitement running through me at the thought—the hope—of seeing Ghent again.

TWENTY-SIX
ARDEN

"**T**HIS IS QUITE THE list," Vel said as he flipped through the page of names.

Leaning against the sideboard, I sipped my glass of Faeries Blood, eyes on Vel. "Of course, it is. It's a Non dominant town."

Vel pushed the papers across the desk and sat back. Crossing the room, I picked up the stack.

"Even so, many may not be worthy to join the Order. Some will fail our physical, mental and emotional requirements."

"All who put their names down were sworn in. I have given them a day, two at the most, to gather their things and come here. As for their worthiness?" I sipped my drink. "Doesn't being a Non make them worthy?"

Vel's nostrils flared.

"There will also be no more capturing of Wielders. No more choice to join. All will be executed."

Vel leaped to his feet. "You have no authority to order that."

Oh Vel. My authority comes from someone much higher than you. "I am the Regulator."

"And I am the Elder. You only order what has been passed down to you. You have overstepped your bounds, Arden."

I snorted. Did Vel think I cared? Did he think I would piss myself with fear from his words? He was weak. Pathetic. He thinks me a young recruit he can push around. Thinks I will jump and say yes sir to him. His days were numbered, I could smell it.

"Do you forget what the Order, the Suppressors were founded on? Do you forget why we were founded?"

Vel's eyes narrowed. "Of course, not."

"Then you would know their deaths will break the binds on our King and he will rule gods and men." I leaned forward. "Blocking their magic does nothing for the Fallen One. Or perhaps you don't want him to break free."

"Of course I do. Why do you think Lillyanna was born?"

I snorted. "Apparently what she was born to do didn't work." I stood back up. "All Wielders will die with or without your order."

Turning, I stalked out of the room, not giving Vel the chance to say more. Walking through the halls, I glared at recruits who scattered as I passed. Drawing up to the library, I stepped inside. It was a beautiful and magnificent room filled with cherry and oak shelves packed with books, with fires blazing in the large fireplaces lending warmth. Windows let in the mid-morning sunlight, and a dozen long tables were scattered thorough the room, recruits seated on the hard, uncomfortable chairs pouring over books.

Striding through the room, the sound of my boots on the black marble floor echoing off the paneled walls, I made my way to the back of the room. I didn't need to search for the books I wanted. I knew where they were by heart. Pulling down the book which contained the history of the Suppressors, I took a comfortable seat in front of a fireplace. Flipping through the book, I caressed the pages filled with Zachariah's neat script, and making myself comfortable, I began to read.

I WOULD LIKE TO say I was surprised at the amount of Nons willing to join my Order, but I was not. I knew the hatred against Wielders ran to the core of those who did not possess magic, though a few embellishments about how bad Wielders were did not hurt. After all, what Non wouldn't be terrified of their daughters being raped to produce more of them? Of Wielders sneaking into their homes at night, killing them in their sleep, or just setting their houses on fire and watching them burn?

Control was about fear. Without fear, there was no compliance and without compliance, there was no control.

But I had it all.

Like others, I read the tales about why Wielders were created. The war between the gods sent Themesis to the Abyss, locked in an obsidian tomb. His binds were held by the magic of the gods. As time went on, the gods decided to make Keepers for the tomb, so they cursed people with magic. Their life and breath kept the binds secure, and the more Wielders born, the stronger the binds became.

But the Nons knew the truth. As Grand Passages went, Nons grew older in appearance while Wielders remained young. They saw them using their magic for simple tasks. A fire Wielder would use theirs to light a forge. A nature Wielder would use theirs to make their crops grow, or to produce rain during a dry spell.

They used their magic in selfish ways. They flaunted it in the faces of the Nons and it made the discord between them grow. They began to question everything.

Blessed by the gods? No. They were agents of Themesis. They were protecting him, acting as his vessel to destroy all Nons and rule.

The Nons came together and went after those with magic, though it was disorganized chaos, and more Nons than Wielders lost their lives. I saw this happening. I saw the anger, the rage of the Nons who lost their friends, their fathers, brothers, and mothers and I put together a plan to use them.

To use that hatred. That anger. That blood lust and formed an organization to suppress those with magic. Suppress the ones who thought themselves superior because they live longer. Suppress the ones who thought their magic kept the Fallen One in his tomb.

And suppress the Nons from knowing the truth.

I was under no illusion Wielders were evil. I kept my own magic under wraps, hidden from those Nons I guided.

No. I knew the tales, the stories thought to be myth, to be the truth, for he came to me in a dream.

Themesis, the Fallen One, the Ruler of the Abyss graced me with visions of the future. He told me what had to be done. Guided my hand with every strike of my sword.

Every Wielder whose life was taken.

Soon, the Wielders learned their plight and begged for mercy. I did not wish to grant it, until we raided a village where an elf was captured. He pleaded for his life, his family's life, giving the means, the tool to block a Wielders power. I forced him to write it down, then I took his head and that of his wife and four children.

And with the knowledge, I visited Karrinian Trounde in Il'Ekhester, striking a deal where they would provide the device, the Sigaa'Lean as they called it, the name which meant Magic Breaker, in exchange for immunity.

Who was I to disagree? For the moment, anyway? They did not know one of theirs gave up the magic. Nor would they. Not until I had perfected it. Not until I could make the Magic Breaker myself. And when I did? All Wielders would die and the Fallen One would rule and I would be raised as a god.

Raised as the one who helped him be free.

F LIPPING BACK, I READ the pages again. Zachariah was given the information on how to make the Sigaa'Lean. Though he may have failed, the knowledge was out there.

A thought entered my mind, and I laughed, the sound echoing throughout the now empty library.

If I could find the spell to make the Sigaa'Lean, I would not use it to trap Wielders.

No.

I had my sights on something bigger.

TWENTY-SEVEN

Sitting in the Great Hall, a large and sterile room devoid of furnishing or any personal touches, I looked around at those seated with me. Of course, Vel, the Elder, would be here. And of course, before us, the previous Elders who now sat on the High Council flanked his Eminence, Quint Farnsworth. Elder Pronce, Elder Dwin, and Elder Bern sat to his left. Elder Clas, Elder Cantell, and Elder Draon to his right. I looked back at Liam and Vel. Liam squirmed in his seat, Vel straightened the cuffs of his uniform, a bored look on his face. I was sure he had something to do with this meeting, coming so soon after Recruitment Day, and our conversation.

Tapping my finger on the chair, I watched Quint sit up, stacking the pile of papers in front of him. The Elders beside sat straighter, hands folded on the table. Quint's eyes slowly pinned each of us in turn. Liam swallowed hard. Vel coughed into his hand, but me? I stared right back into his penetrating brown eyes. I was not afraid of him. He may be Eminence, the highest in the Order, the one who handed down orders to the Elders, but he was as weak and pathetic as Vel. I saw through him. The only reason he was Eminence was because he was a Farnsworth.

When I took control, all of that would change.

"Regulator Rayne." Quint's voice boomed, echoing off the bare walls. "The list you obtained in Voodomecism is impressive. However, how many will join?"

It was the same question Vel asked. I resisted the urge to roll my eyes. I glanced over at Vel whose lips held a smirk. My suspicion was right, though what he thought this meeting would accomplish, I did not know. Perhaps he was trying to show me the power he held. Show me I was nothing more than a lowly Regulator, an underling to push around and try to scare into compliance.

Oh, Vel. You have no idea who you are fucking with.

Propping a leg on my knee, I folded my arms. "All of them. They were sworn in as soon as they signed up. They will be here in the next day or two."

Quint didn't look surprised at my answer. Not that I expected him to, though his eyes narrowed to slits.

"Regulator—"

"They are Nons who would like to see all Wielders eradicated. Why should they not be sworn in? All who signed did so willingly with the same goal in mind." I dropped my foot to the floor, the loud thud made the Elders, most of which looked as though they were falling asleep, jump. I leaned forward in my seat, my eyes on Quint.

"Higher orders insist, all Wielders must die. We will execute them to fulfill the Fallen One's wishes." I bowed my head with respect to the god.

The Elders beside Quint erupted, their voices rising as they talked over each other.

"This is preposterous," Elder Pronce slammed his fist on the table.

"Who do you think you are?" Elder Cantell sputtered.

"You are just a Regulator, You cannot give such orders," Elder Draon snarled.

On and on they went, silencing when Quint held up his hand. "Upon whose orders does this decree come?" His eyes went to Vel.

"It was not mine, Eminence," Vel said. "I am just as surprised as you."

I wanted to laugh at Vel's words. At the way he groveled when Quint was around, all but crawling across the floor to lick his feet.

"It was my own order," I said.

Quint pursed his lips. "You have no authority to do such. Need I remind you who gives the orders here?"

Rising, I stood in front of the table. Folding my arms, I looked down at Quint. "Need I remind you what the Order was founded on? Surely, as a descendant of Zachariah Farnsworth, the creator of the Suppressors, would remember."

An audible gasp rang through the room. Quint clenched his jaw, his face turning red. Placing my hands on the table, I leaned forward.

"Let me remind you. One. Wielders are a plague on this world. Two. Magic is a taint infecting others. Three. Magic is evil born from the Abyss. Four. All magic must be eradicated, and five," I leaned closer, our faces inches apart. "A dead Wielder is better than a captured Wielder." Standing straight, I clasped my hands behind my back, my eyes never leaving Quint. The room was deathly quiet. The seconds ticked by as Quint and I were locked in a game of wills.

I would not look away. I would not show weakness in the face of this pathetic man. Quint's jaw ticked. Dropping his eyes, he fiddled with the papers in front of him. Folding his hands, he looked back up at me. "You have made your point, Regulator Rayne. I have not forgotten our foundation. I have not forgotten Zachariah Farnsworth." Quint looked at Lian, Vel, and the Elders at his side. "Going forward, we will no longer provider Wielders a choice. Their lives are forfeit. Meeting adjourned." Rising, he gathered his papers casting me a look filled with...pride? He turned and exited the room; the Elders followed behind.

Turning, I looked at Vel whose nostrils flared. This time, I did not suppress my smile. Vel turned and stalked out of the room, Liam shuffling behind. My laughter echoed off the walls.

I had won and soon, everyone would see my potential. I'd be handing down the orders.

S TANDING IN THE TRAINING yard, I looked at the pathetic excuse for recruits. The elation I felt hours before had disintegrated, replaced with annoyance and anger. I glared down at the young man on all fours, coughing up blood. He had barely defended himself, though I couldn't say his opponent, who was bent over, hands on his legs, wheezing, was any better. Clearly, I had not been training, or punishing, hard enough.

"Get up," I snapped to the young boy on all fours.

"Please, Regulator Rayne. Just—give me a second."

"A second?" I lifted my wooden sword and slammed it hard into his back. He collapsed onto the ground with a grunt. "There's your second." I grabbed a fistful of his hair and wrenched his head back. "The enemy doesn't give a fuck if you are tired, or injured, or out of breath. You are dead, Tam." I released him with a shove and strode across the arena to select a sandbag. I searched for a sack that weighed about one stone, and I walked back to Tam, who sat on his haunches.

"Get up." I kicked the recruit.

He scrambled to his feet and stood at attention—hands clasped behind his back, stance wide, eyes ahead.

"I want you to hold this above your head until I dismiss you," I said, dropping the bag at his feet. Tam's eyes went to it, and he hesitated. "Is there a problem with my request?"

"Of course not, Regulator Rayne," he stammered as he picked up the bag and held it over his head.

I hid my smile. I knew soon he would be shaking, and I wouldn't be surprised if the bag dropped onto his head.

The small group of recruits held wooden swords. All praying to not be selected for sparring. My eyes lit on a young recruit in his early twenties. The recruit was thin, with blonde hair in a tight braid slung over his... I tilted my head squinting, over his left shoulder. He had an eagle beak nose.

"You." I pointed, striding to where he stood. "Who might you be?"

"Rylee Strahand, sir."

I blinked, taken aback for a moment. The person was female.

I looked around the group comprised mostly of young men. "Why are you here, Strahand?" I peered down at her. My eyes caught the glint of sun off the Sigaa'Lean she wore. "You're a Wielder," I said, grabbing her arm and pushing her shirtsleeve back.

"Y-yes sir. My parents—they sent me here. They wanted me to see the evil of my kind."

I smiled at her words. "And you will learn of it, and you will realize what you have is not a gift from the gods, but rather a curse."

I stepped back and appraised the recruits. The pathetic young men who stood before me. Most were portly and weak, barely able to swing a light wooden sword for any significant amount of time. I glanced over at Tam, who surprisingly still held the sack above his head, though he was drenched in sweat and his arms were visibly shaking. Turning my attention back to the pathetic group before me, my eyes went back to Rylee.

"Rylee and—" I looked about, eyes catching a tall, young, muscular man. "You," I said, pointing to him. "What's your name?"

"Yari, sir."

I nodded. "Spar."

I stepped out of the circle, watching Rylee, who hesitated a beat and the tall young man who grinned and swaggered to the center.

"This should be easy." He flourished his sword. I watched the girl step into the ring and immediately fall into a fighting stance. Yari snorted as he stood casually, face bored.

"Let's get this over with," he said.

I stood back and watched the two fight.

The girl was small and agile. She moved quickly, darting away from Yari's advances and parrying his blows with her sword. More than once, she spun away from a fatal strike, deftly striking out and hitting her opponent with her makeshift blade. Yari scowled, wiping sweat off his brow, and I looked at Rylee, who cocked her head to the side, looking as fresh as a summer's day.

"I thought you said this would be easy." She raised an eyebrow in challenge, and I laughed openly at her words.

Yari shot me a glare, then turned back to her.

"I'm just trying to tire you out," he pushed his hair out of his eyes as he circled her.

"Really? Because it seems to me, you're winded and I... am not." Rylee wrinkled her nose as she also circled. "You smell like a barn and are panting like a tired dog."

Yari scowled, swinging his sword down. Rylee blocked it—just bare-ly—which bolstered his confidence. He swiped the sword across, and Rylee jumped back, stumbling over a rock and falling to her backside. Yari brought his sword down and I held my breath as she blocked the killing blow. Rolling to the side, she swept his feet out from under him and he landed hard on his back. Rylee quickly jumped to her feet and pounced on her opponent. Metal glinted in the sunlight as she pulled a dagger from her boot, striking Yari, who cried out in pain. She slowly stood up, wiping the bloody dagger off on her trousers. I smiled. She was a cunning young woman, and I saw a bit of myself in her.

"Finish the job," I said. "A wounded enemy is a live enemy."

Rylee looked at me and I said nothing as Yari—whose left shoulder was soaked with blood—rose to his feet, gripping the wooden sword. He glared at Rylee's back and still I kept silent. He raised his weapon and lunged at her. Rylee didn't turn, nor did she blink as she dropped to a knee. Spinning around, she blocked the strike with her sword while driving the dagger deep into his thigh. I smiled as I watched him fall to the ground, clutching his leg to stop the flow of blood. Rylee swept a lock of hair from her eyes—a smudge of red marring her forehead—as she rose to her feet.

I had to admit the girl had impressed me in more ways than one.

"Please. Regulator Rayne. I need a healer," Yari cried.

I ignored his pathetic pleas.

"You are all dismissed," I said, eyes never leaving Rylee. "That includes you, Tam." I chuckled at the sound of the sandbag hitting the ground. With any luck, he learned a lesson. Rylee hefted the wooden sword to her shoulder and began to leave.

"Not you."

She stopped and turned to face me. "I did what you asked," she said, glancing down at Yari, whose pallor was turning ghostly white. Her chin jutted out in defiance, and I did not miss how her hand gripped the hilt of her dagger.

"Yes, you did, and I dare say you impressed me." I took a step closer, and her grip tightened. "Few people impress me these days. It seems more and more incompetent fools surround me." I glanced at her hand. "As impressed as I was with your actions, it would benefit you to know you will not best me," I said.

Her eyes narrowed, and she struck fast with the wooden sword. I raised my right arm; the side of the blade slapped the bone. Pain radiated up my arm. Delightful and exhilarating pain. I shuddered at the feel. At the jolt of excitement. Grabbing the weapon, I wrenched it out of her grasp. Light glinted off the dagger as it came down in a slashing motion. Grabbing her wrist, I twisted her arm behind her back and relieved her of her weapon.

"I said you would not best me. No one bests me. Try that again, love, and you will find yourself joining Yari," I said, releasing her with a shove. She turned around and glared at me, her jaw clenched and nostrils flared. I flipped the blade around and held it out to her. Her hand closed around the hilt, and she slipped it into the waistband of her trousers.

"Who taught you how to use a sword?"

She raised her head, chin jutting out. "My brother," she sniffed. "He was training to be a High Council Guard. I would sneak out to his training sessions and watch from afar. Joran caught me practicing—well, more like mimicking his actions—with a stick in the yard. I thought he'd be furious for following and watching but—" her features softened into a smile. "He taught me instead."

"Why do I not know the name Strahand? Was he not competent enough to be a High Council Guard?"

"He was competent enough. He received his letter of acceptance. He—he became ill and passed before he could serve. I offered to serve in his place, but the High Council Guards are only comprised of men," she spat.

"You look masculine enough."

Rylee glared at me. "Joran protected me and my magic. When he was gone?" She shrugged.

"You are where you should be."

"Of course, a Non would say that. You don't know what it's like to have a gift you must hide. To live in constant fear of being taken by the Order. And to be cut off from the one thing that defines us. The one thing that makes us who we are," she said. "Joran—he knew I was special. He didn't hate me for what I am. He stopped my parents from sending me here and when he died—they shipped me off here."

I crossed my arms. "I am a Wielder as well," I said, and for a moment, I wanted to place my hands on her. Only to hear her scream, I wanted to let my magic go. My hands twitched at the thought.

She blinked. "How can you betray your kind?"

I smiled. "It's quite simple, really. I understand the plague we are spreading upon the world. The taint that is infecting society. Magic is not a gift. It is a curse. You will soon learn and understand that."

I knew all too well what a curse magic was. There wasn't a day that went by that I didn't wish I was a Non. Perhaps if I was... I shook the thoughts from my head. Shook the fear that threatened to take hold of me. I would not show weakness, especially in front of a woman.

Rylee said nothing as she fell in step beside me as I walked back towards the barracks beyond the training arena.

"I am going to work you far harder than the others," I said, glancing down at her. "Your skills are excellent, but they can be better. And there may be a place for you as a guard in the future." We stopped at the grand, arching doorway. "You are dismissed."

"Thank you, Regulator Rayne," she said, a small smile forming on her lips.

She nodded and then hurried off through the door without a backwards glance. I watched her retreating back until she disappeared into the dark hall. Turning, I headed back to the main building and to my room and where my Plaything waited.

TWENTY-EIGHT
VEL

I WAS SEETHING. WHO the fuck did Arden think he was? And Quint…how could he be bullied into going along?

"How could you agree?" I shouted, bursting into Quint's study without being announced. He jumped at my outburst. Turning, his brown eyes narrowed on me.

"You do not have an appointment with me, Elder Casteel."

I stalked over to where he stood. "How can you agree with Arden?" My eyes followed Quint, who sat behind his desk, folding his hands in front of him. "What is the point with the structure of the order if we just bend it to another?"

"Regulator Rayne has made a valid point. The Order was founded on the eradication of those with magic. Keeping them alive, allowing them to join, does not follow that objective."

"But Zachariah offered those terms to them," I pointed out.

Quint waved his hand in a dismissive manner. "He was fleshing out the details of the Order and at the time, the numbers of those within were low." A slow smile curled his lips. "And what better way to punish them then to make them go after and kill their own kind?

I shook my head. "And those Wielders who have joined? What of them? Will they be executed too?" I resisted the urge to rub the back of my neck. Rayne and Quint did not seem to appreciate the fact if Wielders, all Wielders must die, it meant those who had joined the Order too. Myself, Rayne, so many had come to the Order out of shame. Out of fear.

"They will stay. For now." He flashed a smile. "As Regulator Rayne said, keeping Wielders alive does no favors to Themesis. The Sigaa'Lean may block them from accessing and using their magic, but it is still there. It is still keeping the binds on our gods tomb sealed." Quint cocked his head to the side. "Do you not want him set free? Do you not want to be rewarded for the part you played in making that happen? Do you not want to be blessed with eternal life in his glory?"

I stood up straight. "Of course, I do."

"Good," Quint said, pulling a blank piece of parchment off a stack and opening a pot of ink. "You are dismissed."

Leaving the room, I made my way to my spacious quarters. Dark walnut furnishings and worn throw rugs in the sitting room made it feel warm. The bookcase spanning the left wall was crammed with books. The light of the setting sun spilled through the panel of windows on the right. Tossing a couple logs on the glowing embers in the hearth, I poured a glass of wine and sat down in a leather chair. Taking a healthy drink, I kicked off my shoes and propped my feet on the cherry wood table in front of me.

Arden's ploy, his orders to kill all Wielders, was done in an effort to undermine me, I knew. He thought himself to be clever, but I knew his game and I tried to stay two steps ahead of him but this? This was something I never could have thought. I knew he was positioning himself to be raised to Elder, though how far he would go to achieve his goal, I did not know.

Sipping my wine, I watched the flames in the hearth grow, the pop and hisses of the wood filling the silence. I thought about what Arden had said about keeping Wielders alive doing no favors to Themesis, and I thought about my daughter, Lillyanna. I often wondered what had happened to her. For all Felicity told me, she was to be Blood Bound to him and he was supposed to break free.

But he wasn't here and the only thing telling me his bonds are weak are the demons that roam free at night. But what of her? What of my Lillyanna? Was she serving him in the Abyss? If she had been Blood Bound to him, if she was his servant, his queen, then why wasn't he completely free? Why was it only demons who have come forth from the Abyss?

I was not proud of going along with Felicity's plan, with the gods' plan, where Lillyanna was concerned. I can readily admit the more I thought about the implications of the Fallen One breaking free, the more I regretted my agreement with Felicity. I loved my daughter with all my heart. I even left her to protect her from the Suppressors. The last thing I wanted was for her to get caught. She never knew of my affiliation with the Order. Even when I left her, I did not tell her where or really why. The look on her face, the tears in her eyes and the question, "Was it me," all but undid me.

When she and Damiyun were brought to Wren's Keep, when I saw the beautiful and feisty young woman she had become, my regret for everything I did grew, but there was nothing I could do. Events had been set into motion, and I was powerless to stop them. And now Arden with blessings from fucking Quint Farnsworth has given the order for all Wielders to be executed, no longer given the option to join. Doing so would facilitate the destruction of the bonds, ensuring Themesis' release.

Something I was no longer sure I wanted.

I had joined the Order for the greater good. I saw the way some wielded their power to do simple tasks, like Damiyun using his to light fires. I saw the way some flaunted their abilities, and I understood why the Nons hated us for it. Though it was a betrayal to my own kind, I saw it as a cleansing of the world.

But when Lillyanna was born, I wanted to protect her with every fiber of my being. Keep her safe and out of the hands of the Suppressors and I began to question myself and why I joined. But what could I do? My only other option was death and that would have done nothing to keep her safe. And now, with the order solidified by Quint, I questioned how safe those who joined were.

How safe was I from having the ax come down on my neck. How safe was that arrogant idiot Rayne? So focused on destruction and torture, he never really thought through the consequences.

A shriek in the night pulled my thoughts back. The room was dark, the light of the low flames cast eerie figures on the wall. I shuddered at the sight, my blood running cold as another shriek, much closer now, echoed outside.

Though the monsters—the demons—seemed to strike those unfortunate enough to be left outside when the sun went down without weapon or fire for protection, I could not help but wonder how much longer we would be safe inside the walls of our homes.

And I couldn't help but ask the question that had been burning in the dark recesses of my mind.

"What have we done?"

TWENTY-NINE
ALLENDAIRE

"**O**ur searches have turned up nothing, Majesty," Krall said.

He sat in the chair opposite my desk, giving me another report of the search for Serafin. I had lost count how many times he has sat before me, how many days—or possibly Moon Cycles—she has been gone. Each report was the same.

Their search turned up nothing.

"Where would you like my men to go next?"

I rubbed my eyes. Was it even worth it anymore? "Let me think on it. You are dismissed," I said, waving my hand. Nodding, Krall rose and exited the room. When the door closed, I let my composure fall.

Rising, I poured myself a glass of wine and looked out the window at my lands. The sun was setting, elves hurried through the gates that would be closing soon. The trenches filled with pitch and the torches around the perimeter would be lit as soon as the sun disappeared, keeping the monsters at bay.

Sipping my drink, I thought about Krall's brief visit. Though I had to keep up the search, each time they came back empty handed, each time Krall said they did not find her nor had anyone seen her, I sighed with relief. Though I did dread the day they rode up with her. When that day came, I would be forced to uphold her sentence. I would be force to execute my own daughter.

I admit her escape made little sense, knowing there wasn't any way she could hurt Lazaro in such a way to flee, I said nothing when he made the announcement. It hurt my heart, my soul, to do what I had done. I loved Serafin, my beautiful daughter born out of a union of love. She was a precocious child, ornery and temperamental. Always she tested my patience. Always I gave in to her, her smiles and kisses winning me over no matter what. And as she grew, I saw more and more of Lillyanna come out. In her headstrongness. In the way she held her head high, ignoring the names thrown at her, though I knew they cut her deep. And in her friendship with Phabian who watched over her, much like he had Lillyanna.

No, I did not want to sentence her to death, but I was left with little choice.

Crossing the room, I sat down in front of the blazing fire. Refilling my glass, my mind went back to that day three Moon Cycles ago, when Mouranda told me of her condition.

The day that changed everything.

She walked into my study uninvited. I was going over the taxes collected with Phabian, who marked down who paid and who did not in the official ledger. We both looked up at the sound of footsteps. She glided into my den, the hem of her black dress trailing behind.

Mouranda always dressed in drab colors. Blacks and browns. Dark greens and drab bronze. She did not wear the bright colors that marked her station. It was just another thing that made me loath her.

"What is it, Mouranda? I am very busy."

"I need to speak with you," she said. Her eyes went to Phabian. "Alone."

"Of course," he said, closing the ledger and putting the stopper on the jar of ink. Rising, his gaze lingered on Mouranda, her narrowed eyes told me he tried to delve inside her mind, but she had blocked him. Neither said a word as he passed by exiting the room and closing the door behind.

Stacking the papers in front of me, I set them aside, folded my hands and looked up at Mouranda.

"What do you want?"

A smile curled her lips, and she caressed her abdomen. The gesture made the hair on the back of my neck rise.

"I am with child, dear husband. I carry your child. The full Shadow Elf prince. The real heir."

I tried to make sense of her words. I had forgotten when the last time we shared a bed was.

I grew cold. Memories flashed in my mind of Mouranda coming into my den at night. Of drinking spirits and smoking Sal'va with her. Of waking up naked in my bed, but I could never remember the act taking place.

But here she was, her hands holding her abdomen in a protective manner.

"How is this possible? You are barren."

She laughed. "The healers tried something new and here I am." She placed her hands on my desk and leaned forward. "And now we have a problem." Her lips pulled back into a smile, and my heart dropped to my feet at the look. "I carry your child, Allendaire. Two Shadow Elves made this babe. He is the heir."

I swallowed. "Serafin—"

"Is nothing. She is the daughter of a whore. A half-breed."

Though the words she spoke were true, the girl was my daughter. My flesh, and I loved her.

"You bent the law for her because I had not produced an heir, but now I have. And now you must uphold the law you hold so dear." She stood up.

I swallowed hard. "No, Mouranda. You can't expect—"

"You to uphold the law? Should I let a small secret out? One you thought none would discover?"

The blood drained from my body. The room tilted, and I grasped the desk, so I did not pitch out of my chair.

"You will do what is right. What should have been done. Upon Serafin's twenty-first Name Day, you will order her death."

And I had done exactly that. Sickness rose. I pushed the dizziness aside, refusing to hear my own voice. The words from my own lips sentencing her to death. I was worse than a hypocrite. She existed merely for my need and want.

And I would never confront Lazaro. Never call him out for what he did because I knew, though he hated her, something deep inside made him set her free. Let her escape.

Perhaps he was unsure of Mouranda's condition, as was I. The circumstances surrounding the act was hazy at best. Something deep inside told me I wasn't the father, but I couldn't be completely sure.

Shaking the thoughts, I went back to my desk and grabbed a piece of parchment, writing out the orders for Krall to fulfill. Orders of where to search for my daughter that would take him on another fruitless chase. Or so I hoped.

And as I sealed the paper, I gave a prayer to the gods Lillyanna believed in, to the Goddess of Nature who she claimed to be her mother, to keep my daughter, my Serafin safe.

THIRTY
DAMIYUN

I GRABBED THE BOTTLE off the night table, pressed it to my lips and tipped my head back. Nothing.

"Damn the gods." I hurled it across the room and the glass shattered, breaking the silence. Sitting up, I ran a hand over the annoying stubble growing along my jaw and glanced over my shoulder at the short, brown hair peeking from beneath the blankets, my aching cock a reminder of the days spent between her legs.

"What was that noise?" Ayelay's voice was thick with sleep as she rolled over, propping herself up on an elbow. The blanket slipped away, exposing her breasts and damn the gods for the desire that bloomed through me, and my cock stood at attention again.

"Fucking bottle is empty." I stood up and worked the kinks out of my body. Gods. Every inch of me was sore.

"Mmm. Leaving so soon?" Ayelay's voice purred as I slipped my trousers on.

"Soon?" I glanced out the window, noting the sun that was sitting low in the sky. "It is nearly evening. The fourth day is coming to a close."

"We have a bit of time," she said. Rising from the bed to meet me, her teeth grazed my earlobe as she slid a hand down my trousers.

"Gods, Ayelay," I groaned, pulling away. I turned around and looked down at her. "You will be the death of me," I said, kissing her softly.

Snaking her arms around my neck, she hopped up and locked her legs around my waist. "So that's a, yes?" She slid her hand back down my trousers and stroked my cock.

"No," I said, disentangling myself from her and planting her on the floor. She crossed her arms below her breasts. A sensuous pout pulled her lips down and I groaned at the look.

"You only have to wait another Grand Passage."

A wicked smile curled her lips, and she wrapped her arms around me again. "Or I can alter the bond and make you stay."

"One Grand Passage. Gods, I take that long to recover. You are insatiable."

She laughed. "All Faeries have a voracious appetite for carnal pleasure," she said, looking up at me. "It is a burden to you, isn't it?"

"What is?"

"Your obligation to me. It seems you try to escape earlier and earlier each time."

I looked down into her violet eyes. Had I not partaken in the food and drink offered to me when I was a prisoner of the Fae, I wouldn't be in the position I was in.

One Grand Passage and four days was my penance. And though I couldn't deny my obligation was a burden, I couldn't rightly say I was trying to escape her.

She cocked her head to the side. "Is it me?"

I gripped her face and pressed my forehead to hers. "No, Ayelay. It isn't you."

She pulled back and looked up at me. "Then who is it? I see the sadness in your eyes, Damiyun. You drink to forget and fuck to ease your pain."

I closed my eyes. Lillyanna's face drifted behind my lids. Tears pricked my eyes and I swallowed hard. "She's no one," I said, my voice cracking.

Ayalay brushed away a tear I didn't know I had shed. "You're hurting."

Opening my eyes, I looked down at her. Concern etched her face, and her eyes searched mine. "I am always hurting. The pain never stops. Who she was doesn't matter." I sighed. "I have been away from home for twenty-one Grand Passages. I am on my way there now and I will no sooner get there, then I will have to turn around and come back." I pulled back and looked down at her. "So yes, Ayelay, it is a burden."

She smiled sadly. "I thought so," she said. "Therefore, I am releasing you from your obligation to me, Damiyun Rayne." She rose on her toes and pressed her lips to mine. I shuddered at the coldness spreading through my body. Any desire, any pull to be with her vanished. My obligation was done.

Sighing with relief, I pulled away and finished dressing. "Thank you, Ayelay," I said.

She smiled sadly. "I hope you find a way to ease your pain, Damiyun. And to lay whoever put the sadness in your eyes to rest."

Pulling her back into my arms, I kissed her softly then exited her room and left the palace. Heading out to the stable, I saddled my horse Xander up and guided him outside. His silver coat shone in the light of the setting sun, making it appear that he was glowing. I pulled a fresh bottle of Serpent's Venom from the saddlebag and took a long drink.

Fuck it all, I needed that. I held out my hand, watching the shaking subside as the spirits warmed me. Stopping the bottle back up and stowing it in my cloak, I swung up into the saddle and guided my horse out, gritting my teeth at the soreness. As always, my departure from here was bittersweet. While I loathed being on the Fae lands—the memory of almost losing my head for what Zedekiah did coming back each time I did—I regretted leaving Ayelay. In the times I had come back here, I had grown fond of her, though leaving was also a bit of a relief.

I had no intentions of forming anything beyond what we had, and I was relieved when she released me from my obligation.

Her companionship filled an aching void deep inside me for the four days I had been obligated to be there every Grand Passage. All because I ate the food of the Fae.

After I left, the void came back. The hurt and anguish filled me. The sadness and guilt over what I had done to the woman I loved.

Shaking the thoughts, I pulled out the bottle and took a long drink of the spirit. It was the only thing that dulled the pain—dulled my senses—and helped me forget.

Forget her.

Shaking the thoughts, the painful memories that sliced through my blackened soul, I finished the contents of the bottle and tossed it into the woods, cursing myself for only having one on me. The memories came unbidden, like they always did and with it, the pain. The anger. I wanted to kill, to tear apart the gods who let her die.

Why? Why was she gone? What was the purpose if only to hurt me? She should be here by my side, but she wasn't.

Fuck.

I screamed into the void until my throat was raw, though it did nothing to make me feel better. The sun dipped closer to the horizon, and I did not wish to be outside when darkness fell. Digging my heels into Xander's sides, I urged him on. I knew from traveling these roads so many times the next village was not too far away, though the rapidly descending sun told me I might not make it.

"Come on, Xander," I urged. The woods were too thick. Too dark. Too frightening and the road too exposed.

Fuck it all. I needed to get to the next village, to the tavern where I would be safe. A scream came from my left deep within the dark woods. The sound curdled my blood.

Wraiths.

A growl came from my left. Red eyes peered out of the darkness. Up ahead, a massive figure loomed in the road. A giant shadow ten stories high with a massive head and wings.

"Fuck."

Xander danced on his hooves, and I struggled to keep him under control. Struggled to stop him from tossing me and bolting to danger.

"Easy, boy," I said in what I hoped was a soothing voice. Pulling my magic close, I reached over my head, my hand grasping the hilt of Shadow Blade, the elven blade given to me by Barlack. The diamond, sapphire, and ruby jewels felt warm in my grasp. The magic contained buzzed. Drawing it, I pulsed the elven magic through, the blade made of the Pyragaty bone glowed blue.

"Stay with me, boy," I said as I jumped off Xander. The last thing I wanted was for him to bolt. He tossed his head and danced on his hooves but did not run. If anything, he pushed closer to me.

The screams to my left grew closer. The wind picked up, whipping dust and debris in the air, and blowing my hair into my eyes, restricting my sight. The Wraiths crept closer, as did the beasts to the right and up the road. I called the flame inside me, warmth rushed through my body. Holding a hand out, a burst of flame shot forth toward the beast in front. It tore right through it but did not harm.

"Gods damn it."

I was surrounded. A touch from a Wraith meant death, but the other beasts? I was sure they would happily make a meal out of me.

A loud ground shaking bellow came from above. Looking up, I saw a demon flying overhead. Wings flapped, stirring up sand. I raised a hand to block the spray. A giant head with pointed ears swung back and forth on a serpent neck. Red eyes scanned the ground. Lethal claws curled at the end of feet on legs the size of tree trunks. Its long tail lined with sharp barbs swung back and forth.

I recognized the beast, though he was usually much smaller.

It was Bel, but why was he here?

"To your right, Damiyun," a voice growled.

Zedekiah. If anyone deserved the name Betrayer, it was him. "Damn it, Damiyun," he snarled. Hands shoved me and I stumbled to the left. My feet tangled with each other, and I crashed to the ground, Shadow Blade flying out of my hand, landing several yards away.

Rolling over, I looked up at him. Smoke surrounded his body forming decrepit figures. Twelve smoky beings formed into solid demons. Skin hung off bones. Jaws hung from sinew and empty eyes looked around.

"Go," Zedekiah commanded, and the beasts took off into the woods.

Bel screeched above, and I looked up, seeing him crash into a demon flying toward him. Bel's claws tore at the beast, pieces of its skin and limbs fell to the ground, the scent of putrid rot filled my nose, and I retched onto the ground. The Wraiths screamed, the sound louder and closer. Leaping to my feet, a glint to my left caught my eye. Shadow Blade. But it was too far for me to get. Wispy creatures drifted out of the woods. Translucent beings floated on the air, the talons on their feet scraping the ground. Wicked claws curled, and black mouths opened to screech, an ear piercing and bowel emptying sound. Coldness washed over me, my limbs shook and I almost collapsed.

I reached for my magic, but it slipped away. I trembled. I tried to calm myself to call forth my magic. Nothing. I watched the beasts float ever closer, claws held out ready to touch.

Ready to kill.

Fear rooted me to the spot and in an odd way, I welcomed the cold death touch of the Wraiths. I welcomed their embrace. After all, what did I have left to live for anyway? The woman I loved, the only one who made me feel like I was worth something, was gone. This world had done me no favors and though I knew my death would put me into an eternity of torment, I had lived that my entire life. Serving Themesis would be no different.

My eyes went to the spirits who beckoned, and I took a step forward. A hand grabbed my collar, yanking me back, tossing me to the ground. Bel screeched from above, the Wraiths shrank back at the sound, disappearing into the dark woods.

Bel flew down, sitting on the ground beside me. His tongue flicked out to lick a wound on his front paw.

I rose and faced Zedekiah. "What the fuck are you doing here?"

Clenching my fists, I let the elven magic flow through my body, and with Zedekiah in my sights, I pulsed it out. Light flew from my body and hit. A concussive thud met nothing.

A fucking barrier. My magic hit a wall and disintegrated.

"Stop, Damiyun."

"Or what?" Warmth ran through me, and I pulled on the flame raging inside. "You betrayed me." Holding my arms out, flames danced on my upturned palms. Zedekiah folded his arms.

"Do what you want, Damiyun. It won't bring her back." His eyes met mine. "I loved her too. I lost another daughter when she died." His voice hitched, and I fell to my knees. Bel screeched. Abraham's eyes looked to the woods.

"Go," he said. "I will keep the demons at bay."

Xander stepped forward and I swung up on his back. Digging my heels in, I urged him on to the village just ahead. And as we raced on, I tried to shake the feeling this journey was another test from the gods.

H ANDING XANDER OVER TO the stable hand, I tossed her a copper and made my way to the tavern.

Gods, I needed drink. I clenched my fists to quell the shaking. The tavern had better be open. If not, I would wake the fucking keep and demand a drink. The chains holding the sign to the tavern and inn made a soft squeak in the light wind. Grasping the door handle, I slipped into The Alchemist's Lair, though nearly empty, it was blessedly open. Finding the proprietor, I ordered three bottles of Faeries Blood, ignoring the raised eyebrow as I pulled the cork from one and took a long pull. The warmth spread through me, the feeling a friendly embrace. Securing a room, I handed over the coin and made my way through the dark hall to the room in the back.

Unstrapping my sword, I removed my cloak and settled on the bed, leaning against the rickety headboard. Waving my hand, the few candles in the room came to life, the flames flickering on the walls in a macabre dance.

Demons meant the binds on Themesis' tomb were still weak. Those who sought to free him still probably wanted a place by his side and immortality. Lillyanna's death had changed nothing.

Scratching the annoying stubble, I slipped off the bed to the cracked mirror hanging above the low table holding a wash basin and pitcher of water. My eyes glowed yellow in the dim light. The Sight of the Fallen One, people called it. It allowed me to see in the dark and looking at the glowing orbs, I could understand why it frightened people.

And it made it clear I was a Wielder.

My long, white hair hung limply around my shoulders. It needed a wash, I needed a wash, but there wasn't much water in the pitcher for that and I did not wish to go outside for more. Not with what is lurking in the dark.

Pulling my dagger from my waistband, I went to task of removing the white gracing my jaw, making me look older than the many Grand Passages I have been in this world. I caught a movement out of the corner of my eye. The shadows undulated, forming a black silhouette near the wall.

"Zedekiah," I said, rinsing my blade, and drying it on my trousers.

Crossing his arms, he leaned against the wall with a sigh. Bel leapt from his spot beneath Zedekiah's beard. Hitting the floor, he scampered across the room, crawled up the leg of the table and sat down, letting out a series of chirps, high pitched squeals and growls.

"Of course you would say that. You're his familiar." I glared down at the little demon. His wings fluttered and he growled again.

"Damiyun—"

"You are not welcome here." I crossed the room, swiping a bottle of spirits off the bed. Pulling the cork, I took a long pull. "Do you think what you did out there erases everything? That I will forgive you?"

Zedekiah rubbed his eyes. "Of course, not."

"So why are you here?"

"It is not your time to die."

I snorted into the bottle. "Right. I don't need your help."

"Clearly."

I took a healthy swig of Faeries Blood. "Leave, Zedekiah. You did your job. There is no need for you to be here."

Bel growled, teeth snapped at me as he leaped across the room to Zedekiah, running up his leg and settling on his shoulder again. Red eyes glared at me. Shadows moved across the floor. Demons formed, wrapping around Zedekiah and then he was gone.

The sight of moving shadows, demons forming from them unnerved me. I didn't think I would ever get used to seeing it.

Rubbing my eyes, I stretched out on the bed. I did not want to think what would have happened to me if Zedekiah—Abraham—had not shown up. Though my contract has not been called, not yet anyway, I had no doubt Themesis would keep me in the Abyss had I been dragged there by his demons.

No, I did not want to admit I was grateful for Abraham's appearance. Nor did I want to admit I missed his companionship, his gruff demeanor and scolding tone. Maybe in time I would forgive him for what he did. For deceiving us, but not now.

The room was silent. Deafeningly so. The only sound was my breathing. Fuck, but I was lonely. The empty hole that had once been filled by Lillyanna was bitter and dark. And though I feared filling it again, feared losing her and her memory if I did, I feared this black and dark loneliness more.

I feared having no one around to mourn my pathetic existence when Death came for me. Shaking the thoughts from my mind, I closed my eyes and reluctantly let sleep claim me, and with it, came the nightmares. The horrific torture from Themesis.

Lil. My Lil.

I watched her walk across the floor, green eyes on Themesis, a soft smile on her face. Her fiery red hair that I loved tumbled down her back in waves. She wore nothing but gold paint that covered her vulnerable areas. Paint infused with magic that made her do Themesis' bidding. I watched her sink to her knees and tilt her head up, eyes closed as he affixed the emerald encrusted slave collar around her neck.

I watched as they were Blood Bound and as he claimed her as his own. All the while Zedekiah stood back, arms crossed, a smirk on his face.

And me?

I was helpless to do anything but watch. And when she looked at me, gods, but her eyes were black and empty, and her words pierced my heart and shattered my soul.

"Thank you, Damiyun, for bringing me to my love. Thank you for bringing me home."

And I watched Themesis wrap her in his arms and claim her again and again and again.

P AIN.

Excruciating and debilitating.

The metal table felt cold beneath my naked torso.

Pain.

The barbed whip bit into my back, tearing flesh and muscle. Bones cracked and broke.

Hammer slammed down on limbs, shattering arms and legs. I screamed in agony.

And then the pain was gone and my wounds were mended.

Only to be torn and broken again.

I BOLTED AWAKE. THE sound of screams—*my* screams—echoed off the wall. My throat was dry and sore, body drenched in sweat, the bed soaked with it.

Themesis' laughter reverberated inside my head.

Weak. Pathetic. Not even worthy of being my servant.

"Leave me alone. Why are you doing this?" I clenched my fists.

You took her from me. My queen. My love.

"She was never yours."

I will break free, and I will make you pay.

"You will never be free. You will never win."

Laughter echoed in my head again. *I already have.*

I gripped my head as the laughter receded. As *he* receded to the back of my mind. A presence that bore down on me. A voice intent on making me mad. His last words played in my head:

I already have.

And I couldn't say his words were wrong.

The grip on my sanity was tenuous at best and with every day, every taunt, every nightmare, I felt my hold loosening.

Picking up a bottle of spirits, I drank until the room swam.

Until there was no more left to drink, and I passed out into a dark, welcome oblivion.

THIRTY-ONE

T HE DAY WAS COLD, the sky cloudy and light flakes of snow drifted down, melting on my eyelashes and cheeks. The wind blew, sending a chill down my spine and I drew my magic close, letting the flame warm me.

I did not sleep much the night prior. Though I drank myself into slumber, the nightmares still plagued me and as soon as the sky began to lighten, I saddled Xander and headed out. Not before swiping three bottles of spirits. I left a generous pile of coin for the proprietor.

The streets were empty at this early time, which made my travel faster. I wanted to get back to Pine Crest Manor as quickly as possible. Though I would have to find a safe place to bed down during the nights.

As the day progressed, the snowfall became heavier and deeper, slowing Xander down. My cloak was wet, and the harsh wind chilled me to my bones. As much as I wanted to call my magic for warmth, I had held it for far too long. I was exhausted, the most recent nosebleed made me fear burning out.

I felt Xander shiver beneath me, and I patted his neck. "I know, boy. We are almost to Voodomecism. I promise you will be nice and warm in no time."

Though I did not wish to stop in this town, the weather left me with no other choice. The streets were busy, the weather having little effect on the people who bustled about on foot and in carriages, though the booths that lined the sides were closed up tight. Navigating Xander through the streets, I found the tavern and inn, an establishment called The Impious Seductress. Locating the barn, I left Xander and headed into the tavern.

A wall of heat hit me as I opened the door from a stone-and-brick fireplace. It instantly warmed my insides. Music drifted over the loud chatter, the tables filled with patrons drinking, eating, and playing games of cards and dice. The packed room was stuffy and reeked of sweat, body odor, and wet dog. Finding an empty table in the back, I removed my sword and cloak, taking a seat with my back against the wall. A serving wench came by, hips swaying and ample bosom spilling out of her top, and I ordered up a bowl of hot stew, bread, and a tankard of ale, kicked my feet out and relaxed. Though I would much rather be on the road, this was a welcome stop. The rations of food I had were almost gone and I had run out of the spirits I swiped long ago.

I dug into my hot stew and sipped my ale, looking up now and again as the door opened and closed letting patrons in and out, along with cold gusts of wind and snow. The door opened again, and with the cold came a feeling of magic. Looking up, my eyes went to a group of two men and two young women entering the establishment.

It was where the surge came from.

Removing their cloaks, they took a seat at a table across the way. My eyes went to one man in the group. He was the only one with a sword and dressed in black. Though I could scarcely see it, I knew what the symbol embroidered on the left side of his chest was.

Two swords crossed over a scarlet "S." The sign of the Suppressors.

He slung an arm around a pretty young woman beside him, drawing her close and nuzzling her neck, eliciting a giggle from her. Sipping my drink, I watched the public display of affection. A pang of loneliness hit my heart. Would I ever have something like that again? Did I even want it? Nothing good happened when I let myself care. Let myself love. Everything sours and dies.

The woman with brown hair said something to the one sitting beside the Suppressor, which caused her to burst into laughter. The Suppressor's eyes met mine, and he rose, stalking over to my table. "Do you have a fucking problem?"

"Other than my mug being empty? No," I said, signaling to the serving wench for another. The woman handed me my drink, I flashed a smile and tossed her a silver. Taking a sip, I looked back at the man in front of me. "Did you want something?"

His nostrils flared. Placing his fists on the table, he leaned forward. "Is there a reason you can't keep your fucking eyes to yourself? I saw you leering at my lady."

I snorted. "Am I supposed to know which of these many women," I gestured with my tankard, "is yours?"

"You know exactly which one is mine. It would serve you best to put your eyes someplace else." He stood up and gripped the hilt of his sword.

It took everything to not laugh. This boy's head would be gone before his weapon cleared the scabbard.

"I would be careful who you threaten." I sat back in my chair, drumming my fingers of the sword sitting on the table.

"Is everything alright, Ghent?"

I blinked. The young man who was threatening me was Ghent Farnsworth? The rambunctious child I had met at Wren's Keep? His arrogance made me believe he was fully under the tutelage of my brother.

Magic pulsed off the young woman who stood beside Ghent. She was a pretty, petite young thing. Her long, white hair streaked with red shimmered in the lamplight and tumbled down her back. Eyes a curious color of green and blue looked up at Ghent. Her features were sharp, narrow nose, high cheekbones, and a prominent jaw line.

"Everything is fine, Fin. Let's go sit back down." Ghent placed a hand on her lower back and led her away.

I shook my head. The girl was playing with a dangerous combination of a Suppressor with a controlling side. Yes. He definitely was under my brother's care. My guess was Ghent did not know she and her friends had magic. I didn't want to think what would happen when he finds out. He would be obligated to bring them in and the women? They would be at the mercy of my brother.

I wanted to warn them, but I kept to myself. The last thing I needed was attention.

Finishing my drink, I tossed coin on the table, grabbed my sword and cloak, and made my way up the stairs to my room. Closing the door, I looked out the small window. The moon shined bright in the sky. That was a good sign. The storm was over and I could leave in the morning.

Though I still had a ways to go, I would cover as much distance as I could to bring me closer to home.

*D*AMIYUN, A DISTANT VOICE said.

Damiyun, it said again.

My eyes snapped open and I bolted up in bed, pulling my magic close. I looked around the small, dark room but no one was here.

So, what woke me?

Damiyun.

The fucking voice was inside my head, though it was not Themesis. It was Barlack. Though Abraham and I communicated through our minds, it was the bond between us that allowed it to happen, along with his connection to the Abyss. I did not know how Barlack was able to speak with me.

I am not coming back, I said.

That is not what I want.

Then why are you bothering me?

Allendaire has a daughter. He sentenced her to death because the queen is with child. She escaped somehow and needs to be found.

I clenched my jaw. *No.*

Damiyun—

No, Barlack. How do you know this, anyway?

That does not matter, he said. *Allendaire has sent soldiers out to find her. If they do, she will be brought back and executed.*

That is not my problem.

Damiyun—

I said no, Barlack. I am not a fucking nanny. Why don't you use your mind invasion to find her?

I don't know where she is and she is likely too far away. We can only go so far. I have no one else. I trust you, Damiyun. Please.

There was desperation in his voice.

I groaned. *What am I to do if I find her?*

Protect her. Keep her safe. When it is time for you to come back, you will bring her with you.

I rubbed my eyes. As much as I did not want to do this, I knew there was no way out of it. *Fine.*

And when Barlack described what she looked like, I knew the task would be far more complicated than I wanted.

Finding her wouldn't be a problem. She was here.

Barlack sighed. *Keep her safe, Damiyun.*

"Fuck it all."

THIRTY-TWO
PHABIAN

I WAS BONE TIRED. My body ached from the saddle and the hard beds at the inn. A few nights I was forced to bed down with Maxamillian in the cold and smelly barn. I was dirty and smelled bad, I knew. I could not wait to get to my quarters and soak in a hot tub of scented water.

The spires of Trounde Castle appeared above the tree line in the distance. Morning sun glinted off the red marble walls, making the palace glow like fire. My body relaxed at the sight, and I heeled Max into a distance eating canter. The oak and iron gates came into view showing Elves standing sentry in a line formation, their swords drawn.

"We have been waiting for you, Phabian," Samel's deep voice said. "The king knew you would eventually return. Get off your horse."

I hesitated a second. While I could use my magic and lay the half dozen Elves out, I knew it would only further my trouble with Allendaire. Swinging off Max, I tossed the reins to a soldier on Samel's right.

"Weapons."

Sighing, I removed my sword from my waist, and daggers from my belt and boot.

"Arm."

"What?"

Samel grabbed my arm, and I felt the cold obsidian of the Sigaa'Lean on my skin. Words were quickly spoken, and my magic rushed from my body replaced with a gaping hole of emptiness.

"Is this necessary?"

Samel glared at me. "Do you think us stupid enough to let you have your magic?"

My nostrils flared. "Do you not realize I could have laid the lot of you out with it just moments ago?"

Samel said nothing, though I could almost hear his teeth gnashing together. Two soldiers grabbed my arms, yanking them behind and secured my wrists with thick rope. Grabbing my elbow, Samel and his men marched me to the palace, securing me inside a dark cell.

And as the door closed and darkness suffocated, I realized the severity of my plight.

I was going to die.

COLD SEEPED THROUGH MY clothes, and the dampness of the dark cell chilled me to the bone. I pulled a threadbare blanket with more holes than fabric tighter around my body.

Twenty days passed in cold, dark, and silence. Only the morning and evening meals broke the monotony.

Though I could not see morning or night, ticking off the passage of time on the wall after each evening meal had become a comforting ritual.

Leaning back against the wall, I wondered, not for the first time, how long I would remain locked behind these walls. Perhaps instead of losing my head, they would leave me to rot. I half hoped for a swift execution instead.

The sound of footsteps outside the door and the murmur of low voices drew my attention. A key scraped in the lock, and the hinges screamed in protest as the door opened. Feet shuffled on dirt as someone stepped into the dark room and I raised my arm, shielding my eyes against the brutal light of the lantern.

"The king wishes to see you." It was Krall.

I pulled myself up to my feet, discarding the rank blanket, and stretched the kinks out of my body.

"Krall—"

Saying nothing, he stalked down the corridor. Sighing, I followed behind. My stomach churned as we moved through the dungeon corridors and up the stairs to the palace, and I wiped my sweaty hands off on my trousers.

"Where are you taking me?" I wanted to be a little prepared for what awaited me.

Again, I was met with silence.

We continued through the halls, and I glanced out the windows as we passed. The sky was painted with brilliant colors—sunrise or sunset, I couldn't be sure. I was sure he was taking me to the throne room. Realization hit when Krall stopped outside a tall, thick door made of oak, the Shadow Elf crest carved into the wood. My mouth went dry, and my hands shook.

A room that was used when the common folk and lesser nobles of our lands had grievances to air, or when matters of governance and law needed to be addressed.

Or when someone was brought before the king and council to be tried and executed.

I summoned what little saliva I had and swallowed hard against the rock in my throat. Krall pushed open the door and strode in. I hesitated a second, then reluctantly followed. The grand room was packed with people. The smooth white marble floor was polished to a mirror shine. The deep, cherry wood panels covering the walls depicted scenes of Shadow Elven history. The master carver who I knew Karrinian had hired worked in the details.

Windows from floor to ceiling broke up the dark panels, letting in the fading sunlight. Lit sconces lined the walls, and a grand, ornate crystal and diamond chandelier hung from the ceiling. Dozens of candles reflecting a kaleidoscope of color over the assembled. Despite the crowded room, the elves remained fairly silent. Nary a whisper rippled among them. A man cleared his throat. A child tapped their toes, impatience showing in their eyes. I followed the line of people to the dais where Allendaire sat. He drummed his fingers upon the emerald serpent's head of the armrest. Light caught the jewels adorning the golden crown, and his cold blue eyes stared death straight through me.

Holding my head high, I crossed the room. The sound of my shoes echoed off the walls as I made my way to the throne and stood in front of him.

"Kneel before your king." Krall said.

I didn't move. He wasn't my king. He wasn't anyone's king.

"I said, kneel," Krall grabbed my shoulder, pain lanced from the pinch down to my arm. I gasped as he shoved me down.

"Phabian Trounde," Allendaire's voice lashed through the silence. I looked up at him, barely containing the deference Krall wanted me to show. Allendaire's cold, blue eyes froze me. "You spoke blasphemous words about your king."

I lifted my head high. "I did."

"You said you no longer respect me. That I am no longer your king."

"I did."

Allendaire gripped the armrests, his knuckles turning white. "Those are traitorous words." His voice echoed through the hall. Someone coughed into their hand, and I nearly jumped at the sound, the crowd so silent I forgot they were there.

Looking up at Allendaire, I licked my lips. "They are, and I deeply regret speaking them." I swallowed back the bile that rose at my words. "It was rash of me to say such things about my benevolent king. I was upset about Serafin, though I know you did what was right." My stomach lurched, and I almost vomited on the clean, white marble floor. I took a deep breath, forcing the rest of my words out. "I misplaced the love for my king on the princess." Gritting my teeth, I pressed my forehead to the floor.

"I subjugate myself before you. I come humbly, asking you for forgiveness at my folly. My love for you never faltered. I spoke out of passion, and I regret my words."

The room was so quiet you could hear a dagger drop. My heart pounded in my chest, my throat was dry, and my palms sweated.

The seconds ticked by; my body cramped from the position I was in.

"Phabian Trounde," Allendaire's voice sliced through the silence. "Though you spoke traitorously against your king, I am a just and loving monarch. You have been a trusted advisor. A loyal subject of my court who has never spoken ill of me before. I can only assume your love for Serafin clouded your judgement. Because of the Grand Passages of loyalty you have shown me, and because I put my trust in you as an advisor, I will spare your life."

I exhaled hard, the tension easing from my body. The room erupted into chaos. Voices shouted for my blood. For my head on a spike.

"However," Allendaire's voice rose above the ruckus. He held a hand up and the commotion came to an abrupt halt. Sweat dripped down my back and I swallowed hard.

"However," his ice blue eyes pinned me, "you will not go without punishment. I will administer one hundred and seventy-six lashes in the square at dawn. Five for your blasphemous words. One for every day you were gone, and twenty-one for every Grand Passage spent with Serafin."

I bowed my head. "Your kindness is overwhelming, and I thank you for sparing my life." *Or simply making my death a slow and painful one.* "I will prove myself a most loyal and humblest of servants once again, my king."

I almost choked on the last words.

"This trial is concluded. Take him back to his cell." Rising, Allendaire stalked past me and out of the room, back straight and head held high. Those in attendance followed behind, voices murmuring as they left, some casting scathing looks at me as they passed.

Krall's had clamped down on my arm, yanking me to my feet, marching me back to my cell to wait for the morning.

"IT'S TIME," KRALL SAID as he swung the door to the cell open.

I said nothing as I rose to my feet and followed him out. The halls were empty. No doubt the inhabitants of the castle were already crowding the square in anticipation of my flogging. We walked in silence, and I didn't try to engage my brother in conversation, knowing he wouldn't answer, though I would have welcomed the distraction. Stepping out of the palace, we made our way down the pathway and through the gates leading to the town. My muscles tightened, and I had to resist the overwhelming urge to flee, though I didn't know where I'd go. I took a deep breath in an attempt to calm myself, to slow my heart.

Krall glanced over his shoulder at me. "You should be losing your head this morning."

"But I'm not."

"Perhaps the whipping will do you in. I can't say I will mourn the death of a traitor."

I clenched my fists at his words. The loyalty he had for the king was blind, though I knew there was nothing I could say to convince him otherwise. Until Serafin was born, I too was blind. My love for my king knew no bounds. When Serafin came, I started to question our ways. Not enough to make a change, but questions emerged. If I had understood Arybelle's tale sooner, learned of it sooner, I might have done more to challenge and question our traditions and laws. A flicker of anger bloomed inside me. Arybelle had stayed hidden so long. Why?

Trudging behind Krall, I kept my head high, hands clenched to keep from shaking as I passed by people waiting to watch my punishment. As we shouldered our way through the throng, to the center square, my pulse raced and my heart pounded in my ears.

I looked around the crowd. At the elves I had known. At the people who had once respected me and saw nothing but hatred and fury within their blue eyes. Voices hissed and cursed me as I passed through.

"Traitor." A voice I recognized as Ryana hissed. The woman was a familiar yet distant aunt.

"Half-breed lover."

"Wilde Elf."

Even more called for my demise.

"Take his head."

"Clip his ears."

"Feed him to the ravens!" A particularly loud Elf screamed. His voice boomed over the crowd.

Stinking garbage hit the side of my face. "Burn him alive."

Dannel spit at me. He was a childhood friend who Krall and I often invited to drink stolen spirits in the woods. I hadn't seen in some time, even before Serafin was banished.

Part of me wondered if the king had changed his mind. My legs gave way and I stumbled. The press of people kept me upright.

When we broke through, I saw the whipping post on the green and fell to my knees, all but weeping in relief. Grabbing my arm and hauling me to my feet, Krall dragged me to the post, stripped me of my shirt and shackled my wrists. My body shook, and I collapsed. I scrambled to stand, but my legs were like water and would not support my weight. A hush fell over the crowd and hearing a shuffle, a swish of clothing, I turned my head to see Allendaire standing behind looking very much the part of a king dressed in his finery. The train of his black fur-trimmed robe fanned out on the ground and the sun glinted off the jewels on the golden crown nestled upon his white mane. In his right hand, he gripped a knout whip and my stomach roiled.

I had never in my life been whipped. Never been beaten and the sight of the whip in his hand made my blood drain.

"Phabian Trounde," his voice broke through the silence, and I jumped at the sound. "For your treason, I sentenced you to one hundred and seventy-six lashes by my hand. Five for your blasphemous words. One for each day you were gone, and twenty-one for each Grand Passage spent with Serafin. Will you speak to your crimes?"

I looked around at the crowd. At the people I had shared food and drink with. At those few who I knew had loved the princess. Who had accepted her as queen but who now stood with hatred and bloodlust in their eyes. Who now were happy to see me whipped—or even executed—when before they welcomed me to their table and to their home and I knew there was something undeniably wrong. I knew it from the moment Mouranda announced she was with child.

I looked back at Allendaire and forced myself to my feet, clutching the post to keep myself upright. "You are a kind king. A fair and just king. A loving king," I said. Allendaire's eyes narrowed. "I am humbled before you and accept this generous punishment for my traitorous ways."

Allendaire's lips curled back into a smile, his knuckles clutching the handle of the whip turned white. He drew back and struck. There was a whoosh as leather sliced air and an audible thud as it hit flesh. I grit my teeth against the stinging pain and locked eyes with Allendaire.

"One," I said.

He struck again with much more force.

"Two." I called between grit teeth.

With each strike, he applied more force and with each strike, I called out the number.

I screamed at strike number sixteen.

Fell to my knees at twenty-one.

My bowels loosed at twenty-five and blackness took me on the thirtieth.

THIRTY-THREE

S OUNDS PIERCED THE DARK. A rustle of clothes reached my ears. Hands touched my back.

I woke with a start, scrambling to sit up.

"Stop," Lazaro's voice drifted to me. His hands grasped my shoulders and gently pushed me back to my stomach.

I was tired. Sleep made my eyelids and limbs heavy which made me compliant. The sound of water splashing reached my ears, but I was too tired to rise again. My back hurt, and I winced as a rag gently touched my skin.

"Sorry," Lazaro's voice drifted through the haze, and I turned to look at him. Pain twisted my back. "Fuck, Phabian. Stay still," Laz snapped. His hands pushed me back down.

"Laz—"

"You should be dead. The beating you took…" his voice trailed off. I didn't need him to say more. "

"I'm alive, Laz. I can feel my magic healing me."

Rolling to my side, I sat slowly up. Laz didn't try to stop me, though his sigh was filled with annoyance. The room spun for a moment, then righted. Stars filled my eyes and I took a deep breath.

"You should lie back down."

"I'm fine."

Though my back hurt and my body felt heavy with tiredness, I would not laze around in my bed. I was sure that was what Allendaire expected. For me to hide in my quarters, licking my wounds, so to speak.

"How long have I been out?"

"Since after the punishment. The healers gave you an elixir to keep you asleep so you could heal."

That explained the heaviness in my limbs and the exhaustion in my body. Rising, Lazaro strode across the room to my desk in the corner. Pulling the stopper out of a jar of ink, he dipped a quill and began writing across a piece of parchment.

"What are you doing?"

He looked up, eyes darting around, and he pressed a finger to his lips. Crossing the room, he held the paper out, and my eyes scanned the words.

I need to speak with you. Meet me at the Broken Wench in Theonaus this afternoon.

Frowning, I looked up at him. Why was he being secretive?

*Laz, what—*A wall came up within my mind, stopping the words I was sending.

My frown deepened.

Laz hurried back to the desk, the sound of the nib furiously scratching on parchment filled the silence between the pops from the fire blazing in the hearth. Coming back to where I sat, he held up the paper again.

Just meet me there, and be careful, Phabian. I do not know who to trust within these walls.

I nodded, and Lazaro sighed with relief. Holding the parchment, a blinding flash of blue lit the room engulfing the paper which disappeared, leaving no trace.

"Now," Lazaro said, gently pushing me back onto the bed. "Let me tend your wounds."

Leaning forward, his lips brushed my chest, and his hand slid between my legs.

"I don't think my cock was injured," I said.

"It doesn't hurt to check, does it?" Lazaro murmured as he trailed kisses down my torso.

"I suppose not," I said, sighing as his warm mouth took me in.

I thought about the last words he had written, about not knowing who to trust. Did that include my own brother? Though he had brought me to be flogged, he was working under the orders of Allendaire. Surely, I could trust him?

Pushing the thoughts aside, I lost myself in my pleasure. I would meet Lazaro in Theonaus and hopefully get to the bottom of what he was talking about.

P ULLING THE DOOR TO the tavern, I slipped inside. It was bustling and hot. A bard stood on a dais in the corner singing in an off-tone high-pitched voice and I cringed at the horrible sound. I looked around the tavern where nefarious looking folk sat eating and drinking. Hands brushed hilts of daggers and swords, narrowed eyes peered from beneath brows, bodies tense and alert, waiting for the chance to brawl. Theonaus was a poor town, and it showed in the clientele with their dirty, threadbare clothing. The look of despair in eyes glassy from drink and the dim lighting did nothing to hide the grime coating tables and countertops.

I scanned the crowd, catching a flash of bright clothing, and pushed my way through the people to a table in the corner where Lazaro sat. A woman perched on his knee and one of his hands clutched a tankard. The other was somewhere beneath her skirts.

"Phabian." He greeted as I pulled out a chair and sat. His face was flushed and eyes bright with drink, and I wondered just how long he had been here. "This beautiful woman is Hannah. This," he said, gesturing with his mug, "is Phabian."

I snorted as I flagged down a serving wench. Laz was far drunker than I thought. The woman who sat upon his knee was anything but beautiful. Her yellow hair streaked with gray was a tangled bird's nest. The stretched out neckline of her faded dress hung open, revealing a wrinkled chest and sagging breasts and the deep ruts carved into her face made me wonder if she had been the first woman to ever sell services to a man. I laughed into my mug of ale at the thought. Milky gray eyes appraised me, brown tongue flicked out and licked lips smudged with paint.

"Oy. I'll give ye both a good price. Ye kin 'ave me at da same time," she said with a gap-toothed grin.

I shuddered at the thought. "Thanks, but no. I quite like my cock and don't fancy watching it rot off."

She glared at me. "I ain't got no diseases. My cunny be clean. Cleaner den any o' dem udder whores," she smiled, and I recoiled at the expanse of brown gums and rotting teeth. "Fer a copper, I'll let ye have a sniff."

"Off with you, hag. We don't want anything you offer."

A snarl curled her lips, and she jumped to her feet. "Think yer too good fer me, eh? Wit yer fancy clothes an gems? Yer no better 'an me. Yer worse. Ye've prolly ne'er worked o' day in yer life." She grabbed my wrist and yanked my arm up, then dropped it with disgust. "Jus as I taught. Smood as a babe's arse. At least I earn a honest livin'." I snorted. She turned to Laz.

"Four coppers fer da feel."

I threw my head back and laughed. "Four coppers for touching that foul thing? You aren't even worth one."

"May the gods curs ye wit a life o' bad luck."

"My luck can't get any worse than it's been. Now off with you," I said, waving my hand in dismissal, watching as she slunk away, eyes already on another hopeless drunk.

"Really, Laz?"

He laughed into his drink. "She wasn't that bad."

I raised an eyebrow as I took another mug from the wench. "She was missing teeth and the few she had were rotten."

"And that's bad? There's no chance of having her bite my most prized possession off then."

I chuckled. "You'll be lucky if your hand doesn't rot off," I said. "Now. Why are we here? What was with your cryptic message?"

Laz tipped back the contents of his drink, then grabbed two tankards off the tray a wench held. Sliding one across the table to me, he took a sip of his own.

"What is going on, Laz? Why do we have to speak here? Why could you not speak in my room?"

Lazaro licked the foam from his lips. "Don't you find the queen's condition odd? Don't you wonder about the way Serafin was condemned?"

I frowned. "Of course, I do. You know as well as any how much I love her. Why do you think I left when I heard?"

"What would you have done if you found her? Bring her back to lose her head?"

It was almost the same question Arybelle had asked.

"I don't know. Maybe I wouldn't have returned. Maybe I would have stayed with her. Protected her from the evils of the world."

Lazaro laughed. "She is a woman of twenty-one. She doesn't need protection."

Flagging down the wench, I ordered two bottles of Serpent's Venom. I had a feeling I would need something stronger than the ale.

"No? It appears she needed it—needed me—on her Name Day. Had I been there—"

"What, Phabian? What could you have done?" Reaching across the table, Laz grabbed my hand, threading his fingers with mine. "I saved her. No one knows how she really escaped, and I distracted the party when she came out. You are the only one who knows the truth. You know in your heart she is safe."

Safe, and doesn't need me. That was the part that hurt the most.

Pulling my hand away, I opened the bottle placed before me and took a long drink. Warmth spread through my body, the tips of my ears burning. "You did not ask me here to tell me what I know."

Lazaro shook his head and took a drink from the other bottle. "No. I don't... none of this sits well with me. How is Mouranda with child?"

I snorted. "Do I have to explain how that happens?"

Lazaro rolled his eyes. "I know how but...how?"

Shaking my head, I rose. "I don't know, but we need to find out. I feel like the fate of the kingdom, of my Little Princess, rests with the truth." I tossed coin on the table. "We need to be careful. I am sure I will be blocked from the minds of those close to Mouranda. We have to come up with a way to get the truth."

"I am on your side, Phabian. Trust no one. Not even Krall."

My heart felt heavy at his words, but knowing Krall's position in the court, it did not surprise me. Nodding, I slipped around the table and headed to the room

I secured. In the morning, I would head back to the castle and I would begin my search for the truth.

THIRTY-FOUR
MOURANDA

"**H**OW ARE YOU FEELING?" Denalla handed me a mug of warm goat milk as she sat down in the chair beside me. A fire blazed in the hearth in my quarters, the wind whipped outside shaking the windows, the sound of snow slashed against the glass. Pulling my blanket closer, I sank deeper into the chair and took a sip of the warm milk, pushing down the bile that rose.

"I am feeling fine," I said. The lie slid off my tongue easily enough.

The babe was active, turning and kicking, often causing me pain. I knew he shouldn't be this active at only three Moon Cycles. When I told the healer I felt him move, she laughed and said it was impossible.

But I know it wasn't.

"Don't lie to me, Mouranda," Denalla said.

Of course, she would see through me. I could never lie to her. "He kicks and claws at my insides."

Denalla frowned. "It is far too early to feel him."

I laughed. "You sound like the healers."

Taking her hand, I placed it on my abdomen. The prince kicked hard, and Denalla's eyes widened for a moment, then concern etched her brow. She had birthed seven children and knew what she felt to be wrong.

"The magic." Her voice was barely above a whisper. Her frightened eyes met mine.

"It was worth it." I clasped her hand and forced a smile, though I wondered if it was.

I didn't feel regret. Not really. What I did ensured the daughter of a whore would be executed. But she wasn't. She somehow escaped. Krall and his patrols failed to find her.

Did I want the girl's blood on my hands? Though Allendaire ordered her death, her blood was ultimately on my head; a fact only Denalla knew. The girl rejected me at every turn, and yet I could not help but try, even though I knew I would be snubbed.

The child moved, pain lanced through my body and I gripped Denalla's hand hard.

"Are you alright, my queen?"

I patted her arm. "My Denalla. My loyal Denalla. You remember. I know you do." As the child turned again, I too, remembered.

Walking through the library, I passed down the rows of books, trailing a hand down the leather spines, making my way to the back where no elf had been for centuries. Cobwebs graced the shelves not cleaned by a maid. I pulled down books, Tomes from past kings. Not Karrinian. No. His Tome was made present in the library proper.

This was a different book. Grasping it, I pulled it off the shelf and though my grasp of the Old Tongue was rusty, I could read enough to know this was a long forgotten book. A book buried in the back of the library never to be resurrected, but I found it.

It belonged to the first king. The Dark Elf king.

Magic pulsed within the Tome dark and delicious. Running my hand down the front, I caressed the cracked leather, the crest barely visible. Tucking it beneath my arm, I hurried through the halls to my room. Locking the door, I sat down at my desk, the book in front of me. The lock was rusted with flecks of red. Flecks easily fell as I flicked my thumb over the metal.

Blood.

Pulling open a drawer I grasped the hilt of the dagger hidden within the confines. Taking a deep breath, I sliced my palm letting the blood run across the lock like so many Elves, centuries before had done. The lock glowed yellow, then sprung, the book opening up before me. Running my hand down the thick, golden pages, I looked upon the words. Words long forgotten, but I knew enough. Flipping through, my blood hit the paper. Light flared, words swirled and damn if the book didn't come alive for me.

I paged through, watching the words swirl on the pages. I scanned the symbols that formed and flipped through until a page caught my eye.

It was a spell.

A way to get me with child, and I copied it along with the ingredients for an elixir, down word for word, tucking it away in my drawer, then hid the book in the dark recesses of my wardrobe.

And then there was my Denalla. My loving, faithful Denalla who would do anything for me, and when I showed her the pages I copied, she agreed to do what was needed.

Though her agreement did not come without question. "My queen," she had said, watching one of my many servants place the red velvet cloak around my shoulders. All she knew was Denalla and I were going out for a walk.

Turning, I looked at Denalla who stood before me in a white dress wringing her hands. "My queen," she said again, falling to her knees. "Don't do this."

"Come, Denalla." I pushed past her.

We made our way out of the palace to the woods, Denalla guiding the way and there she sat.

The woman.

The sacrifice.

Tied to a chair she had no idea what was about to happen to her. She squirmed against her binds, the gag in her mouth keeping her from screaming. Pulling the knife I carried, I made my way to where she helplessly sat.

She struggled at the sight of the knife. Screamed as it cut into her abdomen, and her eyes widened in shock and horror as I held the fetus up and consumed it, speaking the words memorized from the paper in my drawer. I then opened the bottle containing the elixir and drank it.

The wind picked up and shadows crept across the ground. A screech echoed through the woods. Denalla stepped away, and I could not blame her, but me? I knew what this was. What I had done had brought the beasts. The demons.

A shadow rose up in front of me, ten stories high. Leather wings protruded from its back and its fire eyes stared at me.

"A life for a life, Mouranda Trounde," its voice growled. Grabbing my arm, sharp teeth dug into my flesh.

"A life for a life," I said, and though I didn't really understand what it meant, I did not care. It was done. I couldn't take it back. Just knowing I would be with child was all that mattered. Having that daughter of a whore out of my palace was all that mattered. The beast dissipated, and I brushed my hair from my forehead.

I could see the whites of Denalla's eyes in the growing darkness.

"What have you done?"

THIRTY-FIVE
DAMIYUN

T HE BELL ABOVE THE bookstore, Nonpareil Opus rang as I pushed it open. Shaking the wet from my cloak, I stepped into the warmth of the store. If I was going to be stuck in this blasted town, I might as well find something to occupy my time.

Besides a woman on my lap, of which I have not yet found one who meets my taste.

The musty scent of leather and paper filled the air, a comforting smell. Walking through the store, I tilted my head to look at titles.

"May I help you?" A female voice called out from somewhere within.

The young woman I saw in the tavern with Ghent came out carrying a stack of books which she placed on a table. She brushed a lock of hair from her forehead, tucking it into the messy bun on top of her head. Her blue-green eyes met mine, smile faltering as recognition crossed her countenance.

"You." She crossed her arms.

Fuck. What did Ghent say about me? Surely, he could not have remembered seeing me at Wren's Keep so many Grand Passages ago. He was just a toddler.

"I—do we know each other?" It was the safest thing I could think of to say.

She sniffed. "The tavern?"

I shrugged. "I have seen many in the tavern."

Moving past her, I perused the shelves. The soft sound of her shoes on the wooden floor told me she followed.

"Well then. What can I help you with?"

I glanced at her. "I am just here to browse." I moved further down the shelves. I could see her following still out of the corner of my eye.

"Serafin, could you---fuck." A voice followed by a crash came from the back of the store.

Serafin ran through the aisles with me hot on her heels.

"Help." A hand made its way up into the air, fingers wiggling from beneath the stack of books and shelves. Grasping the hand, I pulled the person out from their burial.

"Uma," Serafin cried, rushing forward.

My eyes met Uma's golden ones. Her hand clenched mine tight and her eyes widened. I felt magic surge, visions flashed in my mind and my heart plummeted.

Uma was a seer.

"You." She said.

I pulled my hand from her grasp. "I hope you're alright," I said, stepping back.

Fuck it all. Why did I have to encounter someone like her? I don't need a stranger knowing everything about me.

Serafin rushed to the other woman, pulling her into her embrace, and I took the moment to slip away.

Fucking Barlack. Nothing could come easy.

STANDING IN THE SHADOWS, I watched Uma open the bookstore. Waiting a bit, and not seeing Serafin, I pushed off the wall and made my way to the store, the bell ringing as I opened the door.

"I knew you would be back." Uma's eyes met mine briefly.

I chuckled. "Of course, you did."

"She has friends here. A man that cares about her," Uma said as she navigated around the store, putting books back on shelves. I watched her move around, coming back to the table where Serafin placed the stack of books the day prior.

"I know."

"And you will take her?"

"I don't want to. Believe me of that."

Uma's fingers drummed on the stack of books. Her eyes never left me, and I resisted the urge to squirm beneath her gaze. "She doesn't know you."

"You saw us meet at the tavern. And we met here yesterday."

Uma took a deep breath. "Just know she has—"

"Friends? A man she cares about? So, you said. I don't want to do this, if it's any comfort to you."

"I know but if she—"

"I will guard her with my life." I said. "You know I will."

Uma laughed, a sad sound. "I know."

"You won't say anything to her." It wasn't so much of a question. I did not want the girl to become spooked. She wouldn't run, I knew. Not with the life she built here, but I did not want her avoiding me. Hiding from me.

Uma ran a hand through her brown curls. "When?"

I scratched my chin. "I'm not rightly sure."

It was the truth. I did not know when I would tell her who I was and I was here to take her with me. To eventually bring her to the Wilde Elves. It was a delicate situation.

Which meant I would be stuck in this blasted town for longer than I wanted.

Fucking Barlack and his fucking task. Fuck the gods damned escaped princess. Only, I couldn't leave without her. I made a promise and I am a man of my word.

"Just...just let me know ahead of time so I can spend time with her before she leaves?"

"She's not going far. Just to L'Ochal for a bit. I won't keep her from her friends. Or Ghent," I said, though I would very much like to keep her away from that boy. The less time she spent with a Suppressor, the less chance there was of her being brought to Wren's Keep to my brother.

Uma relaxed. "Alright. But you will—"

"I will tell you."

She nodded with a smile, and I bid her good-by and wandered back outside to explore the town. I might as well get acclimated with it better. The gods only knew how long it would be before I left.

Fuck it all.

THIRTY-SIX
ABRAHAM

T HE HOUSE WAS QUIET; a fresh breeze blew in through the open patio doors. Standing in the doorway, I watched my Palma tend to the flowers she planted in our little backyard. The colors were bright and cheerful in the afternoon sun. She took pride in the garden. The flowers and herbs used for teas and medicine flourished beneath her care. And for her, I made it into a quiet sanctuary with flowering trees and a footpath with a pond full of fish at the end. A gentle waterfall cascaded down rocks, the soft splash of the water calming. Benches sat beneath the shade of a willow tree, facing the serene pond. Palma pushed a lock of hair from her forehead, tucking it into the messy bun atop her head, leaving a smudge of dirt on her face.

Gods, but she was stunning, and my heart skipped a beat as she turned and looked in my direction.

Crossing the courtyard toward her, I pulled her into my arms. "Are you alright?" Palma's head tilted to the side, a concerned look upon her face.

"I have never been better or happier than I have been with you," I said, brushing the smudge of dirt off her face, then pulled the box out of my pocket. "I love you, Palma DuLocke, and I wish to spend eternity with you."

Her eyes widened as I opened the box. Pulling the bracelet out, I secured it around her wrist. "That is, if you will have me?"

"Of course I will have you, Abraham," she whispered, eyes glistening with tears. "I know this was a decision you have thought long and hard on. I understand that and know I would never ask you to forget Lenore. I would never ask you to desecrate her memory," she said, brown eyes on me as she took my right hand—the hand that bore the scar from being Blood Bound to my Lenore—and pressed her lips to it. "She is yours, Abraham. Always."

"Thank you."

Palma smiled and pressed her soft lips upon mine, tongue coaxing. Telling.

"I am yours, Abe," she said, pulling away for just a moment.

"Always, Palma. Forever."

"Then show me you mean it."

I needed no further invitation, no more words. Pulling her close, I kissed her in a slow, teasing way and she melted in my embrace.

I slipped my hands beneath her shirt, soft skin warm upon my rough hands. Cupping her breasts, I brushed my thumbs over nipples that were growing erect. She sighed softly; breath warm upon my face. Pulling away for just a moment, I slipped her shirt over her head and gazed upon her naked torso.

Damn, but she was beautiful and perfect in every way. Plump breasts, small waist giving way to generous hips and the face of a goddess. Soft features, wide brown eyes and sultry lips that could do wonders.

"If all I thought you were going to do was stand there and gape, I would have finished tending my plants. You act as though you've never seen me before."

"Every time I see you is like the first time."

Dropping to my knees, I pressed lips to her stomach, fingers working the ties on trousers, easing them over hips and off. I trailed kisses lower and lower, flicking my tongue between her legs.

Gods, but I loved the way she tasted. She was almost too perfect for me. I gripped her hips and her hands entwined in my hair as I gave her pleasure using fingers and tongue.

"Abe." She gasped, body shuddering with climax.

I sat back and looked up at her.

"My turn," she said, placing a foot on my chest and shoving me back. Straddling me, I pulled off my shirt, and she ran her hands up my chest. I sighed at her touch. She placed a hand on either side of my head and looked down at me. I tucked a lock of hair behind her ear and pulled her to be closer, more entwined. She pulled away, a wicked smile on her face and I settled back, closing my eyes as her lips trailed soft kisses across my chest, moving down, down. Fingers undid trousers, hand slipped inside to stroke, tongue flicked over skin as she moved down, finally taking my length in her mouth. I groaned as mouth and tongue worked. Thrusting, thrusting, giving in to the pleasure until I climaxed. Palma sat up and crossed her arms.

"What?"

"I was expecting more, Abraham."

I laughed and pulled her down beside me. She curled up in my arms, head on my chest. "What am I to do when I have a beautiful woman I desire? Who, with just a touch, can make me tremble? Just a look makes me weak, and a kiss makes me abandon all reason," I murmured, kissing the top of her head. Pulling back, I looked down at her. "Don't worry, my heart. I will give you what you want."

She playfully nipped my chin and propped herself up on an elbow, running a hand down my chest, her touch made me shiver. Fingers traced the brand. The three numbers: Four two four.

My slave number. Her eyes were sad as she traced it. As they always were when we were like this.

"It's in the past, Palma."

She smiled sadly. "I know, but it's a part of you."

"And it's in the past," I said. I felt her gaze on me and turned to look at her. "You know the story." Her eyes never left mine, and I sighed. "My mother was a whore. Her father sold her when she was a child to pay a debt. When she had me, I was allowed to stay in her room at the brothel. I earned coin by running odd errands for the other women. After my mother was murdered, I was taken as a slave. I was given a number, which became my name."

"And what is your name?"

I looked down at her. "Abraham."

She shook her head. "No. Who are you?"

"I am yours."

She laughed. Taking my face in her hands, she looked at me. "No. Who are you truly?"

I clenched my jaw. "Zedekiah, son of Themesis."

Her hand caressed my chest. "And these?"

"You know what they are."

Brown eyes looked down at me. "I enjoy hearing the tale."

"Every day?"

"I never tire of it."

"They are the faces and skulls of those I have delivered to my father."

Her fingers traced one in particular. I didn't have to look to know.

I always knew.

"Jaylynn." She whispered the name of my daughter whose soul I delivered so many Grand Passages ago.

"Yes."

"And this?" Fingers next caressed the wolf on my shoulder.

"Loyalty and Devotion."

"To Lenore."

"Yes."

"And—"

I pulled her close and silenced her with a kiss, pushing her onto her back. "No more words. Did you not ask me for more?"

"Always, Abraham. I always want more."

Looking down into eyes filled with love and desire, I slowly kissed her. Slipping a hand between her legs, I prodded and teased, stopping just before she climaxed, then starting all over again while trailing kisses down chin and neck, tongue flicking over breasts, teeth grazing erect nipples.

She writhed beneath me, grinding herself against my hand, sighing in annoyance and frustration. I pulled away and her eyes snapped open.

"Abraham."

"What ails you, my heart?"

"You know what." She reached for me.

Grabbing her wrists, I pinned her arms above her head. "Now, Palma. You know better than that," I chastised.

"Please?"

"Mmmmm. Close," I said, teeth grazing chin.

"Please, Abe?"

I slid my hand between her legs again, but did nothing. "Better," I said, teeth biting her earlobe. She wiggled beneath me, and I pulled away again.

"I swear to the gods, Abraham. If you don't take me now—"

"What, Palma? What are you going to do? It seems I have the advantage here, no?" I quirked an eyebrow.

"Please, Abraham. I will do whatever it is you want. Please?"

"Whatever I want?"

She nodded emphatically, and I laughed. Releasing her, I flipped to my back. Pulling her on top, I slipped inside her soft warmth. Gripping her hips, I moved in and in, deeper and deeper. Arching her back, head thrown back, she met my thrusts. Her lips parted, a look of ecstasy on her face and she shuddered, and I held her, thrusting once, twice, then lost myself and we came together.

"Damn you, Abraham," she said, falling beside me.

I chuckled and pulled her close, kissing the top of her head. "I love you, Palma."

She turned her head, lips grazing my cheek. "And I you." Turning, she looked up at me. "How is Damiyun?"

I sighed. "Hurting. He hates me." I sat up. "I did not betray him. Or her. I did what I thought was best."

Palma's lips pressed against my naked shoulder. "I know, Abraham."

"What my father did to her...if Damiyun thinks I was a part of that..."

Palma's arms slipped around me. "He doesn't. You know this in your heart."

Leaning back, I caught her mouth with mine. "I love you, Palma DuLocke."

"And I you, Abraham." She pulled away, plopping herself in my lap. "Now, for mine?"

Laughing, I softly guided her to the ground. "Now, for yours."

S TEAM ROSE FROM THE tub, and I lowered myself down into the hot water. Sinking deep, I leaned against the back of the copper and closed my eyes. The heat seeped in, invading worn muscles.

In a scant few hours, I would once again be Blood Bound to a woman I love. To my Palma.

I ran a hand over my face and scratched my beard. It had been a long, long time since my Lenore passed.

Since my little family fell apart.

It had been an equally long time since someone captured my heart—my soul—like my Lenore, but Palma did.

I smiled at the thought of her. Her big, brown doe eyes and ash blonde hair that tumbled down her back. Her small waist and generous hips. The beautiful smile that lit up her face whenever she saw me.

My fingers brushed the bracelet I wore. My Lenore gave it to me on the last anniversary of our Blood Binding.

It was the last time we were happy.

Though my Lenore had long been dust in the grave, I couldn't help but feel a pang of guilt. A pang of betrayal at giving my heart, my soul, and myself to another to be Blood Bound for Eternity.

"I'm sorry, Lenore. I am sorry for everything. I am sorry for who I am and for not trying harder to stop our Jaylynn." I closed my eyes and sighed. "I wasn't the father she needed. I was wrong, but I loved her. I did what I thought was right, and I loved you, Lenore. The gods know I never stopped."

I pulled myself out of the tub and dried off. Wrapping the towel about my waist, I went out on the balcony and looked down upon the flower garden Palma planted and tended, the various blossoms blooming Grand Passages round, her magic keeping them alive.

Like my mother, Palma's magic was pure, a stark contrast to my own. Palma was a healer, her magic coming from nature and all the good in this world. My magic, however, came from the darkness of the Abyss. She was everything I wasn't. Gentle and kind. Pure and loving. Just like my Lenore was.

Removing the bracelet, I clutched it in my hand. "I will always love you, Lenore, but it's time I move on. Time, I make a new life with another I love. I am sorry for everything and I—I hope to have your blessing. And your forgiveness."

I looked down at the bracelet, caressing the words I knew by heart:

To my Abe. Forever into Eternity. Love, Lenore.

A breeze picked up, bringing the scent of honeysuckle and lavender, Lenore's favorite. I breathed deeply of the scent surrounding me.

Let me go, Abraham. Your happiness is all I want. I have long since forgiven you. I will always love you.

Lenore's whisper drifted to me on the soft breeze and my guilt, the heaviness I carried, lifted and floated away with it. I made my way back into the room, pressed my lips to the bracelet, and placed it in a drawer, locking it—and the past—away.

Opening the wardrobe, I pulled out the clothes I had purchased for this occasion and dressed.

In two hours, I would be Blood Bound again.

"WELL, WOULD YOU LOOK at that," Sam commented as I exited the house and crossed the yard. He, Lucas, and Bones stood beneath the arbor where Palma and I would be Blood Bound. It was decorated with daisies, Palma's favorite flower, and Willow's Lace, a lacy white moss, the name taken from the spider which produced a similar web.

"He even bought new clothes for the occasion," Lucas said.

Bones sniffed. "And bathed and trimmed his beard."

"Fuck you," I laughed. Though I wouldn't call these men friends, they were Soul Collectors like myself who I often fleeced with card games. Lucas had agreed to perform the binding while Bones and Sam were there to bear witness.

I took a deep breath and rolled my shoulders.

"Nervous?" Bones said, not a hint of mischief nor malice in his tone.

"A bit."

He clapped me on the back. "That woman loves you. How you scored another perfect mate is beyond me."

I raised an eyebrow. "Meaning?"

"Meaning, she is perfect in every way. She knows you, Abe. The real you and she loves you and accepts you." He shook his head. "I could only hope to be half as lucky."

Well, if she doesn't show, I am nothing short of a fool and perhaps my luck is starting to run out.

"She'll be here," Lucas said.

I glanced at him, heart stopping as my eyes caught sight of Palma stepping out from the house onto the grass.

Gods, she was the most beautiful woman I had ever seen. Goddess-like in the way the sun shone on her, white skin almost sparkling in the rays. The three men beside me inhaled sharply.

"You're one fucking lucky guy," Sam muttered, and I had to agree.

Palma's brown eyes met mine, and she smiled. I took her in as she made her way to where I stood. Her hair was loose, a crown of daisies sat atop her head, and she clutched a bouquet of the same. Her dress was a light blue satin, sleeves cut short and square neckline showing an expanse of skin, a sapphire pendant nestled between her breasts. The garment was fitted at the waist, flowing softly about her hips, the train floating behind on the grass as she made her way toward me. Bare feet poked out from beneath her skirts as she walked, and I chuckled at the sight. Even on this day she forwent shoes, preferring the feel of the grass—of nature—beneath her feet.

"Abraham," she sighed softly as she stood before me.

"Palma."

She cocked her head to the side, eyes amused. "Are you nervous? Did you wonder if I would come?"

Per tradition, we had been apart for a week, and I did fear she would not show. "Yes."

She laughed and placed a hand on my cheek. "Silly man. I am yours, and you are mine."

"Always."

"And now it will be more than just words."

We turned to Lucas, who stood back a bit. "Ready?"

I glanced at Palma, who nodded, and I did the same. I held out my left hand, palm up, and she held out her right. Lucas drew his dagger and made a slice across each hand. We grasped the other and our wrists were bound with a black scarf. I looked down at Palma, who smiled up at me and recited the words to bind her.

"I am yours, and you are mine. Blood, life, and time bind us. I swear to protect you and keep you safe. Until my last breath and my soul leaves this place."

She smiled, fingers squeezing my hand. "To you, I pledge in blood and life. To you, on this day, I become your wife. I trust you with all I am until my bones dry and become sand."

I felt a tingling sensation in the hand that was bound to Palma's. The sensation turned to fire that raced up my arm, piercing my heart. I sucked in a breath and clenched my teeth against the pain. Palma whimpered, eyes closed tight, and then the sensation was gone.

We were Blood Bound for eternity.

Lucas clutched our hands. "So, the words have been spoken that will bind Abraham and Palma for eternity. May the gods bless this union and may you have a long life together."

He undid the bind, and I pressed my thumb to my bloody palm, then marked her forehead.

"I am yours for Eternity, Palma DuLocke."

She smiled and marked my forehead the same. "And I am yours, Abraham."

We then signed the documents in blood, further securing our bond and with that, Palma was my wife for all eternity.

She looked up at me, eyes shining with tears, and I leaned down and kissed her. "I love you."

"And I, you."

"Now that that's over with," Lucas said, opening up a bottle of Faeries Blood, "Shall we celebrate?"

I glanced at Lucas, then back to Palma, who looked up at me through lowered lashes, lower lip caught between her teeth.

The look was seductive.

And very telling.

"No." My eyes never left her face. "I think we will celebrate alone." I reached out, grabbed her, and tossed her over my shoulder. Her breathless laughter floated on the breeze. "My house is yours. You know where to stay. I just ask you not to drink all of my spirits," I said, striding past the trio. Lucas clapped me on the back and pressed the bottle into my hand.

"Just in case," he laughed.

I strode through the house and up the stairs to my room with my bride across my shoulder. When I entered, I placed her on the bed and took a long pull from the bottle, then handed it to her.

"Abraham. You're not nervous, are you?" She took a drink, placing the bottle on the bedside table.

"I might be."

She laughed and floated to me on silent feet, arms snaking around my neck. "We have done this hundreds of times," she teased, teeth nipping my chin.

"I know, my heart, but we have not done this as husband and wife."

She laughed softly. "Is it any different?"

I looked down into her beautiful face and pushed a lock of hair behind her ear. "I gave my heart and soul to you. Now I give you all of me. Yes, Palma. This is different."

She stepped away and disrobed, her dress falling to the floor in a soft whoosh of fabric. I looked upon her naked body, creamy white flesh glinting in the rays of the setting sun, and desire bloomed within.

"You are so beautiful. How did I get so lucky?" My throat constricted, making my words sound thick.

"I believe it is I who is lucky," she murmured.

Picking her up in my arms, I strode across the room to the bed and placed her on it. Brown eyes stared up at me and I smiled.

"Now, it is time to have all of you."

"I LOVE YOU, ABRAHAM," Palma said, lips grazing my cheek. We lay in bed, limbs entwined, her head on my chest.

"And I you."

I felt a tug from the Abyss. *Shit.*

Palma pulled back and looked at me. "What's wrong?" Her eyes searched mine, and her face fell into a frown. "Now? Whatever for?"

I clenched my teeth. *What the fuck do you want?*

You, Zedekiah. Here. Now.

Why?

Get your sorry fucking ass here now, *Zedekiah. Do* not *make me ask again.*

Gods damn it.

I knew he was doing this to be pompous. To prove a point, though what that could possibly be, I didn't know.

Pulling away from Palma, I rose and strode to the wardrobe and dressed.

"What does he want?"

I glanced at her. "The fuck if I know," I said, making my way to where she lay. I sat on the edge of the bed and brushed a lock of hair from her face.

"I will be back soon."

She smiled and pulled me down for a long and lingering kiss. "I will be here, Abraham. I am yours."

"Always."

I pulled the shadows around and slipped into the Abyss just outside the door to the throne room. Bones, Lucas, and Sam stood there, and I noticed others arriving as well.

"He summoned you too?" I said, scratching the head of my demon familiar, Bel who was snuggled next to my beard where he often stayed, a soft purr rumbling in his chest. His forked tongue flicked out and tasted the air. Red eyes peered about and his small wings flapped in agitation. While he was small enough to fit in my palm, he was not one to underestimate, as he could grow up to ten times his size when provoked. Or when protecting.

"Yes, though he didn't say why," Sam grumbled.

"He didn't tell me either," I said. Grasping the handle to the room, I turned the knob. "Let's get this over with. You know how much he hates waiting."

I pushed the door open, and we filed into the throne room to find out what was so urgent.

THE THRONE ROOM FILLED up with Soul Collectors and demons. My eyes went to my father, who sat upon his throne, a garish monstrosity made of obsidian. Griffins made the legs and armrest. The only color gracing the black was a braid of purple along the base.

Nightshade, the name given to the throne itself.

His black hair was pulled back. He was dressed smartly in a coat of deep blue velvet, black shirt, snug leather trousers, and polished boots. His neatly manicured fingers tapped the heads of the griffins, the ruby, emerald and sapphire rings that adorned his fingers glinted in the low lamplight.

Pulling my gaze from him, my attention drifted to the floor, to the triangle within the circle. To the objects and words. The channels ran through to each wall. My mind went to what had happened here almost twenty-two Grand Passages earlier.

To Lillyanna and Damiyun.

"Zedekiah." Themesis' voice pulled me from my reverie. I looked up at him. "Take your place."

My eyes went to the golden throne beside him, stomach dropping, and nausea churning within.

"Is there a problem?" he snapped, blue eyes piercing me.

"Of course not, Father." I bowed my head, then made my way to the seat beside him.

To my throne.

"Jaylynn." He called out, a smile playing upon his lips.

I watched my daughter, who wore nothing but her slave collar and gold paint, which covered vulnerable parts, make her way to us, holding a tray with a decanter of wine and glasses. Placing the tray on the ground, she filled two and handed them to us.

"Good girl," he crooned. I watched Jaylynn beam with pride at the pat on the head and the kiss he placed upon her lips. Themesis waved a hand at Jaylynn. "Fill the rest and tend to whatever—needs—they might have," he instructed, and I watched as she moved through the crowd filling glasses. Watched as hands grabbed at her and then led her away to be used.

And abused.

I ground my teeth, hands clenching the chair. A low growl came from Bel, hidden beneath my beard. "Why are we here?"

Themesis glared at me out of the corner of his eye. "We are here because I am still trapped in this fucking prison." His knuckles turned white, and lips curled back in a snarl. "If I had my queen…" he closed his eyes and took a deep breath, fingers relaxed, and he smiled.

"Well. That is neither here nor there. My binds are still weak. They weaken more with every Wielder killed, but they are not weak enough to set me free."

I took a sip of wine. "And?"

He leaned forward in his chair, steepling his fingers beneath his chin, eyes scanning those who stood before him. "The more Wielders that die, the weaker my binds become. What I want," he cast a look over his shoulder at me, "Is for all of you to go out into the world and kill as many as you can. Set me free."

"That is not our job. We collect the souls of those whose contracts have been called," I said.

"And Wielders don't fall into that category?"

"They're a small part," I snapped, sitting forward. Themesis laughed, the sound grating on my nerves. "You are asking us to kill innocents. Send your demons through and leave us to do our job."

"Are you growing soft, Zedekiah? Has that woman of yours turned you from who you are? Shall I bring you back? Remind you where you belong?" His hands clenched the armrests. His magic rolled off him in waves. He was poised, ready to strike. The threat was evident, and I would let nothing happen to my Palma. I sat back in my chair.

"Does anyone else wish to speak up? Wish to have their loved one become a mindless slave like Zedekiah's daughter?"

No one spoke, and Themesis nodded. "That's what I thought. You all will go out. Hunt down and kill all Wielders. Set me free." His words echoed throughout the quiet chamber. "You are dismissed. Do not disappoint me."

The assembled dispersed. I rose to my feet.

"Not you." Themesis crooked a finger, smiling.

Of course not.

I slowly lowered myself back down.

"You are nothing short of a disappointment." His jaw clenched.

"And that surprises you?"

"You are my son. You are of my flesh."

"And I am of my mother's flesh."

"A whore."

"Who you took to your bed. Who you took away from her insufferable life."

If only for a short time.

"She rejected me. She could have had everything."

I snorted. "I hardly call an eternity locked in the Abyss everything."

Themesis turned toward me, and I felt the air leave my body. My chest constricted and I couldn't breathe. Bel hissed and leapt at my father, who caught him and threw him aside. He hit the ground hard, whimpering in pain.

"Watch your tone, boy. I own you. You belong to me, and you will do what I say."

My vision wavered and darkness crept in.

"Do I make myself clear?"

I nodded, gasping for the breath as he released me. Holding my hand out, Bel scampered to me, tail between his legs. Crawling up my arm, he wrapped himself around my neck, burying his head in my beard. Scratching his back in a soothing manner, he relaxed, and a soft purr rumbled through his body.

"That's what I thought. Now, you will do what I ask, or you will not only gaze upon your daughter who does my bidding, but your new wife as well." Blue eyes pierced me. "Do I make myself clear?"

Gritting my teeth, I pulled myself out of the chair. "Yes. Are we through?"

Themesis waved a hand, his look bored. "We are."

I strode across the floor toward the exit, trying hard to block out the sounds coming from my daughter.

"One more thing."

I paused.

"Bring me Damiyun."

THIRTY-SEVEN
PHABIAN

"**S**OME OF THE FOOD stores are growing low. I will appoint someone to have them restocked."

I sat behind my desk in Allendaire's study going through the food and goods ledgers. Allendaire stood with his hands behind his back staring out the window. The sun began to sink below the horizon, rays of yellow and orange danced on his form.

I studied Allendaire as I marked the ledgers and placed them on the desk. He was thin, posture hunched. Deep lines marred his gaunt face and he looked older than his two hundred sixty-eight Grand Passages. He no longer looked to be the strong, majestic ruler of this vast kingdom, and though I lost any love and respect I had for him when he sentenced my Little Princess to death, his was not the only change.

Mouranda, who was rarely seen, did not look well either. The whole palace felt ill. It oozed from the walls, from the whispers of servants. Even Lazaro felt it, many nights we hunkered down in my bed just for comfort and companionship.

"Allendaire. Did you hear me?" *Do you even care?*

Allendaire shook himself. "Of course, I heard you, Phabian. Where were we?"

"Taxes." I pulled the ledger and opened it, frowning at the blank spaces I saw where payment should have been recorded. "What is this? Why are there no numbers logged?"

Allendaire ran a hand over his face with a sigh. "Times are tough. Some of my elves cannot pay."

I clenched my fists, the quill snapping in half. "Is that not the law?" *Did you not send your daughter to be executed because Mouranda is with child?*

Allendaire glared at me. "Of course, it is," he scoffed.

I shoved the ledger across the desk. "Then why are there blank entries? Does the law, your law," I spat, "not state if the coin is not paid then you are to take the deed?"

"Phabian—"

"The law is the fucking law." Slamming my hand on the desk I jumped up, the chair crashing to the floor behind. "You cannot hold it up for some but not others." I slammed the ledger closed. "Those who cannot pay will be given ninety days to give their coin. If they cannot, then they will go to debtor's prison." My eyes met Allendaire's watery ones. "After all, the law is the law, is it not?"

He held up the fucking law when he sentenced Serafin to execution, why couldn't he hold this one up? Our eyes clashed and finally he dropped his gaze to his hands.

"You are right, Phabian. The law is the law. I will pen a decree, they have ninety days to produce the coin or their deed." He took a deep breath. "And if they cannot pay, then they will be sentenced to debtor's prison."

Nodding, I put the ledger down and crossed the room.

"I loved—love—her, Phabian. I held up the law."

I snorted. "Of course, you did. Just as you are doing now."

"Phabian—"

"Are we through here?" Not waiting for a response, I crossed the room and strode out into the hall.

Fuck Allendaire. He could say and do what he wished because he was the king, but I knew his deceit and I had a goal in mind.

Mouranda.

"**C**OME." MOURANDA'S VOICE CALLED out in response to my knock. Opening the door, I stepped inside the dimly lit room. Her eyes met mine, and I braced for her to tell me to get out, like she had many times before.

"Phabian." Her lips curled up in a snarl, rather than a smile. I took a few tentative steps into the room, trying not to show my shock at what I saw.

She was lying in her bed propped up by a mound of pillows, hands folded upon her bulging stomach beneath the blankets. I blinked at the sight. I had seen my Anya with child enough to know this was not normal for three Moon Cycles. Her normally pale skin was whiter still, the blue of her veins startling. She was also painfully thin. Her face was gaunt. Eyes large in their sockets and arms no more than twigs. I watched a vein on her neck pulse with each beat of her heart, waiting for it to stop. She looked old and tired. As if Death was standing outside her door. When she spoke, her voice was raspy, like the nib of a quill scratching across a piece of parchment.

Her lips pulled back in a smile when, just for a second, I tried to delve inside her mind, coming up against a wall. Well, I had tried.

"Do you think me a fool, Phabian? Do you think I would leave myself open to someone with your abilities?"

I crossed my arms and leveled my gaze on her. "Only if you have something to hide. What do you have on Allendaire that would make him abandon his daughter so freely?"

Her eyes narrowed to slits. "I carry the heir. The true heir."

"Do you? And how did this come to be?"

"You have children. I know it has been quite some time since Anya passed, but surely you haven't forgotten the process."

My eyes went to her bulging stomach. I watched the blanket beneath her hands ripple and undulate, serpent like in its movements. A flash of pain crossed her features, and she cried out, a loud howl of agony as the movement continued. Her hands gripped the blanket and sweat beaded her brow. When it was done, she sank back against the pillows, eyes closed and breath ragged.

"I will find out what you did, Mouranda."

She laughed, a look of pain crossing her face. She opened her eyes and looked at me.

"And do what with whatever information you think you will gather? No one will believe a half-breed lover."

Pursing my lips, I left the room, striding through the halls to the library. I sank into a chair, the plush cushions soft, and the high wingback embraced me in a hug. The scent of leather and musty paper swirled on the breeze blowing through the open window. The room was peaceful.

I understood why the library was Lillyanna's favorite place. My visit with Mouranda solidified the fact something was wrong. The way the child—or beast, I wasn't sure—moved inside her was wrong. I thought about Lillyanna and all the times Serafin moved or kicked, the feeling a soft flutter beneath my hand, the impression of a foot pressing against the womb visible just briefly as she flipped and turned. What I saw with Mouranda was something different. And dark. Even her room felt wrong. There was a heaviness about it. A darkness, pressing and suffocating.

An evil hidden inside.

Running a hand over my face, I pulled myself out of the chair, and crossed the floor to the shelves of books. Scanning the titles, my eyes rested on the Tome of the Kings. Pulling the great volume off the shelf, I sank back down in my chair and laid it on my lap. I scanned the page, then settled back to read Karrinian Trounde's story.

This time, though, with a different mindset.

*A*FTER THREE LONG GRAND *Passages, Il'Ekhester is finally ready to be pop-ulated. I sent my best carpenters and masons to construct everything. I am sad to leave Naar'Glon, but our population's growth forced me to cross the Calgonian Sea to Il'Ekhester. My heart is heavy at having to leave the only home I have known, but I am also filled with hope.*

Arybelle celebrated her eighteenth Name Day three days prior to our leaving. It was the day my hands touched her virgin skin and the day I claimed her. She defied my order to leave, locking herself in her room, the sound of her wailing cries echoing through the halls. She was mine, and she had quickly learned her place.

The journey was hard, the weather making it take far longer than it should have. Arybelle's face was sullen, ruby lips drawn down in a pout, as we disembarked. She didn't cry, no doubt the memory of not being able to sit for several weeks still fresh in her mind, but she let me know she was displeased.

Seeing the spires of the castle, one marking each corner, reaching far into the sky, the evening sun glinting off the snow-white marble, made me giddy with anticipation. Goosebumps pricked my skin as I gazed upon the splendor and beauty. Bright colored rugs littered the floor. Vibrant tapestries and lit sconces of pure gold hung on the walls and heavy, intricately carved furniture lined the hallways.

The sun was well below the horizon when we finished our tour and I left Arybelle at the threshold of her room. Kissing her cheek, I bade her good rest, reminding her of the big day ahead.

On the morrow, we were to be Blood Bound.

*I*T WAS THE DAY *of our Blood-Binding.*

I took care in preparing for the event, my servant bathing me and helping me dress in matrimonial attire. I pulled on a vibrant blue tunic, slipped into a pair of purple trousers and blood red boots of the softest suede laced to my knees. A heavy, fur-trimmed robe of magenta was placed around my shoulders, and my servant presented the ceremonial sword. The Pyragaty bone they made it from was as white as snow. The Elven Crest—serpent wrapped around a single rose—etched on the blade. He then handed me the ceremonial dagger, a smaller version of the sword, which would be used for the Blood-Binding.

Rows of benches filled with my people lined the floor. I walked down the aisle, smiling at the Elves who bowed before me and took my place next to the orator in front of my grand throne. A hush fell over the crowd as the doors opened and Arybelle stepped through.

She was breathtaking in her long, form fitting blood red dress. Black roses were stitched into the fabric, and an emerald serpent with ruby eyes was stitched into the right bodice. The train fanned out behind her, floating as she walked down the aisle. Her white hair was loose and flowed about her waist, the sides secured with ruby clips and her eyes—eyes as blue as the deepest sea—were frightened as they met mine.

Taking her hands in mine, I smiled down at her as the orator spoke, and then I unsheathed the dagger and handed it to him. Holding right hands out, palms to the sky, he slashed the blade across tender flesh, then wrapped a red silk scarf around our hands and spoke the words that bound us in blood for eternity. The scarf was then removed, and we then marked the other with a bloody thumbprint upon forehead, signaling to all that we belonged to each other.

With ceremony complete, it was time for the festivities to commence and though the lure of food, dance and drink was great, I was most eager to solidify the relationship with my queen. Picking her up, I tossed her into the air, catching her, and then throwing her over my shoulder. The room erupted with cheers and whistles, the sound of feet pounding on floor and fists upon the table were like thunder, and I laughed as I made my way out with my young, struggling bride upon my shoulder.

Arybelle fought me when the time came. Tiny fists pummeled me when I pushed her to the bed. Nails scratched when I held her down and spread her legs. A scream tore through her, the sound echoing off the walls of her bedroom when I entered her.

Her screams heightened my arousal. I reveled in the pain, the screams, and the tears as I made her mine over and over and over again.

I SAT BACK AND closed my eyes with a sigh. I felt for the young Arybelle, and shame washed over me for being no better than Karrinian. For claiming my Anya—my own sister—in much the same way he claimed his queen.

For forcing the bond.

For fucking her to give me children who would keep the race alive.

"I'm sorry, Anya," I whispered, though I knew my words were not enough.

Flipping through the pages, I came to the next king.

Bodwin.

*I*T IS WITH GREAT *sadness that I fill the Tome with these words.*

On this day, my father, Karrinian Trounde and my brother, Halston, were both victims of a horrible and tragic hunting accident to which I bore witness.

With the words of our ancestors—go into Eternity as you lived your life—I send them off with a heavy heart. And as a Trounde—and a descendant of Karrinian—I will carry his legacy. I take the throne and will carry on his vision of our bright future, and one day we will move on to dominate.

HOW HAD I NOT seen any of this. Blind loyalty so deep seemed like a weak excuse. Our history lessons were flawed. Fuck, but everything was wrong. Had I not left to find Serafin, had I not seen Arybelle and Vanla with my own eyes, would I still be blinded?

Flipping through the pages I came up on Finlay, Bodwin's youngest son who was the chosen heir and who somehow survived attempts on his life, as did Nehem, Terrin's father. Reluctantly, I flipped to Allendaire's entries.

It saddens me that my father, Terrin, is dead. My sister Rahina fed him poison and now she is locked beneath the palace in the dungeon awaiting death. And those who decided to go against the Shadow Elf Law and procreate outside our race will feel my wrath. They...

"Phabian."

I looked up from the Tome, my eyes meeting Krall's who stood in the doorway, helmet tucked under arm, armor glinting in the sunlight.

I swallowed hard, closing the book I held on my lap.

"Armor up. The king has requested your presence in the search for Serafin."

Fuck.

THRITY-EIGHT
DAMIYUN

SITTING BACK IN THE chair in the corner of the tavern, I sipped my ale. A bard played a wind instrument in the corner, the tune drifting through the crowd and a fire blazed in the hearth, warming the room. The atmosphere was comforting to me. Settling back in my chair, I gazed upon the patrons. A couple toasted their anniversary in the corner, they seemed to have better fare to eat. Across the room a rowdy group sat around their table tossing dice. A man cheered the moment he won, nearly tipping his chair. His companions clapped him on the back. Axes thudded against the other wall.

The door opened and laughter followed. I looked up. It was the wanted princess and her friends. I watched them cross the room, taking a seat at an empty table. Ghent pulled Serafin onto his lap, her arms going around his neck, his mouth catching hers in a long kiss.

Uma's eyes met mine, and I watched her excuse herself. Slipping around the table she weaved her way through the people to where I sat. Flagging the serving wench, I ordered two more drinks. Uma took the empty seat in front of me, hands clasping the tankard set on the table.

"You are here for her."

"No," I chuckled over my drink. "I just happen to be staying at the inn."

Uma shook her head.

"I did not ask to do this," I said.

"But you agreed."

"I had little choice." I looked over at Serafin who looked happy, content, and my heart hurt for her. "No. I do not wish to take her."

Uma opened her mouth to speak when the door banged open. Looking in the direction of the noise, my eyes took in six figures dressed in silver armor; an emerald serpent wrapped around the stem of an obsidian rose was hammered into the breast plate. Helmets with pointed ears sat on heads. The soldiers looked around the crowd, the eyes of the one in front went to Serafin who was oblivious of their entrance.

Fuck.

"Serafin Trounde, by order of the King, you are under arrest," his voice rang loud through the tavern. Murmurs rippled like water as the soldiers strode through. Serafin looked up, her pale skin turning whiter still. The armed elves shoved their way through the crowd to where the princess sat.

"Fuck." Jumping up, I grabbed Shadow Blade and shoved my way over to where she sat, positioning myself between her and them. Uma stood beside me, arms crossed.

"What is this?" Ghent's voice came from behind.

Fuck it all, but he did not know.

"Get her, Phabian." The elf I assumed was in charge commanded. The man to his left hesitated. I held Shadow Blade in front of me, eyes on them.

"Phabian?" Serafin's voice was soft.

The one named Phabian removed his helm. Serafin's eyes widened, and she slipped off Ghent's lap.

Phabian's throat bobbed as he swallowed. "Sera," he breathed, the word filled with sadness and longing.

"What is this?" Ghent asked again. I glanced over my shoulder at him. He slowly rose, eyes going from Serafin to the soldiers and back. She chewed her lip, eyes dropping to the floor.

"I'm sorry," she whispered, and my blood boiled at her words.

"I gave you an order, Phabian."

"Krall," Phabian sighed.

Holding Shadow Blade up, I stepped forward. "If you want her, you will have to go through me."

Krall laughed. "There are six of us and one of you."

I pulsed magic through the sword, the Pyragaty bone becoming engulfed in flames.

"Wielder," a voice called out, breaking the tense silence, and chaos ensued. People jumped up from their chairs, the sound of blades clearing scabbards rang through the air along with curses.

Gods damn it, can't anything be easy? Pulling back my magic, I sheathed my sword and grabbed Serafin. "Let's go," I said, dragging her behind as I pushed my way through the angry crowd to the back entrance.

She yanked out of my grasp. "No." Standing on her tip toes, she looked through the crowd growing angrier by the moment.

"You will either die by the hands of the elves, or by the hands of the Nons if you do not come with me."

"But—"

Grabbing her arm again, I dragged her behind, ignoring the flurry of curses flowing from her mouth. Crashing through the door, I pulled her to a stop, looking up and down the street at the people who went about their day, oblivious of what was happening in the tavern.

"Let me go." Serafin yanked her arm in my firm grasp, angry blue eyes glaring up at me.

"No."

Spinning around, her knee connected with my groin, and I let her go, dropping to my knees. Gritting my teeth against the pain, I jumped up and ran after her. Grabbing her around the waist I dragged her to the ground, straddling her hips.

"Get the fuck off me, you beast." Her fists pummeled me and she tried to buck me off. Grabbing her wrists, I pinned them to the ground, my eyes on the door we came through.

"Listen, Princess. Do you want to die? Because I can assure you if you go back in the tavern or stay here, you will."

She stopped bucking and I relaxed my grip, if only slightly. "But Phabian..."

"I don't care about Phabian, or Ghent, or Uma. I only care about getting your ass some place safe."

Rising, I pulled her up and tossed her over my shoulder.

She struggled in my grasp as I raced to the barn. "What is this? Put me down you brute."

"Hush." I dumped her on the ground, clamped a hand over her mouth, and hunkered down in Xander's stall, pulling her onto my lap. She squirmed in my grasp, teeth grazing the hand on her mouth.

"Stop," I snarled, freezing at the sound of feet inside the barn. Xander stepped forward, his body blocking ours. My eyes watched the soldiers as they entered the stable. I looked at Serafin, shaking my head and putting a finger to my lips. She sagged in my arms, and removing my hand from her mouth I pulsed magic through my body, cloaking us.

"Where the fuck is she?" Krall snapped.

I held Serafin close. There was no fucking way I was going to let her go, especially knowing she would run to Phabian. Her wide eyes met mine.

Don't move and don't say a word, I mouthed.

But what about Phabian? Her voice filled my head and for a brief moment, I faltered, almost letting go of my magic.

"She came in here with that man. I saw him," a soldier said.

Krall and the others were close. I held Serafin closer, my eyes locked on hers. She barely breathed as they walked around the stable, checking every stall, and when they were gone, I released my cloak.

"Princess," I said, looking down at her. Her lips pulled back in a snarl and fingers curled into claws, ready to strike.

"Who are you?"

"Damiyun Rayne. I—"

"I am not going with a Rayne." Her voice shook.

" This is my home. I want to talk to Phabian."

I rubbed my eyes with a sigh. Why can't anything ever be easy? "If you stay here, you will die. If you go find Phabian, you will die."

Serafin tossed her hair. My ears picked up the sound of pounding footsteps in the street.

"Fuck it all." I had enough with her petulance, and we didn't have enough time. Picking her up, I tossed her across Xander's back. She wiggled off with a huff.

"I have a horse."

"Then get the fuck on him and let's go," I snapped, swinging up onto Xander's back.

"It's a she."

For the love of the fucking gods...

"Serafin Trounde," a voice barked from the door. "On order of the king, you are under arrest. Surrender and you will be offered leniency," Krall said, and I wanted to laugh at his words.

"Alright. Let me get Yasmine, and I will go," Serafin said.

I whipped around and looked at her, opening my mouth to speak.

I'm not, her voice filled my head, and I closed my mouth. *I am to be executed. I'm not stupid. I will not go back to lose my head.*

But you wanted to go back to Phabian.

She looked at him, but said nothing. I rolled my shoulders, the tension heavy. There would be a fight, I knew. Clenching my fists, I pulled my magic—the flame and that of the Shadow Elves—close, ready to unleash it at a moment's notice. Serafin stepped out of the stall beside Xander, guiding out a horse the color of snow. Swinging up onto her back, she looked at me.

"Let's go."

I stared at her.

Get on your fucking horse. Her voice rang in my head. Xander stepped forward, shoving me with his head. Grabbing the reins, I swung up into the saddle. Serafin sat tall on her mount and guided her forward.

What was she doing?

Guiding Xander behind, I marked each elf standing in the doorway, and I pulled my magic closer still.

"Serafin Trounde—"

"I know," she sighed, tossing her hair. "The king sent you to get me. Well, here I am."

I kept my eyes on the six warriors as Serafin guided her mount forward. I felt magic surge, but it wasn't from her. It was from the elves standing to Krall's right and left.

I didn't know what was happening, if these two were targeting Serafin or what the fuck she was going to do. I just knew I had to somehow keep her safe. Drawing Shadow Blade, I held it out. "Run."

Serafin glanced at me, her face screwed up in confusion. "What—"

"Run, damn it."

Xander nipped her mount's backside, the horse rearing up and bolting past the soldiers, knocking them to the ground. My eyes marked each elf in the doorway. Krall's eyes narrowed on my blade, which burned.

"How do you have that?"

"It was given to me. I was told it belongs to me."

Krall took a step forward. "That blade was Karrinian's. It belongs to Allendaire. Who are you to think you can wield it? An elven blade forged from—"

"A Pyragaty bone? Etched with the," I pulled my magic back and ran my fingers up the blade. "the Shadow Elf crest?" Reaching behind, I sheathed it. "It was given to me. Apparently, it does not belong to your king." I settled my hands on the pommel of the saddle.

You. A voice rang in my head, my eyes meeting a pair filled with shock. *Rahina's son.*

I am someone's son.

I rolled my shoulders. I was bored, and I needed to know where the Princess was, and that she was safe.

"I'm done here." I heeled Xander forward.

"You aren't. How do you have that sword?" Krall said, stepping forward, the three elves behind drawing closer.

Phabian, and the one to Krall's left, hung back.

Fuck, but I did not wish to hurt anyone, regardless if they were here for the princess.

Go, the voice rang in my head again.

I glanced at him. *Where is she?*

Pictures flashed in my mind in rapid succession and I understood.

You will keep her safe.

It wasn't a question. For the love of the fucking gods, why does this fall to me?

Yes, of course.

Digging my heels into Xander's sides, he leapt forward, running through the elves blocking the entrance. Magic surged behind, but I did not look to see what was happening. Urging Xander forward, we ran through the streets, dodging carts and people, some of which were ready to kill the Wielders. My heart pounded in my chest as I thought of Serafin. She had a head start.

She is fine. She made it home, a voice rang in my head. How the fuck did he know what I was thinking? *Get to her. Keep her safe. Please, Damiyun.*

My nostrils flared at the intrusion as I raced through the roads, finally coming upon a house in the woods. Bringing Xander to a halt, I swung down from his back and looked at the quaint home before me. Sighing, I walked up the steps and raising a hand, I knocked on the cherry door.

"Damiyun," Uma said, pulling the door open. "You told me I would have time with her."

I sighed. "I did not ask for this. Where is she?"

Uma hesitated.

I stepped forward. "If you want the elves to come here, the Nons to take what you have, tell me to leave and I will."

"He's right." My eyes went to Serafin who stepped behind Uma. "I—our—being here is putting you and other Wielders at risk."

Uma turned around. "But—"

"She will be safe with me." She turned back to me. "You will always know where she is and you are always welcome to visit. As I said, I am taking her to L'Ochal first, then Val'I'Victorous." I looked at Serafin. "Pack what you think you will need until we get to my home."

"I'm ready," she said, holding up her saddle bags. "But Ghent—"

"You can pen him when you are settled. I will not keep you from those you are close to." Even though every fiber of my being told me to keep her far away from that boy. And though I longed to go home, I would make that trip as brief as possible, if only to hand the Princess over to Barlack.

"Let's go, then," I said, pushing past Uma. "I suspect it won't take long to find you." Especially since one of the elves used his mind invasion on me to tell me where she was.

Hurrying out to the horses, I swung up on Xander, and Serafin swung up on Yasmine and clutched the reins.

"Where are we going?"

Heeling Xander toward the road, I glanced over my shoulder.

"Home."

THIRTY-NINE
SERAFIN

DIGGING MY HEELS INTO Yasmine's sides, I followed Damiyun to the road. If it wasn't for Phabian's voice in my mind urging me to go with him, I would have fled. Instead, I listened and went back to Uma's to gather my things. Where would we go?

"Sera." A door slammed and Uma's voice rang out through the house. I looked up from the saddle bags I was packing looking at Uma who stood in the doorway. "You're leaving."

I shoved a pair of trousers and a top in the bag. "I have to."

Uma sat down on the edge of the bed, eyes on her hands. "I wish I could tell you what I know." She looked up, golden eyes on me. "But I can't."

I squeezed her hand. "I know."

"He will take care of you."

And I knew that, too. *Go with him, my Little Princess. Trust me with this,* Phabian had said, and though I knew nothing about the handsome man who was going to risk his life for me, I believed Phabian and Uma.

Shaking the thoughts, I guided Yasmine in step with Damiyun. "How far is this L'Ochal?"

"Far enough."

I rolled my eyes. "Alright then. Why should I go with you again? Besides Uma trusting you?"

Damiyun sighed, eyes going to the sky, hands tightening on the reins. "Because the fucking knights you saw and the Nons in this gods forsaken town are after you."

"But why you?"

Damiyun took a deep breath. "Go on back to Uma's house. Hunker down in your bed but I can assure you, the elves will come and the Nons will come. What will you do when that happens, Princess?"

"How can I trust a Rayne?"

Though Ghent was a Suppressor, he never felt like a threat. Admittedly, he did not know I was a Wielder. Not until today. Who was to say this Damiyun wasn't a Suppressor, taking me to the Suppressor Compound? He was a Rayne, after all. Though he also wielded Shadow Blade, a sword lost for centuries. It had disappeared after Karrinian died and rightly belonged to Allendaire. Perhaps my questions should start there. "How do you have Shadow Blade?"

"It was given to me."

"It's been lost."

He snorted. "Apparently not."

I slowed Yasmine down. "Who gave it—"

A screech from the woods cut my words off. Yasmine danced on her hooves and Xander bucked.

"Fuck," Damiyun cursed.

The screech was a sound I remembered from when I was left in the woods to survive on my twelfth Name Day. The sun was rapidly descending below the horizon, and we were outside.

"Damiyun." My voice was just above a whisper, and I tried to keep the fear at bay. I moved Yasmine closer to him.

"We need to secure shelter. We have maybe an hour to set up camp and our perimeter," he said, heeling his mount into the woods.

Another screech hit my bones and a giant beast flew above, blocking out the crescent moon. Yasmine bucked and danced on her hooves. I gently squeezed my legs and patted her neck, then guided her into the woods behind Damiyun. He swung down from his mount. Another scream sounded and I leapt off Yasmine, knocking into Damiyun.

"What was that?" Looking up, I saw a beast flying and once again, I was brought back to my twelfth Name Day, and I shuddered.

"We need to mark a perimeter with torches and light a big campfire. Gather as much timber as you can carry and bring it to me."

While he rooted around for thick logs to jam into the ground, I gathered as many leaves, twigs, and brush I could carry and brought it to him. Wrapping it around the posts, he set it on fire with his magic, then made a large campfire.

Damiyun pulled a few bottles of spirits out of his saddle bags, before he settled down on the ground beside me. Close, but not too close. Our mounts, sensing danger, moved close as well.

"Back to Shadow Blade," I said as he pulled the cork out of a bottle and took a long drink. He rolled his eyes, which glowed a light yellow in the dimming light.

"Barlack Satow, king of the Wilde Elves gave it to me."

I opened my mouth to speak, a screech and the sound of flapping wings above cutting off anything I was about to say. Looking up, a form blocked the crescent moon for a moment. My blood ran cold and I scooted closer to Damiyun. Grabbing the bottle from his hand, I took a long drink. The liquid burned a path down my throat and I sputtered.

"Easy, Princess," Damiyun said, taking the bottle back.

"Why would he give you a sword, which belongs to Allendaire? That sword has been passed down to every heir that has ever sat the Shadow Elf throne."

"And your father is not the heir. My mother Rahina was the chosen heir."

I laughed at his words. "Right. So why did she poison Karrinian if she was to rule?"

"She didn't. That was your father's doing."

I chewed my lip. Though his words were far from what I had grown up believing, how exactly could I doubt them when the king had sentenced me to death and sent soldiers to find me? I was sure Phabian was forced into the search. I know in my heart he would not have gone willingly.

"Look what he did to you, Princess." His voice was soft. He handed me the next bottle and I took a drink. My head swam from the spirits and lack of food, though not in an unpleasant way. It dulled the hurt of the truth he spoke.

"Do you have illusion magic too?" I released the magic that hid my ears.

Damiyun grasped the bottle, his long fingers brushing mine as he took it back. "No. They were clipped when I was born."

"Clipped? How savage."

Damiyun laughed openly as he brought the bottle to his lips. "No more savage than normal."

My ears burned at his words, though I knew them to be true.

Another scream rocked the night, the sound like a child being eviscerated, and my blood ran cold. Wind picked up and Damiyun leapt to his feet.

"Fuck. Wraiths."

Striding to the perimeter he used his fire magic to bring the torches back to life. Holding his hands apart, a ball of light manifested.

Elven magic. He wasn't lying, but was he who he claimed to be?

Another scream pierced the air, and Damiyun threw the light ball into the darkness. Whatever beast it hit wailed in agony. A growl came from behind me and I raced to my feet, pulling my magic and making a large ball of light. My mouth went dry at the sight of the specters. White, formless specters glided through the woods, their wails deafening. Frightening. Long, bony fingers reached out. I watched them advance, and I could not move.

"Throw the ball." Damiyun's voice made me jump. Hoisting the ball of light, I hurled it at the ghastly creatures making their way toward me. The object hit the intended target, the being exploding in a spray of smoke.

Screeches came from behind me as Damiyun fought the Wraiths on his side, throwing balls of light in rapid succession. I quickly formed another ball, my heart dropping at seeing almost a dozen demons advancing from the dark woods beyond. If there were this many coming at me, how many was Damiyun facing? How many were coming from the other sides?

There was no way we could keep this up. No way we could defeat them. Not without burning out.

Or dying.

Another beast roared from the darkness. The sound shook the ground and I knew it had to be enormous.

This was it, I knew. Had I just stayed at Uma's today, I wouldn't be in this situation, facing my death again. I looked over at Damiyun whose magic winked out. Making his way to the campfire, he tossed some logs on and sat down.

"Sit down, Princess. We're safe."

I laughed. "Did you not see all the beasts out there? Did you not hear the one who just roared?"

Damiyun pulled the cork from another bottle and took a drink. "Sit. And yes, I heard. He is on our side."

I slowly sat beside him. "What do you mean?" Holding the bottle out to me, I grasped it and took another long drink in an attempt to block out the wails, roars, and screams outside the fire perimeter. Warmth spread through my chest.

"I mean that beast who rocked the ground is not a foe."

I took another long drink off the bottle.

"Easy, Princess," Damiyun said. Blinking hard, I tried to focus on him as he snatched the bottle from my grasp.

"Explain how that beast isn't a foe." I squinted at him and my words sounded slurred to my ears.

He ran a hand over his face. The light from the fire cast an eerie glow over his features. His eyes looked haunted, and every now and then they glowed yellow.

"It—It's complicated, Princess. Just know you are safe. I won't let anything bad happen to you."

Snatching the bottle back I took another drink, my eyes on him.

"Princess—"

"My name is Serafin, in case you didn't know," I said, tossing my hair over my shoulders. Fuck, but that made the world tilt.

Damiyun chuckled. "I know your name, Princess." He took the bottle back. "I think you've had more than enough."

I glared at him. Who did he think he was? Though he might be right. The world swam before my eyes. Even squinting at him didn't help see better. My stomach lurched, and bile rose up my throat.

I was going to be sick.

Turning away from him, I fell to my hands, my stomach heaving. Hands gently pulled my hair away from my face.

"Let it out," Damiyun said, not unkindly.

My stomach lurched again, and whatever I drank spilled out onto the ground.

"Shit," he swore with a laugh.

I glared at him for a moment before more came up.

"You're alright," he said, gently rubbing my back. I carefully turned my head to look at him. His thumb brushed the corners of my mouth and his eyes searched my face.

"I'm fine," I said. Moving away from the mess I made, I stretched out on the ground, pulling my cloak close. A shiver ran through my body as coldness seeped through, and I wiggled closer to the fire.

Arms circled me and I was pulled close.

"What—"

"Hush, Princess. I'll keep you warm," Damiyun said, a laugh in his voice.

Warmth enveloped me, and I settled into his embrace, despite everything inside that told me not to.

FORTY

Y HEAD POUNDED, MY mouth felt thick, and the rising sun was far
too bright. Untangling myself from Damiyun's embrace, I sat up.
Why had I allowed him to sleep with me? The world tilted and my stomach
lurched. Leaning over, I dry heaved, stomach aching.

"I told you not to drink so much." Damiyun's voice tinged with amusement came from behind.

I shot him a glare over my shoulder. "You did a piss poor job at stopping me."

"Is that so?" He raised an eyebrow as he stood.

"Yes, that is so," I said, rising unsteadily to my feet.

Damiyun chuckled, steadying me with his hand. "You are going to be a handful," he muttered under his breath as he made his way to the horses. Securing his saddle bags to his mount, he swung up into the saddle. I looked at Yaz who seemed so very far away. Clicking my tongue, she walked to where I stood, much to Damiyun's amusement. I swung up onto her back, clutching her neck as the world pitched, along with me, and I almost fell off. Damiyun's laughter filled the silence.

"I am so glad you find me so amusing." I heeled Yasmine forward. "As though you have never had too much to drink before."

"Oh, I have," Damiyun said, falling in step beside me. "It's what helps me sleep and keeps the terrors at bay."

"Terrors?"

He shrugged. "Think about what we battled last night only it's inside your head and within the walls keeping you safe."

"I don't understand."

"No, I don't supposed you would." His words were tinged with sadness and pain, and for an unknown reason, my heart broke.

"So, help me to."

He looked at me, then shook his head. "Tell me, Princess," the corners of his mouth twitched, "What could you have done to make you wanted? And so fiercely?"

I chewed my lip. How much did I want to tell this stranger? Though how would he know Allendaire's name? Or Rahina? And why would he have Shadow Blade if not—I shook my head.

"Does it even matter?" No, I would not tell him.

Not yet, though there was something about him, something tugging on my mind telling me to trust him, and it wasn't Phabian's voice.

"Not to me, no, but to them?" His eyes pinned me. "To them, it matters which makes my job that much more difficult."

"Where are we going?"

Damiyun slumped slightly in the saddle, a longing look crossing his face. "Home," he said, glancing at me. "I have no intentions of claiming a throne."

"But you claimed Shadow Blade."

His jaw clenched. "Not my choice. Nothing in my life has been my choice, Princess. I didn't grow up pampered and loved. In truth, I was beaten almost every day for being what I am, and Arden? My brother? He sent the Suppressors after me on my fourteenth Name Day." Pulling his shirt up, my eyes looked at the "S" branded on the left side of his chest. The same brand Ghent had. "No, I am not one of them," he said, answering the question I was about to ask. "I had no choice."

"I'm sorry, Damiyun."

"As am I."

We rode in silence though I could not stop myself from sneaking glances at him. He sat straight in the saddle; reins held loosely in his hands. He had broad shoulders, thick arms and muscular thighs that gently guided his horse as he rode. Gray eyes scanned the woods. His long, white hair fell just below his shoulders, tied back with leather. A few strands had come loose, framing his face, which I took in. Strong jawline, high cheekbones, and sharp nose, with a slight bump on the bridge. A light pink scar graced his left cheek from below the eye to the jaw, and while it marred his otherwise flawless features, it didn't make him ugly.

Rather, it made him even more attractive.

"So, what's the verdict?"

"What?"

He turned his head, eyes dancing with amusement. "Did I pass your scrutiny?"

"What?"

Dropping the reins, he held his arms out. "Do I meet your approval?" A smile tugged his lips.

Sitting high in my saddle, I dug my knees into Yasmine's sides, guiding her ahead.

"No."

Damiyun's chuckle followed behind and my ears burned at the sound.

Fucker.

IT'S ABOUT FUCKING TIME," Damiyun muttered, heeling Xander into a faster pace down the winding road stretching out before us. He pulled his mount to a halt at the top of a hill, and I reined Yasmine up beside him.

"Home," he said, and I heard the longing and sadness in his voice. Following his gaze, I saw a large house to the left, away from the road, surrounded by woods on three sides. He glanced at me, lips curling up in a slight smile, then spurred Xander into a gallop and raced toward his home. His child-like laughter floated back to me on the breeze, and I couldn't help but smile at the joy radiating from him.

Laughing myself, I heeled Yasmine toward his house, pulling up beside him in front of the manor.

"Master Rayne," a man greeted as he opened the heavy double doors made of oak.

Damiyun jumped off his horse with a smile and embraced the small, thin, and balding man, then pulled away.

"Levin. I am pleased my letter found you."

"I admit I was surprised. It has been—"

"Far too long." Damiyun looked around the property. "You did an excellent job fixing the place up. I admit I let it go."

"Yes, well, it took some work."

Damiyun chuckled. "No doubt, my friend. Shall we?"

Levin nodded, brown, beady eyes looking at me. "I have had your room prepared, though I didn't know you would have a—guest—with you."

"Nor did I," Damiyun said, looking at me.

Swinging down from Yasmine, I folded my arms and leveled my eyes on Damiyun, who turned back to Levin.

"I will settle her in," he said, squeezing the small man's shoulder briefly. "Let's go, Princess," he strode up the stairs and into the house. He paused in the entryway, eyes scanning the surroundings, and I looked about as well. To the left, a grand staircase spiraled up to another level. Black marble graced the floor and wood paneled the walls. I followed Damiyun on down the hall that spilled out into a large sitting room, noting the windows that let in the cheery sunshine and the heavy furniture that graced the room. A set of doors spanned the wall opposite, opening to a patio and courtyard beyond.

I looked around and couldn't help but gape at the opulence. Intricately carved furniture, tables with heavy crystal vases filled with flowers sitting atop. Chandeliers of diamonds and crystal hanging from the ceiling. Sconces made of gold. Expensive tapestries hung in a random way on the walls, and expensive rugs dotted the floor. Damiyun most definitely did not appear to be of the sort to afford such luxuries.

He crossed the room and stood in front of a large clock. The giant pendulum swung; the loud ticking resonated through the room. He looked up at the face, raising a hand and placing it on the glass. His expression was unreadable, though his shoulders straightened, and he took a deep breath.

"Time goes on. The past is done," he whispered, and then stepped away. "Let me show you to your room," he said, striding past me.

I followed him up the staircase to the second floor, whose hall was no less ostentatious. He paused for a beat outside the first closed door on the right. He reached out and softly caressed the oak.

"No," he said softly, and then continued down the hall to the next door. Turning the handle, he pushed the door open and stepped aside, gesturing for me to enter.

I looked around the spacious room. A large, four-poster bed was to my right, white canopy above and thick curtains tied to the mahogany posts. The mattress looked thick and plush, red velvet cover piped in gold graced the top. Across from the bed were doors that spanned the walls, windows looking out upon a small garden within a great lawn and woods beyond. To the right was a seating area in front of a large, unlit fireplace and a wardrobe, chest of drawers, vanity and tables took up the rest of the room and a heavy, porcelain claw-foot tub sat behind a partition.

"I can have your serving girl draw you a bath if you desire," Damiyun's voice pulled me from my awe.

Serving girl?

"Yes, that would be lovely. Thank you."

Nodding, he took a step back. "You can take this eve's meal here or with me if you choose. I will send for you when it's time. For now, bathe and rest."

"Thank you," I said again as he slipped out of the room and closed the door.

I crossed to the doors that spanned the wall and pulled them open, stepping out onto the balcony. Leaning on the stone wall, I looked down upon the garden. It stretched across the lawn toward the woods. The flowers grew lush. The bushes were trimmed into topiary, swans to the left side and another bird I did not recognize to the right. Damiyun was most definitely a man of mystery. While I didn't think him poor, I didn't think he owned estate such as this. I watched the workers tend the flowers and lawn for a bit, then went back in and stretched out on the bed.

It was like sinking into a soft pile of feathers. Sighing, I sank deeper still, sleep taking me almost as soon as my eyes closed.

T HE SOUND OF BIRDS chirping and bright light roused me. Opening my eyes, I momentarily thought I was home. Back in my bed in Il'Ekhester, the white canopy above telling me I was not. A flash of disappointment and longing stabbed at me as I sat up, tossing the blanket off.

When had I grabbed that?

Shaking myself, I looked around, eyes spying a silver tray on a table on the balcony, white card with writing scrawled propped up against it. Curious, I slipped out of bed, padded outside, and picked up the note.

Princess,

I hope you had a good rest. I didn't have the heart to wake you. If you wish a bath, you only have to ask Pietra. If you're hungry, there are pastries beneath the cover, or you can join me in the dining room.

-Damiyun

Putting the note down, I had to laugh at the formal tone of the invite. Days prior, he was making me blush and angering me with his words and questions. Now he was formally requesting my presence for a meal?

I peeked beneath the cover, and, taking a sweet, I washed up in the basin, then crossed the room and opened the door.

"Ah. Mistress Trounde. You're awake. Are you joining Master Rayne for the morning meal?" A young woman, close to my age, stood in the hall, eyes on the pastry I hastily shoved into my mouth.

"Yes, I am," I said. "And please. Call me Serafin. Am I to assume you're Pietra?"

She smiled and spread her skirts out in a curtsy. "At your service, Miss—Serafin."

"Take me to Damiyun, then," I said, falling in step beside her. I looked about as we walked through the house, again taking in the finery. The sturdy furniture had to cost a fortune. Colorful rugs that covered the marble floor. Tapestries on the walls showed hunting scenes. Stained-glass windows with wildlife and forest imagery casting bright colors upon the walls and floor.

Such opulence belied the person I had traveled with.

Damiyun seemed a simple man. Cunning and humble in his ways. Smart and prudent. I didn't take him for the lavish sort.

"Is this all Damiyun's?"

Pietra glanced at me. "Yes."

"How did he obtain the funds for such a place?" *No doubt in a nefarious way.*

"His father was a trader, and when he died, he took over."

"It's quite impressive. A bit grand for one person."

"Oh, he didn't always live here alone."

"So, he has a family?" I knew about his brother, Arden, but that was all. I wanted to laugh. Damiyun was the farthest thing from the family type.

"He was Blood—"

"Pietra." A voice cracked like a whip.

We stopped walking and turned in the direction it came from. A plump, older woman, brown hair piled in a bun on top of her head, stood with fists on hips.

"Do you think it's prudent to be spreading gossip, words of which you know nothing about Master Rayne in his own home?"

Pietra shifted on her feet; gaze trained on the floor. "No, ma'am."

"Then why are you?"

Her eyes met the other woman's, a slight hint of fear in them.

"I apologize," I blurted. "I was inquiring about Damiyun's home. It seems a bit large for one person. Pietra was just answering my questions."

The woman pursed her lips. "Yes. Well. There are some things best left unspoken. Some things left buried," she snapped. "After you have taken Mistress Trounde to the dining room, come find me, please." She turned on her heel and strode away.

Pietra exhaled a shaking breath. "Thank you."

"I only spoke the truth."

Though the woman's words did pique my curiosity, as did the strange words Damiyun uttered when he looked at the clock.

Stopping at a doorway, Pietra motioned with her hand. "The dining room," she said, then scurried away. I stepped inside and looked around. It was a good-sized room. Floor to ceiling windows lined the right side, brilliant sunshine pouring through, sconces and tapestries breaking up the space between. To the left, double doors opened to a stone slab with chairs and a table. A pleasant breeze blew through, the scent of the advancing spring drifted in. Down the center of the room was a large table.

Damiyun sat at the head. A large, unlit fireplace loomed behind him. He lounged casually in his chair, eyes dancing with amusement. His hair was loose, except for the sides pulled back and braided, face clean-shaven. He wore a light blue silk shirt, sleeves rolled up to the elbows, top three buttons undone, revealing his smooth white chest through the opening. Gray trousers and polished leather boots came just below the knee finished the ensemble.

He lounged casually in his chair, eyes dancing with amusement.

Compared to what he was like while traveling, he was light, almost worry free. I took the chair to his left, painfully aware of his gaze and scent. An earthy, manly mix of pine, cloves, and rain. I felt myself heat as the smell drifted on the breeze surrounding me, a small flame of desire blooming inside. He sat forward, placing his elbows on the table, gray eyes on me, a smile on his lips.

"Do I look more... princely?"

I sniffed. "You clean up alright."

He laughed and sat back, arms resting comfortably on the armrests, long legs stretched out, ankles crossed.

"Did you sleep well?"

"I did, thank you."

He nodded, head turning toward a door that opened behind and to the right. A few servants entered the room carrying trays of food. Pastries, bread, boiled eggs. One of them came with a platter of meat, cheese, and a variety of fruits. There was far more food than either of us could eat.

"What's left goes to the servants," he said, as though reading my thoughts. Grabbing a plate, he began piling it with food. "What they don't finish—or want—is taken to feed the poorer section of the village, though it's been quite some time since that's happened."

I shook my head as I made up my plate.

"What?"

I glanced at him, slicing an egg in half, and taking a bite. "You are not the person I thought you were."

"Oh?" He put down his fork and folded his hands. "Tell me, Princess. What sort of person do you think I am?"

Leaning forward, I propped my elbows on the table, resting my chin on fists, and locked eyes with him.

"Cocky. Conceited. Insensitive."

His lips twitched.

"Rude, brutal, and rather annoying." I sat back and folded my arms.

"Is that all?"

"For now. I'm sure my list will grow."

He chuckled softly and cut a piece of meat. "Well, I've been perceived as far worse."

"That's not surprising."

"My turn," he said, looking at me again.

"What?"

"Well, if we're playing first impressions, it's only fair I give you mine."

I nibbled on a cheese pastry and sat back. "Fair enough."

His eyes swept over me as he slowly chewed and damn if my face didn't heat again beneath his intense scrutiny. He placed his fork on his plate. "Hmmm. Entitled. Spoiled. Stubborn." He sat back, finger tapping his lips as he thought. "Rash. Impetuous and rather annoying."

"Is that all?" I said, trying to keep my tone level.

"For now."

"Well, I'd say your perception of me is quite off."

He quirked an eyebrow. "Is that so?"

"Yes, that is so."

"Hmm. Well, I would say fighting me when I was trying to help your ass, impetuous, and quite annoying."

I grit my teeth and he laughed. "Come on. Let me show you around the manor."

Grabbing a peach and another sweet, I rose and followed him out of the room. I hoped my stay here wouldn't be long. The sooner we were on our way to the Wilde Elves, the sooner I would be done with Damiyun.

It was all I wanted. He was boorish. Flames bloomed within my chest and stomach. My breath came short. The burning told me otherwise.

FORTY-ONE
PHABIAN

"**I**'M SORRY." LAZARO'S ARMS slipped around my waist, his lips brushing my ear. "I was dragged into this too. Krall—"

I pulled away from him.

Krall.

Allendaire's most loyal guard. His highest guard. His name made my blood boil.

"You know what I did," Laz said.

I took a deep, calming breath. "Yes, I do, but do they?" I turned, my eyes searched Lazaro's face. Did he tell then?

"I did not betray Serafin, or you. On my life, Phabian, I did not."

While I wanted to believe, I had to know, so I delved into his mind. What I saw was Krall ordering him to armor up and join them on their search, just as he had done to me.

I cupped his chin. "I had to know."

Laz's warm lips brushed mine. "I know, and your brother—"

"Are you loyal to Allendaire?" Pulling away, I looked at him. Though I delved into his mind to see he was a reluctant participant in the search for Serafin, I knew there were ways to block what I saw, if not block me out completely like so many elves do.

Lazaro's throat bobbed as he swallowed. "Once, I was just as you were." His eyes met mine. "I don't know what to believe anymore, Phabian."

I caressed his cheek with my knuckles. "Believe me, Laz. Please. Help me find others that do as well. I feel as though our race depends on it."

Lazaro rested his forehead on mine. "I do, and I will do whatever you ask of me. I am your loyal servant."

Nodding, I pulled away and crossed the room to my desk. Unrolling a piece of parchment, I uncorked a vial of ink and dipped a quill.

Meet me in Theonaus in an hour.

Rolling it up, I passed it to Lazaro as I walked by and stepped out of the room. Before that happened, I needed to see my brother.

K RALL LOOKED UP FROM his armor he polished as I entered the armory.

"Phabian," he said, returning his attention to his helmet. "You should be polishing every piece of armor and weapon here for your insolence."

I clenched my jaw at his words. I needed to tread carefully with him and not let my anger do something I might regret. Though knowing how fiercely loyal to Allendaire he remained, I wasn't completely sure if I cared.

"What does Allendaire gain from going after Serafin? You saw her. She was happy. She had a life, something you destroyed." And she was thriving without me, something that hurt more than I would admit.

Though my Anya gave me eight boys and one girl, I had nothing to do with their upbringing, aside from guiding my boys in asserting their authority over females, something that shamed me now. Serafin was different. Though she was not born of my seed, she was no less a daughter to me. I could not fathom what Allendaire did to her. He professed to love her, fuck me, but he loved Lillyanna, though I should have known how quick he could turn with sending her away. I should have done more, but I was blinded by my love for the king.

But no longer.

How could I have known how much I would love the young woman Lillyanna bore? And I loved her as well. Though my part in what happened shamed me, I tried to get her to leave before she became with child, but she ignored that voice planted in her head. I did what I could for her, if only to ease my guilt. What would she say if she were standing before me now? I did not know. What I did know is she and Serafin helped me to see the error of my—of our—ways and I would find a way to put my Little Princess on the throne.

Krall put his helmet on the bench, his blue eyes pinning me. "He gains an illegitimate cunt not taking the throne. That daughter of a whore should have never been born."

"And you don't wonder, don't question Mouranda who is barren by all accounts of the healer, being with child?"

Krall rose slowly from the bench. "No, I do not." He stepped forward. "Should I tell my king, my brother," he stressed the word and I felt the meaning, "ignores the queen being with child? Ignores the true heir?" He took a step closer, our chests a breath apart.

I stood straight and looked him in the eyes. "I do not ignore the child born of Allendaire's seed, planted in Lillyanna's womb and the princess that was tossed out like garbage." I spat on the floor. I looked at Krall, at my first eldest brother who I looked up to as a child, someone I once respected, and everything I felt for him left in this one moment. "You have made your stance, as have I."

Turning, I left the armory and headed to the stable to saddle up Max and meet Lazaro in Theonaus.

THE BROKEN WENCH WAS hot and stank of sweaty bodies and urine. I had forgotten how nasty this place was. My eyes went to Laz who sat at a table in the corner with a dirty whore on his lap, and I pushed my away through the crowd toward him. Her eyes appraised me, and she smiled a toothless grin.

"Oy. Double the pleasure," she said with a cackle.

I wrinkled my nose. "I happen to like my cock. Who knows where your cunt has been."

Glaring at me, she rose from Laz's lap. "That's four coppers for the feel," she said, holding her hand out. Laz deposited the coin, and she stalked away.

"Really, Laz?" I said as I slid into the seat opposite. "What is it with you and dirty whores?"

He gave a wicked smile. "They will do anything you ask."

I shook my head. Flagging down a serving wench, I ordered two tankards of ale, and sat back in my chair.

"Why did you ask me here?" Lazaro said when our drinks were deposited.

"Mouranda."

"What about her?"

"There is something wrong."

Lazaro sighed. "We went over this." He took a sip of his drink.

"I visited her in her rooms. Mouranda's condition is concerning. At only three Moon Cycles, the child moves as though she were farther along, and the way she looks?" I shook my head and took a long drink.

Like death, really.

Lazaro's hand crept across the table, catching mine. "Do you feel the unease within the walls? A sense of evil?"

"I do," I said, and my mind went to my visit with Krall before coming here. While he was a loyal servant of Allendaire, the captain of his guards and a general in the army, he had felt different to me. As Krall's second in command in our army, I was used to taking direction from him. But when he told me to be a part of the hunt for Serafin, told me to apprehend her, those orders felt like they were coming from someone else. Now I wondered if walking away from him would yield dire repercussions for me.

"Krall is different."

"As are many, I've found," Lazaro said. "Our king...he gets into fits of anger and confusion. I had to ask him why the stores were still low and when I showed him your ledger, he went off in a rage." He took a sip of his drink. "It had nothing to do with what I asked, Phabian. It made no sense."

Leaning forward, my eyes pinned Laz. "I think..." I stopped.

"What?" Laz said. "Phabian, you can trust me. I don't know how I can prove that to you."

"Yes, Krall is different, but I need to know, Laz. What are your thoughts on Mouranda, who by all accounts of the healers, was declared barren, being with child?"

It was what I had asked Krall, but I realized I did not ask Lazaro.

Grasping the fresh drink placed in front of him, his thumb idly stroked my hand. "It's not right. She did something."

Sighing in relief, I leaned forward. "Thank you, Laz, for confirming my thoughts. I need your help."

"For?"

"Mouranda has been sent to the infirmary to be under watch by the healers. I need to get into her quarters and I need your help."

FORTY-TWO

BLINDING LIGHT HIT MY eyes and I threw my arm over my face. Fuck, my head hurt. A heaviness pressed my chest, and biting back the pain lancing through my temples, I looked down at the heads laying on each side. Wiggling out from beneath the burden, I sat up. The room pitched then righted, and I swallowed back the bile that rose.

I glanced over at the couple who lay on my bed. Twins, Tamara, and Tristian snored peacefully, unaware of my extraction. Crossing the room, I poured water into the basin and splashed water on my face, and looked in the mirror. My eyes were bloodshot and the stubble on my jaw made me look older than my hundreds of Grand Passages. Pulling on clothes, I cast a longing look back at my occupied bed, wishing I could kick Trist and Tam off and bury myself back beneath the plush blankets, but I couldn't.

Fragments of my meeting with Lazaro filtered through my mind, but none of how the twins ended up in my bed. Not that it mattered. What mattered was my goal. Breaking into Mouranda's quarters to find out what she did.

Stepping out of my room, I walked on silent feet through the corridors to her quarters where I hoped through the hazy memories filtering through my mind, Lazaro would be somewhere close. As I drew closer to her rooms, I saw figures in the shadows was it Lazaro? Could it be Krall? Was I betrayed?

"Phabian."

The voice was that of Lazaro's, and I sighed in relief.

"What do you need?"

"Be my lookout. If anyone comes, if anyone looks as though they wish to enter, warn me."

"I will have your back, Phabian."

Nodding, I turned the handle to the door, entering her room where I hoped I would find answers to the mystery surrounding Mouranda.

And the evil descending upon the palace.

Holding my breath, I turned the knob on Mouranda's chambers, pushing open the door, breathing a sigh of relief at seeing the empty room. I was not sure if Denalla would be within, though I had a lie ready if she was.

Quietly closing the door behind, I looked around. Though the room was spacious, it was sparsely furnished. A large four poster bed sat in one corner. A wardrobe in another. A wooden partition hid a copper claw foot bathing tub. A desk was situated in front of the windows spanning the wall across from the door. Bookcases lined the wall to my left and right, and a couch, chairs and table sat in front of the cold hearth.

Walking into the room, I decided to check the bookshelves for anything out of the ordinary. Though I did not see anything odd in the titles, I pulled the books off the shelves in the hope of something hidden but found nothing behind nor tucked within the pages. There was nothing amiss with the wardrobe either. Nothing hidden within the depths or stuffed into the pockets of a cloak or buried inside a shoe. There were no papers or books hidden beneath the heavy feather mattress or between the cushions of the chairs.

The only item left to search was the desk. As I crossed the room, I caught a movement out of the corner of my eye. The hair on the back of my neck rose, and I had a sensation of eyes on me. Rolling my shoulders, I glanced around but saw nothing. I shook it off to nerves at snooping around in Mouranda's chambers. Shook it off to a fear of someone getting by Lazaro, sneaking in and catching me in the act. I had no lie ready for that.

Standing at the desk, I pulled open the drawers, rifling through stacks of blank parchment, quills, nibs, and various jars of ink. There was nothing incriminating within the drawers.

Maybe I was just being paranoid. Maybe my love for Serafin was fogging my brain, making me think the worst of everyone and everything. Maybe Mouranda and Allendaire had copulated. Maybe whatever the healers gave her worked.

Reaching for the last drawer, I tugged, expecting it to open like the others, but it was locked. I frowned. For what reason would this one drawer be locked when the others were not? I searched the desk and the drawers again, looking for a key, but came up empty. Pulling out the small knife I always carried, I slipped off the chair. Squatting in front of the drawer, I inserted the tip of the knife into the lock. The feeling of something hot and sharp scraped against the back of my neck. Dropping the knife, I touched the spot, gasping at feeling welts beginning to rise. Coldness washed over me and again I saw movement but when I looked there was nothing to be seen.

Shaking the feeling of being watched, the feeling of oppression and ignoring the burning pain on my neck, I went back to my task of unlocking the drawer. Finally, after what felt like an eternity of frustration, I heard an audible click, and when I pulled the drawer, there was no resistance. Stowing my knife, I looked inside. Seeing a stack of notebooks, I pulled one out and flipped through, noting Mouranda's perfect flowing script.

Journals.

Pulling them out, I spied another book. It was thick, bound in red, cracked leather. There were no words, no title to denote what the book contained. The only marking was a crest in the center. It was of a winged beast, green scales made of emeralds. A ruby and citrine plume of fire poured from its open mouth and glinted in the low lamplight. Obsidian eye flashed evilly, and diamond talons added a lethal touch. The crest was one I was unfamiliar with, and it—as well as the book—piqued my interest. Pulling it out, I set it and the journals on the desk, and sat down again.

Phabian, Lazaro's voice echoed in my head. *Get out. Krall is coming. I will do my best to distract him, but get the fuck out.*

Gathering the books, I jumped to my feet, tipping the chair over, the crashing sound deafening in the silence. I froze, and upon not hearing footsteps racing down the hall, I righted the chair, gathered the books and bolted to my room.

With any luck, the items I took would give insight into what Mouranda had done.

FORTY-THREE

S EVERAL HOURS LATER, I sat behind the desk in my room looking at the items I had found in Mouranda's quarters. Journals, papers that looked to be letters of some sort, a heavy and curious looking book, and a dagger. The weapon was quite plain in appearance, nothing like the jeweled, ornamental one she used to keep at her hip. The blade appeared to be rusty, though when I touched it, the color had flaked off and I realized it wasn't rust at all.

It was blood.

I stared at the items on my desk, unsure of where I should begin, while fighting the urge to return everything back to its rightful place. I wanted to believe I was being paranoid. That my love for Serafin had driven me to think the worst about Mouranda but knowing Lazaro felt something was amiss, made me stay where I was.

As did the strange feeling I was being watched while I searched her room. More than once, I had thought I saw movement out of the corner of my eye. More than once, I searched over my shoulder, sure I would see something, but never did.

Even now, in my room, my shoulder blades pricked, and I cast a look about, seeing nothing.

You're paranoid. It's because you broke into Mouranda's chambers and stole personal items. Nothing more.

Taking a sip of Serpent's Venom, I opened one of the diaries and began flipping through. They were filled with mundane entries, day-to-day dealings, thoughts on visits with people in the village, friends, and family.

I quickly went through a portion of her journals. Sighing, I reached for the next one. I was growing bored with my task. Maybe I was just paranoid. I was close to the end of yet another book, close to returning everything to its rightful place, when the next entry piqued my interest.

*I*T HAS BEEN FIVE *Grand Passages and I have once again failed to provide Allendaire with an heir, though I have been to dozens of healers. Drank my share of horrible potions. Allowed myself to be poked and prodded, stayed in bed for three days to ensure his seed fertilized my egg, even going so far as to thinking of propositioning another female who was with child. I had thought about deceiving Allendaire. Deceiving everyone and paying another to give me their child. Pretend I had birthed it. Pretend it was my own, but I couldn't, in good conscience, do that and I am now forced to accept my defect.*

My imperfection.

Face the truth I will never give Allendaire an heir.

*I*F FLIPPED FORWARD A few pages, skimming as I went, stopping at another entry that caught my eye.

*A*LLENDAIRE WAS FURIOUS *I cannot produce. He flew into a rage. He accused me of doing something so as not to have a child, but what female would do that? It was our place—our duty—to keep the race alive. To give mates children who will carry our name and legacy. I was not pleased with my defect, and it hurt he would blame me for it.*

And I knew what it meant. I was not perfect.

I knew, although I was his wife and queen, he would uphold the law. Our law.

I knew I would lose my head for this.

But I also harbored a secret about my dear husband. It is something I have kept close to my heart. It is a dark secret enough to destroy him

A secret I had hoped I never had to use, but he forced my hand. And so, I told him what I knew. He had poisoned Terrin and blamed his sister. He took the throne through traitorous means.

And I let him know I would tell all upon my last words granted.

And he knew they would believe their beloved queen. Though I was a woman, and nothing to this race, I was their queen. And if there were any doubts? If I still lost my head despite this knowledge? Barlack Satow had explicit orders to show the proof. I knew all about his spies within our walls. I knew all about the child born to Rahina.

I knew my husband thinks me ignorant. Thinks me less because I happen to be female, and that caused him to underestimate me. When I discovered the spies, I confronted Barlack, and he told me everything. He told me of the treachery within the walls and about the child, and I did not believe. I had to see for myself, and so I sought him out and when I saw him, I knew.

He bore every resemblance of the elves—of his mother—save for his clipped ears, and I knew Barlack's tale to be true. Though I should have ended the child's life knowing no one knew of him, knowing he was a half-breed, something deep inside stayed my hand. Something whispered this knowledge might be of use and so I aligned myself with Barlack. I gave him instructions on the chance I met my demise, telling him to reveal Allendaire's treason, and to put the young prince on the throne. Though he was a half-breed, I formed a decree by which he would be recognized and rule.

And I told Allendaire what I knew. I took a foolish gamble with my words, though the look in his eyes and the way he crumbled at hearing this told me I wasn't going to die, and I knew I had him.

I knew that never again would he underestimate me. Treat me as less. As if I didn't matter.

As if I were not queen.

For once, it was I who was in charge.

I CLOSED THE BOOK and sat back.

This was why Allendaire went along with her orders and sentenced Serafin to death. He was too afraid of being outed. I clenched my jaw at the thought.

I found it curious that Barlack had spies in the palace, but also, he would tell her Rahina survived, though she later died, and had a child. Even more so, Mouranda did not end his life. Did Barlack still have spies in the palace, and if he does, how could I find them?

I shook my head. Evening was fast approaching, the shadows growing long on the walls, the screams from the beasts beyond pierced the silence, and I got up and lit my lamps, poured a tall glass of Serpent's Venom, and settled in for a long night.

I opened the next—and final—journal and scanned the pages and what I read within, made my heart ache for Lillyanna.

For my little princess.

And it made my blood run cold. Made my gut clench with fear over the fate of the palace.

And the fate of the Shadow Elves.

FORTY-FOUR

T HE NIGHT GREW LONG as I sat at my desk. The bottle of Serpent's Venom had long been empty. I had read through all the journals I found in Mouranda's chambers, and I wasn't sure what to think. Though she had planned Serafin's birth, coerced Allendaire to form a relationship with Lillyanna, it was clear she did not consider the consequences. Did not foresee Allendaire caring for Lillyanna. She did not think of the reminder the child would be. A reminder of her husband's love for another. A child who was a half-breed and should never have been born.

But she was the one who had planned it. And I went along with it.

Shame filled me when I thought of my part in what happened, but what came of it? What was born was the most amazing woman I had ever known. A woman who I loved and who I knew could—no, would—right the wrongs of our people.

I looked at the final book. It was thick, bound in red, cracked leather. There were no words, no title to denote what the book contained. The only marking was a crest in the center. It was of a winged beast, green scales made of emeralds. A ruby and citrine plume of fire poured from its open mouth and glinted in the low lamplight. Obsidian eye flashed evilly, and diamond talons added a lethal touch. The crest was one I was unfamiliar with, and it—as well as the book—piqued my interest. I pulled on the lock, but it didn't budge, and I cursed myself for not taking the time to find a key. Picking up the dagger, I tried to pry it open.

"Shit." The dagger slipped, pain radiated through palm and blood flowed over the cover. Jumping up, I quickly grabbed a rag and began wiping the blood away, then wrapped my wounded hand.

I heard a soft click and watched in shock as the lock of the book sprang open. Hesitating a beat, I reached forward and opened it, my heart—and hopes—sinking as I looked at a blank page. I flipped through, heart sinking further at seeing the entire book was blank.

Sighing, I closed it and looked out the window at the night. Clouds filled the sky, passing over the crescent moon intermittently. The wind had picked up a bit, and I saw the flash of lightning and heard the rumble of thunder in the distance.

It was nothing more than another diary, awaiting Mouranda's pen. Opening the book again, I ran my hand over the blank pages, cursing the trail of blood my wound left behind on the crisp paper. I flipped through again, hoping to find symbols, words, something. Everything remained blank.

Yawning, I stretched my aching back and began closing the book, though movement on the page made me pause. Blinking, I stared at the paper, shaking my head when nothing happened.

You're tired, Phabian. Your mind needs rest.

I went to close it once more, when again the page shimmered. Symbols and letters swirled and shifted, finally settling on the page and forming words. Though the text was foreign at first, the more I scanned, the more I understood.

This book was not anything written by the Shadow Elves.

I ran my hand over the page, eyes reading the letters of a long and dead language. A language once taught in school. The language slowly came to me as I scanned the pages.

It was the language of the Dark Elves.

A race long eradicated.

A race from which our own had spawned.

"WHAT DID YOU FIND?" Lazaro breezed past me and into my room the next morning.

"Come in, Laz." I rolled my eyes, and closed the door behind.

He flashed a smile over his shoulder as he threw himself down in a chair.

"And make yourself comfortable while you're at it."

He kicked his feet up on the table and laced his hands behind his head. I sat down in a chair opposite.

"So?" His light blue eyes trained on me.

I looked out the window while I composed my thoughts and answer. The sky lit up with the flickering of lightning, followed by the rolling crash of thunder. The wind blew and rain slashed against the window in an angry torrent. I glanced at the pile of books on my desk, then looked back at Lazaro. "Mouranda used dark magic to become with child."

"What?"

I got up and retrieved the book from my desk and placed it on his lap. He frowned, then opened it.

"What is this?"

I perched on the edge of the table and looked at Laz, who flipped through the pages.

"Dark Elf magic."

He stopped flipping, eyes going to me, a confused look crossing his pretty face. "Dark Elf? They've been gone for thousands of Grand Passages. Wasn't everything they had burned?"

I nodded.

"So, how could this be from them? It's just pages filled with symbols and squiggles."

"Do they not still teach their history in school?"

He sat back with a shrug. "I guess. History bores me and I would often skip those lectures."

I took the book back and flipped through. "My grasp of the Old Tongue is a bit rusty, but it came back to me. This book is of dark spells and curses. Mouranda must have used it to have a child."

"How can you be sure?"

"Why else would she have this book?"

Lazaro sighed. "But what does that mean?"

After closing the book, I put it back on my desk. "I don't know. I think I need to pay her another visit."

"**I** WOULD LIKE TO speak with M...the queen." I choked on the word, "alone if I may?" I said, looking at the three healers and Mouranda's maid, Denalla. The four women looked at me, Denalla's eyes holding fire.

"No, you may—"

"It's alright," Mouranda said, her voice like rocks scraping across sand.

"But—"

"Go."

The four women hesitated, then pushed past me and out the door. I looked at Mouranda who looked like death. Her stomach bulged; every now and then a ripple would move across, her face contorting in pain.

"Help me sit up."

Placing the book tucked beneath my arm on a table, I propped the pillows behind her and helped her to a seated position.

"Now, to what do I owe your presence?" She said, settling back against the pillows.

I held the book up. Mouranda's eyes widened. Taking a seat beside the bed, I placed the book on my lap and leaned forward. "I read some of this book." I tapped the cover, "My grasp of the Old Tongue might be rusty, but I know enough." Her eyes did not leave the finger that tap, tap, tapped.

"Where did you get this?" Bony hands reached out, and I sat back, sliding the book toward me and out of her reach.

"You know where, along with your journals that tell what Allendaire did."

I did not care that I was showing my hand, telling her I broke into her rooms. What was she going to do in her condition? Have Denalla come after me, her faithful maid and lover, who would do what?

No. Mouranda had no authority with the position she was in.

"Why do this? Why sentence Serafin to death?"

Mouranda glared at me. "You know why."

"I don't," I said, though I really did. I wanted to hear it from her.

"She never loved me. Never accepted me. As a babe, she would scream when I came near but you? Allendaire? When you came around, she would quiet and demand hugs and kisses from you. Even when she was older, when she fell and scraped a knee, when she had a bad dream, she would go to you. Never would she accept my attempts at being a mother."

"Because you weren't one," I jumped up from my chair. "Where were you when Lillyanna was with child?"

Mouranda glared at me. "Did you really expect me to run to that...that whore and pat her stomach, talk to the child that...that..." she crumpled against the pillows, "that showed me everything I was not?" Her voice was a whisper. Setting the book down, I sat on the edge of the bed. "Go away, Phabian."

"No." I took a deep breath. "But perhaps your...defect...was a blessing. You were saved the horrors of having to produce children one after the other." I looked down at my hands. "I know what sort of person I am—was—and I would never wish what I did to my Anya on another." I looked at Mouranda, at the skeletal figure lying in the bed. "Serafin is the heir. She is the future queen."

"I know now, Phabian. What I did was done out of anger and malice." She swallowed hard, and I poured a glass of water and handed it to her. "I know she escaped. Is she...is she..."

"Yes."

Pain crossed her face, and a scream tore through the room. The three healers and Denalla rushed in, pushing me out.

"Phabian," I turned toward Mouranda. "I'm sorry."

Turning back, I made my way out, Mouranda's screams filling the ward. Her jealousy, her feeling of inadequacy for not being able to churn out babies drove her to use dark magic from a race long gone. Part of me felt sorry for her for not being able to bring forth life, though after what I learned—

Go, Phabian. Go to Naar'Glon.

I stumbled. *What?*

Go to Naar'Glon. All your answers are there.

"WHERE ARE YOU GOING?" Lazaro breezed into my room as I was packing my bag.

"Come on in, Laz," I said rolling my eyes as I secured the buckle. "I am going to Naar'Glon."

"What? Why?"

"I believe the answers lie there."

"Give me a few moments to pack."

Turning, I looked at him. "No. I'm going alone. I need someone I trust to stay here and keep an eye on Allendaire and what is going on here."

"But—"

"I need you here, Laz."

"But how will I contact you?"

I smiled. "Krall and I had special books we used to communicate when we were children. We infused them with magic and the words written in one would appear in the other and vanish upon being read."

Lazaro laughed. "Clever." Lazaro pressed his lips to mine. "Be careful, Phabian," he said, his breath a warm caress on my face. "It would hurt me deeply if anything happened to you."

I cupped his chin and smiled. "I promise I will come home alive and in one piece."

A wicked grin curled his lips. "You had better. There are some pieces of you I am quite fond of."

I laughed.

"I'm serious, Phabian," he said, his tone quiet. "If what you think is true... if this is Dark Elf magic..."

I softly kissed him, and leaned my forehead on his, fingers tracing the curves of his face. "I promise I will be careful, Laz."

"When are you leaving?"

I looked out the window at the storm raging beyond. "As soon as the storm lets up."

Taking my hand, he tugged me toward the bed. "So, we have time then?"

"We have time then," I said, pushing the unsettling thoughts of what was happening here and my trip to the back of my mind as I was lost in Lazaro's pleasure.

FORTY-FIVE

T HOUGH THE WEATHER BROKE allowing me to travel to the Calgonian Sea to hopefully secure passage to Naar'Glon, it did not cooperate for long. Storms of rain turning to squalls of snow hindered my progress. More times than I could count I was hold up at an inn for a day or two. The mud and ice covered roads made the trek slippery and dangerous and I had to guide Maximillian even slower.

When I made it to the docks of Gualazinia, I sighed with relief, though there was a part of me which questioned if the journey was the right one. I stabled Max, secured a room, and then went out to see about buying a captain to take me to Naar'Glon, though I had no idea how to do that. The town was filled with rough working men and sailors whose vessels were being loaded with goods. Whores stood against dilapidated buildings preening like peacocks and showing their goods, male and female alike.

A man with ebony skin and eyes as white as clouds caught my eye. His muscles showed through the tight shirt he wore and the even tighter trousers? Well, I was mesmerized and took a step in his direction, his smile beckoning.

"I wouldn't," a voice said in my ear, hand tugging my cloak.

Turning, I looked at a tall woman with short, brown hair. "What?"

"That lot over there. The whores." Her eyes flicked to where my concentration was before she broke it. "They will offer you a drink then lace it with Themesis Blood."

Clearly, she saw the confusion on my face because she laughed. "It's a drug they slip into drink. It causes paralysis and you lay there awake watching them rob you blind, unable to do anything about it. Not even scream. By time everything is back to working order, they're long gone on the next ship. That is, if they don't decide to take you with them to sell as a slave," she said. "Clearly, you're not from here and I've never seen an elf. Can I touch your ear?"

"What?"

Before I could move, her fingers grasped the tip of my ear and pulled. "What are you doing?" I shoved her away.

"I'm sorry. I've never seen one like you." Her brown eyes went to the ground, teeth biting her lip.

"It's alright."

She looked up, eyes bright. "So, I can touch—"

"No." I jumped back. "You cannot touch my ears. What is wrong with you?"

"I just... your ears are interesting and you're very pretty," she said, and I dare say, I blushed. "I'm Mara." She stuck out her hand.

"Phabian," I said, grasping it.

"I'm sorry."

"It's fine." I held up a finger. "That does not mean you can touch my ears."

She laughed and began to walk with me falling in step beside her. "What brings you to Gualazinia?"

"I need to secure a boat."

Her eyes brightened. "My uncle has a boat. Where do you need to go?"

"Naar'Glon."

"I've not heard of it but maybe... uncle!" She ran down the docks to a... my heart sank at seeing an older man with gray hair stepping off a small fishing boat. The man looked up, browned skin that looked like worn shoe leather wrinkled into what I thought to be a smile.

"Mara," the man said.

"Uncle." Mara engulfed him in an embrace. Stepping back, she looked at me. "This is my new friend, Phabian. He needs passage to—"

"Nowhere," I said, stepping away. "Thank you anyway."

Mara grabbed my arm. "No, it wasn't Nowhere. It was...Naar'Glon. Yes, that was it. Can you take him?"

I pulled my arm from her grasp. I was sure the only reason she was doing this was for coin, and if that was the case? Reaching into my coin purse I pulled out a silver.

"Thank you," I said, pressing it into her hand. I suppose on the morrow I would head back to Il'Ekhester.

"My skiff might not be able to take you all the way to Naar'Glon, but I have a cousin who has a ship that can."

Turning, I looked at the old man and Mara. "Alright. Let's talk."

THE SOUND OF THE gangplank lowering was music to my ears. I had been on this ship for ten days.

Ten days of tossing about on the Calgonian Sea, with uncertain weather and storms.

Ten days of vomiting until the boat landed at the docks. When my feet hit solid land, I wanted to kiss the ground beneath. I was finally in Naar'Glon. It had cost a good chunk of coin to get here.

It felt strange being in the lands from where my own race migrated. I had only heard of this place and was led to believe it was abandoned. Moving off the docks and away from the Vomit Vessel, I made my way through the town, noting the affluence and diversity. Humans and elves crowded the white cobblestone streets. Tall buildings made of the same white stones and red brick lined the road. Vendors selling food and goods drew a crowd. It was hot, and the air was thick with humidity. My shirt clung to me. Sweat rolled down my back, and I was uncomfortable. Pushing on, I looked around what was once my own people's homeland. Tall, thin men and women with their faces covered, dark hair peeking out from beneath bustled about the town. White eyes peered out of the slit on the covering.

I stopped and watched the covered people. My mind raced. White eyes. I had to stop my jaw from dropping as memories from my childhood teachings flooded my mind. I was looking at Dark Elves.

My blood ran cold at the realization, my mind going back to the attack on Allendaire and his hunting party. One soldier had said it was an unknown assailant, heads covered showing only white eyes.

But how could that be?

I shook myself as I began to again realize much of what I knew, possibly everything, I wasn't sure at this point, was a lie. My blood ran cold at seeing people from a race long thought dead.

Like Arybelle and Vanla were.

I continued through the throng, searching for a place to rest my head. Though the town was diverse, amongst the covered Dark Elves, I stood out like snow in the summer, and I tried hard to ignore the eyes that followed me. Ignoring the feeling, I pushed through the crowd, sighing with relief when I found the inn. I entered and quickly made arrangements for a room, a meal and some Faeries Blood. There were few people in the common room. Even so, I had no interest in social interaction. I holed up inside to eat my meal.

I pulled the book out of my satchel and opened it up, reading the words in the Old Tongue. I knew that the book I held concealed dark words.

Dark magic the Dark Elves possessed. I still was surprised to see them alive. Putting the book aside, I pulled out another. Opening to a blank page, I grabbed my quill.

The Dark Elves live, I wrote. *I saw—* The door to my room burst open. Four men, faces covered, shouldered their way in. I leapt up, eyes on the intruders.

"It is best you don't try anything," one intruder said. Another strode forward, snatching the dark magic book off the bed.

"Where the fuck did you get this?"

"I—" The other two lunged forward and grabbed me. My arms were jerked behind my back and tied, and they tossed a pillowcase over my head.

"It doesn't matter. You will answer to Lord Rah."

R OPE BIT INTO MY wrists, and the chilly dampness of the dirt floor seeped into my bones. I had no idea where I was. Or exactly how long I had been here. I just know that the Sigaa'Lean was put on and I traveled blind and on foot and was shoved into a cell. The door scraped open, and I turned in the direction, squinting from the lamplight.

"Lord Rah has decided to see you," a voice said. The hooded man strode into the cell and jerked me to my feet. I stumbled as they shoved me through the door.

"What—"

"Shut up, you filthy, in-bred freak." My captor snapped. Snickers echoed off the walls. My face and ears burned, and I couldn't help but wonder if this is what Serafin felt like when she was taunted at the palace as they guided me through the halls. What I had assumed was a grand palace was a large manor. Unlike the palace in Il'Ekhester, it was modestly furnished. Subdued colors, worn furniture, and threadbare rugs. Heavy curtains covered the windows, and the walls were devoid of any sort of tapestry, though dispersed around the halls was what I now recognized as the Dark Elf crest, winged beast with scales made of emeralds, ruby and citrine plumes of fire poured from its mouth, obsidian eyes looked at me, and the diamond talons glinted in the light.

My guard pulled to a halt outside double doors. Knocking once, he pulled them open. I hesitated a moment, stumbling as they shoved me through. The ornate doors belied the room within. It was a small dining room, informal in nature. A table fit for eight graced the middle. A sideboard sat to the right. Thick, velvety, cream-colored curtains concealed the windows spanning one of the walls, soft moonlight spilling through the gap. There was a man with short, black hair at the head of the table. White eyes looked at me as the guards led me inside.

"Sit," he said, motioning to the chair on his left. "Cut his binds," he said to the other man.

"Sir?"

The man—Lord Rah—smiled. "He won't cause any trouble."

The guard hesitated a moment, and then I felt the ropes fall away.

I said nothing, eyes on Rah, as I rubbed my raw wrists.

"You can go." He waved a hand in dismissal to the man. The sound of his shoes echoed in the silence, followed by the click of the door closing. "You must be hungry." He gestured to the food on the table.

"I'm not, thank you," I said, trying to ignore the painful void in my stomach.

Rah chuckled. "The pride and stubbornness of the Shadow Elves will be your downfall," he said, grabbing a plate and filling it. "If you think the food is poisoned, rest assured I have no reason to kill you." He flashed a smile. Sharp fangs glinted in the light. "Yet."

Fangs?

Long, graceful fingers cracked and peeled an egg which he delicately ate. Hesitating a second, I grabbed a pastry and took a bite. My stomach growled in satisfaction as the sweet confection hit it.

"Tell me..." Rah started, raising an eyebrow.

"Phabian," I said, grabbing an egg and cracking it.

"Tell me, Phabian," he began again, teeth pulling a slice of meat off his fork. "What are you, a Shadow Elf, doing in Dark Elf lands? Did your king send you to spy?"

"No," I said, chewing a bite of cheese. "I did not know your race was still around. I had thought you were long eradicated."

"And yet, here I am." He sat back and spread his arms.

"Yes, well, I am learning much is not what it seems or how it was where my people are concerned."

Rah quirked an eyebrow but said nothing. "How did you come upon this?" Fingers tapped the heavy book that sat beside him.

"I found it in Mouranda, the queen's, quarters. How she got it, I don't know."

"This book has been missing for centuries."

I shrugged. "As I said, I don't know how it came into her possession. Perhaps Karrinian took it when he traveled to Il'Ekhester."

Rah's finger continued to tap, tap, tap the book cover. The sound grated on my nerves.

"Hmm. And what would your queen be doing with such a book?"

I folded my hands and leveled my gaze on him. While I was hesitant to divulge what I knew, I also bore no loyalty to Allendaire or Mouranda. Considering I had come all this way for answers, and I was sitting with a thought-to-be eradicated race, I felt I had nothing to lose.

"I suspect she used a spell to become with child."

"And why do you suspect her of doing that?"

"Because she was barren. I can only surmise magic was at play."

Rah laughed. "Why do you suspect magic? Many women think they are unable to conceive only to one day be surprised."

"This is true. My Anya and I tried for several Grand Passages before she gave me a daughter and then produced seven more sons."

"So, this was a blessing from the gods."

I snorted.

"Ahh. Right. I forget your kind does not believe."

"It was known she was barren. The healers even deemed it so."

Rah shrugged. "So, they were wrong." He pulled the book in front of him and folded his hands on it. "Now. What is it that makes you think this book," his pinky tapped the cover and the garnet in his ring flashed in the light, "holds answers? What makes you think we do?" He sat back in his chair. "That is why you are here, is it not?"

I leveled my gaze on him. "Because I read some of what it contains and though my grasp of the Old Tongue is rusty, I know enough. The magic contained within is dark."

Rah sighed. "What does this have to do with me? With the Dark Elves?"

"I was hoping to find out more about what the book contains."

Rah laughed. "Right. And why should I trust you? Your people nearly eradicated our race. For all I know, you're a spy for Allendaire. There could be ships waiting to come and attack."

"I'm not a spy." *Not exactly.* "I assure you, I am here alone. Send out your own scouts to see if what I speak is true."

Rah opened his mouth to speak, when the sound of the door burst open and a woman wearing a yellow gown rushed in. Rah jumped up and quickly crossed the room at the sight of the petite redhead.

Human. Interesting.

"Bethulda. What is it? Is it Cassion?"

"He's awake. Come quickly, Rah, before he falls unconscious again," she said, lifting her skirts and rushing out of the room, Rah behind.

Curious as to what was going on, I rose from my seat and followed on silent feet. They rushed through the nearly empty halls, drawing up to a door. Rah glanced at Bethulda and slipped his hand in hers. They entered the room, with me trailing quietly behind.

"Cassion," Rah said, his voice soft as he rushed across the room. My eyes followed him to the bed where a young man lay. His skin was white as snow and had the waxy look of death. Strands of white hair clung to his sweaty face. I quietly crept closer.

"Cassion," Rah said again, clutching his hand. Cassion's head turned, blue eyes looked at Rah as he sat down on the edge of the bed.

"Father."

"How are you feeling?"

"It hurts. And I'm cold. So damn cold."

"The healers are trying. I need to know what happened," Rah said.

Cassion licked his lips and closed his eyes.

"Cassion?" Rah gently shook him. Cassion's eyes opened again.

"I told you. I don't know. We were out at the tavern drinking. The room spun and then I was here." He took a deep breath and closed his eyes again. Rah leaned down and pressed his lips to his forehead.

"Rest, son. I promise I will figure this out," he said, rising to his feet.

"What if we can't?" Bethulda's face was creased with worry. Rah pulled her into his embrace.

"We have to." He turned back, eyes locking on mine. His jaw clenched, and he released Bethulda. "What the fuck are you doing here?" He demanded, stalking over to where I stood.

Shit. I held up a hand. "I mean no disrespect."

"This is a private matter. You," he snapped, pointing at a man leaning against the wall. "Take him back to his cell."

The man pushed away and advanced toward me.

"Wait. Please, Lord Rah," I said quickly as the man grabbed my arm. "I might be able to help."

Rah's eyes narrowed on me. "How can you do what no healer has been able to?"

"I can delve into his mind. Go into his memories and possibly see what happened," I said. "Let me at least try."

"Why would you do this? What will you ask for in return?"

"Nothing." I was not entirely lying. If I found something in this Cassion's mind, I could use it as leverage to save myself or obtain Rah's help.

"There has to be something you want in return. Your lot is cunning and deceitful. I will never trust a Shadow Elf's word."

"Rah," Bethulda's soft voice said. He turned and looked down at her, face softening. "Let him try. What could it hurt? The healers have come up with nothing and if he does as well?" She shrugged.

Rah smoothed his hand over her hair. "Bethulda, darling. We don't need the help of a filthy Shadow Elf. They tried to eradicate our race."

"Thousands of Grand Passages ago."

"And it has taken us that long to rebuild."

Bethulda shook her head. "My love. Cassion is our only child. We must find out what happened to him and why."

Rah sighed. "You know I cannot say no to you," he said. His eyes went to me. "I will allow you this, Phabian, but do not think I will do anything in return."

I sighed in relief. "Of course not," I said, though I held onto the hope he would. Rah nodded to the man who held my arm, and he released me. Rah strode over, grasped my arm, and pulled my wrist up. He spoke softly, the Sigaa'Lean opening with a click. I rubbed my wrist as I made my way to the bed and sat down on the edge. This differed from my normal delving. I could usually see into a person's mind without contact, but this time I needed to go back into the past. Taking a deep breath, I placed my hands on either side of his head. Closing my eyes, I cleared my mind and sent a wash of magic through.

Images flashed through my mind, flickering quickly like lightning. Fighting in a training ring. Helping his mother in the kitchens. Intimate moments with men. Then... There. One scene flashed. The room tilted and then there was blackness. Holding onto the moment, I pulsed more magic through, bringing me back. I was sitting at a table with several other men. I looked around the table. Drinks were flowing. Serving wenches bounced on laps and merriment was all around. My uncle, Bethos, sat to my right. He pinched the backside of a serving wench that walked by. She gave him a scathing look and swatted his hand. The table erupted in laughter. My hands grabbed the mug of ale shoved in front of me and lifted it. I peered down into a cloudy white liquid. I knew something was wrong with it, but my mind was already fuzzy from spirits. After I tipped it back, the room pitched, and darkness engulfed me.

"Poison," I said, opening my eyes and removing my hands.

Rah frowned. "What?"

I stood up and looked down at Cassion. "He was poisoned. I don't know who did it, but his last mug of ale didn't look right and shortly after he drank it, he fell into darkness."

Rah shook his head. "He has been like this for weeks. It's got to be something else."

I shrugged. "Perhaps someone is feeding him the poison, so he stays this way."

"What sort of poison?"

"I don't know."

Rah ran a hand through his hair. "For what purpose?"

Bethulda placed a hand on Rah's arm. "We will find out." She turned to me and smiled. "Thank you, Phabian."

I nodded, my eyes going to Rah. "I'm ready to go back to my cell."

Rah's lips pursed into a tight line.

"Rah," Bethulda said. "He helped us."

"But he did not tell us who or what. What he gave us is about as useful as not knowing."

"I am sorry, Lord Rah," I said. "I only see things through the person's eyes. It is impossible to see what they cannot."

"We will figure this out, my love. Have all quarters searched and have anything suspicious be brought to you. Change who cooks and let me bring food to Cassion."

Rah smiled and softly kissed Bethulda's forehead. "As always, my darling, you are wise." His eyes went to me once again, and I held my breath. "You will not sit in a cell. For now, anyway. I will have quarters made up for you and you will stay here, under watch, until I decide your fate."

I exhaled, my body relaxing at his words. "Thank you," I said, bowing my head. Striding across the room, he grabbed my arm and put the Sigaa'Lean back on, speaking words Rorla'rro ho rloagha rma'rl ho Waorcom "remove the magic from the Wielder", and it receded and I sighed. Rah waved his hand, and the man who had previously apprehended me strode out of the room with me in tow.

For the second time, my neck had been spared.

I only hoped my luck hadn't run out.

FORTY-SIX

I STOOD OUTSIDE ON the balcony overlooking a small courtyard. The Calgonian Sea scented the air along with flowers I'd never seen before. The manor was walled off, but beyond that, I could see the outline of the buildings and houses of Naar'Glon. The sun slipped slowly below the horizon. The sky lit up with pink, yellow, and orange, the colors illuminating the low clouds in a spectacular display.

Reaching a hand out, I pressed my fingers against the barrier that flickered. Iridescent swirls shimmered beneath my touch. The landscape beyond wavered as though I was underwater. A barrier of magic enclosed the balcony. The door to the room was locked with guards standing watch on the other side just in case.

Just like I knew they stood watch outside below.

Though I wasn't locked in a cell, the room, as it was, was still a prison. The Sigaa'Lean a reminder I was not a guest.

Though I had helped as much as I could, discovering Rah's son Cassion had been poisoned, he did not trust me. I could not blame him. After all, it was Karrinian who had tried to eradicate his race.

A soft knock on the door drew my attention, and I crossed the room, waiting for the sound of a key, the audible click telling me the door was unlocked. Grasping the handle, I pulled it open. Two guards stood as they always did, sharp swords crossed in front of the opening. My eyes went to Bethulda who stood in the hall.

"Phabian," she said, a smile forming on her lips. She nodded to the guards who sheathed swords. They stepped inside, flanking me, and grabbed my arms in a vice-like grip.

"Is this necessary? I have no weapons or magic."

"You are a cunning and deceitful race," one of the guards said.

"What am I going to do? You know she is here, and you would no doubt have my head before I could even think of doing harm."

Bethulda's amber eyes pinned me. "It's fine."

The guards hesitated. "My lady?"

She looked at them and motioned with her hand. "He did what our healers could not. He is the reason Cassion will get the chance to live."

They released me and moved across the room to stand in front of the open door. Hands rested casually on hilts. They seemed so calm, but I knew by the tension in their muscles, their jaws, each was ready to strike me down.

"What are you doing here?" I crossed the room to the table where a carafe of wine and glasses sat. Though I was a prisoner, I was at least treated fairly. I poured two glasses and handed one to Bethulda who settled down in a chair, arranging her skirts and tucking her feet beneath.

"I wanted to thank you for what you did."

I settled into a seat opposite, glancing at the guards who casually moved further into the room.

"Have you discovered what was used?"

She shook her head and took a sip of her drink. "No, but we now have a new cook, and I bring him his meals. His situation seems to have improved some, though we are still searching for the poison so our healers can administer the antidote."

"Why are you here?" I kept my eyes on her while trying to ignore the other gazes that penetrated. "Surely it wasn't just to thank me." I gestured with my glass.

"To extend an invitation to dinner tonight."

I laughed. "Extend or order?"

She took a sip of her drink and smoothed her skirts. "Extend."

"I'm sure Lord Rah," I gave a mock bow at the name, "would be delighted to see me."

Bethulda held out her empty glass, and I obliged her with a refill. She took a sip and settled back in the comfortable seat. "You must understand. My husband, well, he is a Dark Elf. Descendant of the First," her eyes locked on mine. "Descendant of your king, Karrinian."

I chuckled into my glass as I sipped. "Tell me, Bethulda. If we are descendants of your race, why would we have tried to eradicate you?"

A smile curled her lips. "I will let Rah tell you," she said, rising to her feet. I put my glass down and rose as well. "So, you will join us?"

"Do I have a choice?"

"No," she said as she crossed the room, the two guards quickly flanking her.

"Would it be possible to be granted a little freedom? I tire of these walls."

She stopped. "I will bring it up with Rah."

So that's a no.

"Rest, Phabian. You will be summoned when it is time for the meal," she said as she crossed the threshold into the hallway. The door closed, and the lock clicked.

Sighing, I poured another drink, and sat down to wait for the summons to dinner.

"**T**HANK YOU FOR ACCEPTING my invitation," Rah said, sitting back in his chair. Long, elegant fingers gripped his glass of wine. The diamonds and rubies on his ring glinted in the lamplight. My eyes went to Bethulda who sat to his left. She wore a plain, short-sleeved dress of powder blue. A cuff in the design of the Dark Elf crest wrapped around her right arm—a winged beast with scales made of emeralds, ruby and citrine plumes of fire pouring from its mouth, obsidian eyes glinting in the light—and a necklace of rubies nestled between her breasts.

I laughed, taking a chair to his right and picking up the glass of wine placed there. "How could I refuse?" Sipping my drink as I appraised Rah.

His black hair was slicked back, white iris's shifted and swirled as they looked at me. He was dressed smartly. Velvet waistcoat in gray with black lapels covered a white, silk shirt. Gray trousers and polished black boots completed the ensemble. His gaze penetrated me, and his finger tapped the glass he held. I felt insignificant, dirty, and underdressed. I had not had a proper bath, and my clothes were in need of washing. I had no doubt it was done on purpose to show me who was in charge.

To show me I was nothing more than a filthy in-bred Shadow Elf.

"Bethulda has told me you wish to have more freedom," Rah said as he filled his plate with food. "What makes you think you deserve it?"

"What makes you think I don't?"

Rah's eyes narrowed. "I would watch my tongue if I were you. Your cell is still available."

"As I told your wife, I have no weapons and no magic." I lifted the arm with the Sigaa'Lean. "What can I possibly do?"

"Flee."

I laughed. "In a land full of Dark Elves? Do you think me foolish?"

Rah raised an eyebrow. "You are a Shadow Elf. Your kind isn't the brightest."

"We were smart enough to eradicate your race."

Rah chuckled. "Not completely. Like I said. Not the brightest."

I glanced at Bethulda who sat quietly eating her meal. "If you're that concerned, give me a guard. Your wife was in my room earlier. Did I harm her?"

Rah pursed his lips.

"Let him have guarded freedom for a few days." Bethulda's voice drew my attention. "If he proves not to be like his kind, there is no harm in making it permanent."

Rah opened his mouth to speak. Whatever he was going to say was cut off by the sound of the door being thrown open. Looking in the direction of the sound, a man, who bore a striking resemblance to Bethulda, stood on the threshold flanked by two armed guards. His wrists and ankles were shackled, and he stumbled, nearly falling, as he was pushed inside. He glared at the guards, then flicked his head, tossing a lock of red hair out of his eyes. His back was straight, and his amber eyes looked at Rah and Bethulda who leapt to their feet.

"What is the meaning of this?" Bethulda's eyes flashed with anger.

"My lady, this was found in your brother's room," one of the guards said, holding out a vial. Bethulda hesitated a moment, then crossed the room to where the shackled man stood. She took the vial and peered at it.

"What is this?"

"Raven's Blood, my lady." The man said.

Raven's Blood? I knew it to be a very potent poison, though it was slow acting. It made the victim sick and slowly attacked their organs, eventually turning them into liquid. It was a horrifically painful way to go.

Bethulda looked at her brother who stood ramrod straight, face stoic.

"What is the meaning of this, Bethos? Why would you have this poison?" He stared at Bethulda but said nothing.

"Answer her," Rah strode across the room to stand next to his wife.

"Did you give this to Cassion?" Bethulda crossed her arms.

Bethos smiled. "Yes."

Rah's jaw clenched "Why would you do that? Why would you poison your own nephew?"

"You know why," Bethos' eyes narrowed on his sister. "Do you want a son who is like them?" He jerked his head in my direction.

Bethulda and Rah glanced at me.

"He is my son. He is nothing like them," Rah spat. "But what would you know? You know nothing of my people. Of what we have been through."

"At the hands of those like Cassion. They left you to die. He will be no better than them." His eyes went to me again.

"He is my son. Our son," Rah said, pulling Bethulda to his side. "And your nephew, who you poisoned."

"I am just sorry he hasn't died," Bethos said. His head snapped to the side, the sound of the slap Bethulda delivered, echoed off the walls.

"You are not my brother," Bethulda said through clenched teeth. "You are nothing to me. Dead to me." She spat on the floor. Her eyes went to one of the guards. "What of the antidote? Is there one?"

The guard nodded. "The healers are working on it."

Bethulda nodded "Good," she said, turning hate-filled eyes on her brother. "Lock him in a cell. He will be executed in two days' time," she ordered. The guards nodded and pulled Bethos back.

"You will regret this." he said, as he was dragged away.

Bethulda said nothing, and Rah pulled her into his embrace.

"I am sorry," he said.

She pulled away and looked up at him. "Cassion will live," she said. Her eyes went to me. "If it weren't for Phabian, he would be lost to us."

Rah's white eyes turned in my direction. "Perhaps," he stated. He crossed the room to where I still sat. Rah filled our glasses and sat back in his chair and sipped his wine. "You saved my son with your mind invasion, and I am grateful. I will tell you what you wish to know. And more of which you probably do not."

I sat back in my seat and, for the second time since Serafin had been gone, was I told a tale that went against everything I was taught, and everything I knew.

FORTY-SEVEN
DAMIYUN

I BOLTED AWAKE. My body and bed were soaked with sweat, the sound of my screams echoed through the dark room. The door opened, and I turned to see Serafin standing in the doorway. The soft lamplight poured in from the hall, shining through the silk shift she wore, the outline of her body silhouetted beneath, and I cursed her, and my own traitorous body.

"Damiyun. Are you alright?"

I rubbed a hand over my face and nodded. "Yes. I'm fine. Just a nightmare."

It's your reality. You will never escape it. Never escape me.

Gritting my teeth, I shut the voice out and pulled my body out of bed, trying to hide the wince from the pain inflicted during my slumber. Crossing the room, I poured a glass of water. My hand shook as I brought it to my lips, water slopping over the side and onto the floor.

"You're shaking." Serafin's voice came from beside me and she put her hand on my arm.

"I'm fine."

"Do you want to talk about it?"

I poured more water and drank it. Gods, but I needed something far stronger. I was stupid for not drinking myself into oblivion like I did every night. For not dulling the pain. The agony. For not making the torture bearable.

"No."

"Damiyun. You were screaming in terror. You're shaking and drenched with sweat. You are not fine." She reached for my face, and I pulled away.

I ran a hand through my hair and slipped out onto the balcony. The breeze was cool upon my naked torso. I took a deep breath and looked up at the star-lit sky.

"It's nothing to concern you. I have them every night. I've grown quite used to them."

Serafin hopped up on the stone railing, face a mask of concern. I leaned against the wall and looked at her. Gods, but she was pretty, even more so with her tangled hair and heavy, sleep-filled eyes.

Don't even go there. You don't want to get tangled up with her.

Themesis' laughter echoed in my head. *What's wrong, Damiyun? Afraid you'll kill her too?*

I gritted my teeth and winced at the words. At the bitter truth within them.

"Are you sure you're alright?" Serafin's soft fingers brushed my arm.

"Are you going to keep asking me that? I told you. I am fine. There's no need to concern yourself with me."

"Forgive me for being alarmed when I am woken up by someone screaming. Next time I will leave you be," she sniffed, a hurt tone in her voice as she hopped off the wall and began moving away.

I sighed. "I'm sorry, Princess. I appreciate your concern." She stopped and looked at me. The soft moonlight shining upon her skin made her look ethereal.

Damn the gods. Why must they torture me so? I clenched my fists, resisting the urge to pull her into my arms. Resisting the flare of rising desire. Rubbing my eyes, I sighed again, crossing the balcony, and throwing myself down in a soft, cushioned chair. Serafin perched on the edge of a chair opposite.

"I'm sorry," I said again, though for what, I wasn't sure. The need to break the silence was there. "I don't much talk about myself."

I don't much like to.

"That's fine. I was just concerned. I thought something horrible was happening."

I laughed. "It was. It's Themesis. He torments me in my sleep. And my waking hours."

She cocked her head, lips drawn in a slight frown.

"Right. I forgot your kind don't believe in the gods. Themesis is the Fallen One. He rules the Abyss."

And I would have ruled the world if not for you.

"Ah. Those mythical beings that drive your actions. Continue," she waved a hand. Amusement played on her face as she sank back into the cushioned chair, dangling her legs over the arm. "So why does he torment you?"

"Because he owns me." I locked eyes with hers. "I am far from a good man. Far from being the kind, decent and moral sort. My rest lies in the Abyss when my time here is through."

"What does that have to do with your nightmares?"

"He is showing me what my eternity will be. An Eternity of agonizing torture. Of being healed, only to endure it again and again."

"So why would this... god..." Serafin smirked, "do this?"

"Because I sold my soul to him."

She laughed. "Your story gets more unbelievable as you go on."

Will you tell her why you sold it? Tell her you killed your wife shortly after? Will you tell her you killed your former lover too? Themesis chuckled. *You don't even know who she is.*

I frowned.

What will you do when you find out and you realize she never loved you? Lillyanna?

No one could ever love you, Themesis whispered, his voice fading, retreating to the dark recess of my mind.

"So why does this—Fallen One—own your soul?"

"Go to bed, Princess." I rose to my feet.

"Damiyun—"

I pulled her out of the chair, tipped her chin, and looked down at her. "Go to bed, Princess. I'm fine. My pains are not your worry."

Her tongue flicked out and licked her lips. I stifled a groan and stepped back a pace. "We can talk more on the morrow if you wish. I—I need to be alone for a bit."

She opened her mouth, then closed it and brushed past me. I let out a puff of air when I heard the door shut and looked up at the star-filled sky again.

Fuck it all. Why did I agree to do this?

I rubbed the stubble on my chin and went back inside the room. Climbing back into bed, I pulled the covers up and tried to ignore the beautiful woman across the hall.

I LOOKED UP AS Serafin crept into the dining room. She wore a silk periwinkle dress, fitted at the waist, the skirt flowing down to the floor like a waterfall. Shortly after she settled in, I sent for the tailor to make her a wardrobe. She protested when dresses, trousers, and shirts of silk, satin, and cotton arrived along with warm cloaks, shoes and boots made of soft calf's leather. I was not going to make the same mistake with Zenith's clothing. Her hair was loose, falling to her waist in soft waves, the light from the sun glinting off the red streaks, making them glow like fire. And damn, if a picture of her from the night before standing in my doorway with her hair tousled from sleep, the lamplight shining through her sleep dress outlining her body make its way into my mind.

She stepped shyly into the room, as though we had spent the night together, something I had wanted. For a moment.

Laughter rang in my head. *You have no idea who she is.* He said the words he spoke the night prior. Gritting my teeth, I looked at Serafin who hesitated a beat, then strode into the room taking the chair to my left. The silence stretched as she piled food on her plate, and I did the same.

"Last night," she said, cutting into an egg. Eyes that were more green than blue today looked at me. Why did they look so familiar?

Taking a bite of a pastry, the sweet strawberry jam filling my mouth, I looked back at her. "I told you. I have terrors at night." *And the only damn thing that calms them is drinking myself into oblivion.*

She chewed her lip, an innocent gesture, yet one that made her look desirable, and I looked away. Fuck me, but I couldn't do this. I took a deep breath and looked back at her. "I killed my wife." *And Lillyanna who I loved with every fiber of my being.*

Serafin put down her fork. "What?"

Sighing, I sat back in my chair. I might as well get this over with as I was sure it would come up eventually. Perhaps this confession would create a divide between us. I could only hope.

"I walked in my wife Zenith's room and saw her in a passionate embrace with another man. She threw a dagger at me and I—I died," I said, rubbing my heart where the weapon hit. I took a sip from the glass of juice before me, wishing I had something stronger, or at the least, that the juice was laced with it. "I sold my soul because I loved her."

Serafin took a sip of her juice. "But...but you killed her."

I rubbed my eyes. "She—her words were hateful." And as I said it, I realized how weak and pathetic they sounded, as did Serafin who jumped up, her chair crashing to the marble floor.

"So that made it fine to kill her? Because her words were hateful?" Her eyes, now a deep shade of blue, glared at me. "I think you are a boorish brute. Will you kill me now?"

Heat raged through my body at her words. Slowly rising, I placed my fists on the table and leaned forward. A flicker of fear passed through her eyes, and I suppressed a smile. Good. The more fearful of me she was, the better. "Who are you to judge what I did? You, whose race fucking kills anyone who puts a foot on your lands? You, who never should have been born?" Standing, I glared down at her and damn if her set jaw and defiant eyes did not cause a traitorous stirring within me, a vision of tossing her over my shoulder, throwing her on my bed, and having my way with her entering my mind. I pushed it back as quick as it came. "You, whose father sentenced his own daughter to death because why?" I leaned forward still, "a barren queen is with child, and here you stand in my home telling me what a monster I am?"

Gathering her skirts, she turned and stalked out of the room. I rubbed my eyes. Fuck me, but this was going to be harder than I thought. I only hoped Barlack would tell me to bring her to Val'I'Victorous soon.

A tinge of guilt needled its way into my conscience for speaking to her the way I did, and I rubbed my face. Sighing, I crossed the room and up the stairs to apologize to the petulant princess.

FORTY-EIGHT
SERAFIN

"P RINCESS?" DAMIYUN'S VOICE CAME from the other side of the door.

"I do not wish to speak with you," I said as I stuffed clothes into my saddle bags. The hinges of the door groaned, and I turned to see his six foot, broad shouldered frame fill the doorway. His long, white hair hung just below his shoulders, the top buttons of the black shirt he wore were open, and I glimpsed an expanse of smooth, white skin, and snug trousers that left little to the imagination sheathed his legs.

"I didn't say you could come in."

He raised an eyebrow, his gray eyes sparked with amusement. "In case you didn't know, this is my house."

I stopped stuffing clothes in my bags. Crossing my arms, I glared at him. "So that means you can just burst through closed doors when you want? Wonderful."

A low chuckle rumbled through his chest, then his face turned serious. "Princess…"

"Serafin."

"Princess." The corner of his lips twitched. "I came to apologize for my outburst. It was uncalled for. I am sorry."

Turning, I buckled the bags and hoisted them on my shoulder. "You don't have to worry about that. I'm going back to Uma's."

"Is that so?" Damiyun folded his arms.

"Yes, that is so."

"You can't."

"I didn't ask you to bring me here," I said, brushing past him. He grabbed my arm.

"Princess—"

"Master Rayne," Levin's voice called out as the man hurried down the hall toward us. "There is a Suppressor at the door inquiring on Miss Trounde. What do I do?"

My heart flew into my throat. "Ghent." Tossing the bags to the ground and pulling from Damiyun's grasp, I raced down the hall.

"Wait," Damiyun's voice called after me, but I didn't stop, even when I heard footsteps pounding behind.

Racing down the curved staircase, I flew through the house to the front door. Pulling it open, my eyes went to Ghent who stood on the covered porch. Dark curls blew in the light breeze, hazel eyes met mine, the corners crinkling up in a smile. It had been nearly a Moon Cycle since I had seen Ghent.

"Fin." Stepping forward, he pulled me close, crushing me against his chest, his mouth catching mine in a kiss that left me breathless. "When Uma told me you left, and who you went with," his jaw clicked and nostrils flared, "I about lost it. I wanted to follow, I really did, but I had to get back to Wren's Keep before night fell. I came as soon as I was able." He pushed a lock of hair behind my ear. "I am here to bring you back."

I took a step back. "I am capable of making the trip myself. "After all, I did travel here alone from Il'Ekhester. "I was about to leave before you showed."

Ghent smiled. "Good. Let's go." He took my hand, but I pulled free.

Something didn't feel right about this. How could I be sure he was taking me to Uma's and not to the Suppressor Compound? The presence of elven soldiers who knew my name gave me away as a Wielder. And Ghent was a Suppressor whose loyalty laid with the order.

And Arden.

The thought of meeting that man again put icicles in my blood.

Ghent's questioning eyes looked back at me. "Fin?"

"She is not going anywhere," Damiyun's deep voice came from behind.

My jaw clenched, and for a moment, however brief, I wanted to defy him and go with Ghent. However, my uncertainty of his intentions kept me rooted to the spot and I stilled the remark on my tongue.

"She just told me she was leaving."

Damiyun stepped out onto the porch. Gray eyes glanced at me for a moment, and then went back to Ghent. "I am aware of what she thinks she is doing and where she thinks she is going. Just as I am sure you are aware she is not safe there. Vel may very well send a patrol back to that town with Feelers and she will be taken." He folded his arms and widened his stance. "What will you do when that happens, and it will happen."

Ghent's nostrils flared. "I won't let it."

Damiyun snorted. "Do you think you can stop Arden?"

Ghent took a step forward. "Why does it matter to you anyway? Why did you bring her here?"

"Because her life was in danger." Damiyun glanced at me again. "And I have been tasked with keeping her safe."

Ghent's eyes narrowed for a minute, and then he looked at me. "Fin?"

What was I supposed to say? I trusted a boorish brute of a stranger more than I trusted the man I said I loved? It was, in part, truth.

"I don't...I need..." I shook my head. "Damiyun, can you give me a moment?" I turned to him.

"Of course," he said, not moving and not blinking, eyes on Ghent.

Taking Ghent's arm, we made our way down the steps and out of earshot of Damiyun. I glanced back to where he still stood. He made an imposing presence and I wondered what he would do if Ghent tried forcing me to go with him. Would he get physical? Would he toss me over his shoulder and run me into his home for safety? My heart fluttered at the thought. I couldn't deny feeling a thrill when he picked me up in the village, and when he pulled me onto his lap.

"Fin?" Ghent's voice pulled me back from my unwanted thoughts. "You said you were about to leave."

"I did, but I realize that would be a rash move. There are things you don't know about me."

He shrugged. "You're an elf. The soldiers gave that away." He flashed a smile, then pulled of the sleeve of his right arm, the sun glinting off the smooth obsidian of the Sigaa'Lean he wore. "I am a Wielder too," he said, and I felt it was only to ease my mind. He was still a Suppressor, and I knew many joined to save their own lives. Though he told me he had no choice, that he was in it because of his bloodline, he was still one of them.

"Damiyun is right. There is no reason for Arden to not send a patrol back to the village." The thought that I put the life of Uma and who knows who else at risk by being there, being outed, made my stomach turn. For all I knew the Suppressors were there already. Uma could be dead. Tears pricked my eyes at the thought.

Ghent tensed. His eyes flicked to the porch and I had to resist the urge to turn around. Was Damiyun still there?

"I don't like you being here. You're not safe."

"He put his life on the line for me," I said. Ghent had been absent when Allendaire's elves tried to take me. He had not stood up for me. The man who I all but let claim me, who said he loved me, did not protect me. A stranger did. It made me wonder all the more.

"I know Damiyun. He thinks with his cock and loves nothing more than a pretty face. What is to stop him from going into your room and forcing himself on you at night?"

I chewed my lip. He did just walk into my room earlier.

Ghent gripped my hand. "I don't trust him, Fin. If you are apprehensive about returning to Voodomecism, we will find another town. Any place but here."

I stole a glance over my shoulder. Damiyun still stood on the porch, arms crossed, stance wide, and body rigid. He looked dark. Threatening. And so damn sexy. He was a coiled viper ready to strike if Ghent so much as breathed wrong.

He protected me. He was ready to strike down the king's soldiers. He was ready to lay down his life for me, but where was Ghent? I could not stop the thought, and yet I could not ask the question. I loved him and perhaps that stopped me because there was a part inside that did not want to know the answer.

He was a Suppressor, after all.

I took a deep breath. "I am going to stay here until Uma assures me it is safe to go back."

He ran a hand through his hair, eyes flicking to Damiyun. "Fin—"

"I will be fine. He protected me."

"He is a womanizer and you, a beautiful young woman, are just his type."

Would it be so bad if I did end up in his bed? I chased the thought away.

"Ghent," I said, and his features softened. "I love you." *Did I?* "I am going to stay." His eyes darkened and I quickly pulled him close. "Uma will tell me when things have settled." If she was alive.

His hands gripped my waist hard, almost painfully and he looked down at me, expression hard. "I don't like this," he snarled, and then his expression and his grip softened. "I will come back in a couple days. If anything happens—"

"I will be fine."

Turning, he made his way to where his mount waited. Swinging up into the saddle, he took one last look at me then heeled him down the road. As I watched Ghent leave, I was filled with mixed emotions. Sorrow because he was gone, a strange relief for the same, and a tinge of fear that he would show up with a troop to come get me.

"Are you alright, Princess?" Damiyun's soft voice came from behind. Taking a deep, cleansing breath, I turned around. He was close, only a hands width away. Heat radiated off his body. Did he always feel this way? Was his skin hot to the touch? My face heated at the thought, and I took a step back.

"Stop calling me princess."

"Is that not what you are? I could call you Her Royal Pain In The Ass. So far that's been accurate."

I glared up at him. "Fuck you, Damiyun."

He gasped and held a hand to his chest. "My lady."

"Fuck off, Damiyun." I pushed past him, his hand grasped my wrist, and I whirled around, ready for a fight but my eyes only met a concerned face.

"Are you alright?" He asked again, and those words and the damned concern in his tone undid me. Clutching him, I cried into his shirt. My tears ran for everything I had gone through in my life. For the hatred of the elves. For the king sentencing me to death. For giving up who I was for Ghent, and for fear that Uma might be in danger.

"Serafin," Damiyun said, voice soft.

"It's princess." My hands curled into his shirt, my tears soaked the fabric.

Damiyun's arms held me close, his hand rubbed my back. I knew I should have pulled away, but he was a comfort.

"You're alright, Princess. What can I do?" His breath was a warm caress in my ear.

"Not kill me?"

Damiyun tensed, and then a chuckle rumbled through his chest. Pulling away, he tipped my chin. "Princess, I think every day with you will be a test." He pulled away and I pushed down the brief feeling of disappointment. "It's early and there is a festival in town. I'm not a healer, but I have heard they make sad people happy."

"Is there food?"

"Lots."

I smiled. "Then let's go."

AFTER STABLING YASMINE AND Xander, we walked through the crowded streets. Carts filled with food and trinkets lined the sides. Men and women on stilts juggled balls and swallowed fire. It reminded me of the solstice festivals on my lands and a pang of sadness hit me. Damiyun slipped his hand in mine, giving a gentle squeeze as he looked down at me as though he felt my sadness.

"What is this for?" I gestured around.

"It's the Festival of the Gods. It used to happen once every Grand Passage, but as people stopped believing, they stopped celebrating. It has just recently started up again," he said as he dodged people in the streets, dragging me behind.

"Here." He pulled to a stop in front of a food cart. "The best food at the festival."

The man behind the cart smiled and nodded to Damiyun. I watched the man press out two discs of dough, dropped them in boiling oil for a moment, then liberally sprinkled sugar on top. Handing them to Damiyun after he passed the man coin, he held one out to me. I took a bit of the hot treasure, the dough melting on my tongue and the sugar adding just the right amount of sweet.

"What is this?" I said as I finished mine, eyeing the small bite Damiyun had left. Laughing he gave it to me and I popped it in my mouth.

"I don't rightly know what it's called, just that it's delicious and my favorite."

We walked down the road, stopping at booths selling trinkets and baubles. Damiyun picked up a necklace. It was a single stone that was blue or green, depending on how the sunlight hit it, set on a delicate chain of gold.

"How much?" He asked the man behind the booth.

"Oy. That be two silver."

Damiyun reached into his pocket.

"Damiyun—"

"Will this make you smile?"

"Well, another one of those delicious treats might."

Chuckling, he handed the man the coin. Turning around, I lifted my hair and he secured the necklace.

"You didn't have to. My sadness is not your concern."

Taking my hand again, he gave a gentle squeeze. "Maybe not, but while you are in my care, Princess, your happiness is." He looked around the street. "Where to now?"

My eyes lit on a small stage where children were gathering. It was a puppet stage, much like the one at my Name Day celebration.

"Can we watch the show?"

Damiyun followed my gaze.

I remembered Phabian chastising me for wanting to watch it and my face heated with embarrassment for wanting to watch another. "Never mind. It's for children," I said.

A smile curled Damiyun's lips. "If it's what you want to do, then we shall."

We pushed our way through the crowd finding two spots in the front. Again, my mind went to my Name Day when Cwella and I sat in front of a puppet stage. Before the demons came.

"Princess?"

I looked at Damiyun. He cupped my chin, thumbs wiping the tears I did not know I shed. "I'm fine."

"You're not. Do you want to go home?"

The curtains opened and puppets on strings loped onto the stage. "No."

I watched the puppets bounce about, telling the tale of the humans past. Of their gods past. Of a man named Themesis who wanted to control the world, the only god worshiped. He gathered lesser gods and waged a war. Though the gods lost many, they prevailed, tossing Themesis and those who helped him to the Abyss where he was entombed in the obsidian beneath Kraagswell Mountain. I watched the puppets dragging the one called Themesis below the stage. A black paper mountain popped up with him inside.

A female puppet drifted out on stage. She wore a blue dress; her long blonde hair flowed down her back in soft waves. I couldn't take my eyes off her, and had I not known any better, I would have thought the puppet's blue eyes looked straight at me.

The crowd cheered as the puppet drifted across the stage, voices yelling "all hail Felicity, the Goddess of Nature."

"He will forever be locked in the Abyss. We will bless humans with magic, and the life and breath of them will keep him locked way for eternity," Felicity declared, and the cheers rose to a crescendo.

I glanced at Damiyun whose eyes were on the puppet, his jaw clenched. The curtains closed, and people began to leave.

"If the magic of Wielders keep him entombed and the Suppressors are killing them, what does that mean?"

Damiyun's jaw clenched. "That his binds will weaken and he will break free."

"Is that why there are demons at night?"

"Yes. I thought your kind didn't believe in the gods?"

I shrugged. "My people are narrow minded and only believe what they are fed by their king. I have learned this from being off my lands." I looked at him. "What happened to me, what I have seen and learned in the four Moon Cycles I have been on my own has made me more open minded. I may not believe in the gods, but I will not look down on those who do."

Damiyun looked at the sky. "There are a few more hours of daylight before the festival is over. What would you like to do next?"

I thought for a moment. "I would like to play some games."

"Alright, Princess. Games it is. Just know I am very competitive and dislike losing."

I grinned. "As am I. Bet?"

"I'm always up for something to up the stakes. What are you thinking?"

I skipped backwards, eyes on him as I thought for a moment. "The loser cooks dinner for the winner for a fortnight, whatever they request."

Damiyun arched an eyebrow as he casually followed me, hands clasped behind his back. "Are you sure about having to do something you know nothing about?"

I smiled. "Yes, because I don't plan on losing," I said.

Though I knew what Damiyun thought of me, he wasn't completely wrong. I was a pampered princess with servants at my bidding, though he had them as well. Phabian, for reasons unknown to me, made sure I knew how to do basic things, including cooking. Though I could not make a gourmet meal, I could make almost anything. Almost.

Perhaps somewhere inside he knew I might be turned out and he was preparing me on how to survive on my own without servants to do everything for me, though I was sure he did not think I would be sentenced to death.

"Neither do I," Damiyun said. Holding out his hand, we shook on our bet and made our way to the first game.

Over the next few hours, Damiyun and I competed in all sorts of games. Tossing axes to see who could get closest to the center, hitting a hammer to see who could make the boulder go the highest, and firing arrows at a target, the bullseye a tiny feather that had to be pierced, which Damiyun was far from good at. Though if I were to be truthful, Damiyun cheated once or twice, though in the end our score was even.

"Even score, Princess. What does that mean?" He said as we entered the stable.

I looked up at him. "Well, you cheated more times than I could count but I forgive you," I flashed a smile and swung up into the saddle. "One week of cooking for you, whatever I want, and one for me, whatever you want."

Damiyun swung up onto Xander and we guided our mounts to the road. "I didn't cheat, but your deal is fair. Just be careful what you wish for."

DARKNESS FELL, AND THOSE awful noises pierced the night as we made our way up the stairs.

"Did you have a nice day, Princess?" Damiyun said as we stood in the hall between our rooms.

"I did."

Damiyun took a few steps closer, closing the gap and my breath caught. "Did this make you happy?" His fingers brushed my skin as he held up the stone he bought.

I licked my lips. "Yes."

"Good." He cupped my chin. "I only want you to be happy. Sleep well, Princess." Turning, he went to his bedroom, leaving me alone feeling...I wasn't sure what I felt. It was confusing for sure, and some place deep inside of me said it was right.

FORTY-NINE
DAMIYUN

CLOSING THE DOOR, I ran a hand over my face. Fuck me, but that was the most fun, the happiest, I had been in a long time. Serafin was a breath of fresh air with her chatter, her questions, and just her. She made me forget. She made me happy, if only for a moment, however brief.

Stripping out of my clothes, I washed up in the basin and slipped beneath the bed covers to the nightmares that will never leave.

"DAMIYUN, WAKE UP."

I heard a voice from far away. Female in nature.

Hands shook me and I winced from the touch. The pain inflicted still fresh. The wounds still new.

"You're having a nightmare. Come on. Wake up."

I focused on that voice. On the warm hands upon me and pulled myself from the darkness.

"That's it. Come back to me, Damiyun."

Opening my eyes, I saw a face looming above, concern etched in emerald eyes. Moonlight glinted off of red hair spilling over the woman's shoulders. A smile curled her lips.

"It's alright. You're safe. You're in your bed. It was only a nightmare."

"Princess?"

"You were having another nightmare."

Laughter echoed again. *It is your reality.*

I leapt out of bed. I was tired of the nightmares. Tired of the taunts. My hold on my sanity was slipping. "Why are you doing this? Why won't you leave me alone?"

A look of concern and fear flashed across Serafin's face.

You know why.

"She was never yours."

But you are.

"Then why don't you take me? Why don't you end my existence? Have Zedekiah call my contract."

Oh, I will. When you crawl on your hands and knees begging me for it.

Stabbing agony shot through my head. My vision wavered. I fell to my knees.

Pain throbbed. My skull was slowly being crushed. I held my head and screamed.

Beg me for it.

Pulsating. Aching. Debilitating. I couldn't see.

I howled in agony.

Whip bit into the flesh of my back.

I fell to my hands.

Crawl to me. Beg me for it.

"No."

Pressure. Squeezing, pressing on my chest.

Whip bit again, and the crushing, debilitating pain stabbed my head. Lights flashed behind my eyelids.

Beg me for it.

My screams echoed off the wall. Bones broke beneath the hammer.

Crawl to me.

Shaking hand moved forward, sliding across stone, followed by my leg.

That's it, Damiyun. Crawl to me. Beg me for it.

Legs followed hands as I slowly dragged myself across the floor.

Laughter echoed inside my head. Pain throbbed and radiated through my body.

I couldn't take it. I wanted it to end. I felt sick. The smell of urine hit my nostrils.

"Please."

Ask me for it.

Tears and snot dripped from my face onto the floor. My trousers were soaked with piss. I slowly crawled forward.

"Please."

I screamed again as more pain tore through me. Ripped me open.

I just wanted it to stop.

Say it.

"Please," I sobbed. "Please take—"

"No." A deep voice snapped from far away.

Hands, soft and gentle, touched my bare back. I shivered as a wash of cold spread through me, followed by a blanket of warmth. The feeling was like that of an embrace. The pain receded, and I took a long, gasping breath of air. Sickness rose, and I vomited on the floor until there was nothing left. Until my sides ached from heaving.

"It's alright, Damiyun. You're safe." A soft, feminine voice disrupted the torture. Not Serafin.

I slowly sat back on my haunches, wiping my mouth with the back of my shaking hand, and looked into a pair of kind, brown eyes.

"You're all right," she repeated. A smile spread across her face. She rose to her feet, and I looked up at her.

Who was this woman who had saved me? How did she get here?

I looked to her left.

"Abraham."

His face was drawn into a frown, though black eyes held concern, and one hand slowly stroked the close-cut beard he wore.

I began to rise, my legs giving out, and I collapsed back to the floor.

"Easy, Damiyun," Abraham said, offering a hand. I grasped it, and he hauled me to my feet. I looked down at where I had been, shame filling me at seeing the vomit.

And piss.

"I... I need to change." I averted my gaze.

Fuck. My legs shook beneath me, and I didn't know if I could walk. I clutched Abraham, who led me to the washbasin at the table. My eyes went to the bed as I slowly shuffled across the room.

To Serafin, who sat there, knees drawn to her chest, a look of pity and pain on her face.

Shit. I had forgotten she was there. Shame and embarrassment flooded me. I let go of Abraham and took the clean pair of trousers the woman with him offered and then washed up.

"You don't have to do that," I said, watching as she grabbed a towel and cleaned up the mess I had made. She smiled up at me but said nothing. Serafin slipped off the bed and padded over to my side.

"Are you alright?" Eyes filled with concern searched my face.

I ran a shaking hand through my hair and nodded. "I'm fine, Princess. Why don't you go back to bed?"

She stayed where she was. Slipping her hand in mine, she gave it a gentle and reassuring squeeze. "Why are you here?" I turned my attention to Abraham.

"You were about to give yourself over to Themesis."

"So, you're here to call the contract, then?"

He folded his arms. "No."

I laughed. "Right."

"It's the truth," the woman's soft, melodic voice said. "Abraham felt your pain. We came here to save you."

"Who are you?"

"My wife, Palma," Abraham said, and I did my best to hide my shock.

"You should have left me. End my insufferable misery."

He quirked an eyebrow. "Do you think your misery will end when he claims you? This is but a small taste of what your eternity holds. Palma?"

The woman stepped forward and placed her hands on either side of my head. Icy fingers caressed me, I shivered at the feel. When she removed them, the presence of Themesis, though still there, was less.

"I put in a bit of a block. I can't hide him completely, but it should be enough to let you rest for a few nights." She stepped back next to Abraham. "I will make you an elixir to take at night. It will essentially do the same. It will also contain a potent herb to help you rest. Abraham will bring it tomorrow."

"Thank you. You are too kind. I don't deserve it."

Palma smiled. "Everyone deserves kindness, Damiyun. Even you."

I watched the shadows envelope Palma and Abraham, crawling from the corners, demon shadow beings swirling around them in an inky mist, and then they were gone.

Dropping Serafin's hand, I crossed the room, grabbed a bottle of Serpent's Venom, and stepped outside. The air was cool on my hot skin, and I breathed in the damp earth and mud scent of spring. The night sounds, frogs, crickets, and other animals were a soft and soothing symphony, though interrupted by the screeches and screams of faceless beasts in the woods. I sank down into the plush cushions of a couch, tension slowly easing from my sore and weary body. Serafin padded across the stone floor and perched on the armrest opposite me. Pulling the cork from the bottle, I took a long drink, then offered it up to her. "Are you alright?" Her soft voice broke the silence.

Was I? I couldn't rightly say. I was ready to give up. Give in to Themesis. Let him claim me. When Abraham stopped me, I'm not sure what I had felt.

"Damiyun?"

"I'm fine, Princess. Just tired. And sore."

"What was that? What was happening? It looked—and felt—so real."

"Because it was. It's what awaits me when I leave this world."

I got up and walked over to the wall and looked out over my lands. Gods, my body hurt. Though Palma had dulled Themesis, I still knew he was there. Waiting to torment me more.

"Fuck it all. Why are you doing this to me?" I yelled out into the darkness. A hand laid upon my back made me jump. I looked down at Serafin. "It's Themesis." I made my way back to the chair and sat. Serafin lowered herself beside me.

"The fallen god?"

I nodded, grasping the bottle she held and taking another drink. "Abraham may carry the contract on my soul, but he… he owns me. It was a mistake I will forever regret."

"I'm sorry." She reached out, her fingers trailing across the tattoos on my chest and I shivered. "Tell me about these."

I was sure her question was more to distract, and I was grateful for it. "Well, the one on my back, the sword, represents strength and protection, while the serpent is for transformation. This one, the phoenix," I touched the brightly colored bird on my right chest and shoulder. "This signifies rebirth and the raven on the skull," I glanced down at the black ink that covered my shoulder and left arm, "loss of a loved one. And no fear of death."

Her fingers softly traced the brand, the ugly "S," on the left side of my chest. "You were a Suppressor."

"Yes. Not by choice. Arden sent them when I was fourteen."

"I'm not surprised," she said, and I laughed. "And the scars?"

"My father and the Suppressors," I said, brushing a hand over the back of my shoulder. "The others?" I shrugged. "Being on the wrong side of a sword."

"You've been through a lot."

I rubbed my eyes. She didn't know the half of it. Turning, I looked at her. "I don't…I don't want to be alone," I said, my voice sounding pathetic to my ears.

Serafin bit her lip, and I suppressed a groan. "I understand. What happened to you, it looked terrifying. But—"

"Sleep, Princess. That is all." *For tonight.* "I just…I don't want to be alone," I said again. The thought of it, of more nightmares terrified me.

"Alright, Damiyun. I'll stay."

Rising, I held my hand out and pulled Serafin to her feet and we made our way back to my room and slipped beneath the covers. Serafin curled into me, her head on my chest, an innocent act, but damn, it felt right. Slipping my arms around her, I held her close and hoped I would slip into a dark and blissful sleep.

FIFTY
ABRAHAM

"**H**ERE IS MY ELIXIR to help Damiyun sleep," Palma said, walking into the sitting room.

"He doesn't know the girl is Lillyanna's daughter." Damiyun referring to her as princess told me all I needed to know.

"No, he doesn't." Palma sat down beside me. "She has made him happy in the short time she has been with him."

Fuck. I ran a hand over my face and scratched my beard. "What am I to do?"

Palma touched my knee. "Would it be so bad to let him have this?"

"She is Lillyanna's."

"But not his." She took my face in her hands and turned it toward her. "Why would you end his happiness?"

Pulling away, I stood. "Because it is wrong."

I heard the rustle of clothes as Palma rose as well. "Like Jaylynn and Arias? Did you disapprove because he was Fae? Do you disapprove because Serafin is Lillyanna's daughter?"

My jaw clenched, and my heart pounded. "I disapproved because he stole my daughter," I roared. Bel chirped, his little wings fluttered.

A hand gripped my arm, and I looked down at Palma. My rock. My heart. "He did, and Themesis took what Damiyun loved. He loves again, just as you have. Why would you take that from him?"

"He needs to know."

"He does but not now." Palma wrapped her arms around me.

I rested my forehead on hers. "I love you."

She pulled away. "And I, you. Give them a chance. It might not last, but if it does, his love for her will be pure and not because she is Lillyanna's."

"He will hate me."

Palma smiled. "I suspect he will, but he will come back."

Kissing her upturned mouth, I pulled the shadows to me and made my way to Pine Crest Manor.

"**I**S KNOCKING NOT A thing anymore?" Damiyun closed the book on his lap and tossed it on the table.

"Would you have let me in if you saw me?"

"It's common decency."

I laughed. "When did that ever concern you? Where's the girl?"

"She went into town to buy food to make me dinner."

I raised an eyebrow, and he laughed. "It was a bet we made on games at the festival."

I placed the vial on the table and sat in a plush chair. "Palma's elixir. How do you feel?"

"Better than I have in my life. Thank you, for what you did."

"I did nothing. It was Palma. I just brought her."

"Which you didn't have to."

I laughed. "Saving your sorry ass isn't anything new. I might start charging if you keep it up."

Damiyun chuckled. "Blood Bound, eh? What magic did you use on her for that to happen? I can't imagine a woman as pretty as that would hop into bed with an uncouth brute like you. Not willingly, anyway."

I couldn't stop the smile that tugged my lips. "Fuck you, Damiyun."

He got up and poured two glasses of spirits, handing one to me. We fell into a comfortable silence, much like those between us before.

I took a deep breath. "I—I'm sorry for everything that happened, Damiyun."

He took a sip of his drink. "I know you are."

"I was playing a part. I had to be convincing. If I broke character even once, if one of his demons caught me, if either you or Lillyanna did something..." I shook my head.

"There is nothing we can do. We can't bring her back."

No, but she lives on in her daughter. Gods, but he has a right to know.

"Damiyun?" A voice called out as the front door slammed shut.

"Parlor," he called back. Footsteps echoed through the halls and the girl stepped into the room. She wore a white, long sleeved peasant top, leather trousers, and purple suede boots. Her hair was piled on top of her head in a messy bun, tendrils of white and red curled around her face. Gods, but she was pretty.

"You were here last night," she said.

"Yes."

"I'm Serafin." She smiled warmly. "Thank you, for whatever you did."

"Did you find everything on my list, Princess?" A smile tugged Damiyun's lips and his grey eyes danced with amusement.

The girl crossed her arms and glared at him. "Did you purposely put alabaster root on it so I would look like a fool asking for something that doesn't exist?"

Damiyun laughed. "Maybe."

She put her hands on her hips. "Is that so? Well, maybe I will add a surprise to your meal and maybe we will see how you like it." She huffed, turning on her heel and flounced out of the room.

Damiyun chuckled, his eyes filled with fondness, and perhaps a bit of love, as he watched her leave.

No. I won't tell him who she was. It could quite possibly destroy him.

I rubbed my eyes. "As you know, Themesis' binds still weaken. Too many Wielders have been captured or killed. He has ordered the Soul Collectors to hunt and kill Wielders so he can break free."

"Including you?" He finished his drink and poured more into both our glasses.

"Including me. When that happens, when his binds break and he is free, I will kill him."

"Are you sure that is what needs to be done? Are you sure there isn't another way to achieve your goal? If you despise him so much, why haven't you ended his life? Why must he break free for this to happen?" He gestured with his glass.

"Because that is when he will be the most vulnerable."

"But, does his blood, his magic, not run through your veins? Surely you can destroy him."

I rubbed my eyes and took a drink. "I am his son, something I wish to forget. He owns the Abyss. His magic draws from it. As long as he is within the obsidian walls of his tomb, he is far more powerful than I am. Why do you think my magic did not hurt him? You know the gods cannot be in the mortal world for more than one Grand Passage and a day. They begin to get weak the moment they come here. You know my father is a narcissist. He has been locked up in the Abyss for thousands of Grand Passages and would never return. When he is mortal, I will be able to kill him."

"But Lillyanna, her death was supposed to strengthen the binds. Why didn't it work?"

I shook my head. "I do not know the answer to that. Perhaps his binds have weakened past the point of noreturn."

Damiyun filled his glass again. "But surely Felicity, the other gods, would have known this. Why have Lil be Blood Bound to him?"

I rubbed my eyes. "I don't know, Damiyun." I took a deep breath. "Themesis wants me to bring you to him."

He laughed. "If you knew he wanted me, why did you save me last night?"

"Because you will not go there without me."

Damiyun rubbed his eyes. "When?"

Putting my glass on the table I rose. "Now."

WE STOOD OUTSIDE THE door to the throne room. Damiyun swallowed hard, his skin turning pale and I squeezed his shoulder.

"It is not like last time." I said. His hand squeezed mine. "Make it believable." I pushed opened the door. Themesis sat upon Nightshade. His black hair was pulled back, and he wore a velvet coat of royal blue over a black shirt, black trousers, and boots polished to a mirror shine. One finger idly tapped the Griffin's head that made up the armrest, while the other scratched Jaylynn's head, who sat to his left. I clenched my fists at the sight. Taking her chin, he softly spoke to her. Jaylynn nodded, then scurried away.

Damiyun's eyes were glued on the center of the floor.

"Easy," I said, voice low. He took a deep breath and strode to where Themesis sat.

"You brought him."

"Of course I did. Did you doubt me, Father?"

"Based on your previous betrayal? Yes.'"

Crossing the room, I poured two glasses of wine, handing one to my father and taking the golden throne beside him.

"What are your plans for him?" I gestured to Damiyun with my glass.

Themesis smiled. "He will kneel before me, swear his allegiance and pledge his loyalty."

Damiyun glared up at him. "For what purpose?"

"I won't readily call your contract and I will lessen the torture I inflict."

"No."

Themesis laughed. "You were so ready to give up last night. You crawled across the floor, crying and pissing yourself like a baby."

Damiyun's jaw clenched. "And now it is the light of day. I know better. I will not submit."

Themesis sighed. "I grow bored with your theatrics. Let's see how brave you are when the whip is real." He held out his hand and a whip with razor sharp barbs appeared. "Zedekiah?"

Taking the whip, I went to where Damiyun stood. Kicking behind his knees, he fell to the floor. I pulled back the arm that held the whip and struck. Once.

Twice. Three times. Damiyun's screams tore through me like the barbs that tore through his flesh.

"I swear," he panted. "You have my loyalty and my promise."

Themesis laughed. "I thought I would. Now, crawl to me, dog, and lick my boots."

"Is that necessary?"

Themesis' eyes narrowed on me. "Perhaps I should have you do the same to show your loyalty."

Pursing my lips, I watched Damiyun crawl the short distance to the throne, tongue flicking out to lick his boots. Themesis patted his head with a laugh. "Good boy."

Waving his hand, the wounds I inflicted disappeared, as did the whip I held.

"Now to seal our agreement." Pulling out a knife, he sliced his palm, squeezing the blood into his goblet. Holding the knife out to me, I grasped it. Grabbing Damiyun's wrist, I sliced his palm and squeezed his blood into my goblet of wine. Handing my glass to my father, I grasped his and gave it to Damiyun.

"Drink."

Damiyun hesitated a second before bringing the goblet to his lips, eyes on Themesis as he drained the contents.

Themesis smile "It is done. You are bound to me in blood and soul, Damiyun Rayne." He leaned forward. "I own you." Sitting back, he waved his hand. "You are dismissed."

Pulling the shadows, I brought us back to Pine Crest Manor. Damiyun stumbled across the parlor floor. Grabbing a bottle of spirits, he pulled the cork and took a long pull, wiping his mouth with the back of his shaking hand.

"You should have let me give myself over last night. He owns me anyway."

"And your existence would be far worse than anything he has ever done to you. At least you are alive and not serving him in the Abyss. He would turn you into a twisted monster. That is what most of his demons are. Men who were broken and twisted and turned into something gruesome and evil."

He ran a hand over his face with a sigh. "So, what now?"

"You do whatever he asks. Torture Wielders. Kill them. Whatever my father requests, you will do," I said. Pulling the shadows close, I drifted away from Pine Crest Manor and back to Howling Cove to my Palma.

FIFTY-ONE

"Zedekiah." A voice said, calling from the distance.

Not my father. No, it was female in nature.

I stood in a dark void and tried to pull the shadows close, but none came.

"You are nowhere, Zedekiah. You cannot call what is not here."

I looked around, my eyes going to a pretty woman with short black hair framing her heart shaped face.

"Samanka."

"Zedekiah." She bowed her head in reverence, sinking down into a deep curtsy, blue skirts billowing on the floor.

"What is this?"

"Zedekiah, Son of Themesis, the god of all gods, this is your dream."

I paused. I had not had a dream in my life.

Samanka laughed. "No, Zedekiah. You have not. This is the only way I could speak with you." The dark void shimmered and Felicity's gazebo appeared. Samanka took a seat on the ground, arranging her skirts. I slowly sat across from her.

"What is this about?"

"Felicity did not send her daughter to seal the binds. She sent her to free him. If Damiyun had not killed Lillyanna, he would have broken free."

How could I not know this? I shook my head. "But it didn't work. Demons roam the lands. His binds weaken still. Surely you know this."

"Of course, I do."

"Then you know when he breaks free, he will wage a war on the gods."

"Yes, with Felicity and Sarlay joining him."

I rubbed my eyes. "S'aehe will fall."

"Yes, as will the world with the three strongest gods ruling." Samanka bit her lip. "We need your help."

I rubbed my eyes. What was I to tell her? She was a god and they were all deceitful. Despite her bringing me to the plain of the dreams to ask my help, I can't say I trusted her.

I held my cards close to my chest. In an actual card game, I could bluff, knowing I would always win but this? Samanka was a god, and I was a lesser, though she gave me the honorific of the title I shed long ago. No, I did not trust her.

"Help with what? Do you wish me to wage a war like my father did? Send Felicity and Sarlay to the Abyss to live with him?"

"Of course not. Your magic grows stronger. His demons are slowly accepting you as their king, a sign of Themesis' growing weakness. It is why Felicity and Sarlay will join him. He cannot launch an attack on S'aehe alone."

I looked up at the ceiling. "What does all of this have to do with me?"

"He needs to break free so you can defeat him. You are the only one who can do it."

"I already plan on doing just that." I rose to my feet. "Is that all?"

Samanka rose from her spot against the pillows. Her eyes met mine and she bowed her head. "No. Zedekiah, Son of the Fallen One, god of gods, king of kings, we need you to rule."

B OLTING UP IN BED, I grabbed the blankets. Bel screeched from the corner where he slept, eyes on me, and I knew he saw.

"Abraham?" Palma's voice was thick with sleep. Her arms slipped around my waist and warm lips kissed my shoulder.

Always she was there for me.

I took a deep breath, turned my head and kissed her forehead. "No, my heart. No longer Abraham. I am Zedekiah."

FIFTY-TWO

SERAFIN

Tʜᴇ ᴛᴀᴠᴇʀɴ ᴡᴀѕ ʜᴏᴛ and crowded, the bard's music rising above the din of chatter. Damiyun and I sat at a table in the corner.

"I'm sorry," I said, looking down at my hands. It was my last day of cooking for Damiyun, and it was a disaster. The bread burned, the venison roast came out like shoe leather, and the cheese pie he wanted as dessert was a complete flop.

Damiyun laughed as he reached over and grasped my hand. "I may have had a hand in that disaster."

I looked up, his gray eyes danced with amusement. "What do you mean?"

He rubbed his hand on the back of his neck. "I admit your cooking skills surprised me. Whatever I asked for, you delivered. I just maybe thought you could use a break."

"So, you sabotaged my last meal for you? Wasted food?" I rose from the table. "Enjoy your mutton stew and I'll enjoy my ruined meal." I turned and began walking toward the door. Damiyun grabbed my arm stopping me.

"Sit." He was so close, his breath hot in my ear and damn if a fire didn't ignite inside me, heat running through my veins. "All your meals were good but if I told you not to cook the last? I would lose, and I hate losing."

I couldn't stop the laughter that bubbled inside. "But the food—"

"Will go to those in need in the poorer part of the town. Now sit, Princess."

And damn if I did not obey those words. He refilled my glass with wine and leaned back in his chair. I didn't know what to say, how to act. All I could think about was the heat radiating from him when he was beside me and I wanted to feel more.

The bard started a jaunty tune and tables were pushed away as people spilled out. Skirts lifted and legs kicked as patrons danced. Jumping up, I held my hand out to Damiyun.

"Dance?"

"No, Princess. I don't dance but you go on."

Hoisting my skirts, I pushed my way through the crowd to the people who were jumping, spinning, and clapping hands.

"Oy, lassie,' A man called out. Taking his hand, he twirled me around through the crowd. I had no cares. No problems as I danced, and then the song stopped, turning to something slow. Looking up, my eyes met Damiyun's who was striding toward me. I swallowed hard at the intense look in his eyes as he drew up before me.

"I thought you didn't dance."

"Not to that, no." He pulled me close, crushing me against his broad, hard chest. Damn, but he was a wall of solid muscles and smelled of cloves and cinnamon. "You realize you're a complication," he said, pulling back and looking down at me.

"How so?"

A chuckle rumbled through his chest and I clung to the vibration. "In every way." He took a deep breath. "On the morrow we will push on to the Wilde Elves."

I knew this was going to happen, though I wished it wasn't. "Twice, I've been comfortable in a new home and twice, I am forced to leave."

"I will be with you. I won't leave you there alone."

I looked up at him, the warmth he radiated encompassed me in a way I could not explain. His gray eyes met mine, and fingers brushed a lock of hair behind my ear. Did the music stop playing or did we just stop dancing? I did not know anything but Damiyun.

"Such a complication," he murmured softly. His hand curled in my hair and he dipped his head, lips meeting mine.

"Fin, what the fuck?"

Whirling around, I saw Ghent pushing his way through the crowd. Damiyun and I pulled away, though our hands were still entwined. How did he know I was here?

"What is this?" He stood in front of Damiyun, hands clenched. "I told her to leave but you? You wouldn't let her."

Damiyun laughed. "Let her? I hold no reins on Serafin. She comes and goes as she pleases."

Ghent's jaw ticked. "If that were true, she would have come with me."

"And go where? Wren's Keep? A Wielder, a fucking elf at that who is not protected by her lands?"

"I would protect her, and she could hide herself like she hid from me."

Damiyun laughed. "And when a Feeler gets close to her, what will you do?" Damiyun took a step closer to Ghent.

"Let's go talk," I said, grabbing Ghent's arm and dragging him out of the tavern and to the street.

"So, you're fucking him," he said, yanking his arm from my grasp.

"What? No." Though I had shared Damiyun's bed a few nights here and there, nothing happened, much to my dismay. He was every bit the gentleman, doing nothing more but holding me close. His tears often soaked my sleep dress, but I never brought it up when the sun woke.

Ghent laughed, a hollow sound. "Right. So, him holding you close, kissing you," his nostrils flared, "was nothing?" He shook his head. "Now I know why you wouldn't give yourself to me. All those times together—"

"All those times?" I took a step closer to Ghent, my magic flaring at his words. "Where was Damiyun all those times, Ghent?" I clenched my fists, magic swirled around my forearms. Ghent's eyes went to there and back to me.

"Fin—"

"No." I shoved him in the chest. "Damiyun wasn't at Uma's. He wasn't anywhere until the soldiers came for me."

"And he took you from me."

"No, Ghent, he didn't. He saved me. You were nowhere to be found."

"I came to take you back."

"To where? Voodomecism? To the Suppressors?" My magic burned. The sound of thunder rumbled in the distance and lightning forked through the sky. Power surged in my veins.

Do it. Use your magic. Kill everyone. A voice whispered deep in my mind. It was dark. Seductive, and for one moment I wanted to unleash it and annihilate everything. Annihilate Ghent. Taking a deep breath, I shook the thoughts, my magic retreating.

"Princess?" Damiyun's voice came from the door behind. Ghent's eyes went to him, and I held my hands out to keep them apart.

"I'm fine." I turned to Ghent. "Why are you here?"

"Brother," a voice called out. Damiyun's head snapped up and I followed his gaze. A dozen Suppressors marched toward us and my blood ran cold.

"Ghent—"

"I—I didn't."

"Get out of here, Serafin," Damiyun's voice was low as he brushed past me. I was rooted to the spot, my eyes on Arden who sauntered through the streets. Damiyun pulled Shadow Blade, the Pyragaty bone glowed orange with flame. He glanced over his shoulder, eyes on me for a second and said one word:

"Run."

FIFTY-THREE
ARDEN

"**Y**OUR BROTHER IS CUTE," Rylee said. I cast her a look and she laughed as she drew her sword. "In a I can't wait to taste his blood sort of way." She sliced her blade though the air and I dare say pride bloomed through my chest at seeing her eagerness. Is this what Zachariah felt when he gathered the Nons and went after the tainted? I would like to think it was.

Though the elf bitch ran, that did not bother me. I would find her. I knew she could not be far.

"Arden," Damiyun said, lowering his blade like the sap he was. I waved my hand, and he grunted, the flame encompassing the blade winking out, just like his magic. He stumbled back, angry eyes on me. "I don't need my magic to defeat you."

I laughed. "Then why not strike me down?"

He sheathed his blade. "Because you are my brother."

His words dug into me like a knife. Leaping, I grabbed him around the neck. "You are nothing to me. You took everything from me." I snarled, spit hitting his face. "Rylee." My faithful recruit stepped forward, sword at the ready. "Bind him. We are going to the camp."

Nodding, she placed the tip of her sword beneath my brother's chin. "Try anything and I will run you through like a pig," she said, and I could not hide my smile. But there was one loose end I could not let go.

"Ghent."

"Sir." He stood erect, legs spread, arms behind his back, eyes forward.

I walked over to him and leaned forward. "Get that elf bitch."

SETTLING INTO MY CHAIR, behind my desk, I clasped my hands, waiting for the guards to bring Damiyun in.

"For all your talk about Damiyun, he didn't put up much fight." Rylee stood in the door of the tent, arms crossed.

"Was there something you needed, Suppressor Strahand?"

Flashing a smile, she turned to leave, bumping into the Suppressor who brought my brother in. I admit I was a bit disappointed that he did not put up a fight. I was looking forward to seeing him be pummeled.

"Have a seat, Brother." I nodded to the chair opposite me. Grasping the decanter on the desk, I poured two glasses. Handing one to Damiyun, I settled back in my seat. I watched him raise the glass to his lips, and then slowly bring it back down.

I blinked, my face a mask of innocence. "Do you think I would poison you?"

"I wouldn't put it past you."

I clucked my tongue. "You hurt me, Brother. I thought you knew me better. Do you think I would end your life in such a simple manner?"

I sipped my drink trying hard to keep my composure, keep my control on the situation. My brother always had it about him to remain in control of any situation. He could hold his head high in the direst circumstances.

Like right now.

I wanted to pummel him, stab him with my dagger for the way he sat sipping his drink.

Controlled.

Composed.

I raised my cup in a salute and took another sip, eyes on him as he tentatively drank. He propped a leg on his knee and folded his hands. "Why am I here? No guards. Unbound. Aren't you afraid I'll kill you?"

"You have no magic."

He quirked an eyebrow. "Is that the only way you think I can kill you?"

I locked eyes with him and pushed my quill across the desk. "Go for it then, Brother."

He looked at the quill and leaned forward, eyes locked on me. *Try it*, I silently willed, hoping he would. I clenched my fists.

"Are you worried, Arden?" he said, hand closing around his glass and sitting back.

You would love to think that, wouldn't you? I took a healthy sip of wine. "Not at all."

"You could have killed me many times over. Why haven't you?"

I leaned forward. "Because your pain gives me great pleasure. Your screams are a symphony to my ears." A ripple of pleasure coursed through me. My hands twitched with the want of being placed upon him. Of unleashing my magic. I closed my eyes at the thought of hearing him scream. Hearing him beg me to stop.

I shuddered at the thought. I looked at him and smiled. "Don't worry, Brother. I will have your head."

Damiyun sighed. "When will you stop blaming me, Arden? For what purpose would a babe want his own mother to die? Why would I want to grow up and not know the one who birthed me?"

Because you're a selfish prick. You never should have been born. I should have done something about it. "It doesn't matter." I slammed my glass down on the desk. Shards sliced through my hand as it shattered, and I shuddered at the pain. "You took her from me."

"I took nothing."

"You took everything." I jumped up, placing my hands on the desk, and glared down at Damiyun, who didn't even flinch. *Arrogant fuck.* "You have no idea. You don't know what I went through before Father found me. You know nothing about what happened to me before Father brought me home."

He looked up at me, his face a mask of sadness. "You're right, Arden. I don't know. In fact, I know nothing about you."

"You don't need to know. I don't need your fucking pity."

"I pity no one," he said. "All I ever wanted was a brother."

I laughed and sat back down. "And all I wanted was my mother."

"And you think hurting me will bring her back? That having Father beat me would make it right?"

"No. I only want you to feel the pain I have felt every second of every day that she has been gone. Your suffering gives me great pleasure. I loved her. She loved me."

Damiyun refilled his glass and sat back. "As any mother should."

"You know nothing about it. She loved me and I loved her." Gods, just the thought of Rahina filled me with longing. The feel of her arms around me as she held me tight, her breast a soft pillow beneath my head. Lips warm as they kissed me goodnight.

He shook his head. "You are delusional, Arden. If you think... that's just sick."

I clenched my teeth. Heat filled me and I leapt up from my chair, knocking the decanter of wine over. Damiyun jumped up as the red splashed onto his lap. "I am not sick. I am unique. I am special."

"What happened to you, Arden? What did your parents do to you?"

"I told you. I don't need your pity." I would not tell him what happened. No one needed to know the humiliation I suffered. No one needed to know inside, I was nothing more than a scared, weak child.

"Let's play a game." I waved my hand. Damiyun grunted, a look of pain crossing his face as his magic filled him again. "The one we played as children."

Damiyun sighed. "I do not wish to kill you, nor do I wish to try. Why must we be like this, Arden? Why can't we be brothers? That's all I ever wanted. I love you. Help me to understand you."

I glared at him, his pity grating on my nerves. "You know we are not brothers. We never were."

"Arden—"

His words were cut off when the door opened. We both looked in the direction of the noise. I smiled at seeing Ghent dragging the Elf Bitch inside.

FIFTY-FOUR
DAMIYUN

I watched Ghent drag Serafin into the tent and fury heated my veins.

"I found her sneaking around outside," he said, tossing her to the floor. Serafin glared up at him. My magic flared and I lunged at him, grabbing him around the neck.

"You fucking shit." I gripped harder and his hands clawed at mine.

Good.

"You brought her here? The woman you claim to love?" I shoved him away. He stumbled backwards, catching himself before he fell. "Right. You're a Suppressor. You only do what you're told."

I squatted next to Serafin. "Princess?" Green eyes burned and I knew that look.

Damiyun?

Yes, Princess?

You have magic. She slowly rose, her face not giving anything away.

For the moment, yes. I rose as well.

Let's burn this fucking place to the ground.

My lady.

The corner of her mouth twitched.

I had been here for what felt like an eternity. The only thing breaking up, no, not breaking up, stopping, the violence that was sure to erupt, sure to cause me pain was Ghent dragging Serafin into the tent.

And when I saw her, I wanted to do exactly what she said: burn this place to the fucking ground. Serafin invoked something in me I had not felt for a long time. Something deep. Something primal and lasting. Fuck me, but those nights I held her close, it was just for comfort, but when I kissed her, damn but it unlocked something buried deep inside me. Something I hoped never to feel again.

And now? Seeing her look down her nose at Ghent and Arden, eyes filled with defiance, her posture regal, it made me want to fall to my knees and worship her like the queen she was.

A roar pierced the silence.

Demon.

Screams echoed through the night.

Suppressors fleeing for their lives.

My eyes went to Arden, who was snapping orders to those around him and I grabbed Serafin's hand.

"We have to go."

We raced out of the tent into the chaos unfolding in the camp. Suppressors ran screaming in terror. Some in pain as they were picked off, torn apart, or eaten.

"Damiyun?" Serafin gripped my hand, her scared eyes looked up at me, and I had no reassurance to give.

Thunder rumbled in the distance and lightning sparked the sky. Serafin stepped away from me. The wind picked up as the storm rumbled in the distance drawing closer. I looked at Serafin, her hair whipped around her head looking like fire and lightning. Her eyes and veins lit up and something so very familiar stirred inside me. It was like when Lillyanna called the lightning.

Another roar came from above, pulling our attention, the storm retreating as quickly as it began. We looked up and I sighed with relief at seeing a large demon circling above, barbed tail whipping from side to side.

Bel.

Smoke and demon shadows drifted to where we stood, coalescing into a human form.

Abraham.

"Take Serafin," I said, shoving her at him.

"No." She tried to pull herself from Abraham's grasp, but he held tight. "Damiyun, I can help."

My heart ached as the demon shadows surrounded them and she was whisked away, but I knew she would be taken to my home. Taken to safety.

A scream came from within the tent.

Arden.

Racing back to the tent, I saw a man standing in front of Arden who was curled up in a ball on the floor.

"Stand up, boy." The demon snapped. The sound of his belt clearing loops filled the air and my mind went back to when I was young and I almost crumbled.

"No. Please?" Arden begged, his voice bringing me out of my memory.

"You know what you need to do. You know what I want."

Arden buried his head in his arms, body heaving with his sobs. "No. Please, Father. Don't."

And with those words I knew why he did not tell me of his past. Of what he endured at the hands of his own father and my anger filled me. I should not have cared. What Arden did to me as a child, and as an adult, and what he convinced our father to do should have made me walk away.

But I couldn't.

No. All I saw before me was a child terrified of what his father was going to do, and the knowledge sickened me.

"Please?" Arden's voice was soft as he begged his father, no, the beast, who strode forward, one hand smacking the belt on his leg while the other fumbled with the ties on his trousers. I watched him walk around the desk and though a part of me wanted Arden to suffer, the part that cared, the part that loved him, would not allow it.

"Stop."

I pulled my magic, and the beast stopped. Turning, he changed from Arden's father to my Lil.

"Damiyun," she sighed and for a moment, I faltered.

But I knew it wasn't her.

"Don't you love me?"

I drew my magic, feeling the warmth race through my veins. "No," I said, unleashing a stream of fire that engulfed the beast turning it to ash.

Arden's sobs filled the tent, and I made my way around the desk. My eyes went to my brother who lay on the floor in a ball, body wracked with sobs, his trousers soaked with piss.

"You're alright, Arden. It's dead." I knelt beside him and placed a hand on his back. He bolted up, angry tear-filled eyes on me.

"Do not fucking touch me."

I held my hands up. "I'm sorry," I said, though I wasn't sure if I was apologizing for touching him, or for what he went through as a child. Though none of it excused what he did to me, it explained why he was the way he was. Why his feelings, his love for Mother was twisted. I understood now that he misunderstood her motherly love, having none given to him from his birth parents.

"Regulator Rayne." A female voice said. I looked at Arden whose face was streaked with tears and who stank of piss.

"Lie down and close your eyes," I said, voice low. He hesitated for a second, then did what I told him.

A young woman with blonde hair stood over us. "Is he dead?" She jerked her head at Arden.

"No. One of the demons tossed him. He hit his head on the desk and knocked himself out."

"Pity," she said with a sniff. "When he wakes up from his nap, let him know we secured the perimeter." She turned and strode out of the tent.

"She's gone."

Arden sat up. "Why did you do that? You had an opportunity to embarrass me, to expose me as a coward but you did not."

I rubbed my eyes. "Because I am not like you, Arden. I do not derive pleasure through another's misery."

Rising, he crossed the tent to a chest and pulled out a clean uniform. "I will grant you leave. For the moment."

I hesitated for a moment.

"I'd leave if I were you. It'd be a pity if I changed my mind."

Standing, I ran out of the tent and into the camp. Looking around, my eyes spied Yasmine's snow-white coat, and I made my way to where she was tethered.

"Damiyun," Ghent's voice called out. I clenched my fists at the sound and pushed my magic back.

For the moment. Stopping, I turned and looked at him.

"I—I'm sorry," he said, fingers sweeping his hair off his forehead.

I took a step forward, smirking as he shrank back. "Are you? Can you even comprehend the danger you put her in? You know what sort of person my brother is. You know what he would have done to her."

"He gave an order."

"And you could have told him you couldn't find her."

"And when someone like Rylee found her, then what? That bitch would have roughed her up."

My nostrils flared. "Forgive me for not being thankful it was you." I pushed past him, making my way to Yasmine.

"I do love her," Ghent said softly. "Can you...can you tell her that and that I am sorry for...for everything?"

I said nothing as I swung onto Yasmine's back, turning her toward home. Movement on the ground caught my attention and I pulled my magic close, releasing it when I saw it was Bel. Scampering up my leg, he leapt to my shoulder. Wrapping his tail around my neck, he settled against me, letting out a series of chirps and growls.

"Well, I appreciate your watching over me," I said, scratching his head.

As I rode back to L'Ochal, back to Pine Crest Manor, my mind kept going back to Arden and what I saw and I could not help but pity him. I could not help but feel sorry for the terrified child I saw curled up on the floor, lying in his own piss, crying and begging for his abuser to stop.

And anger at the ones who stole his childhood. The ones who were supposed to protect him. Keep him safe, but instead they were the ones who hurt him. My understanding of him grew, though I could not excuse his actions.

I shook the thoughts, heeling Yasmine into a gallop as the manor came into view. Settling Yasmine in her stall, I gave her feed and entered the manor making my way to the parlor. My eyes went to Serafin who was curled up on the couch sleeping, a blanket tucked around her. Abraham sat in a chair, feet up on the table and a book open on his lap. A fire burned in the hearth warming the room.

Making my way to the sideboard, I poured two glasses of spirits. Handing one to Abraham, I sat in the chair opposite him.

"Thank you for taking care of her, Abraham."

He sipped his drink. "She refused to go to bed. She was worried about you. I can't tell you how many times I had to stop her from going back. She fell asleep about an hour ago," he said. He took another sip, his black eyes on me. "I am no longer going by the name Abraham. I am Zedekiah."

I lowered my glass. "What?"

"I have spent my entire life rejecting who I am. Changing my name did not erase the fact I am Zedekiah, Son of Themesis. A name does not change who I am."

I scratched the stubble on my jaw. I wasn't rightly sure what to say.

"I am the same person I was, Damiyun."

"I know."

"Damiyun?" Serafin's sleepy voice pulled my attention. Rising, I squatted beside the couch.

"I'm here."

"I was worried."

I pushed a lock of hair behind her ear. "I know."

She sat up, stretching her arms over her head. Her hair was mussed, eyes heavy with sleep and damn, if my body did not react to her.

Rising, I held my hand out. "Let's get you to bed," I said, pulling her to her feet. She stood inches from me, eyes on mine. Zedekiah cleared his throat, and I took a step back, dropping her hand, and damn, if disappointment did not flash in those eyes. I glanced at Zedekiah whose lips were pursed, expression unreadable, and followed Serafin through the house and up the stairs. I was tired, and I was not in the mood for a discussion.

"Sleep well, Princess. Tomorrow we will have a talk about what you did." Kissing her cheek, I turned toward my room, her hand on my arm stopping me.

"Stay with me."

It wasn't question, and I can't rightly say it was a request.

Turning, I looked down at her. "I—I'm not sure that's a good idea."

Stepping forward, she wrapped her arms around my waist. "I am," she said, voice soft. Rising, she pressed her lips to mine.

Untangling myself from her embrace, I stepped back. "I'm sorry," I said. Hurrying to my room, I closed and locked the door and took a deep breath. Thank the gods we were pushing on to the Wilde Elves on the morrow. I would do my best to distance myself from Serafin on the journey, though I knew it would be difficult.

Fuck me, but why do these things always happen to me?

FIFTY-FIVE
SERAFIN

T HE SOUND OF THE lock clicking into place on Damiyun's door left me feeling...I wasn't quite sure. Perhaps I misunderstood the tender way he would brush my hair back from my face. The way his gray eyes softened as he looked at me and perhaps, I misunderstood the kiss we shared, though briefly, in the tavern.

Perhaps I misunderstood much where Damiyun Rayne was concerned.

Shaking the thoughts and ignoring the burning inside I went into my room. Slipping out of my dress, ignoring that I wished it was Damiyun removing it, I pulled on my sleep dress, and slipping beneath the luxurious covers, I burrowed deep into the feather mattress and went to sleep.

S OMETHING PULLED ME FROM my slumber. Not the screams of demons or the howling of wolves. I had become used to those. This was something else. Rubbing my eyes, I sat up, listening for what it was. Hearing nothing, I settled back in my bed when a sound broke the silence.

A soft knock on my door.

Tossing the covers off, I slipped out of bed, padding to the door my heart in my throat. Grasping the handle, I pulled the door open, my eyes on Damiyun who stood on the other side, his eyes glowing yellow in the dark. He wore only sleep trousers and I couldn't stop my gaze from traveling over his muscular chest.

"Dam—"

His arms came around me pulling me close. His mouth crushed mine hot and demanding. Pulling back, he held my face, forehead resting on mine, his ragged breath warm upon my face.

"I want you, Serafin. May the gods help me, but I do. I tried hard to stop the feelings, but I can't. I thought locking my door would lock you away, but I couldn't stop thinking about you." He pulled back; his eyes searched mine. "Tell me to leave. Tell me to go back to my room. Tell me this is wrong."

I licked my lips, and he groaned. "I can't."

He lifted me in his arms, kicking the door closed behind him and he tossed me onto the bed. He looked down at me, and I shivered at the look in his eyes. The wanton lust and raw need on his face. He slipped out of his sleep trousers. The moonlight pouring through the windows shone silver upon his body.

My eyes took in the hard muscles, the brand of the Suppressor and the tattoo of a phoenix on his right shoulder and the raven on a skull on the left. He looked perfect and beautiful, and my heat mounted. Sitting up, I ran a hand up his chest, pressing my lips to his hard abdomen. He shivered at my touch and pulled me to my feet. Mouth captured mine once again, teeth grazing my lip, tongue dancing with mine. Hands grasped the hem of my nightdress. I pulled away, and Damiyun pulled it over my head. The air was cool upon my skin, causing bumps to form on my arms. Damiyun's eyes raked over me.

"You are just so beautiful," he breathed. Hands gently pushed me back onto the bed.

His mouth was hot on my cool skin, his tongue flicked over nipples and his fingers parted my legs. I gasped as his finger entered me. He teased my mouth, my breasts and skin as he brought me to climax. His lips met mine, urgent and persistent as his body covered me. He settled between my legs, and I felt pressure, a slight sting as he pressed forward, and I tensed up at the feel. Damiyun stopped and pulled back, eyes meeting mine for a moment.

"Fuck." He cursed, removing himself and sat up, back facing me. "You're unclaimed. I thought Ghent…Why didn't you tell me?" He turned his head and looked at me.

My face heated, and I sat up. "I… I didn't know it would be a problem."

He ran a hand over his face with a sigh, stood up, and pulled his trousers on. "It would have been nice to know."

I got up, conscious of my nakedness, and yanked my nightdress over my head. "Why is it a problem?" I inquired as I followed him out to the patio.

"Because you don't want me as your first. This isn't the way it should happen." He rested his arms on the wall and looked out at the moonlit sky.

"Why? How should it happen?"

He turned and looked down at me. "With someone you love. Or at least care about. Not someone who… not someone like me."

"What's wrong with you?"

He chuckled softly. "There are not enough hours in the day to explain everything wrong with me." He shook his head. "You don't want me for your first.

It should be memorable. It shouldn't be with someone out to simply... simply satisfy an aching desire."

I hopped up on the wall and looked at him. "Was your first time memorable and with someone you loved?"

A ghost of a smile flitted across his lips. "Love? No. But I cared about her." He shook his head. "I can't rightly remember how we met, but I was thirteen when it happened. She was older and the most beautiful woman I had ever seen. She taught me things I... gods, she was something else. It was the best Grand Passage of my life. I shouldn't have bothered you." He stepped away. I reluctantly hopped off the wall and followed him back inside. "I don't want you to go."

He groaned, hand on the doorknob. "If I stay ... I can't rightly say I can keep my hands to myself."

"But you did all those other nights we spent together."

He let out a puff of air. "That was different," he said, though he didn't turn the handle.

"Why?"

His eyes held mine. "Because I didn't want to fuck you then."

I couldn't help but laugh, though I understood what he was saying because I felt the same. That didn't change the fact I wanted him to stay regardless. I bit my lip and looked up at him. "Please?"

He groaned. "Fuck me, Princess. Don't look at me like that." He dropped his hand from the handle, and I knew I had won. "Alright. I will stay. You have my word I will be a gentleman."

We crossed the room and slipped into bed. His arms slipped around, and he pulled me close. I curled into him, resting my head on his chest. His lips brushed the top of my head, and I closed my eyes, pushing back the disappointment and want that filled me.

I knew he would keep his word, and I would behave myself so as not to make him break it. Tonight, anyway. After all, tomorrow was another day. As I drifted off into sleep, Damiyun's arms tightened around me, his lips brushed my temple, and he uttered one thing:

"Such a complication."

FIFTY-SIX
ALLENDAIRE

I LOOKED DOWN AT Mordecai, the child laying in his crib. He did not stir. Did not look up. He did nothing.

Not like Serafin who, when I walked into the nursery, she would hold out her arms wanting to be picked up, somehow knowing I was there. Or, when she was older, would bury her face in her pillow and giggle and I would pretend she was hidden, looking around her room, checking her wardrobe, calling out her name as I sat down on her bed in mock defeat. And then she would pop up, laughter in her eyes as she held her arms out to me, and I would hold her close; clutch her against my chest and speak of her mother.

Of Lillyanna, and the wee child often had questions I could not answer. *Where is my mother?*

Serafin was a breath of fresh air and so much like Lillyanna in so many ways and I cherished the moments when she sat on my lap, snuggling close as I read her that blasted book *The Story of Jayne*.

Phabian took a liking to her; took her beneath his arm like she was his own. And I admit I was envious of their relationship, the way Phabian held her when she had a scrape. The way she ran to him when the Elves said nasty things to her, and the way she went to him when she had a bad dream.

Yes, that hurt me.

I was her father, but for all the little things that hurt, that plagued her, she went to Phabian. Not me.

Her father.

Shanking the thoughts I looked down at Mordecai who slept peacefully in his crib.

The child that I was not sure was mine.

Though my memories came and went, and they were of Mouranda and me in my bed, I could not say we copulated. Though the child in the crib, though Mouranda's bulging stomach told me perhaps the healers elixirs worked, I still could not say he was mine. Black hair and milky white eyes brought forth a memory long tucked away and forgotten. A history hushed and never spoken.

I tucked the blanket around the sleeping child, and had I not known better, I would have sworn he growled, sharp fangs flashing in the lamplight. But he was just a wee babe born not long ago. He couldn't have teeth.

Not yours, the voice in my head called out. Most likely it was my own.

The guilt of what I did to Serafin kept me up at night. Those green eyes so much like Lillyanna's haunted my dreams and damned my soul.

Slipping out of the nursery, I made my way to my den. Pouring a glass of sweet wine, I sat behind my desk. What would Lillyanna say to me if she stood before my desk? It wasn't the first time I wondered, but it was the first time I thought about what I would say, though "I'm sorry" sounded weak and pathetic.

I could almost see her green eyes flashing with anger and accusation, chin jutting out, and I could hear her voice.

You fucking coward. You useless man. How could you condemn our daughter to death? You said you loved me, but that was a lie, wasn't it.

My eyes burned and as if she stood before me, I spoke. "No, Lillyanna. It was not a lie. I did—I do—love you. Our child was born of that love. My—our—Serafin was—is—the best thing I ever had besides you." Taking a long drink, I refilled my glass and rubbed the tears from my eyes. "She is the heir, Lillyanna. The child, Mordecai... he—"

"Who are you talking to?"

A voice cut through my thoughts and the image of Lillyanna faded away. Apparently, I had drunk far more than I thought. Looking up, my eyes met Krall's who strode into the room.

"What news do you have for me?" I said, straightening papers on my desk.

"We've come up empty once again. Wherever she escaped to, she is doing a good job at hiding."

When I heard she escaped capture, running off with a man who was ready to fight for her, I had to contain my elation. I knew if Krall had found her again, if he was able to capture her, he would have gleefully dragged her into my den. "The search is ended."

"What?"

I looked up at Krall. "I said, the search is ended."

"But...but she is alive and could come here and claim the throne."

My eyes did not leave him. "She would not," I said, though a part of me, a big part, hoped she would. Though I sentenced her to death due to Mouranda and our law, I did not see the boy as the heir. And I did not think upon his twenty-first Name Day I would name him as such.

No. My heart and my soul named Serafin, and I would not revoke her claim, despite whatever consequences that decision might bring.

"Do you want to search all of Ay'Arina and beyond to find her?"

Krall's jaw clenched and his nostrils flared. "If it means finding where that daughter of a –"

I leaped up from my chair. "Think long and hard about the next words you choose to speak lest you find your head gracing a spike." I placed my fists on the desk. "The search is done and if you decide to continue it on your own time, I can assure you my threat will become a reality for you and any you convinced to help."

"Of course, my king," Krall said, bowing his head. "Is that all?"

Sitting back down, I folded my hands. "No. Find Phabian and tell him to come here."

Krall's brow furrowed. "I have not seen my brother since the trial."

Krall's words gave me pause. Though Phabian had missed the petty grievance meetings, Lazaro told me he was checking the boarders. I was sure he wasn't being truthful.

"Fine then. Send me Lazaro."

Bowing again, Krall strode out.

I knew Phabian was not pleased with what happened, his attitude and defiance, his denouncing me as his king told me as much. But when he came back from wherever he had gone, there was an air about him that told me he discovered something, and for a moment I wondered if it was my buried secret. I quashed the thought as soon as it had entered my mind. There was no way for him to know.

But he had left again, and I knew he was not here checking the borders. Even if he was, there was no reason for it. No alarm was raised suggesting any had wandered close to our lands, and with that knowledge it made me wonder where he truly was and I hoped I could somehow get Lazaro to tell me what was going on and where Phabian was.

"**Y**OU WISHED TO SEE me, majesty?"

I sprinkled sand on the fresh ink, folded the parchment, and sealed it with wax. Wiping the nib on a rag, I put the stopper in the bottle of ink. "Sit," I said to Lazaro, gesturing to the seat in front of my desk.

He folded his muscular frame into the chair. His eyebrows drew down in concern.

Folding my hands on the desk, I looked at him. "Where is Phabian?" I wasn't going to waste time with pleasantries and idle conversation.

Lazaro licked his lips. "He has been patrolling the borders during the day and helping keep the demons at bay at night."

"He must be exhausted, having no sleep for a Moon Cycle," I said, my eyes not leaving his. Lazaro shifted in his seat and dropped his gaze to his hands folded in his lap.

"Where is he, Lazaro? Did he...did he find her? Is he with her?" I tried to keep the hope out of my voice.

Lazaro's eyes met mine. "No, majesty. He is not with her," he said, and my heart sank, but I showed no emotion over it.

"Where is he?"

Lazaro ran a hand through his hair, and I could see the conflicting emotions running through him. Betray his lover, or lie to his king? A tough choice, I was sure.

"Phabian is in Naar'Glon."

My eyes widened. "Why would he go there?"

Lazaro took a deep breath. "He found a book in the queen's chambers. It came from Naar'Glon. It is written in the Old Tongue and from what little I could understand, which isn't much, it looked to be a book of dark spells."

I blinked. What was Mouranda doing with a book written by the Dark Elves? And a spell book at that? My mind went to the nights she visited me in my den, pouring wine and smoking Sal'va. Of taking her to my bed and waking up naked the next morning with no recollection of copulating with her.

And then, days before Serafin's Name Day, she comes into this room, telling me she was with child. I did not believe her then and seeing the child, Mordecai, I did not believe he was mine. His hair was black. His eyes a milky white. He looked like a ...

"Dark Elf," I said out loud.

"Majesty?"

I leaped from my desk. "The child is not mine. It is a Dark Elf."

Lazaro looked up at me. "Phabian did not believe the queen became with child by natural means. He went to Naar'Glon to get answers." Lazaro paused and took a deep breath. "Sir, the Dark Elves still live."

"How can you know this?"

"I communicate with Phabian through a magic notebook. He told me they live. He is also a prisoner there."

What was Phabian thinking?

I rubbed my eyes. "Thank you, Lazaro. Please keep me updated when he contacts you. And keep anything that was said here to yourself."

"Of course, sire," he said, bowing his head. Rising he exited the room, and I made my way to the sideboard. Pouring a glass of spirits, I threw some logs on the fire and sat in my worn, leather chair.

I suspect Phabian thought—just like I and all the elves did—they had been completely eradicated. That they still lived, that Mouranda used dark magic and birthed one…I did not want to think about what any of that meant.

I took a sip of my drink. Did Mouranda know the child would be a Dark Elf, or was she so consumed by her hatred for Serafin, for Lillyanna, that she was willing to do anything to become with child? And what did she do to make that happen, and more importantly, at what cost?

Ever since she became with child, a strange darkness seemed to have settled over the palace. The feeling intensified after he was born. Shadows moved, or at least I caught movement out of the corner of my eye, but when I looked, nothing was there. And my mind was foggy more often than not. I was tired and found myself sleeping more and more and when I woke, I could not say what day it was or what time it was.

And when I slept, the nightmares came. Nasty beasts with sharp teeth and claws, razor sharp dorsal spines, and barbed tails. They tore flesh and ripped limbs. A river of red flowed through the palace. And watching it all, commanding it all, was Mordecai seated on the Shadow Elf throne.

But that wasn't the worst. No. The worst was my daughter leading a massive army to attack Il'Ekhester, fury filled eyes on me as her sword pierced my heart.

I shook the thoughts from my head and rolled my shoulders. I needed to confront Mouranda. Find out what she did. I feared the fate of the Shadow Elves depended on it.

FIFTY-SEVEN
MOURANDA

THE DOOR TO MY study banged open, and I jumped, spilling hot tea on my dress. Who dares come into my personal space unannounced, and in such a violent way? Placing my cup on the table beside me, I rose, my eyes going to Allendaire who stalked across the room. The red shirt he wore matched the color in his face. His jaw and fists were clenched. A white light pulsed off him.

"Allen—"

He grabbed the front of my dress and yanked me off the floor. He pulled me forward, our faces inches apart. "What did you do, Mouranda?" He spat between clenched teeth.

Swallowing down the fear knotting my stomach, I dug my nails into his hands. He released me with a rough shove. I stumbled back, my feet tripping on the edge of the throw rug, and I landed hard on my backside. I glared up at him as I rose, smoothing my hands on the silk fabric of my dress as I composed myself.

"What did you do?" he said again, taking a menacing step toward me.

"You need to be more specific, dear husband. I do a lot of things." I smiled sweetly at him.

His nostrils flared. The light pulsing off him grew brighter. Would he use it on me? Would he kill me? Though I did not care, not really, I was not certain of what awaited me on the other side. Would it be the beast from the woods? The demon who visited my dreams? I shuddered at the thought.

Turning, I crossed the room and poured two glasses of wine, placing them on the table beside the two chairs in front of the crackling fire.

"Sit. Have a drink," I said.

Allendaire did not move. "I know the child, Mordecai, is not mine."

I froze, the smile on my face nearly faltering. I forced a laugh. "Dear husband. Do you forget how children are made? Do you forget the many times you took me to your bed in the Moon Cycles prior to my being with child?"

"I remember you coming into my den. Plying me with wine and smoking Sal'va. I remember waking up naked in my bed, but I do not remember copulating with you."

I laughed, a real laugh this time. "That is because you were so drunk, so drugged, you passed out right after the act was completed."

His eyes narrowed, and he took a few steps closer, and I had to stop myself from taking as many back.

"The lies pour off your tongue like water," he said. "I know you did something. I know about the spell book from the Dark Elves you have in your possession."

I froze. A bead of sweat slid down my back, and my palms became moist. How could he have possibly known about that book?

I licked my lips. I could not lie my way out of this one. "I found it in the back of the library. It was hidden, covered in dust and cobwebs. I did not know it was there. When I saw it, well, naturally I was intrigued. Why would a book from the Dark Elves be in the depths of the Shadow Elf library? So, I took it and read it."

"And you did not think to bring it to my attention so it could be destroyed?"

"No." I frowned. "How do you know about it?"

"Lazaro told me," he said. "What did you do, Mouranda? How did you become with child?"

I would not answer his question with the truth. I would take that secret to the grave. "You know."

His nostrils flared. "The boy is a Dark Elf. Or have you failed to notice?"

I said nothing. Of course, I noticed the black hair and milky white eyes that marked him as such. When I used the spell, it did not occur to me my child would be a Dark Elf, but there was nothing I could do about it now.

"Where is the book?" Allendaire's voice brought me back.

"Phabian has it. Go ask him to see it."

Allendaire crossed his arms. "Phabian has gone to Naar'Glon to unravel what you have done," he said, and took another step closer. We were a mere hands width apart. "The Dark Elves live, and Phabian is being held prisoner."

I swallowed hard. I had sent Phabian there to find answers. I did not know the Dark Elves still lived. I did not know he would be taken prisoner. I had let my anger and my hatred for Serafin and Lillyanna get the better of me. I let it consume me. Eat away at me. It was what drove me to do what I did, but now? Now I wished I could take it all back. I did not even think of the consequences of my actions. Denalla had advised me against it, but I did not listen to her, and now? I did not know what was to be.

"I sentenced my daughter, the rightful heir of the throne to death because you carried what I thought to be my child. But it isn't, and now the daughter I dearly love is lost to me because of your jealous hatred."

I had no words to say because I could not deny his.

"There is no telling what the ramifications of your actions are," he said. "You very well might have sentenced the Shadow Elves to death." Turning, he stalked out of the room, slamming the door behind.

My legs gave out and I collapsed to the floor.

What have I done?

FIFTY-EIGHT
PHABIAN

Standing on the balcony of my room, I gazed out at the Dark Elf lands but not really seeing anything. While the magical barrier was still in place, Rah allowed me a bit more freedom. If being shadowed by guards could be considered free.

I took a sip of my drink, God's Truth, a bitter and sweet spirit that warmed me and dulled the ache in my head. Rubbing my eyes, I sank down into the soft, plush cushions of a chair. I thought about the tale Rah had told me. Though it sounded outrageous and laughable, I couldn't completely dismiss his words. Not after everything else I had learned.

Propping my feet up on the table, I sank deeper into the chair and closed my eyes. I went over everything I had learned about the Shadow Elves, my own race. Things that contradicted everything I had learned. Everything I knew. Everything that had been written in the Tome of the Kings since Karrinian Trounde, the first Shadow Elf King, had laid nib to paper.

I took another sip of my drink and thought about everything I had found out. Arybelle, Karrinian's wife, and her daughter, Vanla, were thought to be long dead and yet I met them both. Rahina Trounde, Allendaire's sister, was thought to have poisoned their father, Terrin.

I shook my head. "And then Allendaire took the throne, waged a war on his own people, banishing those who procreated outside their own race," I said out loud. I wasn't surprised, considering what he had done to Serafin.

I rubbed my temples, trying to relieve the pulsing pain. And now I sit in the manor of Lord Rah. A Dark Elf. A race that Karrinian had eradicated when he settled in Il'Ekhester.

Opening my eyes, I poured more God's Truth and took a healthy drink. The sound of knocking pulled me from my thoughts. Crossing the room, I waited for my guards to unlock and open the door. I looked past the guards who held swords across the opening to the young man who stood behind.

"Cassion." My eyes met his blue ones. His red lips curled up in a smile.

I took him in as he stood there. He was a few inches taller than me, with a slight build, and absolutely beautiful. His white hair was loose and flowed about his shoulders. My hands itched at the thought of running them through his flowing locks. His clothes were simple. A plain white shirt that was open, revealing a glimpse of his smooth chest, brown trousers that hugged his legs, and black boots polished to a mirror shine. My face heated at the thoughts that went through my mind, and I averted my gaze as I stepped aside.

The guards lowered their weapons, entered the room, and flanked me.

"There is no need for that," Cassion said as he crossed the threshold, closing the door behind. The men hesitated a second, then stepped back and stood in front of the door, hands on the hilt of the swords they had sheathed.

Cassion followed me out to the balcony. We settled into the chairs after I poured him a drink.

"I wanted to thank you for what you did." he said.

"I admit my reasons to be self-serving."

Cassion chuckled. "Of course they were," he said into his glass. "You still saved my life. You didn't have to."

I laughed. "I told you. My reasons were self-serving. Had I not done that, I would not have gained Rah's trust, as little as it is. After all, I am nothing more than a filthy, inbred Shadow Elf."

Cassion said nothing. The silence stretched, the only sound that of the two guards shifting on their feet, and the night creatures waking up.

"It is true Karrinian tried to eradicate us. But I can't blame you for something that happened thousands of Grand Passages ago."

"Rah does."

"My father tends to hold on to the past, and he tends to hold grudges," Cassion grasped the decanter and refilled his glass. "You have to understand my father's kin were among those eradicated."

"And you have to understand I had nothing to do with that."

I refilled my glass with a sigh and settled back into the soft chair. "Tell me about this... affliction that has affected your race. Rah told me very little."

Almost nothing at all, really.

He only told me there was a defect in their blood. There were those born without it, and they tried to keep their blood clean by procreating within their race. It had worked, and that was the reason the Shadow Elves were inbred. It kept our race pure.

Cassion took a long drink and settled back. "I don't know much about it, really. I only know that it makes us age faster. We often become exhausted after doing anything, and it makes us sensitive to light. It's harsh on the eyes and burns the skin."

"That's why you keep yourselves and the windows covered."

Cassion nodded.

"So, how were you born without it?"

"I don't know the answer to that. There hasn't been one born like me in a long time." He placed his glass on the table and rose. "I should go. I'm sure you wish to rest."

"How long am I to remain here?" I looked up at him.

"That's up to my father."

Of course it was. Which meant I might be here forever.

"Thank you again for what you did. Have a good night, Phabian," he said as he crossed the room and exited, the two guards following.

I rested my head back on the chair and looked up at the sky. The stars shined bright, looking like diamonds glittering on a field of black. Like everything else I have been discovering, Cassion's visit only left me with more questions. The more I asked, the more frustrated and confused I became with the cryptic answers and silence.

Rubbing my eyes, I finished my drink and went back into the room. The notebook I had used to communicate with Lazaro glowed a faint yellow. Picking it up, I sat on the bed and opened it.

Have you figured out what the queen did?

I picked up the quill, unstopped the bottle of ink, and dipped the nib. *Not yet. They took the book away from me.* The words I wrote disappeared and moments passed without a response. I was about to close the book, when words glowed across the page.

Something isn't right here. I feel darkness within the walls. I see shadows moving. My mind is foggy. I would swear the child is only four Moon Cycles, but my memories tell me he has had his first Name Day. I don't know what's going on, Phabian.

I stared at the now blank page, my mind churning over what he said. When I was going through Mouranda's quarters, it felt like someone was watching me. It seemed as though all of this began when she became with child. It was becoming imperative I find out what she did. I picked up the quill and dipped the nib again. *I will try to find out what Mouranda did. She told me if I came here, I would have my answers.*

Please keep me updated. And please find a way to come home. I miss you.

I smiled, though a pang of loneliness hit me. *I promise to update you as soon as I know something. And I miss you too, Laz.*

Closing the notebook, I put it in the drawer next to the bed. Changing into my night clothes, I slipped into bed. Lazaro was right. I needed to figure out how to go back home.

And Cassion might be that ticket.

FIFTY-NINE
SERAFIN

"**G**ood morning, Princess."

Looking up, I stretched my arms above my head and smiled at Damiyun. He laid on his side, head propped up on a hand, eyes on me, a smile tugging his lips.

"Good morning."

"Did you sleep well?"

"Yes." *No.* I couldn't ignore his presence, his body pressed against mine, and I couldn't ignore the want that burned through me.

The need for release was strong but I could do nothing. Not with him lying beside me. Not without making him break his promise.

Laughing, Damiyun settled back against his pillows. "Did you know when you lie your eyes become a curious shade that is not quite blue and not quite green?"

"Lie? What do you mean?"

Damiyun placed a finger beneath my chin and tipped my head up. "With the way your hands wandered in your sleep, I had to change my trousers."

I blinked. "What?"

"It was fine. I quite enjoyed it."

My cheeks burned like fire as a dream I had came to my mind. But if he enjoyed it and didn't stop me... Straddling him, I placed my hands on either side of his head.

"Princess—"

"You enjoyed it." I slipped a hand between us, stroking his length that grew hard.

He pulled my hand away and I could not hide my disappointment. "I am not the one for you, Princess."

"I am not asking you to be Blood Bound to me."

Damiyun chuckled. "No, but—"

I pressed my lips to his. "You want me."

"Yes, but—"

I kissed him again. "And I want you."

He pulled away and held my face in his hands. "It is not that simple." He took a deep breath. "There was someone I loved very much and I...I hurt her. I promised myself I wouldn't get close, wouldn't get involved with another. It just hurts too much when...when they're gone." Tears glistened in his eyes, and he swallowed hard.

"I'm not going anywhere."

"I'll hurt you."

"I won't let you."

"Princess," he sighed, breath warm on my face. He pulled me close, our lips joined, tongues entwined as he kissed me deep. Pulling away, I sat up and pulled my sleep dress over my head, tossing it to the floor. Damiyun inhaled sharply, eyes that glowed a faint yellow raked over my body. Bumps rose on my skin at the look of desire within the depths. Grabbing me, he flipped me onto my back. His warm lips pressed against my stomach, kissing a trail slowly, painfully so, down my body. I jolted at the feel of his tongue between my legs. Gasped as fingers entered me, gently bringing me pleasure. Closing my eyes, I gave into the sensations coursing through my body.

It wasn't like when I was with Ghent. No, this was different. The pleasure I felt, the tingling though my body was euphoric. Lifting my hips I moved with Damiyun's fingers, burying my hands in his hair. I gave into the sensations, my body shaking, legs clamping around his head as I climaxed hard.

Pulling away, he slipped out of his sleep trousers, towering over me hands on either side of my head. His mouth teased me, the scent and taste of myself ignited a fire inside.

"Are you sure about this?" His voice was soft. Pulling back, he looked down at me. "We can't go back once we do this."

Grasping his face, I pulled him close, kissing him deep. "I'm sure."

I felt him between my legs, his eyes never leaving mine as he pressed forward. I felt a pressure, a slight uncomfortable feeling. A stinging sensation and I inhaled sharp and winced.

"Am I hurting you? Do you want me to stop?" His tone was concerned, and he started to pull away.

"No." I gripped his arms. "Please, Damiyun?" I wrapped my legs around his waist and pulled him close. Gripping my hips, he drove himself inside me. I gasped at the light pain and fullness. Clutching him tight, I gave into the pleasure as he thrust once, twice, and upon the third, he held me close, grunting as his body shuddered. Pulling out, he laid down beside me.

"I'm sorry, Princess, but I couldn't hold back." Propping up on an elbow, he looked down at me. "Are you alright? Did I hurt you?"

I pressed my lips to his. "I'm fine."

"I promise to make it up to you," he said, lying back down and pulling me close. I snuggled into his arms, resting my head on his chest. The sound of his beating heart and the steady rise and fall of his chest was a calming comfort.

"Do we have to go to the Wilde Elves?"

Damiyun sighed. "We do."

"I don't want to go."

"Believe you me, there is nothing more that I want than to stay here. Unfortunately, I made a promise to Barlack."

Pulling away, I sat up and looked down at him. "What could he possibly want with me?"

Damiyun reached up, fingers idly twirling a lock of my hair. "I don't know, though he somehow knew what happened to you."

I frowned. How could a Wilde Elf know anything about me? Their lands were far from the Shadow Elves and I knew none would dare step foot there.

"I won't leave you there alone. You have my word," Damiyun said.

I looked at him, at the gray eyes that softened whenever he looked at me. I thought about the feelings he awakened inside me. It was different than what I had felt with Ghent. Though I loved him, or thought I did, what I felt when I was with him was lust, I knew, but also wariness. He was possessive and his jealous anger came out where Damiyun was concerned, and it worried me.

And I could not forget how he did not raise a hand or a sword when the soldiers came for me. Nor could I forget the Suppressors that appeared while he was there.

But Damiyun? I knew he would have given his life for me, a woman he did not know and the feelings he evoked in me? It was a primal wanting need. Raw and real and unlike what I felt with Ghent.

It was more than wanting to feel his hands on me, his skin and lips on mine. I wanted to be near him. I wanted to hear his voice and make him laugh. I wanted to take the sadness from his eyes.

I wanted to make him happy, and I realized I cared about him.

A sharp stabbing pain lanced through my head. Crying out, I closed my eyes and held my head. Blinding light flashed behind my lids. The pain was crushing. Debilitating and I screamed.

"Princess?" Damiyun's voice came from far away, and then I heard him howl in agony.

And just as soon and rapidly as it happened, it stopped.

I looked at Damiyun, whose face held a frown. I could feel the confusion in him, feel his presence deep within my mind, and I knew.

"What was that?"

I took a deep breath.

"We are mates."

SIXTY
DAMIYUN

"WHAT DO YOU MEAN we are mates?" I said, slowly sitting up, eyes on Serafin. She chewed her lip, and I stifled a groan at the look.

"The elves, when they find their mate, the person who is the other half of them, a bond is created. It binds their souls, and they become a part of each other. What one feels, the other does as well and they will always know where each is." She ran a hand through her hair, her eyes turned a dark green and her nostrils flared. My body grew hot. The want to destroy the room was overwhelming and I knew it was coming from Serafin. Reaching out, I took her hand and gave a gentle squeeze. The feeling subsided, if only slightly.

"The Shadow Elves...I don't know that a bond has ever occurred naturally. The males would force the bond on the female they wanted to claim."

"How do they do that?"

Serafin shrugged. "I don't know. I am sure the males are born with some magic to allow that to happen. They force themselves on the female, so why not have magic that forces the bond?"

"I'm sorry, Princess."

"The Shadow Elves are nothing but savages. My mother, she protected me from that. When I was in her womb, she made a bet with Allendaire over a game of Capture the Pegasus. If she won, he had to promise I would be queen and not rule in name only. My mating bond would be allowed to occur naturally, and I would decide how many children I would bare and not be forced to churn them out." A small smile flitted across her lips. "She won, of course."

"Your mother sounds like a smart woman."

The smile fell and sadness tore at my heart. "I wouldn't know. I never knew her."

I kissed the back of her hand. "It appears we have something in common. I never knew my mother either," I said. "Her bond, though, it came into place with my father."

Serafin's eyes widened.

"I take it bonding with a human isn't normal?" I said.

"I really don't know, since we don't allow outsiders on our lands." She took a deep breath. "If I were to be queen, I would change everything about my race."

I tucked a lock of hair behind her ear. 'You will be queen, Serafin. We might have to raise an army and attack your people, but you will sit on the Shadow Elf throne."

And I would make sure of it. I knew in my heart Serafin would do good for her race, possibly uniting the Shadow Elves with the Wilde Elves. She has told me in not so many words that she does not agree with the things her people do. The laws, which sent her to her death and the way the men treat the women, something which made my blood boil. And for a brief moment the thought of my taking the Wilde Elf Throne, if only to facilitate the joining of the divided races, passed through my mind.

Something I dismissed immediately.

I did not care my mother named me heir, and then Barlack. I was no fucking king. What did I know about lording over an entire race of people? Shaking the thoughts, I tossed off the covers and sat on the edge of the bed.

"We need to press on," I said. The sooner we left, the sooner we could come back, though something told me it wouldn't be that soon.

Serafin's arms came around me, hand slipping between my legs. "Do we?" Her teeth grazed my ear.

Pushing her away, I rose, willing my cock to calm down. "We do."

I stifled a chuckle at hearing her grumbling as she slipped out of bed and opened the wardrobe.

"Take only what you can pack in you saddlebags," I said. Striding across the room, I exited. Leaning against the door, I let out a hard breath. Fuck me, but I could feel her in the back of my mind. Another presence. Though it was better than Themesis, it was almost as bad.

Shrugging the feeling, I strapped Shadow Blade to my back and slipped daggers into my waistband and boots. I stuffed clothes into my own saddlebags, then made my way through the manor to the kitchen. Grabbing another bag, I loaded it with hard cheese, cured meats, dried fruit, and hard bread. Then I filled two water skins and swiped four bottles of spirits.

"Going someplace?" Levin's voice came from the doorway.

I glanced up at him. "I am taking Serafin to Va'l'Victorus. I can't say how long I will be away. You are in charge in my stead."

"Very well, sir," he said with a nod.

Tying the bag and stuffing it into my already bulging bags, I headed out to the barn where Serafin was checking the saddle straps and securing her own bags across Yasmine's rump, then swung up onto her back.

Balancing my bag on my shoulder, I swung up behind Serafin, slipping my arm around her waist. Yasmine tossed her head with a snort, hooves pawing the ground. Serafin muttered some soothing words, patting Yasmine's neck who let out a low whinny. Digging her heels into her sides, we made our way toward town where Xander was stabled.

Saddling him up and securing my bags, I gave the stable hand two silvers. Swinging up on Xander's back, I led him out of the barn and to the road to begin our journey to Va'l'Victorus, a feeling of unease settling between my shoulder blades.

"Are you alright?"

I looked at Serafin, whose face and eyes held concern. I could lie to her. I could smile and tell her all was well, but I wasn't sure what she could feel through this damn bond. And there was a part of me that did not want to lie to her. I did that enough with Lillyanna. Had I just been forward with her from the start, perhaps we never would have entered into a relationship. Perhaps I never would have fallen in love with her.

Perhaps the truth would have saved me from so much pain. So much sorrow. So much wrong I did to my Lil. So much hurt.

So much hate from her, all of which I deserved. Losing her was my fault, but killing her? Fuck. Her eyes haunted my dreams. Her begging stabbed at my heart. Her words brought me to my knees. *Do it, Damiyun. Do what needs to be done. End this. End him. Do it before this place claims me. Before I am lost to you forever.*

Shaking the thoughts, I reached a hand out to Serafin and clasped hers. "No, Princess. I am not alright."

"What's wrong? What can I do? Is it me?"

"By the gods, no. Why would you think that?" I brought Xander to a halt. Yasmine slowly stepped forward. Stopping, she nuzzled Xander.

"I—I don't know. What we did and the bond?" She waved her hand, and I laughed.

"Princess, my Princess." I squeezed her hand. "Never could you do anything to make me angry. Annoyed?" I laughed again. "Most definitely. But angry? No." I ran a hand through my hair and scratched my chin. "No. There is something here. Something not right."

"Suppressors?" She tensed up, and I felt her alert through that blasted bond.

"No, not them. Something else."

Rolling my shoulders and shaking off the feeling, I gripped Serafin's hand and led our mounts forward, though to what? I did not know.

SIXTY-ONE
ARDEN

BRACING A FOOT ON the wall behind me, I crossed my arms and looked at the pathetic recruits that I was in charge of.

None could wield a wooden sword, let alone know which end was which. I watched them hit each other as if it were a game and my annoyance grew.

"This lot is pathetic," Rylee said. I glanced at her. Though she was insufferably annoying, she had proven herself and earned a spot beside me, though that did not elevate her rank. "They seem to get more and more pitiful. Why even join if you don't know which end of a sword to use?"

I couldn't disagree with her, though I would never let her know that. Pushing off the wall, I strode to where the group fumbled around.

"You all are a fucking embarrassment to the Order. Zachariah Farnsworth may the gods bless his eternal soul," I said, bowing my head and kissing my index and middle finger, I pressed them to my heart. "is probably clawing his way out of his grave as we speak." My eyes raked over the half dozen recruits. They were a rag tag bunch of young men who were fat to those who were tall and gangly.

"None of you know which side of a sword to use. Perhaps I should explain." Pulling my own sword, I ran it through the nearest recruit. Gasps and shouts erupted from the others. "It's the pointed end."

Wiping the blood off on the dead boy's uniform, I sheathed the weapon. "Get this body out of here and when you are done, I want all of you to grab a forty-pound bag of sand. You will carry it up and down Shale Hill one hundred times. If you drop the bag, you will start over from one."

Striding away, I looked over my shoulder. "With me, Suppressor Strahand."

Rylee fell in step beside me. "That punishment was a bit harsh, don't you think?"

"Harsh? I thought it was quite tame. Are you getting soft Suppressor Strahand?"

Rylee snorted. "Of course not. Where are we going?"

"On a raid in Voodomecism."

"WHAT ARE WE DOING here?" Ghent looked around, when two days later we entered Voodomecism.

I glanced over at him. "I have it on good authority that there are Wielders hiding amongst the Nons in this town." I scanned the people, who looked with open curiosity as our party ambled through. "We cannot have that, can we?" I glanced at Ghent.

"Of course not, sir."

"I have heard you put in for the position of Taskmaster."

"That's right."

"From what I gather, Elder Castille approves. The only thing standing between you and your promotion is me." I pulled Storm to a halt, stopping our group. "This is your chance to convince me you are worthy of the title." I eyed the small crowd that was gathering.

"Sir." A Feeler named Kanton called out. I turned my attention to him. "There are Wielders in the crowd."

I couldn't help but grin. "Well then. Suppressor Farnsworth, it looks like it's time to impress me."

Ghent gripped the hilt of his sword. His jaw was clenched so hard I was sure I would hear his teeth cracking from the pressure.

"What do you want me to do?"

"Tell your Feeler to find them and bring them to you."

He licked his lips. "Find the offenders and bring them here."

I smiled and swung down from Storm, Ghent and Rylee following off their horses. Two Feelers marched four people forward, three men and a woman. I recognized one of the men and the woman from being with the Elf Bitch.

They struggled against the hands that held them, murderous eyes on us.

"You fucking prick." The woman's angry golden eyes were on Ghent.

Rylee strode forward and struck her across the cheek. "Watch your mouth, cunt. You will address him as Regulator Rayne."

The woman spit at Rylee, which earned her another slap. I could barely hide my smile of pride for my protégé.

Stepping forward, I stood in front of the woman whose eyes held fire and anger. "Order their execution. But not this one." I grasped her chin and jerked her head up. "This one is mine."

Eyes narrowed, and I felt her spit hit my face. Rylee's hand came up, but I caught it before she could hit her again. "Oh, but I cannot wait to break you."

She turned her attention back to Ghent. "How could you do this?"

"I'm a Suppressor, Uma. My job is to rid the world of people like you."

I laughed. "On second thought, I want you to take care of the other three."

Ghent hesitated. I stepped in front of him. "Is there a problem, Farnsworth?"

"Of course not."

"Then why the hesitation? Have you not taken care of Wielders on your patrol? Or was that just an excuse to run off and be with your little bitch?"

Hazel eyes met mine. "I am a Suppressor. My first and only obligation is to the Order," he said, drawing his sword. He stepped forward and stood in front of the blonde-haired man I had seen with the Elf and the other woman.

"Don't do this, Ghent," She begged, struggling against the Suppressor that held her. Ghent pulled back, plunging his blade into the blonde man's stomach. Uma screamed and collapsed to the ground. I smiled as Ghent swiftly ran the other three through, wiped his blade off, and then stood back.

I reached into my pocket and pulled a pouch filled with coin out and addressed the crowd. "There are more filthy Wielders in this village. Gold will go to anyone who turns them in to us." Murmurs rose through the crowd, then they turned and scattered.

I looked at the other Suppressors. "Take their heads and place them on spikes in the square so all Wielders hiding will know of their fate." They nodded and swiftly did as they were told.

Turning to Ghent, I smiled. "It's time to see if you are worthy of that promotion," I said as I swung up on Storm's back. "Kill that bitch," I said, nodding to Uma, and heeling Storm forward through the village to eradicate the world of more Wielders.

"THIRTY-FIVE WIELDERS FOUND IN a Non-town?" Vel looked up from the list I had provided him.

"Yes. I suspected something was amiss when I held my recruiting event," I said as I sat down in the chair across from him.

Vel grunted, then pushed the papers across the desk at me.

"I heard Farnsworth has put in for Taskmaster and has your approval?"

Vel removed his glasses, folded his hands on the desk, and looked at me. "Yes."

"Well, you do not have mine."

"Oh? And why is that?"

I propped my leg on my knee. "He is incapable of handing down orders, hesitating far too often when I gave him instructions for his men. He is weak."

"Well. Lucky for me, I don't need your approval."

I narrowed my eyes. "Yes, you do."

He laughed, the sound only served to fuel my annoyance.

"I will not have a subordinate who cannot relay orders." I said.

"Then I will make him Elder."

I clenched my fists. "He is not fit for a promotion. He should remain a Suppressor."

"His birthright says differently."

"Birthright." I spat. "Something that bastard waves in everyone's face. That rule is antiquated. Everyone else rises on merit. Why shouldn't Ghent?" I dropped my foot to the floor and leaned forward. "Most of the rules of this Order are antiquated."

"Such as?"

"The ridiculous treaty with the Elves. Why should they get a pass?"

"You know why. They provide the Sigaa'Lean."

"So? That means they go untouched? Are they not Wielders?"

His lips pursed into a tight line. "It's the way it has been. Just as Ghent rising—upon merit or not—is how it has been. He is being promoted, with or without your approval."

"If I were Elder—"

"But you're not, now, are you, Arden?"

Not yet. "Are we through here?" I grabbed the papers and rose. Vel waved his hand absently, his attention already returned to another stack of papers on his desk.

Clenching my jaw, I strode out of the room. I would become Elder with or without Vel or Quint's consent. I smiled as an idea began to form at the forefront of my mind.

"Oh, Vel. You will learn that no one fucks with Arden Rayne. I will be the one giving the orders. I will be the one controlling this Organization. I will make sure Zachariah Farnsworth is worshiped as the god he is. I will bring the Order back to its former glory and you will be helpless to stop me."

SIXTY-TWO
PHABIAN

I HAD BEEN IN this place, Black Root Manor, for over a Moon Cycle per my tracking of the orb in the sky. Though I was granted some freedom, I was still nothing more than a prisoner. Cassion visited me more often than not and I was starting to look forward to the time when he would arrive.

Looked forward to him.

He was a sweet young man and by how eager he was to speak with me, I knew he was starved for attention. The few times he was present at any of the meals I was forced to go to, I could tell he was ostracized by his father, simply in Rah's mannerisms and the way he spoke to Cassion. I was sure it had to do with how much he looked like me, like the Shadow Elves, but why?

"Are you listening to me, Phabian?"

Cassion's sweet voice pulled me back and I brought my attention to where he sat on the other side of the table on the balcony. His posture was casual and relaxed, feet kicked up on the table, arms folded behind his head. His blue eyes met mine and a smile curled his lips. He was pretty. So, damn pretty. My gaze dropped to his lips then back to his eyes. His long fingers combed through his hair and I wondered, for a brief moment, what they would feel like on me.

"I'm listening," I said, quickly chasing the thought away.

His smile widened and his light blue eyes danced with amusement. "So, what did I just say?"

"I—" shaking my head, I laughed. "I honestly don't know. I'm sorry, Cassion."

Cassion laughed as he rose from his seat. "Come with me."

I rose slowly. "Where?"

Pausing, he looked at me over his shoulder. "Town."

"You know I can't leave your lands."

He waved his hand in a dismissive manner. "Don't worry about that. You are with me."

"But—"

"You wish to know what your queen did to become with child, do you not?"

I frowned. "Yes but—"

"Then come with me and I will tell you." He paused for a moment then crossed to where I stood. "It is not safe to speak what I know here, Phabian." His voice was low and he cast a look over his shoulder toward the door. "Trust me."

Cassion's words were close to what Lazaro had said to me. I really had no reason to distrust Cassion. I needed answers and this would get me out of this blasted castle if only for a short time.

"Lead on, then."

THE TAVERN WAS NEARLY packed with elves and humans alike. Sweat trickled down my back; the open windows did nothing to relieve the oppressive heat. Or let out the gagging stench of sweat and body odor. A bard stood in the corner strumming a lute and singing a tale that had the Dark Elves casting scathing looks at us.

They sought to break us
To bring us down
They magicked a plan
And sent a plague on our town
On a ship
They took to the sea
A foreign land
Was where their home be
Upon his head
They placed a crown
And called him king
And they all knelt down
As our people died
As villages burned
As our people survived
And the tides had turned
There would come a day
When we would rise again

The voices of elves rose, tankards slammed on tables and murderous looks pinned us.

"Maybe we should go someplace else," I said, placing a hand on Cassion's arm.

He said nothing as he pushed his way through the crowd to a table in the back, ignoring the slurs cast at him, and it made me think of Serafin. Of how she would hold her head high in the face of her adversaries, but bury her face in my chest, her hot tears burning my skin, later when we were alone.

Cassion sat down, placing the satchel he carried beside him. I took the seat opposite, my back to the wall, something that made me more comfortable. I had a good view of the tavern and could see if anything nefarious were to happen toward us. Flagging down a serving wench, Cassion ordered us two ales. After the drinks were delivered, he pulled a book out of his pack. I could not stop my jaw from dropping at seeing the book that was taken from me when the Dark Elf soldiers barged into my room.

It was the book I found in Mouranda's quarters.

"What is this?"

"You know what it is."

I looked around the tavern, breathing a sigh of relief that no one was paying attention to us any longer.

"What are you doing with it?"

Cassion took a long drink and tapped the cover. "The answers you seek are within these pages. I found it, Phabian. I found what your queen did."

"We should go back. If Rah finds it missing..." Shaking my head, I began to rise. Cassion reached out and grasped my wrist.

"Sit, Phabian."

"But—"

"You fascinate me," he said. "For one so confident, so regal, for one who goes head-to-head with my father, you worry about a book?"

"Because my head is on the line if he finds it missing, not yours. My freedom will be revoked, not yours."

Cassion chuckled, sitting back as the serving wench placed fresh drinks in front of us. "Haven't you ever done anything naughty in your life, or have you always been so perfect?"

"I am not perfect, Cassion."

He folded his hands on the table. "So then. What naughty things did you do?"

I crossed my arms, a memory coming to me of my brothers and half a dozen other elves. "My brother Krall and I used to steal spirits and hide them in the hollow of a tree in the forest. Some nights, my brothers and a bunch of others would sneak out and have a party."

Cassion burst out laughing. "That's it? That is the worst you have ever done? I was right. You are perfect."

I shook my head and took a long drink. Another memory entered my mind. One far darker and far more shameful.

"No. I have done much worse. Once... once my brothers and I held our little sister down and shaved her head. Another time we took her favorite doll and made her watch as we tore it apart and set it on fire." I swallowed hard. "Mother was livid over what we did and Father... Father praised us for asserting our dominance." I looked down at my hands. Tears burned my eyes. "But that doesn't compare to what I did to her. That... that was far worse."

"What did you do?"

I looked up at Cassion. My heart hurt and I blinked back my tears. "I did what all Shadow Elves do. I claimed her against her will. Forced the mating bond and our Blood-Binding. I forced her to give me eight children. She took her life and my only daughter's five Grand Passages ago. I don't blame her for it. I was a beast because that is what I was taught. I'm not proud of what I did. If only I knew..." I clenched my fists. "My Anya would have been cherished, not abused. I never would have done what I did. I would have protected her like I did Serafin. Everything we do is wrong. And for what? A pure bloodline?"

Cassion's eyes held sympathy, and he reached across the table and grasped my hand. "Perhaps your king didn't want to risk his people having the same affliction."

"He is not my king," I spat. "He is nothing more than a bloody tyrant. A selfish bastard who cares nothing for his people. For his own daughter. And would it be so bad if people were born like your race? At least our women wouldn't be forced to breed. At least Serafin wouldn't have been sentenced to death." I shook my head of the thoughts. "Now, the book?"

Cassion took a seat beside me and puled the book forward. Opening it, he flipped through it, stopping on a page. "Here," he said, pointing to a section on the page. "This is what your queen did. Can you read it?"

I pulled the book close. "I'm rusty, but I'll get by," I said, pulling the book forward and reading. When I was done, I looked at Cassion. "I don't understand. This is nothing more than a fertility spell."

"How well does your queen know the Old Tongue? How well do any of the Shadow Elves know it?"

I shrugged. "I don't know. There's no reason for any of us to speak it. Karrinian came up with his own language. It was another way to mark us as different." Though there were some words interspersed in our language that came from the Dark Elves.

Cassion looked at me. "How do you know it?"

"When we were taught of your—of our—race in school, I found your language to be fascinating. It's harsh and guttural where ours is softer and more melodic. I studied it and learned some of it. Why does it matter?"

"Because." Cassion pulled the book close. "These spells are specific. If a word or two are spoken wrong, the spell is changed. Take, for instance, this." Cassion pointed at a sentence in the spell. "Read it."

"U dhark Av dho vank. The woman with child."

Cassion laughed. "You are rustier than you thought."

I clenched my jaw and shoved the book at him. "Why does that matter? So, I got a few words wrong."

Cassion put his hand on mine, and I looked at him. "Because, Phabian. As I said, the spells are specific. Wrong words change them."

Pulling my hand away, I took a sip of ale. "So, what should it say?"

"A child in the womb," he said. Pushing the book at me again, he pointed out a sentence before the one I read.

"Must make a sacrifice," I said.

"No. Vadh dhoko valkk, u dhark varr klav means with these words, a child will grow. So basically, if your queen wanted to be with child, speaking these words along with taking an elixir," he pointed to what looked like a list of ingredients, "would have given her what she wanted."

The serving wench deposited more drinks, and I took a long pull. "But she was with child, so the spell worked."

"If her words were "must make a sacrifice of a woman with child?" If she got the elixir wrong?" His eyes pinned me. "Then she unleashed something dark. Something born from the Abyss."

I thought about my conversation with Laz earlier. How he felt something lurked inside the castle. How the child, who was only four Moon Cycles, had his first Name Day. And the feeling of unease, of eyes watching me when I was in her chambers making me want to run. Not from her room but flee Il'Ekhester.

"And if everything was right?"

"A child would grow in her womb still, but it would have been made from love and want."

"Not revenge."

Cassion shook his head. "No, which makes the mistake in wording that much worse."

Draining my glass, I signaled another round. My mind whirled, and not just from the spirits consumed. It whirled from the knowledge of what Mouranda had done. What if she purposely spoke the words wrong? Made the elixir wrong? What if she somehow knew what it would do?

I shook my head of the thoughts. She may have done this out of revenge and anger over Serafin, but I knew she truly wanted to be a mother. That Serafin rejected her only amplified what she could never be. Though I did not love Mouranda, I could not see her doing something this evil on purpose.

"Everything is wrong, Cass. Why have you done this?" I said, gripping the book. Cassion removed my hands then pushed the book to the side.

"My father's condemnation of you is not fair. What happened is in the past. He will never give you answers, Phabian, so I did." Cassion licked his lips and grasped my hand. "I have no siblings. No friends. The way I was born frightens the others. It makes them think of the past. My own uncle tried to kill me."

"Why do you think you were born different? Why were Karrinian and the others?" It was a question that plagued me since arriving here.

Cassion shook his head, his thumb lightly rubbing my hand. "I don't know."

"Will your mother bear any more children? Could it be something to do with her being a human?"

"It was a hard labor for her. My father fears losing her if she were to become with child again. We will never know if she would have birthed another like me."

I ran a hand over my face. "I need to go home, Cassion. I have been here far too long and there is no purpose to my being a prisoner."

Cassion chewed his lip. "I know. I can't take you. My magic...it's not as strong as the others. I need to know where I am going. Even if I looked at a map..." his cheeks turned pink and he ducked his head.

"So, a boat then."

Cassion sighed. "You will never find a captain who will take you to Ay'arinia. Not even a human one."

I rubbed my face. Fuck, this was going to be harder than I thought. Draining my mug, I rose from my chair. "We should get back before your father comes looking for me. The last thing I need is to have my privileges, however little they are, revoked."

Cassion tossed coin on the table and stood, and we pushed our way through the crowd toward the door. When we got outside, Cassion grabbed my arm.

"I will figure out a way for you to escape, Phabian," he said softly. "It...it might take some time, but I will help you. You have my word."

"Thank you," I said. Slipping my hand in his, we made our way back to Black Root Manor.

Even if Cassion could not find a way to get me back home, I would do my damnedest to find a way.

SIXTY-THREE
SERAFIN

THE LATE AFTERNOON SUN dappled through the budding leaves on the trees. Damiyun and I picked our way through the underbrush, leading Xander and Yasmine to a stream. Damiyun spread his cloak on the ground, and we sat, having a small meal of the food he had packed. The soft rush of water and the clacking of the tree branches in the wind was a soothing sound.

Being out here in the woods, with nature, made my magic come alive inside me, begging to come out and join with nature. To create.

To destroy.

The destructive part of my magic frightened me as much as it thrilled and excited. It has come out on its own accord, the most recent time at the Suppressor camp. It had rushed through my veins without me calling it. It was almost as though the demons were coaxing it out. Begging me to let it loose and destroy all, something I instinctively knew I could do.

And something which, for a brief moment, I wanted.

Damiyun's arm slipped around my waist. "Are you alright, Princess? I felt your magic flare."

I leaned into him. "I am fine. It's this," I waved my hand, "Being in nature makes it want to come out and play. It wants to call the animals and make things grow."

And destroy. Do not forget about that, Serafin. You know you want to let it loose. To send out a path of destruction that will annihilate everything, a voice whispered in my head and the destructive side pushed the good down and rushed through my veins, the feeling delightful.

The wind picked up and thunder rumbled in the distance.

That's it. Use it. Destroy everything. Destroy Damiyun. He will only hurt you. He kills those he loves. Destroy him before he destroys you.

"No," I whispered, and the destructive magic receded. The wind died down and the thunder stopped. Who was that in my head? The voice frightened and thrilled.

"Princess?"

Turning my head, I looked at Damiyun, whose eyes questioned, and face held concern.

I reached up and touched his face. "I'm fine, Damiyun."

He licked his lips.

"Did you do that? The wind and the thunder?"

I chewed my lip. Was he angry? I could not tell by his tone, and the bond gave nothing away.

"Yes. It's another part of my magic. It comes without me calling. It bursts forth without my control. It frightens me, Damiyun." *And thrills.*

The magic thrummed deep inside, and I had to concentrate to keep it back. Why was I doing this now? The only time it came out was when I was in danger. Not at a tranquil time like this.

Damiyun's face turned white. "No. It can't...no." He jumped to his feet and ran a hand through his hair.

"Damiyun?" I slowly rose, my stomach churning. "What's wrong?"

"Your mother. Who was she?" He paced back and forth.

"She was a human who wandered onto our lands. She—"

Damiyun lunged, grabbing my arms and gripping them in an almost painful manner. "What was her name?"

I blinked. Damiyun shook me. "Tell me, Serafin. What was her name?"

"Lillyanna."

Damiyun's eyes widened. Pain flashed within the gray depths. He released me and crumbled to the ground. "Fuck the gods damned gods. Why must you do this to me? Why can't I have anything good? Why won't you let me be happy?" He yelled to the sky, hands clenched at his sides.

I felt pain and anguish and hatred through the bond. A picture flashed in my mind of him storming Trounde Castle and lighting everything on fire, but why?

"Damiyun?" I sank to my knees beside him, tentatively placing a hand on his arm. He looked at me, eyes filled with tears. "What's wrong?" I swallowed hard and for a moment, I wished I could take my question back.

Damiyun licked his lips. "Your mother. I—I knew her." He swallowed hard, his eyes never leaving mine. "We were lovers."

Coldness washed over me. It felt as though someone dumped a bucket of water over my head. "What?"

Damiyun shook his head. "Fuck me, I wish I had known this. I never..." Shaking his head he leapt to his feet again. "I never would have...gods damn it all."

Anger rushed through the bond. My magic flared and I had to struggle to push it back.

"What do you mean?" My eyes followed Damiyun who stalked back and forth. "Damiyun, stop moving. Come sit back down," I said in what I hoped was a soothing tone.

He stopped walking, and sank down in front of me, folding his legs. His hands rubbed his legs in an agitated way.

"What do you mean? How did you know her?" I kept my voice soft. Damiyun seemed like a skittish horse, and I did not want him to flee.

He took a deep breath. "Her mother, your grandmother," he spat the word, "is Felicity, the Goddess of Nature."

I remembered the puppet show from the Festival of the Gods. Of the crowd cheering for her and chanting her name, and the feeling that the puppet looked right at me.

"She put me in charge of Lillyanna," he said.

"Why?"

"To take her to the Abyss. She was a pawn in a fucking game her cunt of a mother was playing. The only reason she was born was to defeat the Fallen One."

Closing my eyes, I took a deep breath and slowly exhaled. Though I didn't want to ask the question, I had to know. Opening my eyes, I looked at Damiyun, and my heart broke at what I saw. His eyes swam with tears. His hands rubbed his legs in a rhythmic manner, and the pain and despair I felt through the bond shattered my heart. Rising, I sat beside him and took his hand.

"I—I think I know what you're going to say, but I need to hear it. How was she to do that?"

Damiyun took a deep, shaking breath. Tears spilled down his cheeks. "She had to die." His voice was barely above a whisper.

Though a fire burned inside me to find her, a voice deep inside me whispered she was gone and that, along with Phabian, kept me from pursuing my quest. But hearing the words, hearing Damiyun confirm what I thought ignited a torrent inside me. My heart pounded in my ears and I felt that dark magic rush though my veins. The wind kicked up again, more violent and fiercer than before. Clouds rushed across the sky, lightning lit up the clearing and thunder crashed. My body burned, and I looked down, gasping at my veins that glowed silver.

"Princess, stop." Damiyun's voice came from far away. I turned and looked at him. His face was ashen, and he gripped my hand hard. "Please. Push your magic back. You will destroy everything, including yourself. Please stop, Serafin."

Don't listen to him. Let it go, my princess. Kill everything. Make the world pay for your sorrow.

It was that voice again. Deep and smooth and so very enticing.

Damiyun gripped my chin, his eyes bore deep into me. His fear tugged at the back of my mind. "Please, Princess," he begged again. "I lost one woman I cared about. Please don't make me lose another. I know I can't take it."

His words broke through my rage, through my want for destruction and I pushed my magic back, though it was a struggle.

Don't listen to him, the voice hissed in my head. *He doesn't care about you. He is only saying that to keep you in his bed. He cares about no one but himself.*

I shook my head of the voice as my magic fully retreated, stopping the torrent I was causing.

"I'm sorry."

Damiyun pushed my hair from my eyes. "That magic is dark and destructive. It draws from the Abyss. From the Fallen One. Your mother wielded it. I almost lost her too, though in the end that didn't matter. I lost her anyway."

"How did she die?"

Damiyun dropped his hands to his lap and hung his head, his hair curtaining his face. "I killed her."

I inhaled sharply at his words and swallowed back the bile that burned my throat.

"I had no choice." His voice cracked. "The Abyss was claiming her. Themesis was claiming her. Her blood had to spill to secure his bonds. At least that is what I was told. She begged me to do it. To end her suffering." He lifted his head and looked at me. Tears stained his cheeks, and my heart felt heavy. "I did what she wanted, and it was like I had turned the knife on myself." He wiped his nose on his sleeve. "Not a day goes by where I am not haunted by what I did. Haunted by her."

I brushed a tear from his cheek. "What about me? How did I come to be?"

Damiyun sighed. "I betrayed her, and she fled."

Though I wanted to know more, I knew what he told me to be painful for him, so I did not ask.

"Did you know about me?"

Hearing about his relationship with my birth mother made me now wonder if he knew I existed. The thought he might have left a sour taste in my mouth.

"No," he said, and I almost cried with relief. "She never told me about you. I suppose whatever she went through in Il'Ekhester, having to give you up.... it was probably too painful for her to talk about."

"She didn't have it easy."

I thought about everything Phabian had told me about her stay at the palace. Her sadness at having to hand me over to Mouranda right after I was born. Of being turned out and then sacrificed in some game orchestrated by the gods made my blood boil.

Twice I was denied a mother and those who put her fate in their own hands, who used her for their own agenda, sat untouched. My father could have let her go, but he kept her as a prisoner. A pet. For all I knew, my birth was planned from the start. And Felicity? The Goddess of Nature, her own mother sentenced her to death.

My magic pulsed again, and I pushed it down. "Where is this Goddess of Nature?"

"S'aehe."

"Is it a place we can go?"

Damiyun blinked. "I don't…" he started, then stopped. His nostrils flared and his eyes narrowed. "Yes, it is a place we can go."

Nodding, I rose to my feet. "Good. Take me there."

Damiyun rose and clutched my hands. "Princess, I truly am sorry for what I did. I loved her. I honestly did but now?" He shook his head. "I don't rightly know where to go from here. I care about you but…" he rubbed a hand over his face.

I understood what he was saying. It was all so very confusing. I cared about Damiyun too. I gave myself to him, but now, this knowledge, though it did not quell the burning desire I had inside me, it certainly complicated things.

"I need to let what you told me sink in. I'm not sure if I am in shock or denial, but I need time."

Damiyun nodded. "I understand."

"We can talk more about it when I am ready and figure out where to go from here."

Damiyun let out a breath. "That's all I can ask."

Making our way to where Yasmine and Xander stood, we mounted our horses and guided them back to the road.

To S'aehe to pay the Goddess of Nature a visit and to give her a piece of my mind.

SIXTY-FOUR
ZEDEKIAH

P ULLING OPEN THE DOOR to the Drunken Dragon, a tavern in Karstollan, I stepped inside. The crowd was lively, clapping their hands and stamping their feet to a jaunty tune a bard was strumming and singing in the corner.

It was warm, and I shrugged out of my cloak as I weaved my way around the tables. I could hear the muted sound of an ax thudding into a wall, the cheers rising above the clapping and stomping. Stopping beside a table piled with coin, I saw Damiyun holding an ax and eying the large target hanging on the wall. Pulling back, he threw the weapon. It tumbled end over end, landing just inches from the bullseye. A cheer rang out amongst groans, and a young woman with white hair streaked with red jumped up and threw her arms around him. Damiyun spun her around with a laugh, then turned toward the table. His eyes met mine.

The girl's eyes went to me and she smiled. "Abraham."

"Actually, it's Zedekiah."

She frowned. "But you said your name was Abraham."

"It is a long story you do not need to know. Suffice it to say, I am going by Zedekiah."

"What are you doing here," Damiyun said.

I had struggled hard with the knowledge of who the girl was and Damiyun's obvious affection toward her. The way he gazed at her, the way he lifted her in his arms told me as much.

"We need to talk. Alone," I said.

Nodding, Damiyun dug into the pouch, fished out coin and handed it to the girl. "Go on and keep playing. Apparently Zedekiah has something he needs to discuss with me."

The girl snatched the coin, then turned back to the people she was playing with. Turning, I pushed my way through the crowd to an empty table, Damiyun following behind.

My eyes went to the girl who hefted her ax, throwing it at the target. A stunned silence fell over the group, then they burst into cheers. She had hit the bullseye. Damiyun laughed, and I saw softness in his eyes.

Love.

"She's pretty damn good at this game,"

Sighing, I waved down a serving wench.

"What did you need to discuss? Does it have to do with Themesis?" Damiyun said, turning his attention back to me.

Two bottles of spirits were placed on the table. I sent the other over to Damiyun as I pulled the cork and took a long drink. The Fairies Blood burned a path down my throat, hitting my stomach in an almost painful way, and warmth spread through me.

I shook my head. "No." Though that was not completely true. My father had sent me here to gather Damiyun to go after Wielders. Two families. I was sure he chose them specifically, being a father myself, and it was a test of my loyalty. A loyalty I was breaking as I would not massacre children, and I knew Damiyun would not either. I knew the punishment from my father would be harsh, but I would take it with a clean conscious.

Damiyun took a long pull of his drink. "Zedekiah—"

"There is something you need to know about the girl, Damiyun. Something that will change whatever is starting between the two of you."

Damiyun slowly lowered his bottle and placed it on the table. "You know. You know she is Lillyanna's."

My hand froze halfway to my mouth, and I blinked. How in the name of the gods does he know? And how long has he had this information? Taking a long pull, I placed the bottle on the table. "How did you find out?"

Damiyun sat back and folded his arms. "How did you?"

"It was when you were with the healer after the Pyragaty injury. She told me herself."

Damiyun's nostrils flared. "And you didn't think of telling me? Didn't think of letting me know a child, a piece of my Lil was out there?"

I breathed a sigh of relief at knowing he did not know who she was all along. Though that did not make whatever was going on between them less problematic.

"That night, the beast said my name. My real name, and she heard. Naturally she had questions which I answered. She promised not to tell you about me, and I promised not to tell you about the girl."

"Wait. She knew about you, about who you really are, and she kept that from me?"

"She promised, Damiyun, as did I. You, of all people should know what it means to keep your word."

Damiyun took a drink. "Did she...did she know what was going to happen to her? What he would make her do?"

"No, she didn't. Nor did I." And it was the truth. I did not know my father was going to use magic to control her and make her debase herself.

Damiyun took another healthy drink, as did I.

"I suppose there really is no point in being angry. What's done is done," he said.

"How did you find out?" I sat back in my chair as the serving wench placed two fresh bottles in front of us.

"It was about two days ago. We were resting from travel and... I don't rightly know why, but she started to call the lightning. It sparked a memory of Lil and I asked her who her mother was."

I rubbed my eyes and took another drink. "How far has whatever you have with her gone?"

He took another long drink but said nothing.

Fuck. Just as I thought. "You realize this is a complication?"

Damiyun laughed. "It gets worse. We are mates."

"How?"

He ran a hand through his hair. "I don't rightly know. Maybe it's because we are Shadow Elves or maybe it's because I bedded her. She doesn't know the answer either. And I realize this is a complication, but I care about her. She brightens my day. When she isn't around, I miss her incessant chatter about absolutely nothing. I miss her presence. I miss her. She makes me happy, Zedekiah." He took another drink. "I just... I fear I might be falling in love with her."

"Well, you did fuck Felicity. Then you entered a relationship with her daughter, despite all my warnings. I suppose fucking Lillyanna's daughter keeps you about on track."

Damiyun chuckled. "Fuck you, Zedekiah."

We sat in silence drinking our spirits and listening to the bard's mournful tune about a sailor lost at sea and the distant woman who waited for his return.

"I am giving her time to think about what I told her. When she is ready, we will have a talk and if she decides on friendship?" He shrugged. "I will take what I can get." He paused for a moment. "I was taking her to the Wilde Elves, but after what I told her, she wishes to go to S'aehe to confront Felicity. That is where we are going first."

I took another drink. "Rightly so. She was the one who sentenced Lillyanna to death. She deserves to know why." My eyes met his. "As do you."

"Damiyun." The girls voice came from behind, and she made her way to the table. "I won." She grinned, holding a fat pouch in her hand

Pushing back his chair, he tossed coin onto the table. "Let's go to our room before someone tries to relieve you of your winnings," he said

I watched them push their way through the crowd to the door that led to the rooms. I ran a hand over my face. Conflicted feelings churned inside me. The girl being Lillyanna's daughter made everything wrong, just as his entering into a relationship with her mother was wrong. But the girl did make him happy. I saw it when he looked at her and felt it through our bond. After everything he has been through, he deserved to be happy.

Pulling the shadows once more, I drifted on the wings of darkness and demons back to Howling Cove.

Back to my Palma who would be waiting and who would make me feel better about this night.

SIXTY-FIVE
DAMIYUN

ROSSING THE SMALL ROOM, I sat down on the edge of the bed and Serafin lowered herself beside me. The tension in the air was thick. We had been traveling for a number of days and if there wasn't silence, there was polite and slightly strained conversation. None of the banter. None of the teasing which I dearly missed. But when we were playing axes, the tension disappeared, and we fell into familiarity. And when she threw herself into my arms after I won? Gods, it felt so good to hold her.

"I suppose I will start with explaining Abraham, so you better understand things. Zedekiah is his real name. Abraham was something he called himself after he escaped slavery. He is Themesis' son, though why he has now decided to take his true name is beyond me." I knew there was more to his reason than what he told me, but I was not going to ask.

Serafin said nothing, and I continued. "As you know, Zedekiah owns my soul and through him, I am tied to the Abyss. Though in many ways, I already was." And now I was bound to Themesis in blood. "What happened..." I took a deep breath. "What happened twenty-one Grand Passages ago didn't work."

Serafin exhaled sharply, and I felt a flash of anger through the bond.

"So, my mother was sacrificed for nothing." Her voice was low. Deadly.

I turned to look at her. The low light from the candles cast shadows upon her face making her look menacing. Evil. Though I knew it was the light, I couldn't help but wonder if she was tied to Themesis in some way too.

"Yes."

Her nostrils flared. "This gives me even more reason to confront that bitch of a grandmother," she spat, and I suppressed a laugh.

"Hold onto that anger, Princess. Use it when we get there."

"She will wish she never did what she did."

This time, I did laugh. "I have no doubt of that." I took another deep breath and continued. "Themesis wants to break free and as you can imagine, he was not pleased of the events that unfolded in the Abyss. He ordered the Soul Collectors and his demons to hunt down and kill Wielders."

"Is that why they come out at night?"

I shrugged. "I suppose so, yes. And to generally terrify the people."

"Isn't there a way to keep him sealed?"

I shook my head. "The Suppressors have killed too many Wielders, and now the demons are doing the same. I fear there is no way to reseal the binds." Rising from the bed, I grabbed the bottle of Serpent's Venom that sat on the dresser and took a drink. Serafin took the bottle from me and took a healthy pull.

The silence between us stretched, uncomfortably so, and I felt a jumble of emotions from her.

Serafin placed a hand on my leg. "I'm sorry, Damiyun. I can't imagine what you are going through. Or what you've been through. It makes what I went through small in comparison."

I placed my hand on hers. "Thank you. I hope you never have to endure what I have." I ran a hand through my hair. "Princess, we need to talk about this. The silence, the strained conversations, I can't take it." *My heart can't take it.*

She bit her lip. "I know, Damiyun. I want to see Felicity before we do that. I fear if we talk, if we settle things between us," she gripped my hand. "Which I really want to do. This is hurting me too, but I fear I will change my mind about going. I want to keep the anger, the hatred I have inside. I want her to know what she did to me."

"I understand," I said, though I wasn't rightly sure I did. I feared this visit might bring us ever further apart.

"Princess, can I sleep with you tonight? I don't...I just need comfort," I said, my cheeks burning with embarrassment.

Every inn we stayed at, I made my bed on the floor. The few times we were forced to make camp, I spent the night keeping the demons at bay. And watching Serafin sleep. But tonight, I did not wish to make my bed alone on the floor, though if she says no, I will respect her answer.

"Of course you can," she said softly.

We climbed into bed, and I laid on my back looking up at the ceiling. I would not touch her. I would not hold her. All I wanted was to be near her. Her presence, her scent, and the heat of her body next to me was a quiet comfort. It was all I needed.

Serafin rolled over, placing her head on my chest and wrapped an arm around my midsection.

"Princess—"

"For comfort, Damiyun. For both of us."

Threading my fingers with hers, I closed my eyes. Perhaps this gesture, however small, was a start to our healing.

A start to our rising above our obstacle together.

SIXTY-SIX
SERAFIN

"**P**RINCESS."

A voice pierced the darkness of my slumber.

"Princess."

It came again and I was shaken awake. Opening my eyes, I saw Damiyun sitting on the edge of the bed, yellow eyes looking at me.

"Go away." I pulled the blankets over my head and burrowed back into the warm, lumpy bed.

He snatched the blankets back. "We need to get going."

I glared at him. "It's still dark out."

"Yes, but it will take the better part of the day to get there."

Knowing if I burrowed back into the bed Damiyun might very well drag me out, I tossed off the covers. Shoving him away, I rooted around in the dark room, pulled clothes from my saddle bags, and dressed. Damiyun pulled the blankets off the bed for bedrolls, and strapped Shadow Blade to his back. Hoisting our saddle bags, we exited the inn, saddled our mounts and began the journey.

A thick fog choked the road. Droplets of mist clung to my hair and soaked my shirt. It was a miserable ride, the deafening silence between Damiyun and I made it worse. Ever since discovering Damiyun's prior relationship with my mother, it seemed the silence, the chasm between us grew. When we did speak, we were careful. Polite. When we shared the bed the night prior, it felt normal and right, but when I woke, the heaviness and caution returned.

I hated it.

"Damiyun," I said, looking over at him. He sat rigid in the saddle, eyes ahead. His jaw ticked, and his hands clenched the reins. Was he feeling the same tension between us? He looked at me, and I held my hand out. Grasping it, he gave a gentle squeeze.

"We will get through this," I said.

He smiled and kissed my knuckles. "I know."

And I truly hoped we did get through this. I had feelings for Damiyun long before this complication reared its ugly head and though the news should have turned my stomach, should have made me want to flee, it didn't. Nor did it change the fact I still cared about him.

I shook the intruding thoughts and focused on what lies ahead. I thought about what Damiyun told me about my mother, her death, and who was responsible for it. Heat rushed through me. My magic pulsed inside my veins, heightening my senses. I could see the individual water droplets in the mist. Hear the sap running through the fir trees. Feel the heartbeat of woodland creatures and hear the soft patter of their feet as they woke.

And bubbling beneath the surface of the good, I felt the darker power. The one I had used earlier, and I struggled to keep it down.

"Hold onto that feeling. That anger," Damiyun said.

I forgot he could sense my magic. Did he feel the dark one brewing deep inside too? I glanced at him, his relaxed look telling me he did not. Taking a deep breath, I pushed the dark and good magic back, though I held my anger close.

"I won't let it go. It is the only thing pushing me forward on this journey," I said. Damiyun squeezed my hand, and we continued on in silence.

At around mid-day, we traveled up a steep and winding path which gave way to a clearing beside the opening of a cave. Damiyun swung down from Xander, and I followed suit. Using Shadow blade, he hacked a branch from a nearby tree.

"What now?"

Damiyun gestured to the cave. "That is how we get to S'aehe."

"But our mounts." I scratched Yasmine's nose.

"They will be fine. Demons don't dare come here and no human knows of this place," Damiyun said.

Removing our saddles, bags, bridles, and weapons, we placed them inside the cave. Damiyun rummaged through his bag and pulled out a soiled shirt Wrapping it around the branch, he used his magic to light it and began walking.

"Stay close," he said, his hand grasping mine. "While some passages lead to an exit, one being Il'Ekhester, many more will cause you to become disoriented and lost where you will die a slow and painful death. It is the god's way of protecting S'aehe."

"So, Felicity summoned you?"

Damiyun took a deep breath. "Yes. She called me here to discuss Lillyanna and what my part was."

I said nothing, and we walked on for what felt like an eternity until finally, a sliver of light appeared up ahead. As we walked closer, the exit to the cave appeared, along with the silhouette of a large man hefting a broad sword.

"Who dares enter the Cave of the Gods?" His deep voice echoed off the walls.

"I do," Damiyun said, stepping into the light.

The man lowered his ax at seeing him. He looked at me, eyes widening with a gasp. "The Goddess of Nature is in her garden," he said, voice shaking.

Damiyun nodded and pushed past the man with me in tow. Stepping into S'aehe, I shaded my eyes from the brilliant white light. As we walked the marble path, I looked around. Beautiful flowers of every color in full bloom lined the sides and dotted the blanket of green that stretched out as far as my eyes could see, the scent of flowers tickled my nose. People lounged casually on the grass, some in intimate embraces, some playing games, while others dozed.

I gazed around, not fully comprehending I was in the realm of the gods. The same gods the Shadow Elves did not believe in. I shook my head and laughed.

"What?"

I looked up at Damiyun. "I can't believe the gods are real. That I am in their realm." I shook my head again. "The Shadow Elves are so stuck in their history, in what they've been told, so secluded in Il'Ekhester they fail to open their minds and see past their own nose. When I am queen, I will open their minds to everything." And I would. I would show them there was far more outside our lands and I would research the gods and do my best to prove they were real.

Damiyun smiled. "I know you will, Princess. You will be a mighty queen," he said, and I warmed at his words.

We walked a bit more when a large structure of marble and oak with a high peaked roof came into view. A beautiful woman with long blond hair held back by delicate combs, the diamonds and pearls twinkling in the white light, lounged against a pile of pillows. A man stretched out beside her, his head in her lap, catching the grapes she dropped into his open mouth. He said something to her, and she laughed, the sound like bells tinkling in the wind.

I could not help but stare at her. Her beauty was mesmerizing. The way she moved was fluid and perfect. I knew I was looking upon Felicity, the Goddess of Nature and my grandmother. The puppet at the Festival of the Gods did not do her justice.

I shook myself of the awe I felt. This woman sent my mother to her death and here she sat, feeding grapes to someone and laughing. Not that I expected her to be wearing mourning garb, but I would think the death of her daughter would have changed her in some way.

She laughed again, fingers of one hand brushing a lock of hair on the man's face away, the other toyed with a jewel nestled between her breasts in a flirtatious and seductive manner.

A bitter tang filled my mouth. My body heated and my magic raced through my veins.

Damiyun softly squeezed my hand. "Easy, Princess."

"How can she be happy when her daughter is dead?" I couldn't imagine feeling joy if I lost a child, no matter how many Grand Passages went by.

"She's a narcissistic cunt. She cares for no one but herself, as all gods do," Damiyun spat.

We took a few steps forward. Damiyun's boot scraped on the polished marble. Felicity paused in her feeding, a frown drawing her supple lips down, and she turned. Her eyes widened with surprise as she looked at Damiyun, her frown turning into a slow smile. The man in her lap rose. His black eyes narrowed on Damiyun briefly, then turned to me, his expression turning from anger, to disbelief, then shock. He shook his head, muttering to himself as he settled down against the pillows.

"Damiyun, darling," Felicity purred as she rose. She wore a royal blue gown, the neckline plunging obscenely to her belly button, the shimmering fabric hugging her hourglass figure. She slowly walked to where we stood, her hips swinging provocatively, blue eyes on Damiyun.

My anger, and my magic, surged.

"I wasn't expecting you," she said, looking up at him. "This is truly a pleasant surprise."

"He is not here to see you, Grandmother. I am," I said. Her head snapped in my direction and her eyes narrowed. "Didn't you know your daughter had a child?"

Regaining her composure, she smiled at me. "Of course, I did. Welcome..." her voice trailed off.

My nostrils flared. That bitch didn't even know my name. "It's Serafin."

"Yes, of course." She waved her hand in dismissal and turned back to Damiyun. "Why did you bring her here?" She hissed.

"Why did you send my mother to die?"

Felicity looked at me. Hatred raged in the blue depths of her eyes. "I did not send your mother to die."

I laughed. "Is she here?"

Her nostrils flared. "Listen, Serenity. There are things in the world you cannot possibly understand."

I crossed my arms, my eyes never leaving hers. "It's Serafin, and I understand my mother is dead. I understand she was sacrificed in the Abyss on your order." I took a step in her direction. My magic bounced around inside me. It raced through my veins. I had to struggle to keep it back. "I understand her death did nothing. Her sacrifice was for nothing." My tone was low. Dangerous. Fear flashed in Felicity's eyes, and she took a cautious step back. I had to stop myself from laughing.

The Goddess of Nature was afraid of me. Good.

"Easy, Princess." Damiyun's voice was low. I had forgotten he was here. Ignoring him, I held my magic closer. I glanced behind Felicity at the man lounging casually against the pillows sipping a glass of wine. He looked at Felicity with amusement, his amusement turning to fear when his eyes met mine again.

So, two gods were afraid of me. Though which god he was, I did not know but I could sense he was powerful and commanded a presence.

And he was afraid of me. I bit my cheek to keep from laughing.

Felicity regained her composure and looked at Damiyun. "I was not the one who sacrificed her. Perhaps you should be speaking with Damiyun about this."

"Clearly, I have. Why else would I be here?" I took another step forward. Felicity took one back. "This is not about Damiyun. This is about what you did."

Felicity's eyes narrowed. "I did nothing."

Damiyun laughed. "You are certainly right about that."

Felicity glared at hm. "Like Selene said, this is not about you. Go have a seat in the garden."

I clenched my fists. It was getting more difficult to keep my magic back.

"Hold onto it, Princess. Know I won't stop you from destroying this fucking place," Damiyun whispered in my ear.

"My name is Serafin, and Damiyun is not going anywhere. Now tell me why the fuck my mother was born."

Felicity swallowed hard. Fear flashed in her eyes for a moment, then her composure was back. At least it appeared she was composed. I saw the way her hands shook. The way she took slow, controlled breaths.

"Why don't we have a seat and talk about this like civil people?" There was a tremor in her voice.

She's afraid of me, I sent to Damiyun as we entered the structure. Felicity settled next to the man, and Damiyun and I sat against the pillows opposite. A table with fruit, cheese, and wine divided us.

As she should be, Damiyun said as he reached across the table and poured four glasses of wine.

So is that guy.

Damiyun's eyes flicked to the man as he handed me my drink.

That's Sarlay, the God of War.

I smiled into my glass. *The God of War is afraid of me.*

Damiyun grasped my hand and squeezed. *They all should be.*

"Why was my mother born?" My voice broke the silence. I would not stop asking the question until I received an answer.

Felicity's eyes looked at me, then settled on Damiyun. "She was to set Themesis free."

Damiyun stiffened. "You told me to bring her to the Abyss to defeat him. You said her blood would seal the binds." His voice rose and he leaned forward.

Easy, I sent to him, placing a hand on his arm. He glanced at me and relaxed, if only slightly.

Felicity laughed. "Would you have gone if told you the real reason?"

Damiyun leaped from his seat. "No. You know that. I loved her. If I had known—"

"What, Damiyun? You would have taken her away to live a quiet life somewhere? Do you really think that was to be?"

"Yes," Damiyun said, slowly sitting back down. I could feel the pain, sadness, and rage through the bond we shared. Slipping my hand in his, I gave a gentle squeeze.

"How was she supposed to set him free?" As long as Felicity was talking, I might as well try to get as much information as I could.

"Her Blood Binding with him would have made him stronger, but you," her blue eyes glared at Damiyun. "You had to kill her. All of this has been planned since Themesis was tossed to the Abyss. The Suppressors, the termination of your kind, it didn't take much to convince Nons Wielders were evil. A whisper here. A dream there. You mortals are so very easy to manipulate.

Damiyun took a healthy drink of wine, then refilled his glass. "So, why toss him to the Abyss? Why didn't you just let him have his way?"

Felicity's lips curled into a snarl. "Because he wanted to rule. He would have destroyed us. We could not allow that to happen."

I shook my head. "None of this makes any sense. You tossed him to the Abyss because he wanted to rule, yet now you want him to break free? Won't he just wage another war on you? Aren't you just sealing your own fates?"

Felicity looked at me. "What would you have done, Sela? Your kind doesn't even believe in us."

I clenched my jaw. "My name is Serafin. Am I not sitting with the gods right now?"

Felicity's nostrils flared. "The mortals long stopped believing. They destroyed the temples and statues in our honor. They stopped praying to us. God's Day is hardly celebrated."

"You wanted him free too," Damiyun said, eyes on Sarlay.

"You mortals will crawl to us. Beg us to help you. To save you, and when we do, you will worship us again."

I couldn't believe what he just said, nor could I stop the laughter from flying out of my mouth. Felicity's and Sarlay's eyes narrowed on me. "You truly thought unleashing what I presume to be an extremely powerful god on the world would make mortals crawl to you? You barely beat him once. What makes you so sure you can beat him now? You said yourself; my mother's blood would have made him stronger."

Felicity's nostrils flared and she clenched her fists. "Who are you to question what we do? Why we do it? You, whose race does not believe. Who are you to come to S'aehe, demanding answers on things you know nothing about?

Sitting up straight, I locked eyes with Felicity. "I am Serafin Trounde, daughter of Lillyanna, granddaughter to the Goddess of Nature," I said. "Or did you already forget?" Felicity's eye twitched, her composure began to crumble. "You took my mother from me." My anger came rushing back, along with my magic.

"I was not the one who plunged the dagger into her chest," Felicity snarled, her beautiful face crumbling into something ugly and wicked.

"No. You just sent her to the Abyss to be Blood Bound to fulfill your fucking agenda. She was nothing more than a puppet for you to control." Rising, I drew my magic closer. Damiyun rose as well. I knew he felt the magic within me, but he did not say or do anything to calm me.

"I hope Themesis breaks free. I hope he wages a war on S'aehe and I hope you all die. Especially you." Light circled and crackled around my wrists. Felicity licked her lips, her eyes going to the energy I harnessed.

"Sawyer—"

"My name is Serafin." Pulling my magic, I sent a pulse of light and energy out. It hit Felicity in the chest, lifting her into the air and tossing her to the ground in an unmoving heap. Sarlay leaped to his feet.

"I suggest you think long and hard about what you think you are going to do, lest you wind up like her," I said. Sarlay's nostrils flared, but he did not make a move.

The sound of voices yelling echoed in the air. Damiyun took my hand. "I think we should go."

I did not argue, and we raced through S'aehe and through the cave, not stopping until we were through the other side, bursting out into the pitch-black clearing. How long had we been there?

"Fuck me, Princess. I didn't think you would do it," Damiyun said, and I detected a hint of pride in his voice.

"Neither did I, but that bitch deserved it."

Damiyun chuckled. "I'm not denying that."

Looking around the dark clearing, I caught a flash white. Whistling, Yasmine trotted to where I stood. Stepping back into the cave, I grabbed our saddle bags and began loading mine onto Yasmine's back.

"What are you doing?"

I looked at Damiyun who was gathering sticks and logs to build a fire.

"Shouldn't we leave? Won't they come after us?" After all, I did attack a goddess. Surely there were consequences for that.

Damiyun shook his head as he used his magic to light the wood. "Doubtful. No mortal has ever attacked a god. My guess is they're either not sure what to do or are too afraid to come after you."

Picking up his saddlebags, he folded his lean frame on the ground and rummaged around, pulling out dried meat, cheese, and a bottle of Serpent's Venom. Sitting next to him, I grabbed the bottle and took a healthy pull.

"You were right. Felicity is a narcissistic cunt. She couldn't even get my name right." Tears stung my eyes. While I did not know what to expect, I did not think it would have been a cold and uncaring woman.

"I know," Damiyun said, handing me some food. I chewed a piece of meat, my eyes on the fire.

"Nothing of what she said makes any sense." I looked at Damiyun. The shadows from the fire danced on his face making him look menacing. His yellow glowing eyes only added to the look. "If she was sent to be Blood Bound to Themesis, why make you take her? Why didn't Zedekiah just do it?"

Damiyun took a long pull from the bottle and handed it back to me. "I don't rightly know."

"Did you—did you know what was to happen?"

Damiyun looked at me. Reaching over, he pushed a lock of hair behind my ear. "No, Princess. I was told my job was to sacrifice her, though again, I do not know why it had to be me. She begged me to do it, Princess. I was ending her misery."

Tears poured from my eyes. Damiyun wrapped his arms around me and pulled me onto his lap. Burying my face in his neck, I let out a torrent of tears. Damiyun rubbed my back and whispered nonsense words that somehow soothed.

"It's not fair." I sat up and wiped my nose on my sleeve. "What happened to my mother and what happened to me. If she were allowed to stay in Il'Ekhester, I know I would not have been sentenced to death. I am sure Allendaire planned everything the minute she stepped onto our lands. Just as I am sure Felicity planned everything when she was born. She truly had no choice with anything. Her fate was determined for her."

Damiyun kissed the tears on my cheeks but said nothing, his silence an odd comfort.

"Come, Princess. Let us get some rest. It has been a very long and very tiring day."

Nodding, I slipped off his lap and rummaged through my bags pulling out my bedroll. Spreading it on the ground in front of the fire, I laid down. Damiyun stoked the fire, then laid down beside me. Curling into him, I laid my head on his chest. His warmth enveloped me and the steady rise and fall of his chest was hypnotic.

I was grateful he took me to S'aehe. Grateful he was there for me then, and now. He was a silent comfort. He was my rock.

And I realized I did not care he had a prior relationship with my mother. My feelings for him rose before any of that came to a head. Today showed me just how much he cared about me and just how much he meant to me.

And when his breathing became even, when I knew he was asleep, I kissed his chin and said the words I knew to be true: "I love you, Damiyun Rayne."

SIXTY-SEVEN
MOURANDA

I SAT IN A chair in the great room, watching Mordecai play with his blocks and dolls. The child seemed much larger, more advanced and far more aware than one of just four Moon Cycles.

At least I thought it had been four Moon Cycles. Since giving birth, my mind had become increasingly foggy. What I thought had been just the passing of a day, some Elves claimed it had been two, sometimes more. It was getting increasingly difficult to know.

There was something odd about the child. Something wrong. His eyes were too alert. His face often held a sinister smile. Several times I had to chastise him for throwing rocks at the hunting dogs and when I breast fed him, it was painful. The child drew blood, something he seemed to like more than my milk. I tried to push aside what I did. Tried to forget the child was a Dark Elf, remembering he was mine, but it was difficult to do. Difficult to love the toddler who might one day destroy us.

And there was a darkness inside these walls. I would often see shadows move out of the corner of my eye, but when I looked, nothing was there. A figure would stand at the end of my bed and when I blinked, it would be gone, and I couldn't be sure of what I saw.

And my nights were restless at best, my dreams plagued by nightmares. The woman I had taken the fetus from haunted me. I saw her face. Saw the hatred and accusation in her eyes. And then came the beast that appeared in the woods that night. Sharp claws tore through skin. Wicked teeth crushed bones. *A life for a live, Mouranda Trounde.* The hideous beast would growl.

Always, I woke up screaming, heart pounding in my chest, my sweat-soaked sleep dress clinging to me.

Mordecai stood, tottering over to the fire raging in the hearth.

"No," I called out, leaping up to chase after him. The child tripped on the rug and I watched in horror as he tumbled headfirst into the flames. I screamed, rushing to the fireplace and stopped, watching as he stood up and tottered out unharmed, with the exception of his burnt clothing.

"My queen. Are you alright?" Krall said as he rushed into the room. I turned and looked at him. His eyes went to Mordecai, who sat down, picked up his dolls and continued playing.

"Why is the prince's clothing burnt?"

I swallowed hard. "He...he fell into the fire, but it didn't harm him." I went to where he sat and squatted down. I touched him to make sure he was real. Make sure it wasn't another one of my nightmares, and I felt flesh and bone. I checked him for burns, some sign other than his burnt clothing and singed hair, anything, but could find no marks.

No evidence, but I know what I saw.

Krall squatted beside me and placed a hand on my arm. "My queen. Perhaps you should go lie down. I know you have not been sleeping. I hear your footsteps. I see you wandering the halls all hours of the night. You need to rest."

I looked at him. "I don't..." I shook my head. "You're right. I am tired. Will you watch Mordecai?"

Krall smiled. "Of course, majesty."

Krall sat cross legged on the floor. He picked up a doll and began playing with the child. I looked at Mordecai who was dismembering one of his dolls, a smile on his face as he ripped off the limbs. Rising, he tossed the parts into the fire, his laughter filling the room. It was chilling.

Evil.

"Mordecai. Don't destroy your toys," Krall chastised. The child looked at him, baring his teeth and growled. A shiver ran up my spine. Krall, oblivious to the wrongness of the child, growled back. Grabbing him, he picked him up, lifted his shirt and blew on his stomach.

Slipping out of the room, I walked slowly through the halls. How could Mordecai have come out unscathed, after falling into the fire? It did not make sense. Opening the door to my quarters, I breathed a sigh of relief at seeing the empty room. I needed to be alone to think. I did not have the energy to put on a smile and act as though everything was fine for Denalla, though I knew she would see through me. She always did.

Crossing to my desk, I poured a glass of spirits and tossed back the thick, sweet liquid. Warmth spread through me as I tossed back another. Grabbing the bottle, I stoked the embers in the hearth and sank into the plush cushions of the couch. Taking another pull off the bottle, I leaned my head against the back of the couch, my body relaxing and the spirits warming.

I caught a movement out of the corner of my eye. Turning my head, I saw the shadows move. My heart raced as I followed the movement.

"Who's there?" I called out, trying to quell the shaking of my voice. A low growl came from whatever lurked in the shadows and I grew cold. But then the shadows stopped moving and I wasn't sure what I had seen.

It wasn't the first time I saw movement in the shadows. Heard a growl, a hiss. I even heard my name spoken. It sent chills down my spine. I knew I had somehow unleashed something evil when I did what I did, but it did not make sense. It was nothing more than a fertility spell, and though my grasp of the Old Tongue was poor at best, I was sure I had translated it right.

And the child? Mordecai? He was far more alert and aware than a child of... I paused in thought. I was certain I had birthed him only four Moon Cycles ago, and yet I remember celebrating his first Name Day. Elves packed the grand ballroom. Urns and vases of flowers dotted the corners and sat atop tables, the fragrance heady. Bright colored streamers hung from the six-tiered chandelier. A string quartet played in a corner. Servants carrying trays of food and drink circled the crowd. One table was piled high with gifts wrapped in bright paper and tied with big bows, while another held a five-tiered birthday cake.

Mordecai, dressed in a bright pink shirt, yellow trousers, and red booties sat on Allendaire's lap. A line of elves stood before the king and prince, bowing and holding their presents out.

I stood in a corner of the room and watched the festivities. Watched the Elves lay gifts on the table and at the boy's feet. Watched Mordecai look around at the crowd, eyes far more alert than a child of one Grand Passage should be, though I was not exactly sure of his age. A distant memory of me birthing him floated in the fringes of my mind. Something told me an entire Grand Passage could not have gone by, surely, I would remember something during that time, but my mind was foggy and here we all were, celebrating his Name Day.

You don't know what you have unleashed, a voice whispered in my mind.

"Mouranda." I jumped at the sound of Denalla's voice pulling me from my memories. Picking up the bottle, she poured what little remained into a glass and took a sip.

Did I really drink that much? My swimming head and blurry vision told me I had.

"I put Mordecai to bed. He fought me the entire time," Denalla said.

I looked around the room at the lit candles in sconces and holders. When had I done that? My eyes went to the windows. The sky was black, a smattering of stars winked in the night sky. Shrieks and wails echoed in the distance. I rubbed my eyes. It was late afternoon when I left Krall with the child. How could so much time have passed?

Denalla sat beside me. "Krall said he had an accident?"

I felt her eyes on me. Was she accusing me of hurting my own child? "Yes," I said. "He took a fall near the hearth."

I could feel the heat of her gaze. "Near, or in?"

There it was. The accusation in her tone. The underlying meaning that, even though I birthed a child, I weas still incapable of being a mother. I looked at Denalla, my eyes widening at seeing scratches and dried blood on her face. A vision of Mordecai baring his teeth and growling at Krall floated in my mind. I was sure Denalla's injuries were a result of the child putting up a fight.

Placing my glass on the table, I rose. "I am going to retire," I said. Slipping out of my clothes, I pulled on my sleep dress. Undoing the pins in my bun, I unraveled my hair and began brushing. I heard the rustle of clothes. Looking in the mirror I watched Denalla slip out of the room without a kiss. Without wishing me a good night. Without a backwards glance.

Putting my brush down on the dresser, I doused the candles, stoked the fire and slipped into bed. Pulling the covers up, I looked at the still shadows and as I closed my eyes, I sent out a prayer to the gods I do not believe in that whatever demons and monsters clung to the shadows did not get me this night.

I feared the day would come when I would not wake from my terrors.

SIXTY-EIGHT
ARDEN

T HE SUN BEAT DOWN on my naked torso. Sweat soaked my skin and burned my eyes. I struck hard and fast with my sword, Rylee barely deflecting my strikes. Sweat dripped from her chin and plastered her hair to her face. She lifted a hand to wipe the droplets, and I took the opportunity to strike, the tip of my blade grazing her midsection, cutting through her shirt and leaving a trail of blood across flesh.

I did not strike too deep, not this time. It was just enough to get her attention. Her eyes widened, and she looked at the blood that dripped. Again, she let herself become distracted. Sweeping her feet out from beneath her, she landed hard on her back. I placed a foot on her chest, pressing the tip of my blade against her neck

"You became distracted. It has cost you your life."

Rylee glared up at me and the next thing I knew, I was flat on my back. She straddled me, and my chest constricted. I couldn't breathe. My mind went to being pinned on the ground as a child. Nausea clenched my gut. Bile rose in my throat. I felt closed in.

Vulnerable.

Helpless.

Just like when I was a child.

Rylee placed the tip of her dagger beneath my chin. My heart pounded in my chest.

"And with my last, dying breath, I will take you to the Abyss with me," she said, breath hot on my face.

"Get the fuck off me," I said, regaining my composure and tossing her off. Jumping to my feet, I picked my shirt off the ground and strode through the soft grass of the training field back to the Compound.

"What's the matter, Arden? Are you sore because you lost?"

Her laughter echoed off the walls. Fire raced through my veins at her words. At her laughter. Turning, I stalked back to where she stood, a mirthful smile on her face. Grabbing her around the neck, I pulled her forward, trying not to laugh at the look of panic, the look of fear in her brown eyes.

"I did not lose. I never lose. You had best remember and if you ever mock me again," I squeezed tighter, "You will feel pain the likes you have never known, and you will wish you were dead." I released her with a shove. She stumbled back, falling on her ass.

"Forgive me, Regulator Rayne," she said, her voice quivering.

"Get up."

She scrambled to her feet and stood at attention, legs wide, hands clasped behind her back, and eyes forward.

"You have potential, Strahand. You are shrewd. Cut-throat. Cold. You will go far in this organization."

Her lips twitched. "Thank you, Regulator Rayne."

"Go change your uniform and meet me out front. We are going on a trip."

Nodding, she picked up her sword and hurried across the field. Picking up my own sword, I trailed behind. It has been about five days since I let my brother go. I was sure he was secure in his home in L'Ochal. I was sure he has let his guard down by now, like the fool he was.

Now it was time to pay him, and the elf bitch a visit.

AFTER A DAY OF travel, we entered the town of L'Ochal as the sun began to peek above the horizon. Though I did not wish to be out at night, the memories of the prior demon attack, the embarrassment of being stripped emotionally bare in front of my brother was fresh in my mind, but we had no choice. This time I made sure to make a strong perimeter. To have blazing bon fires to keep the monsters at bay. I shook off the invasive thoughts. The fear that clenched my gut.

Fear was for women.

As my group of ten marched through the streets, I looked at Ghent who rode to my left. He sat ramrod straight in the saddle, hands clenching the reins of Abigale, and his jaw ticked. The rage that flashed in his eyes when I told the gathered group where we were headed almost made me laugh.

As we marched through the waking village, people eyed us with wary looks. Mothers clutched their children and others ran. It warmed my heart to see the fear we instilled in the people.

"Nice town. Any Wielder's here?" Rylee's voice came from my right. Her eyes scanned the people, and her face held a scowl.

"A few, though it's primarily a Non town."

She looked at me. "Why haven't you run a raid here or held a recruiting event?"

It was a good question, though it was one I had no answer for.

"We need all the forces we can get. We should—"

"When did you become Regulator, Suppressor Strahand?"

She pursed her lips and said no more.

Finally, after navigating our way through the streets of the town, Pine Crest Manor came into view from the crest of the hill. It was a large house with a sprawling lawn turning a deep emerald as spring set in. Colorful flowers dotted beds, and trees were starting to bloom. The blatant show of opulence disgusted me. Of course, after our father died, something I still had questions on, Damiyun took over his shipping business, reaping the benefits of the coin earned. In the past, he would hold elaborate balls for the higher society, showing off his disgusting wealth.

I did not need the flash. The mountains of coin. I preferred my simple life in Wren's Keep. My simple room where everything was as it should be. A regimented day where I knew exactly what I was to do every hour, though on occasion, such as today, I deviated from my order, if only to have a bit of fun causing terror and pain.

Pulling up to the front of the house, we dismounted. The front door opened and a small man with a balding head stood in the doorway.

"Suppressor Farnsworth," I said, turning to him. "Take Suppressor Ewes, and Suppressor Lynt and search the house."

He hesitated a second, then nodded, marching up the stairs with sword drawn, pushing the little man out of the way. After a few moments, the three returned empty handed.

"There is no one here but servants, sir," Ghent said, returning to my side. I detected a bit of relief in his eyes.

I turned my attention to the man on the porch. "Where is he?"

The man said nothing. Striding up the steps, I grabbed him by his shirt and pressed the tip of my dagger beneath his chin. "Tell me where he is or I will slit your throat."

The man swallowed hard. "They left a few days ago. They are on their way to the Wilde Elves."

Smiling, I released him. 'Thank you. And for that, I will spare your life," I said. I was in a magnanimous mood.

Mounting our horses, we heeled them back to the road, beginning the trek to Va'l'Victorus.

I would search every town, every tavern, and every inn until I found my brother.

And this time I would not let him go.

SIXTY-NINE
SERAFIN

M Y MIND WAS CHURNING through my visit with Felicity. I didn't know what to expect really. It certainly was not the coldness and indifference I received. It was clear she had no love for my mother.

Or for me.

And though knowing that should have hurt, I was used to rejection. Used to being ignored. I would do what I have always done. Put on a smile and pretend I'm fine.

"Are you alright, Princess?" Damiyun's voice broke through my thoughts.

I looked at him sitting astride Xander and shook my head. "No, I'm not," I said. Though I could pretend to myself everything was fine, I could not pretend to Damiyun. Something about him made me want to be truthful with him.

He pulled Xander to a halt, and I stopped Yasmine. Swinging down, he guided his mount into the woods, and I followed. Sitting on the ground, he took my hand and pulled me down beside him.

"I don't understand. How could Felicity be so cold? So uncaring?"

Damiyun's thumb rubbed the back of my hand in a soothing manner. "The gods are self-absorbed, and Felicity, she's—"

"A narcissistic cunt?"

"My lady," Damiyun chuckled. "Have I said that out loud?"

"You have and you're not wrong." I sank into Damiyun. Though the silence stretched, it wasn't uncomfortable.

"We still have to talk about your mother. And me," he said.

I took a deep breath and pulled away. Hearing how Damiyun had a relationship with my mother was disconcerting. Did he want me because I was hers? Did he see her in me? Was he trying to hold on to what he had with her by holding on to me?

"I cared about you, long before I knew who you were. Who your mother was." He cupped my chin and brought my face up.

I took a deep breath. "I care about you too."

He dropped his hand and hung his head. "What do we do now?" His voice was soft.

What do we do? Damiyun made me feel safe and loved. He made me see I wasn't an outcast.

Not the half-breed daughter of a whore. Not someone who should be executed for who I was.

He was like me. Half human, half elf. No more, no less and though he told me he had a relationship with my mother, though he sacrificed her to the gods, I did not care. I gave him what I had denied Cal and what I denied Ghent. I gave him me.

All of me, and he took what I had to offer with kindness.

With love.

And we were bound as mates. Two halves of a whole.

Taking his hand, I pressed my lips to his knuckles. "What do you want to do?" I looked into his gray eyes. "I know who my mother was. Who she was to you, and I..." I shook my head.

Damiyun pushed a lock of hair behind my ear and cupped my chin. "I want what we have. Fuck me, Princess, but you make me happy. I love you Serafin, and I know it's wrong, but I don't care."

My lip trembled at his words. "I don't care either."

His lips brushed mine, and I folded into his embrace as the kiss deepened.

"Brother. Am I interrupting something?"

The voice made me freeze. We pulled away and turned, seeing Arden sitting astride a midnight black horse, the reins to Yasmine and Xander held loosely in one hand. Damiyun slowly rose, his eyes on his brother.

"I paid you a visit at your manor. Your man servant was kind enough to tell me where you were heading."

I slowly rose to my feet. Damiyun glanced down, then stepped in front of me in a protective manner. A twig snapped and my eyes went to five suppressors guiding their mounts into the woods. My eyes went to Ghent who was among them. His jaw was clenched, and he gripped the hilt of his sword hard, the knuckles on his hand turning white.

A homely young woman with blond hair braided tight sat on her horse beside him. Her fingers drummed the hilt of a dagger, a smile curled her lips, and her eyes were bright with excitement.

"Why are you doing this, Arden?" Damiyun's voice, though tired, held an edge.

How did he find us? Levin only knew we were going to the Wilde Elves, not to Felicity. How did he get here so fast? I sent to Damiyun.

Time moves slower in S'aehe. The few hours we were there was over a day here.

But how did he know we were here?

The roads converge. Yasmine and Xander were wandering free, he said, though I still didn't understand. *When I say run, I want you to run fast and run far. Try to get Yasmine if you can but please, for the love of the gods, do as I say.*

Why don't you just kill your brother? I reached behind my back, fingers brushing the hilt of the dagger tucked into my belt. *He is nothing but dreadful to you.*

Damiyun's shoulders slumped. *He is my brother.*

I watched the Suppressors shift in their saddles, the female bouncing in hers. Ghent's angry eyes were on Arden, his jaw clenched and unclenched. Arden dropped the reins of our mounts and swung down, folding his arms.

"Did you think I would let you go for eternity?" He took a few slow steps toward Damiyun. "The Order owns you, Brother. It is time you come back home where you belong."

"Wren's Keep is not my home. It never was," Damiyun said. Arden's eyes narrowed and he pursed his lips.

"It's now or never," I said under my breath. Pulling my dagger free, I pounced forward, slamming the blade into Arden's chest. Blood spilled over my hands as I pulled the weapon out. Arden's eyes widened in surprise.

"Princess." Damiyun's voice was filled with shock.

"Yasmine, to me," I called out, and she ran to where I stood. Grabbing the pommel of the saddle as she raced by, I swung up onto her back. Hooves pounded, and I glanced over my shoulder seeing Damiyun racing behind while four Suppressors gave chase.

Including Ghent.

Damiyun drew up beside me as we raced through the woods, Xander and Yasmine leaped over felled trees and we weaved and ducked beneath branches. I looked over my shoulder, my heart sinking at seeing the men closing in.

An explosion erupted on the forest floor in front of a Suppressor. Horse and man screamed as they were tossed into the air, hitting the ground with a thud.

Reaching behind, I unstrapped my bow, quickly strung it, and nocked an arrow. Aiming at the Suppressors who drew even closer, I let loose the arrow which found it's mark in the neck of the closest man. His eyes widened, and he pitched off his horse.

There were two men left, one of which was Ghent. I did not want to hurt—let alone kill—him, but I would do what I had to in order to save our lives. Energy hissed and crackled as Damiyun drew his elven magic. I nocked another arrow. Ghent's hazel eyes met mine. Pulling his sword, he ran it through the man beside him.

"Go," he commanded, pulling his mount around and racing back the way we came.

Damiyun heeled Xander into a gallop, and I raced behind. His eyes scanned the woods, body tense as we pounded through the brush, bursting through to the road as the sun dipped below the horizon. We slowed our mounts who were frothing, and I listened for any hooves following.

"They are most likely taking my brother back to their camp."

Nodding, I led Yasmine down the road, not looking at Damiyun and not saying a word about what I did. Afterall, I plunged my dagger into his brother's heart. I looked down at my bloodied hands, the memory of the warmth pouring over them and the look on the man's face as my arrow hit his neck. Whether or not he lived, I didn't know.

My stomach heaved, and leaped off Yasmine, tossing the contents into the brush.

"It gets easier, Princess." Damiyun's voice was soft in my ear. Turning, I wrapped my arms around him and rested my head on his chest. "It's alright, Princess." His words undid me.

"I'm sorry," I sobbed. "I didn't mean to—"

"Kill my brother?" Damiyun pulled away. I couldn't look at him. I buried a dagger...fuck, but the bile rose again, and I emptied whatever was left in it onto the ground.

"Princess," Damiyun said, and I looked up at him.

"I'm sorry."

His arms went around me, and he pulled me close, the stubble on his jaw scratched my face.

"Don't be sorry, Princess. You did what I could not."

Pulling away I looked up at him. "I want to go home. I don't want to go to the Wilde Elves and see this Barlack," I said. And I didn't. The time spent with Felicity, the brief encounter with the Suppressors again, it left me emotionally and physically drained.

Raw.

I had no idea what Barlack wanted from me, or how he even knew about me for that matter. I was tired of traveling. Of barely sleeping at night, spending my time helping Damiyun keep the monsters away. I wanted to go back to Pine Crest Manor, another home I was taken from.

A place where I felt safe.

"Believe me, I know the feeling, but I made a promise to him." Damiyun ran a hand over my hair. "We have fifteen more days, maybe less if the weather cooperates and we push our horses hard. The sooner we get there, the sooner we can go back home. With any luck."

We swung up onto our mounts and resumed our journey. "What does he want with me anyway?"

Damiyun shrugged. "I can't say, though I suspect it has something to do with your birthright."

A birthright I wasn't so sure I wanted any longer. The Moon Cycles I had been away allowed me to think for myself. Do what I wanted. Wear what I wanted. Say what I wanted. I wasn't forced to attend balls. To accompany the king when he collected taxes and to sit in on boring meetings and petty squabbles. I didn't have to wear gowns and a crown or watch what I said when in the presence of high elves and other nobles. The only time I was free to be myself was when I was with Cwella. Or Phabian, but those times were fleeting.

I sighed. It was clear I had no choice in this matter. I would see what Barlack had to say, and then I would go back to Pine Crest Manor and spend the rest of my days with Damiyun as my own person.

Not some puppet on a string.

SEVENTY
ARDEN

You're safe, Arden. A voice whispered to me through the haze. Long, white hair curtained my head. Bright blue eyes looked at me with love, and red lips curled up into a smile.

"Mother?"

You're safe, she said over and over again, voice fading. I sat up. Hands grabbed me, intent on pushing me down.

I was awake. My eyes went to the offender. "Don't touch me."

Her hands grabbed my shoulders, and I struggled against them. "Stop, Arden," she said. Her eyes darted to the right. Another came and panic took me.

"Drink this," the other voice commanded. I turned my head away.

"No."

"Please," the blond begged.

A glass was shoved between my lips. I pushed it away, spilling the contents.

"Gods damn it," the woman cursed. Another glass was brought forth. I turned away again. Hands gripped my head, wrenching it back. The glass was brought to my lips and poured into my mouth. Hands clamped over my lips and fingers pinched my nose. I had no choice but to swallow.

Anger welled up inside. Anger quickly quieted as sleepiness descended upon me.

Whoever this woman was, she would regret treating me like a child.

I walked through the halls of Wren's Keep. Though I had walked these paths countless times, they felt different.

Unfamiliar.

Though the floors were the same there were no paintings of Elders and Eminences past on the walls. No busts in prominent positions. And the people who scurried about did not wear the black uniform of the Suppressors, nor did they have the insignia—two swords crossed over a scarlet "S"—on the left breast.

No. The people who scurried about were wearing regular clothes. I frowned at the sight. What was going on?

Up ahead I saw a man with blond hair brushing his shoulders coming out of a room. His brown eyes met mine and a smile curled his lips. I stumbled, mouth going dry. How could I be looking at the man I looked up to? The man I worshiped? The man who was higher than a god to me? Had that Elf Bitch killed me? If I were dead, I would gladly spend eternity here with Zachariah Farnsworth.

"Arden Rayne," his voice boomed as he sauntered toward me.

Dropping to my knees I bent forward and pressed my forehead to the floor. "Eminence Farnsworth." My voice shook.

"Rise," he said, and I scrambled to my feet. Though I wanted to look at him, I kept my eyes trained on the floor. I did not wish to offend him by staring.

"You are my most loyal, my most faithful of disciples," he said. My body filled with warmth at his words. "You understand my vision and what the Order is about. You uphold the Five Principles and One Hundred Articles. I dare say you even know our history better than me." He chuckled. Pride blossomed within, and I could not stop the smile from forming on my lips.

"Thank you, Eminence. I do my best to follow in your footsteps, though I feel I do not do you justice. I will never rise to your grandeur." My cheeks burned at my words. At the realness of my self-deprecation.

As devoted as I was, as much as I knew and tried to instill in the recruits, into the Order, I was a poor substitute for the wondrous man who stood before me.

"The recruits are pathetic. Elder Castille's oversight is weak." As was Quint's but I held my tongue. I did not dare offend Zachariah.

"Yes, the leadership is a mockery of what I have built but you, Arden Rayne. You understand. You see the goodness in what the Order does."

I looked at Zachriah, whose eyes were filled with pride. My heart swelled at the look and I stood straighter.

"I do. I live by your words, Eminence. I try my best to follow in your footsteps," I said. "In that vein, Wielders will no longer be given the option to join. They will all be eradicated."

Zachariah clasped his hands behind his back and rocked on his heels. "No."

I blinked. "Eminence—" he held up a hand and I closed my mouth.

"We need as many numbers in the Order as we can get. We need an army of unimaginable size to march beside the Fallen One when he rises."

I frowned. "Blocking a Wielder's magic does him no favors. The magic still runs in their veins. It still keeps the binds held. He has told me to kill all Wielders."

Zachariah stared down at me, and I regretted the words I spoke. But he did not chastise me. He did not walk away in anger and disgust. No. Zachariah Farnsworth smiled.

"I know how to make the Sigaa'Lean. I was given the information long ago, but you knew that, didn't you?" His brown eyes held mine.

"Yes."

"The thing with the Sigaa'Lean, Arden, is it was made by Wielders. Of course, they would want something to temporarily block magic. Something that would not take it away forever. Wielders think they are smarter. Better. They think they are blessed because they were put in charge of keeping the Fallen One secure in his tomb, but you know as well as I that magic is a curse. A plague that chokes the land."

Gods, but his words were the ones I spoke. The ones I lived by.

"The elves, as they made the bracelet, conveniently left out one important element. One important word in the spoken spell. They conveniently left off what would take a Wielders magic permanently."

My eyes widened. "You have figured this out?"

Zachariah nodded. "And I want you, Arden Rayne, to produce the right Sigaa'Lean and use it on all who are captured as you build my army."

"Where are the instructions?"

"They are buried within the words in the History of the Suppressors. I am sure you have seen them, though you did not know what it was at the time. Go back and read, Arden Rayne. Decipher the words and destroy all magic. Do this, and you will be rewarded and rise higher than any in the Order."

M Y EYES SNAPPED OPEN, and I stared at the blood-red canopy above. I was in my bed. Apparently the Elf Bitch hadn't killed me after all, but the dream—if it was a dream--was still fresh in my mind. The image of Zachariah. His voice, strong and deep.

And the last thing he said to me before I woke. I could find how to make the Sigaa'Lean within the words written in the History of the Suppressors. Perhaps I was on the edge of death, that is the only thing to explain the dream, the reality, I had.

And within that moment between life and death, Zachariah came to me. He knew I was devout. Faithful. He knew I upheld what he created, and he entrusted me with making the bracelet. With eradicating Wielders and setting the Fallen One free.

Smiling, I sat up. Pain ripped through my chest, and I gasped for breath, collapsing onto my back.

"Damn it, Arden. Stay still. You are going to reopen your wound."

Turning my head, I saw Rylee stalk across the room to the bed. She pushed open my sleep shirt. My heart pounded in my chest. The room spun and nausea made my stomach roll.

Get it together, Arden. You are not weak. Zachariah would be disgusted with you.

Grabbing her wrist, I twisted. Rylee's face contorted in pain.

"Don't fucking touch me."

She yanked her arm free and rubbed her wrist. "I need to make sure you didn't reopen the wound."

I glared at her. "Are you not a healer? Are you so unskilled you need to worry about your stitching?"

Rylee glared at me. "In case you forgot, a dagger was plunged into your chest. The wound was deep."

Shoving her away, I sat up, biting back the pain. I would not show weakness in front of a woman. Swinging my legs over the side, I rose and crossed to the wardrobe. Opening the doors I pulled out a fresh uniform and my boots.

"Where do you think you're going?"

I glanced over my shoulder at Rylee who stood with her arms crossed, a scowl on her homely face. I said nothing as I pulled on my clothes.

"Get back in your bed. You need rest if you are to heal," she said.

"I don't take orders from a woman." *Or anyone else.*

I strode toward the door.

Rylee moved, blocking my way. "You are my charge."

Oh, you would love to think that, wouldn't you?

"Get out of my way." I took a step closer.

Rylee smirked. "Or what?"

Placing my hands on her, I called my magic. Pain ripped through my body, searing and debilitating. Screaming, I fell to the floor. I did not have look at my wrist to know she had put the Sigaa'Lean on me.

"What is the meaning of this?"

"Your magic inhibited my healing. Every time I touched you, it burst out. I was forced to put it on, or let you die, which was my first choice. Unfortunately for me, I took an oath and was forced to spare your life."

"Take it off."

"Or what? You'll run and tell your mother?" She laughed. "It was quite pathetic how you cried for her while having fever dreams. Do you suck your thumb and wet the bed still?"

I struck her hard across the cheek, driving her to the floor. Rubbing her face, she glared at me. Grabbing her hair, I yanked her head back. I could not contain my smile at the fear in her eyes.

"Do not fuck with me. You have no idea who you are dealing with, Love. Now, take the fucking Sigaa'Lean off me if you wish to not have your throat slit," I said, releasing her with a shove. Taking my arm, she whispered the Elven spell releasing me. I pushed past her and strode into the hall, making my way to the library to read the History of the Suppressors once again.

I would find the information hidden within the text, and I would make the new Sigaa'Lean. I would humble myself before Vel and Quint. I would tell them I have reevaluated my prior proclamation. I would tell them about building an army. Tell them it aligns with Zachariah's vision, and they would have no choice but to agree with me.

I would keep the Sigaa'Lean a secret, until I became the Elder. Then I would lead an army across Il'Ekhester, Va'l'Victorus, and Willowshire where the Fae resided, and I would capture and enslave every being with magic. And when Themesis' binds finally crumbled, when he finally emerges from his prison, that will be the last surprise no one would ever see coming.

Not even Themesis himself.

T HUNDER CRASHED, LIGHTNING LIT up the sky, and the wind howled, shaking the panes of glass in the many windows spanning the library. Rain pounded on the roof above. Monsters and demons howled in the night. My back ached from hunching over the open book on the desk. I had spent hours in the library reading the history over and over again. My eyes burned, the candles burned low, and a headache began to form in the back of my head.

But my perseverance had paid off in the end. Just as Zachariah had told me, the instructions for making the Sigaa'Lean was buried deep within the words I read. Closing the book, I folded the parchment and tucked it in my pocket.

The day of reckoning was coming, and soon, I would have everything I ever wanted.

SEVENTY-ONE
MOURANDA

ALLENDAIRE AVOIDED ME AFTER his visit. He also avoided Mordecai, only holding his hand or putting him on his lap for public display, but I saw the stiffness in his body. The fake smiles and the way he could not wait to hand him over to me.

Could not wait to get away from him.

I did not blame him for it. Did not blame him for the hatred he had for me. The daggers in his eyes when he looked at me froze my blood and I could not help but wonder if a dagger would find itself imbedded in my chest while I slept.

"Mouranda? Are you alright?"

Denalla's voice pierced my thoughts. "Of course," I said, forcing a smile. It seemed I was doing that a lot these days.

Denalla bounced Mordecai on her lap, tickling his chin and cooing nonsense words at him. Did she forget about what I had done? She had stopped looking at the child with trepidation. Stopped speaking to me of what I had done. Stopped speaking of her fears.

Where she had shied away from the boy, she was now eager to hold him. Eager to cuddle. As though what she was a part of had been stricken from her mind.

"Denalla," I said, touching her knee. She stopped the kisses she peppered on Mordecai's face. Her eyes met mine, as did his.

Ever alert.

Ever aware.

As though there was something—or someone—far older residing inside the body of a child.

"Denalla," I said again, forcing yet another smile. My face was beginning to hurt from it. "It is late. Perhaps you should put Mordecai to bed and come back here when you are done."

Nodding, she rose, cuddling the child in her arms as she exited. Pulling myself to my feet, I crossed the room and poured a glass of spirits and tossed it back, letting the fire burn its path down my throat while the warmth enveloped me. Pouring another, I sat down in front of the cold hearth. After a bit, I heard the door open. Turning, I watched Denalla cross the room to where I sat.

"Mouranda," she said sitting beside me and taking my hand. "Are you alright? I have noticed you spend more and more time in your room. You hardly ask for the prince and when I bring him to you, well, you neglect him."

I looked at Denalla. The woman who was once my loyal servant. The woman who shared my bed on occasion. The woman who tried to make it so Serafin would never be born. The woman whose neck I protected from the sword when Lillyanna was attacked in her bed. She looked at me once again as though I were an unfit mother.

As though she did not participate in Mordecai's birth.

My head swam and I knew it was as much from the spirits I consumed as it was the confusion creeping into my mind, trying so hard to make me not see what was plain. And again, I truly regretted what I had done, but now there was no taking it back. I only held onto the knowledge that Serafin was alive somewhere and I hoped, no, I prayed to those gods who I did not believe in, she stayed that way.

And I prayed too, that she would one day come back to claim her birthright before the Shadow Elves were no more.

I patted Denalla's hand. "I'm just tired. I fear I have had too much spirits." I held up the nearly empty bottle. Did I really drink that much? Perhaps. Perhaps not. It was hard to tell what was true and what was an illusion.

And that was what all of this was. An illusion. I only hoped those who it had not affected yet, Allendaire and Lazaro, stayed that way long enough to stop whatever was to come. And though I longed to ask Denalla if she remembers how Mordecai was born, I knew what her answer would be and I knew she would look at me as if I were losing my mind.

Perhaps I was.

Rising, I made my way to my bed and slipped beneath the heavy covers. Denalla no longer came with me. No longer shared my bed. No longer was she a comfort.

My maid, my friend, my lover was a shell of who she once was. Much like so many of the elves in Il'Ekhester.

Closing my eyes, I let sleep take me, and with the darkness of rest came the nightmares. The beasts with sharp claws ready to tear. The woman whose unwilling sacrifice gave me what I wanted.

And the dark figure with red eyes peering out from the folds of its hood. White fangs glinted in the ethereal light of dreams.

Of nightmares.

A wind blew my sleep dress around my legs. I heard beasts step closer. Growls Hisses. The click of teeth, but I could not take my eyes from the one who stood before me. The specter that appeared after I did what I did.

And though I was truly sorry, I knew the words would have no effect. They would not rectify the atrocity I committed.

"A life for a life," the beast said, rising up, towering over me, red eyes never leaving my face.

"A life for a life," I replied.

With those words, I knew the nightmares I feared had come, and I knew I would not wake up.

SEVENTY-TWO
ALLENDAIRE

ELVES CROWDED THE EXPANSE of grass, spreading out by the Na'almlo River. I watched the blue balls of flame sent out across the water to land upon the kindling in the wooden raft that floated upon the choppy waters, engulfing it in flames.

Engulfing Mouranda Trounde's body.

The sound of weeping and wails punctuated the silence. Elves grieving the death of their queen. I dug the tip of the small knife I held into my leg, biting back a curse and letting the tears wet my cheek.

Mouranda's cold, lifeless body was found early in the morning. Denalla's shriek at her findings echoed through the halls. I rushed to her chambers and upon seeing the waxy pallor of her skin and the stiffness in her body, I knew nothing could be done.

The queen was dead.

I checked her over and did not see any self-inflicted wounds. Whether she used poison, I could not guess though even that felt wrong. Mouranda was a strong woman and the last thing I knew she would do was take her own life. I could only guess that perhaps her fate came from what she did.

Mordecai stirred in my arms, and I looked down at him. A smile curled his lips, and a giggle bubbled from within him as he looked at the fire on the river.

A chill ran through my body.

I wish I knew exactly what Mouranda had done. Was there a way to even reverse it? Would killing the child do that?

Mordecai looked up at me, milky white eyes narrowed, and my mouth went dry. Did he hear my thoughts?

When the burning body was just a wink of light at the bend of the river, elves began to disburse, heading I knew for the grand ballroom where the celebration of the queen's life would take place. Searching the crowd, my eyes found Denalla, and I strode to her.

"Denalla, would you be so kind as to take Mordecai?" I jammed the small blade deeper into my leg. Tears stung my eyes. "I can't—I just need to be alone for a bit," I said, forcing a quiver to my voice.

Denalla bowed her head. "Of course, my king," she said, smiling as I deposited the child into her arms. As she walked away, his eyes narrowed on me for a moment before a slow, evil smile curled his lips. A rush of cold washed over me. It felt similar to when Phabian would delve into my mind. Knowledge swam in the child's colorless eyes. Chills ran down my spine and a curl of frost billowed from my mouth for a moment, and then Mordecai looked away as Denalla headed to the place and the chill dissipated.

Pulling the fur cape, I wore close, I followed the elves into the palace, though instead of heading to the grand ballroom, I instead headed to my quarters. Closing the door, I poured a healthy glass of Serpent's Venom and sat in a chair in front of the cold hearth.

I thought about Mouranda. About the woman I had chosen for my mate and wife. I had done so because she was cunning. Calculating. She never did anything without a plan. She was a strong front for a queen.

But she could not give me the one thing I desired. The one thing that every king procured.

She could not give me an heir and though that was enough to end her life, she knew about what I had done and I took her threat to spill all at face value. Though I could easily have done away with her through the use of poison, I was sure she had given Denalla instructions in the event of her demise. After all, they shared a bed.

Pouring more spirits, I rubbed my eyes. A brief flash of the child flickered through my mind. The smile. The feeling I got when I looked at him on the bank of the river.

And the feelings I had since Mouranda announced she was with child and since giving birth. Often times my mind was fuzzy. Often times, there were images of things that happened, such as the celebration for his first Name Day. Though I do not remember it, brief flashes of images within my mind told me it happened.

Mouranda did use dark magic to conceive. At least that is what Lazaro had said and I had no reason to not believe.

Draining my glass, I rose. Removing the cape I wore, I adjusted my crown and headed to the door to make my appearance at the celebration.

MUSIC, LAUGHTER AND VOICES echoed off the halls. The grand ballroom was packed. Elves crammed the room and still more poured out onto the patio and lawn beyond. Servants carrying trays filled with food and drink weaved their way around the bodies.

I was not a fool. I knew none were here for their queen to celebrate her life. They were here to simply celebrate. Any reason to drink to excess, eat until overstuffed, and dance until feet hurt, my elves would be there. I did not wish to be here, but I had to put on a show as the king.

I pushed my way through the crowd that parted, silence following as I walked to the center of the ballroom. I turned in a slow circle, eyes on those who gathered, waiting for me to say something profound.

"Carry on," I called out. "Your queen would have wanted it that way." There was a slight hesitation before the music picked up again and people began dancing, talking, and laughing once more. I was not sure what they expected from me, but I was relieved the festivities continued.

Circling the crowd, I grabbed a glass of wine and took a sip. I saw Denalla spinning around, Mordecai in her arms. She kissed his cheeks and held his hand as she danced. The memory of his smile, the coldness that washed over me was fresh, as were the other confusing memories and visions that flashed in my mind.

I knew I could not in good conscious let this child sit upon the throne. He was not the heir, not yet, and I feared if something was not done, I would end up naming him as such. Or thinking I did. Who would dispute whether or not I had spoken the words if everyone thought it so?

I shook the thoughts as I looked around, my eyes finding Lazaro who had cornered a pretty female elf, and I pushed my way through the crowd toward him.

"Lazaro," I said.

Glassy eyes looked at me. "Majesty." His words were slurred.

"A word, please."

Turning, I made my way through the doors that led outside. Entering the labyrinth, I navigated my way to the center to the bench in the middle. After a bit, Lazaro stumbled into the clearing.

"Majesty. Are you alright?" His voice held concern, and he cautiously walked to the bench and took a seat beside me.

"No," I said. "I need you to do something for me, Lazaro. I know you do not respect me. I know you do not have any love for me, and you should be hanged a traitor for it."

Lazaro swallowed hard. "I... I don't...I'm not..."

"You will not be hanged," I said, and he relaxed. "You told me Mouranda had a book from the Dark Elves and though I would like to think, like to believe, she did not use their magic, I cannot deny the child looks like a Dark Elf."

"He does, though..." Lazaro shook his head.

"Speak."

He took a deep breath. "I am not sure of much anymore. My mind, my memories are fuzzy. The only thing that keeps me grounded to what I think and what I know is my conversations with Phabian in the notebook. Even then, sometimes I look at the words and wonder who has written them." He looked at me. "It is troubling."

"It is. I have felt the same, and that is why I need you, Lazaro. I trust you. You are the only one within these walls who thinks something is amiss. Everyone else, well, they believe Mordecai is the heir. They have forgotten everything before, and only know him."

"What is it you wish of me?"

I looked at Lazaro and took a deep breath. "Find Serafin. Bring her here. I fear all of our lives depend on it."

SEVENTY-THREE
ZEDEKIAH

S ITTING AT THE TABLE in the tavern in Howling Cove, I pulled the cards toward me. I did not have to look to know they were a winning hand, but I picked them up and looked all the same.

Four knights and a serpent.

Tossing coin into the pot at the center of the table, I eyed the three Soul Collectors who graced the table. Lucas, whose brown eyes studied the cards he held. Long fingers swept a lock of brown hair from his face. Sam's brow furrowed, wrinkles stacked up on his wide forehead, and Bones, whose name I could not recall, only knowing him as Bones because of the skin that clung to his thin, boney frame. His face was gaunt, and his black hair hung in lanky, greasy strands.

We met here once or twice a Moon Cycle and on a normal night, I would be happy to play and take their money. Except for tonight. I wanted to know their thoughts about my father. Placing my cards down, I folded my hands on the table, something that got their attention.

"Abe—"

"Zedekiah," I said, glaring at Sam. They might as well know I am going by the name Themesis gave me.

"Why are we here if not to play cards?" Lucas tossed his cards down.

"I called you here for a reason."

I looked at the three Soul Collectors. They did what my father said. Call a contract, take a soul. But I was not sure if they were loyal to him.

Not completely.

I was made a Soul Collector not by choice. He took my soul and made me what I am. Made me take the lives, the souls, of the humans.

A human like I once was.

But Sam, Lucas, and Bones? They became Soul Collectors of their own volition. I was not quite sure how loyal they were. Or if they served him truly. Whatever he offered them in the afterlife might have enticed them enough to give up their own souls. Their own lives to serve them.

Though there were other Soul Collectors who worked for my father, I was closest to these three, though I would not call them friends. I also knew I had to tread carefully with my words and probing.

I did not completely trust them, either. Knowing who I truly was would be enough for a betrayal, if only to be praised and raised ever so slightly by Themesis.

No. This was a delicate situation.

"So?" Sam tapped his fingers. Bones and Lucas took a sip of their drinks. All three men's eyes were on me.

"Why did you become Soul Collectors?"

"Why did you?" Lucas folded his arms and sat back in his chair.

"It was not my choice. It was, however, yours."

Sam shrugged. "Eternal life."

"Which you gave up everything for. You had a wife and child," I said.

"I did her a favor," Sam said, though there was doubt in his voice.

Good.

"And you, Lucas?"

"The same. Eternal life."

My eyes went to Bones who shrugged.

"And when he calls your contract, what then?"

Silence.

Just as I had figured, they had not thought it through like many who sold their souls. At least Damiyun knew what awaited him if that day came.

I prayed it did not.

I could tell the three men were thinking about the choice they made so long ago.

Good. It was time to add to their uncertainty. Picking up the tankard of fresh ale, I took a long drink, letting the silence stretch. Letting their thoughts sink in. Folding my hands, I leaned forward, my eyes going to each man and back.

"What do you think will happen to you when he breaks free? Do you think he will keep whatever promises he spoke when you gave up everything to serve him?"

The men shifted in their seats and glanced at each other. Their discomfort was palpable.

"You will fall just like everyone else. Themesis never keeps his promises," I said, sitting back and taking another sip of ale.

Lucas' eyes narrowed on me. "But you won't, will you Zedekiah?"

It was the exact question, the exact opening I was hoping for. "No."

The silence following that simple word was deafening.

"What can we do?" Bones' normally raspy voice was so low I almost didn't hear the words.

Almost.

All eyes were on me and I smiled.

I had them.

S TEPPING OUT INTO THE warm night, I pulled Bel from beneath my beard. He yawned, wings fluttered, and red eyes glared up at me.

I chuckled. "So sorry to disturb your slumber, but I need you." Bel perked up, sitting back on his haunches, eyes alert. "I need you to get the higher demons from the Abyss, however many you can find, and tell them to meet me in the woods at the edge of Howling Cove."

Bel let out a series of clicks and chirps, then scampered away. I made my way through the streets of the village. They were empty this time of night, the people tucked safely away inside their homes or the inn.

Safe for now, anyway. It was only a matter of time before the sanctuary of their homes would be destroyed by the demons and monsters. I made my way to the woods at the edge of the village and waited. I did not want to go to the Abyss to address the beasts. My father could feel my presence and wonder why I was there.

I could not afford to raise his suspicions.

The sound of feet shuffling, the huffing of breaths, and deep, guttural growls pierced the silence. I watched two dozen grotesque beasts and demons move from the shadows. Red eyes looked at me.

"Zedekiah."

"King."

"God of gods."

The words rippled through the night. Some beasts bowed their heads. Others dropped to their knees before me.

"Why have you asked us here?" One beast closest to me hissed.

"You have spent thousands of Grand Passages in servitude to my father. You have done his bidding. Obeyed his words. You have destroyed lives. Killed Wielders, all in his name.

The demons snarled and snapped their jaws. One stepped forward and circled me, hot breath reeking of death and decay filled my nostrils. I pushed down a gag.

"What do you want?" The beast hissed as he continued his slow circles.

"You call me king. God of gods. Both are titles I am willing to wear in exchange for the loyalty of every demon, every beast, every monster who walks these lands and resides in the Abyss."

The demon stopped its circling and dropped its head down, eyes level with mine. "For what?"

I stared back at the beast. "Release from your imprisonment to Themesis. Your souls to be sent on to Eternity should you choose. If not, you will stand by my side as your god of gods. Your king. As the ruler of the Abyss."

The beast before me growled, then dropped to a knee with head bowed. "I pledge my loyalty to you, Zedekiah. King. God of gods," it said, and I watched the others drop to their knees and pledge the same.

My plan was beginning to fall into place.

SEVENTY-FOUR
DAMIYUN

IT WAS AS IF a dark cloud lifted from my shoulders after speaking with
Serafin. Though I did not care who she was, who her mother was, but if
she did? Though it would hurt like someone ripped my heart from my chest,
I would let her be.

But she felt the same long before we found out. As did I. And she made
me feel like a young buck. Every chance we had to rest the horses, I could
not stop myself from grabbing her. And her laughter, the flirtatious way she
pushed me away telling me *later* only made me want her more.

Love her more.

And then we were in Gavina, a town just a scant ten miles from Va'l'Victorus, a place we stopped for the night. We both stood at each side of the bed,
and I felt like the young boy I was when I was just thirteen, with the woman
who made me a man. Why did Serafin make me feel this way?

"Do you... Do we...?" Serafin's blue eyes met mine.

"I will sleep on the floor."

She swallowed. "Is that what you want?"

There were plenty of nights on the road when we had to sleep in the forest,
spending hours keeping the demons at bay, and when the sun crested the
horizon, we fell into sleep. And there were the times we spent in inns where
it was an unspoken agreement I slept on the floor.

But tonight? Tonight, something was different.

"No, it's not what I want," I said.

She crawled across the bed to where I stood. "What do you want,
Damiyun?" Her eyes searched mine and fuck me, if I didn't want to take her
and have my way with her. "I know you don't want to just hold me tonight."

Those damn blue eyes did not leave mine. "I know you want more. Tell me
you want me, because I want you. Those nights together? I wanted more. I
want what I gave you that night. Please?"

Her words undid me. I pulled her into my arms and buried my face in her
neck.

"Princess," I sighed.

She pulled away and removed her shirt. Guiding her onto the bed, I looked down at her. She was so perfect. So beautiful. I trailed kisses down her torso. Hooking my fingers in the waistband of her trousers, I pulled them down.

Serafin grabbed my head, bringing it up. "No. I just want you. Now."

She was going to get no complaints from me. Slipping out of my trousers, I looked down at her. Grabbing my head, she pulled me down, lips meeting mine in a hungry manner. She bucked her hips against me, and I pulled away.

"Is there something you want, Princess?"

She glared at me. "You know damn well there is." Hands grasping my length, she stroked. I groaned, leaning down and biting her neck as I slid inside her.

"That's better," she sighed, lifting her hips and meeting my thrusts. We moved together, our breathing, our sighs and moans, the only sound in the room. The passion, hunger, I felt from her through the bond fueled my own desire and our pace quickened. Her legs locked around my waist, and she raked her fingernails down my back, something that ignited my passion further. I drove myself deep inside her, letting out a guttural cry, teeth biting her neck as I spent myself inside her.

Flopping onto my back, I pulled her into my arms. "Fuck me, Princess, but you drive me crazy," I said. She burrowed deeper into my embrace, head on my chest.

"I love you, Damiyun."

"I love you too, Princess." I pressed my lips to the top of her head and offered up a silent prayer to the gods that this woman, this happiness, wouldn't be taken from me.

T HE NEXT DAY WE pushed on. I could not forget the feel of Serafin in my arms. I shifted in the saddle, the pain in my groin reminding me of how many times I claimed her until she begged me to stop.

And for the first time, the fact I was sterile bothered me. With Zenith? Knowing she would have relieved herself of my offspring, I was happy to not provide one. With Lil? Gods, I would have wanted nothing more than to have a family with her, but knowing what I had to do? What sort of father would I have been without my Lil by my side?

But Serafin? Fuck. I could see us together with a child or two toddling around Pine Crest Manor.

I shook the thought from my mind. The image of me tossing a little girl in the air, and catching her, her giggles of joy echoing in the air. Showing a boy how to use a sword, laughing as his sister picked up a stick and challenged him.

No. That was not mine to have.

Not with Zenith.

Not with Lil.

And certainly not with Serafin.

"Are you alright, Damiyun?"

I looked at Serafin, whose eyes held concern. Reaching out, I grasped her hand. "I have never been better." I kissed her knuckles. "We should be arriving in Va'l'Victorus late this afternoon."

Serafin sighed, an annoyed and frustrated sound.

I squeezed her hand. "We will stay only as long as you wish. If you say the word, I promise we will leave."

She flashed a wan smile but said nothing.

We rode slowly down the empty road, and I frowned at the eerie silence that descended. It was like the silence that came at night before the demons and monsters slunk out of their holes. But I knew there were no demons. No monsters.

Xander balked for a moment, feet dancing and I had to keep him from bolting. My shoulder blades pricked. It felt as though someone were watching. I pulled Xander to a halt and scanned the dense woods on either side of the road.

"What is it?" Serafin asked, pulling Yasmine to a halt.

"I'm not rightly sure. Possibly nothing." I scanned the woods again, frowning at a movement. A light flicker. A figure wearing black stood off in the foliage. White eyes peered out from the black scarf wrapped around their head. Another flicker, and they were gone, and I wasn't rightly sure what happened. Or what I saw.

Rolling my shoulders, I heeled Xander forward again, trying to ignore the unease slowly blanketing me. We continued through the day, stopping on occasion to rest and water the horses. The ill feeling still clung to me, though it was nothing more than a dull annoyance. Finally, as the sun hung lower in the sky, the city came into view. Oaken Leaf Castle loomed above on a hill. The rays of the setting sun glinted off the white marble. Pulling Xander to a halt, I looked at Serafin.

"Ready?"

She glanced at me and tossed her head. "No," she said, guiding Yasmine forward and heeling her into a trot. Kicking my heels into Xander, I followed behind. I did not know what Barlack wanted with Serafin. I could only guess he had something up his sleeve. Whatever it was, I would be there for her, and we would face it together as a united front.

SEVENTY-FIVE
SERAFIN

W E GUIDED OUR MOUNTS down the street of Va'l'Victorus. Elves and humans rushed to close down their booths and scurried home as the sun sank down. I looked around at the people.

At the elves and humans living in harmony. Some elves bowed their heads to Damiyun. Others muttered the words "prince." Many females giggled as they ran by.

Annoying. Their titters grated.

I glanced at Damiyun as a young woman paused a moment, doe eyes looking up at him. My magic flared, and Damiyun chuckled.

"You have nothing to worry about, Princess." He took my hand and kissed the knuckles.

"No?" I tossed my head and eyed the bevy of young women who trailed behind us, and I glared down at them. They scattered like mice, and I smiled to myself.

"Feel better?"

I sniffed. "Yes."

Damiyun laughed.

I looked up at the palace set atop a rock mass. It was an imposing structure. Elves walked the walls, bows slung over shoulders in what looked to be a casual manner, but I knew an arrow could be knocked and let loose in seconds. The setting sun glinted off the white marble spires and the metal signal fire bowls. Drawing up to a rocky footpath, Damiyun dismounted. I followed suit and we made our way up to Oaken Leaf Castle.

It was eerily silent, the only sound that of our feet crunching on the crushed stone. After a bit, partially closed iron and thick oak gates came into view. Guards stood at each side nodding at the people who filed through.

"Damiyun." One guard greeted when we approached. "You were not expected so soon."

"I know. I promised Barlack I would bring Serafin, the Shadow Elf princess, to him."

The guard's eyes met mine, and he bowed his head. "Welcome, highness. We will take care of your mounts."

Handing over the reins, Damiyun took my hand, and we stepped through the gates that clanged shut behind. We walked through a vast and empty courtyard. Flowers bloomed in beds, the scent intoxicating and various fruits grew on trees. Striding up the white marble steps leading into the palace, Damiyun pulled open the cherry wood door and we stepped into the atrium.

It was a vast, circular room with high, vaulted ceilings, painted with pictures of nature. Stained glass windows at the peak glowed from the setting sun. Carved into the floor in the middle was a massive stag with antlers made of gold and rubies for eyes.

The Wilde Elf crest.

I looked around at the expensive hand-carved furniture, the blood red marble floor with the gold inlay and could not help but feel a bit of disgust. The eight Moon Cycles I had been on my own away from my own ostentatious palace made me see a different side of society. Uma's home was quaint and simple, the nicked-up furniture and thread bare rugs all signs of love and use.

Though Damiyun's home was grand, there was also something quaint and cozy about it, the worn furnishings blending well with the fine ones. But this? This was a garish disgusting display of hoarded wealth.

"Damiyun," a voice called out. Looking in the direction it came, my eyes going to a male elf striding toward us. White hair spilled just below his shoulders, the sides pulled back with golden combs. He wore a plain white top, gray trousers and black boots. His attire was a vast difference than what the Shadow Elves wore.

His eyes met mine and he bowed his head. "Princess Serafin Trounde. I am Barlack Satow, king of the Wilde Elves. Welcome to Oaken Leaf Castle." He turned his attention to Damiyun. "I did not call for you."

"No, you did not. I thought it prudent to bring Serafin here sooner, rather than later."

"Of course. The evening meal will be starting shortly. Will you join us?" His eyes went to me, and I moved closer to Damiyun who slipped an arm around my waist. The corner of Barlack's mouth twitched.

"I'd like to freshen up a bit, and I'd like to take our meal in our room. I am a bit exhausted from not having proper nights rest," I said.

Barlack bowed his head. "Of course. Whatever you wish will be yours."

Damiyun nodded and led me through the halls. Servants paused as we passed. Some bowed their heads, others muttered the words prince and princess. And still others called us king and queen.

Drawing up to a door, Damiyun pushed it open. "This was my mother's room. The gods only know why Barlack makes me stay here," he said, closing the door behind.

I looked around the large room. A bed was tucked into the corner, comfortable looking chairs and couches were arranged in front of the cold hearth. A wardrobe spanned a wall, and a vanity was tucked into another corner. Shelves crammed with books and paper spanned the wall to the right of the door. Across the room, double doors led out to a grand balcony.

Though Damiyun had told me who his mother was, I didn't really believe him, nor did I believe this room and these things belonged to a woman I had been told was dead.

"How do you know she was here? How do you even know she was your mother? You lack the ears of an elf."

"I told you. They were clipped when I was born."

"Were they, or is that what Barlack told you?"

Though Damiyun told me about what Allendaire supposedly did to his own sister, I wanted to believe he was not that calculating. That he wasn't the sort of man who would sentence his sister to death and wage a war on his own people.

Despite what he had done to me, I had no doubt Mouranda had a hand in what happened and yet...yet he went along with it. He handed down the sentence to take my head, only Lazaro saved me. My heart still ached knowing my father wanted me dead.

"I want to speak with Barlack."

Damiyun blinked. "What?"

"Now. I want to talk with him."

"But I thought you wanted to rest and take our meal in the room."

I did, but we traveled so far and are here now. I want to know what he knows before I change my mind and leave."

Damiyun nodded. "Of course, Princess."

Exiting the room, we walked in silence to find Barlack. I had to know the best way forward. Leave my people forever or take my birthright as the Shadow Elf Queen. Either road might be long, but I had to take one.